AKBAR SHAH II., *last of the Moghul Emperors to die in Delhi, holding his Court in the Diwan-i-Khas, about the year* 1820.

From a Painting by Shekh Alam, now in the India Office.

# STRANGERS WITHIN THE GATES

# STRANGERS WITHIN THE GATES

GABRIELLE FESTING

GYAN

*Published by*

Gyan Publishing House
5, Ansari Road
Daryaganj, New Delhi-110002
Phone: 011-47034999, 9811692060
E-mail: books@gyanbooks.com

*Distribution Network*
gyanbooks.com
India, USA, Canada, UK, Australia, France



ISBN : 978-81-212-4073-4 (PB)
First Published, Edinburgh, 1914

2nd Impression 2020

*Printed at:* Gyan Press, Delhi.



**Strangers within the Gates**
Author: Gabrielle Festing

*To F.*

*AND*

*TO THE MEN WHO ARE DOING THE WORK.*

# PREFACE.

AFTER the publication of 'When Kings rode to Delhi,' I was asked to write a sequel, giving the story of the struggles for supremacy in India which followed the break-up of the Moghul Empire.

The sources of the story are too numerous to be given in full. The principal are:—

For the general history — H. G. Keene's 'History of India'; G. B. Malleson's 'Decisive Battles of India'; volume VIII. of the 'History of India as Told by its own Historians'; J. C. Marshman's 'History of India.'

For the struggle between French and English— Malleson's 'History of the French in India,' his 'Dupleix,' and his 'Final French Struggles in India'; Tibulle Hamont's 'Dupleix,' and his 'Fin d'un Empire'; 'Les Mémoires Historiques de M. de La Bourdonnais'; S. Hill's 'Three Frenchmen in Bengal'; and several lives of Robert Clive.

For events in Mysore—Husain Ali's 'Hydur Naik,' and his 'Tipu Sultan'; W. Kirkpatrick's 'Selected Letters of Tipu Sultan'; A. Bowring's 'Haidar Ali and Tipu Sultan'; and R. Hook's 'Life of Sir D. Baird.'

For the Marathas—Grant Duff's 'History'; Keene's 'Madhava Rao Sindhia,' and his 'Hindustan, 1770-1820'; W. Francklin's 'Reign of Shah Aulum'; Sir J. Malcolm's 'Central India'; Colonel Sleeman's 'Rambles and Recollections of an Indian Official'; some of the Maratha Series of 'Selections from the State Papers preserved in the Bombay Secretariat'; 'Military Memoirs of Colonel James Skinner'; Gurwood's Wellington Despatches; H. Compton's 'European Military Adventurers of Hindustan'; and Colonel Tod's 'Rajast'han.'

For the Nepal War—A translation of the 'Vansavali'; T. Smith's 'Five Years' Residence at Nepaul'; R. Gillespie's 'Memoirs of Major-General Gillespie'; and the Private Journal of the 1st Marquess of Hastings.

For the Sikhs—Sir L. Griffin's 'Ranjit Singh,' his 'Rajas of the Punjab,' and 'Punjab Chiefs'; W. L. Macgregor's 'History of the Sikhs'; Sir H. Lawrence's 'Adventures of an Officer in the Punjab'; Carmichael Smith's 'History of the

Reigning Family of Lahore'; Raitt's 'Life of Hugh, Viscount Gough'; and Sir H. Edwardes's 'A Year on the Punjab Frontier.'

For Afghan history — Mountstuart Elphinstone's 'Account of the Kingdom of Caubul'; Mohan Lal's 'Life of Dost Mahomed'; Vincent Eyre's Journal; Mackenzie's 'Storms and Sunshine of a Soldier's Life'; J. W. Kaye's 'History of the War in Afghanistan'; Malleson's 'History of Afghanistan'; J. Greenwood's 'Campaign in Afghanistan under Pollock'; C. R. Low's 'Life of Sir G. Pollock'; G. R. Gleig's 'Sale's Brigade'; and a manuscript diary kept by Lieutenant Richard Frere, one of the "Illustrious Garrison."

For Sind—Sir J. Outram's 'Conquest of Sind'; W. F. P. Napier's 'Conquest of Sind'; Sir F. J. Goldsmid's 'James Outram'; and Captain Trotter's 'The Bayard of India'; T. R. E. Holmes's 'Four Soldiers'; A. Innes Shand's 'General John Jacob'; and J. Martineau's 'Life of Sir Bartle Frere.'

As before, I have to apologise for inconsistencies in the spelling of Indian names. To quote an authority to whom I have been indebted continually, "There are Indian words which have taken their place in British history, consecrated by the glory of great deeds or by the pathos of great suffering." It would be impossible, for instance, to write "Bhurtpore," "Lucknow," or "Cawnpore" in any other form than that used by the men whose daring and endurance will be associated for ever with those places. But names with less sacred associations appear under one or other of the forms approved by modern historians.

The Frontispiece is reproduced by permission of the Secretary of State for India in Council, from a very curious painting by Shekh Alam, now in the India Office. It represents Akbar Shah II., last of the Moghul Emperors to die in Delhi, holding his court in the Diwan-i-Khas, about the year 1820. Near him stand the royal princes; by a polite convention of the artist, Sir D. Ochterlony, the British Resident, figures among the omrahs in attendance on His Majesty.

My thanks are due to Mrs Perrin for her criticism of the MS., for finding a title for it, and for suggesting the subject of the Epilogue; to Mr Foster, Superintendent of Records at the India Office; to Mr Ellis, Assistant-Librarian, for his kind help and advice; and to the officials of the London Library.

*August* 1914.

# CONTENTS.

# PROLOGUE

# WHEN THE ENGLISH CAME TO DELHI

# PROLOGUE.

## WHEN THE ENGLISH CAME TO DELHI.

On the banks of the Jumna stands a marble pavilion on a marble platform.

Two hundred and fifty years of Indian sun have given to the outside the mellow tints of old ivory or old lace. Within, the light comes through pierced marble screens, to show the glory of flowers and foliage decorating panel and arch and pilaster, and the gold lettering above the narrow arches on the north and south, which proclaims, "If a Paradise be on the face of the earth, it is this, it is this, it is this."

Much has passed in Delhi since the time when craftsmen from France and Italy decorated the Diwan-i-Khas (Private Audience Hall) for the Emperor Shah Jahan. Three scenes stand out clearly from many others that have been played in the Hall.

The first was when its glories were new, when the Moghul Emperor's throne was set upon the marble slab at the back of the Hall. Robed in the priceless stuffs made within the walls of his palace, his gold turban ablaze with diamonds, his flowered tunic almost hidden by the soft gleam of his pearls, he sat upon a golden throne. Behind him sapphires, rubies, emeralds glowed from the outspread tails of two peacocks, between them stood the parrot wrought from a single emerald, and from the pearl fringes of the canopy hung the Mountain of Light, the great diamond that brings sovereignty to the possessor.

Above his head was the silver foliage, inlaid with gold, with which Austin of Bordeaux had overspread the ceiling. On the walls twined the flowers of East and West, inlaid in green serpentine and blue turquoise or lapis-lazuli, in jasper and agate and cornelian. Beside him eunuchs waved peacock-feather fans, and before him bowed rajas, and omrahs, and ambassadors, standing on the silken carpets with which the marble floor was strewed.

Among those who stood in the presence of the King of Kings, the Lord of the World, were two or three men, light-skinned and plainly dressed, scarcely to be noted among the magnificent courtiers, whose brightly coloured robes gave the assembly the air of a vast flower-bed. The English, it was well known, were a barbarian race

—"fisher-folk," said some well-informed persons—who lived far away overseas, and existed on sufferance of the Emperor, who gave them leave to trade in certain places of his dominion. They were fit for nothing but petty trade, and less esteemed at the Moghul Court than the Portuguese, who had long held possessions in India, or even the Dutch.

The next scene is a hundred and fifty years later. The Peacock Throne is gone; gone, too, is the ceiling, and bare places on the walls show where the more valuable stones in the inlay have been torn out, to buy food for the Emperor and his children. The walls are stained by bats and birds. Under a tattered canopy, in wretched garments, sits a blind old man, and with the feeble voice of age he calls down blessings upon the sturdy red-faced soldier who stands before him. The despised traders have rescued the descendant of Shah Jahan from misery and bondage.

Pass over more than fifty years, and the third scene opens. It is Sunday morning, September 20, 1857, and the Diwan-i-Khas is full as in the days of Shah Jahan, but with a different audience. Men with white faces stand where rajas and omrahs stood of old, and instead of silken robe and jewelled turban they wear uniforms of cloth, torn and stained. The omrahs made obeisance with extended arms when the Emperor spoke, crying,

"Wonderful! wonderful!" These men cry aloud, to another than the Emperor, "Not unto us, O Lord, not unto us, but unto Thy name be the praise."

The English had come in their might to Delhi, and to them had fallen the sceptre over a dominion wider than any Moghul Emperor had ever ruled. The story of how it came into their hands is a long one. Only fragments from it are here set forth, and the reader who would know it all must turn to those who played some part in it, or who watched as it was in the making.

# I.

# A DREAM OF EMPIRE—1720-1749

"On admire beaucoup, et l'on cite souvent l'Angleterre pour avoir résolu ce grand problème de gouverner, à quatre milles lieues de distances, avec quelques centaines d'employés civils et quelques milliers d'employés militaires, ses immenses possessions de l'Inde. S'il y a quelque nouveanté, quelque hardiesse, et quelque génie politique dans cette idée, il faut reconnaitre que l'honneur en revient à Dupleix, et que l'Angleterre qui en recueille aujourd'hui le profit et la gloire, n'a eu qu' à suivre les voies que le génie de la France lui avait ouvertes."—M. X. RAYMOND.

# I.

## A DREAM OF EMPIRE—1720-1749.

On a tempestuous March day of 1707, the Emperor Aurangzib breathed out his soul into the storm.

He had ruled over a greater part of India than any monarch before or after him. But he had not the power to weld his conquests together, and, even before his death, his empire was falling to pieces. The wisdom of his son and successor did no more than to avert the catastrophe for a few years. The men who followed him were shadows, who sat on the Peacock Throne, each in his turn, till pushed aside by rebellious kinsman or intriguing minister.

Nearly two hundred years before the death of Aurangzib, Babar, sixth in descent from Timur, invaded India with an army from Kabul, and founded the Moghul empire of Delhi. The sturdy northern stock was enfeebled by intermarriage with Hindus, the northern blood ran thin as one generation after another grew up on the Indian plains, far from the hills and the snows whence their Moghul ancestors came. The Moghuls no longer could hold India; even Hindustan was beyond their powers. The great vassals of Delhi, such as the Nawabs of Bengal and Oudh, and the Nizam of the Deccan, though still calling themselves the Emperor's men, were independent in all but the name. From the north came Persian and Afghan invaders to shatter the Moghul empire, and Marathas, Sikhs, and Jats tore at the fragments. If order were ever to come out of chaos, it must be established by the strong hand.

Not one of the rival powers in India was able to keep all the rest in check, though once or twice it seemed that the great Maratha Confederacy was about to do it. The hand must be that of a stranger.

None of the invaders of the eighteenth century, who came down to India, like Babar, through the gates of the north, was capable of rebuilding Babar's empire. But there was an old prophecy, made to the Emperor Aurangzib, that a white race from overseas should conquer Delhi.

At the beginning of the eighteenth century, four white races from overseas were represented in India. The first of these were the Portuguese, whose day was already past, though a Viceroy still held a mock Court at Goa, where empty churches and ruined palaces keep the memory of the time when Albuquerque's Christian city was wealthier than any other in the continent.

The Dutch, who came next, had succeeded in ruining the Portuguese dominion, and, characteristically, had founded nothing in its place. Then, as in all times of their history, their aim was to put the greatest amount into their own pockets, and to keep all competitors from trading, but the making of an empire was no part of their speculations.

Spited alike by Portuguese and Dutch, an English trading company, formed in the last years of Queen Elizabeth's reign, had succeeded in establishing factories at one or two points on the coast. After sixty years of precarious existence, the marriage of Charles II. with a Portuguese princess, Catharine of Braganza, who brought the town and harbour of Bombay as part of her dowry, had given them a more secure foothold. Even then, with many hundred miles separating Bombay from their trading stations on the Hughli river in Bengal, and at Fort St David in Madras, it seemed unlikely that the East India Company would ever play any other part than that of the peaceful trader which they originally claimed.

Last of all came the French, whose Compagnie

des Indes Orientales, founded by Colbert, had acquired a compact territory round about Pondicherry in the south. An eastern empire was no impossibility for them. One man all but succeeded in founding it, and his story is the first act in the long drama which was to end in the proclamation of the White Queen in the streets of Delhi.

## I.

It was the summer of the year 1746. In Scotland, Butcher Cumberland was laying waste the Highland glens with fire and sword, and the Prince for whom the clansmen had died was hunted like "a partridge in the mountains."

On the Continent, Marshal Saxe had torn himself from balls and operas in Paris to lead his victorious army once more against Maria Theresa and her allies.

In the south-west of India, workmen were labouring day and night, as they had laboured for two years past, upon the fortifications of Pondicherry, and among them, directing, encouraging, controlling, moved a tall figure with head erect, and dark penetrating eyes under a lofty brow, glancing now upon the sea-wall, and now upon the vivid blue of the sea.

The struggle between French and English was being fought out upon the Continent; it was also to be fought out in India, where the issues at stake were far greater, though no man had the wit to realise them save one—Joseph Francois Dupleix, whom the Compagnie des Indes Orientales had appointed Director-General of the French possessions in India. Sent away from home in disgrace as a boy, because he preferred roaming about the valley of the Sombre and playing the violin to giving his mind to commerce, he had risen to be a prince in India, bearing honorific titles granted by the Emperor of Delhi. While making a vast fortune for himself, he had brought prosperity to the Compagnie, which under his management carried on a thriving trade with China and the Persian Gulf, as well as with the interior of India, and he was upon excellent terms with all the native rulers, whom he impressed with his state and charmed with his courtesy and tact.

The war with the English was a hindrance to the Compagnie's business, but when once it was over the way would be clear for Dupleix. While others thought of increasing dividends, he dreamed of building an Eastern Empire for France. The times were ripe; let him sweep aside these traders and the road lay open to Delhi and the throne of the Moghuls.

So he dreamed, walking up and down the fortifications. Victory must be on his side. The English in Madras had only six hundred European troops to bring against him, and it would be no easy matter to send reinforcements from Bombay or Calcutta. It was true that his masters at home had nearly ruined the game ere it was begun, writing to him just before the outbreak of the war that he must not load another ship or spend another *sou* upon fortifications. But the ships went off in their season as usual; Dupleix paid for their cargoes, as he paid the workmen who repaired the crumbling fortifications of Pondicherry; and when they heard what he had done, his Directors altered their mind and approved everything.

Then Cardinal Fleury, the Minister, had committed what might have been a fatal blunder, ordering all French vessels at the Isles of Bourbon and France [1] to return home at once. The possession of those islands as a "half-way house" gave an incalculable advantage to the French settlements in India, and as soon as the Cardinal's orders were obeyed, an English squadron could sweep the Indian seas, snapping up French merchantmen and blockading Pondicherry. Had it not been for the friendly Nawab of the Carnatic, who forbade the English in Madras to attack the

[1] Now better known as Réunion and Mauritius.

French settlements, the game must have been lost for Dupleix.

As it was, while the Nawab's prohibition kept off the English, Dupleix had sent the only vessel remaining to him to the Isle of France to ask for help from the Governor.

Bertrand Thomas Mahé de la Bourdonnais made his first voyage as a common sailor on board a merchant ship before he was ten years old. When he had risen to be Governor of the Isles of France and Bourbon, he had transformed them, single-handed and with no assistance from France, building magazines, arsenals, and barracks, constructing harbours and fortifications, laying out canals and aqueducts where had been desolate wastes, and raising substantial houses in place of mud cabins.

All these labours had made him such an expert in the art of manufacturing bricks without straw that when Dupleix's messenger arrived he managed to invent a fleet where there was none. Without warrant, he detained every vessel that passed the Isles; he laid hands on every man he could find and trained him by force into a carpenter, a smith, a soldier, or a sailor; and in July 1746 Dupleix at last beheld the long-expected fleet coming into Pondicherry.

There were nine ships, and they had gained one victory already, for they had encountered an

English squadron on their way, and beaten it back to Ceylon. Dupleix saw his dreams about to be fulfilled; the hour had come to drive the English from Madras.

The hour had come, but not the man. La Bourdonnais, who could achieve impossibilities, alone, upon his islands, would do nothing in India to work out another man's scheme, lest that other man should have all the credit. From the moment of his landing at Pondicherry he took offence because he was required to take the secondary place. He complained of the Governor's "airs of superiority," and it is easy to imagine that there could have been no sympathy between two men, one of whom relieved his feelings with fantasias upon the harp, while the other gave vent to the coarsest seaman's oaths.

When at length the urgings of Dupleix and the whole Council of Pondicherry obliged La Bourdonnais to advance upon the town of Madras, he had little difficulty in obtaining its surrender, since only two hundred men out of the garrison were fit for duty. Then — influenced, some said, by a substantial bribe from the Madras Council—he undertook to admit the town to ransom. Dupleix refused to sanction the agreement. "In the name of Heaven," he wrote, "in the name of your children, in the name of your wife, listen to persuasion, finish as you have begun, and do not spare an enemy whose sole aim is to reduce you to the last extremity." La Bourdonnais stubbornly refused to recognise any authority in India superior to his own, and arrested some of the Commissioners sent by Dupleix to Madras.

The deadlock was ended by a terrible hurricane, which, suddenly sweeping along the coast after a cloudless day, scattered La Bourdonnais' squadron in all directions, drowning four ships with twelve hundred men on board, and damaging the remainder past hope of repair even by his ingenuity. Under protest he signed the form of treaty approved by the Council of Pondicherry, and, having patched up the remnants of his fleet, departed from Madras amid another fearful tempest which threatened to overwhelm them. Soon afterwards he was on his way home to France.

## II.

As the last sail of those storm-tossed vessels sank below the horizon, Dupleix must have felt that with them vanished all his dreams of empire. The French fleet was destroyed, the English fleet intact; his sole English conquest, Madras, was threatened by the Nawab of the Carnatic, who had become jealous of the growing influence of the French.

To the keen imagination and the fine sense of the dramatic which are the natural heritage of his race, Dupleix united the dogged inability to know when he was beaten commonly attributed to the Englishman. Deserted by the man who should have been his mainstay, and attacked by the ally upon whom he had reckoned for protection, he faced the crisis. Already the French garrison at Madras were in great straits, the Nawab's cavalry having cut off the water supply, when Dupleix sent four hundred men and two field-pieces to the rescue. The Nawab's cavalry had massed together to ride down the little force, when the guns fired, and, before the charge could be resumed, fired again. Now, one shot in a quarter of an hour was then the maximum to which Eastern artillerymen could attain, and the cavalry halted in a doubt which was speedily changed to terror when a third discharge crashed through their ranks, followed by a fourth. Headlong they fled, leaving seventy men behind them, while the French remained in possession of their tents and baggage without the loss of a single man.

Two days later M. Paradis, the only competent officer whom Dupleix could command, with a force of less than a thousand men, not a quarter of whom were Europeans, and no guns, came upon the Nawab's army of ten thousand, drawn up on the north bank of the river Adyar, near St Thomé. Over the river he led his men, sword in hand, and the soldiers, "refreshed by the water," flung themselves upon the enemy, who broke and fled back to the town. Thither Paradis followed them, driving them from point to point; their very numbers were a disadvantage in the narrow crooked streets, and they wavered and turned, and fell over each other while the French muskets raked them. When the remnant had struggled beyond the walls of St Thomé, it was to find another enemy upon their flank—the French garrison of Madras, who had sallied to the help of Paradis. The battle became a massacre, and the retreat a panic-stricken flight.

"Of all the decisive actions that ever were fought in India, there is not one more memorable than this." "The battle of St Thomé first proved the absolute and overwhelming superiority of the disciplined European soldier to his Asiatic rival."[1] No longer would French or English come suppliant to Nawab or Wazir to ask his protection; it would be the native rulers who would entreat the help of the Europeans. "Les balles de Saint-Thomé avaient brisé leur sceptre."[2]

Only one thing now hindered the establishment

[1] Malleson. [2] Hamont.

of the French empire in India; the head to devise was there, but not the hand to execute. Dupleix could draw out a masterly plan of campaign, but he could not himself translate it into action, and the officers at his disposal could not even obey orders, much less take the initiative at need. Four times did he attempt to drive the English from Fort St David, and four times did he fail from various causes—an incapable officer allowed himself to be surprised, a storm drove back the boats that were to attack upon the sea side, the right moment was allowed to pass and an English squadron came from Calcutta to the relief of the Fort, another incapable officer was beaten back from the walls.

The Fort was the last refuge of the English in Madras, and within it was a young writer in the Company's service—a sullen, quarrelsome fellow whom no one liked, though one or two of his superiors reckoned that he had some ability. When the fourth attack was repulsed with heavy loss, Dupleix did not guess that there was no more hope for himself or for the Compagnie des Indes Orientales.

It was far more serious to him when, shortly afterwards, Paradis was killed during a sortie, while a combined English and Dutch fleet, with "the largest body of Europeans till then amassed on Indian soil," was besieging Pondicherry. Only one efficient helper was left to him, the wife whom he had married six years previously. The child of a French father and a Portuguese mother, Mme. Dupleix had lived all her life in India, and probably had some Hindu blood in her veins. Mistress of several Indian languages, and understanding native manners and prejudices, she could penetrate where Dupleix could not, into the women's apartments, where the fate of princes and peoples is decided as often as in the Council Chamber. She was her husband's secretary, his prime minister, his diplomatic agent.

It was her spies who brought news that after five weeks the siege was to be raised. There is a story that during the course of the siege a bomb dropped within the defences, putting to flight soldiers and sepoys. Dupleix walked up to it, and, as the dust and smoke of its explosion subsided, said with perfect calmness: "You see, children, that it does no harm." Except for the death of Paradis, the besiegers had done no more harm than their bomb. They were dropping with sickness, the rainy season had begun, and the English admiral feared that the monsoon might shatter his fleet as it had shattered that of La Bourdonnais. So he destroyed his batteries and provisions and sailed away, leaving over a thousand dead behind him, while Dupleix and his garrison sang a "Te Deum."

In the following year the Peace of Aix-la-Chapelle ended the war, and either country being obliged to restore what it had taken, Dupleix found himself obliged to give up Madras that France might regain Cape Breton. In the height of their disagreement, La Bourdonnais had insisted that it was better to hold the town to ransom, since it would be taken from them before long. He was not there to triumph, having been thrown into the Bastille on his return to France, on the charge of treason, disobedience, and the misappropriation of funds, but the memory of his prophecy may have clouded the elation of Dupleix when congratulatory letters poured in from the princes of India, including the Emperor of Delhi himself.

Nevertheless, the road must be clear now, since none was likely to withstand the man who, single-handed, had defied the Nawab of the Carnatic, and beaten off the combined forces of Great Britain and Holland.

Two men had been left out of Dupleix's calculations.

One of them sat alone in the Bastille, and, deprived of ink and paper, wrote his "Mémoires" with a bent *sou*, dipped in a compound of soot and coffee-dregs, upon handkerchiefs stiffened with rice-water.

The other, the writer in the East India Company's service, having served as a volunteer in an expedition to the mouth of the river Coleroon, shortly after the Peace of Aix-la-Chapelle, was nominated Commissary to the Army. His name was Robert Clive.

# II.

# CHECK TO THE FRENCH—1749-1752.

"Mr Robert Clive, who has lately been very serviceable in conducting several parties to camp, offering to go without any consideration to pay, . . . it is conceived that this officer may be of some service."—*Records of Madras Council*, 1751.

## II.

## CHECK TO THE FRENCH—1749-1752

### I.

The War of the Austrian Succession had ended in Europe. The French and English settlements in India were compulsorily at peace, each impatient to extend its boundaries, each burdened with the support of an increased number of European troops. Such conditions were impossible, and Dupleix, always quick to grasp a situation, found a way by which French and English might settle their differences, in spite of the Treaty of Aix-la-Chapelle. There were continual wars around them—a disputed succession, or an attempt by some prince or chief upon a rival's territory, continually disturbed such peace as India could know in the days of the later Moghul Emperors. The battle of St Thomé had taught the native princes the value of European soldiers. If the French were to lend their troops to one side in a dispute, it was inevitable that the other side should call upon the English for help, and then the hereditary foes could decide between themselves who was to be master upon Indian soil, without troubling as to what might be laid down by diplomatists in Europe.

The occasion soon presented itself. While Dupleix had been making futile attempts upon Fort St David, the Viceroy of the Deccan died, having nominated his grandson as his successor. One of his sons made a counter-claim, and the grandson appealed to the French. At the same time Dupleix was implored to aid the cause of Chanda Sahib, the rightful Nawab of the Carnatic, now a prisoner in the hands of the Marathas, while another — the enemy whom Dupleix had beaten at St Thomé—usurped his power.

It was a magnificent opportunity, and Dupleix seized upon it. To have his nominees governing the Deccan and the Carnatic would be to give France the control of all Southern India. Chanda Sahib was ransomed, and the usurping Nawab was slain in a battle in which his troops suffered a total defeat. One of his sons fled to the English, who as a matter of course were preparing to back the claims of the Deccan Viceroy's son against the grandson whom the French protected.

Again the plans of Dupleix were ruined by those who should have carried them out. His officers proved incompetent and cowardly, their men mutinied on the eve of a battle, and his claimant to the Deccan, after throwing away several opportunities by stupidity and inaction, actually surrendered to his uncle and rival, who behaved in a manner worthy of all the cruel uncles in romance or tradition. He flung his nephew in irons, and when he went out to battle against the French, he mounted the hapless youth upon an elephant, with the executioner behind him, and brought him to the field.

In the midst of the fight the uncle saw some of his allies retiring, and gave orders to the executioner to strike off his nephew's head. By an error in judgment, instead of waiting to see the operation performed, he started in pursuit of the fugitives. The executioner hesitated. As the nephew waited, trembling, for the sword to descend, a bleeding head was laid before him—the head of his uncle, who had been shot down by one of the deserters as he was pouring abuse upon them.

Raised from a prison to the throne of the Deccan, the new Viceroy's first act was to send a message to Dupleix promising to do nothing without his advice. Lands and money were freely bestowed upon the Compagnie and upon its Governor, and a body of French troops was selected to escort the Viceroy to his capital, and to be maintained at his expense for so long as he should have need of them.

Except in his resolution to be guided by Dupleix, the young prince had exhibited very little wisdom up to this time, and he gave the last proof of his folly by getting himself killed on the way to his capital in a skirmish with the chiefs who had deserted his uncle on the battle-field. Once more Dupleix pieced his broken webs together. Three young uncles of the dead man still survived in captivity, and one of these was released and set upon the throne, to prove a loyal friend to Dupleix at all times.

Dupleix was now to all intents and purposes the ruler of Southern India. Though he had declined the title of Nawab of the Carnatic in favour of Chanda Sahib, he was master there, as in the Deccan, and his influence was felt in the kingdoms of Mysore, Tanjore, and Madura. He had at last a competent general in Charles Joseph Patisier de Bussy-Castelnau, who, coming out to India "with no fortune save his pedigree and his title of marquis,"[1] had proved himself "an eagle among the sparrow-hawks," and was loved by Dupleix

[1] Hamont.

as his son. Bussy's capture of the fort of Gingi, till then held to be impregnable, had confirmed the general belief that nothing could withstand the French arms.

It seemed of little moment that Mohammad Ali, son of the usurping Nawab who had died in battle for the Carnatic, refused to surrender Trichinopoly, and was backed up in his refusal by the English. Bussy was fully occupied in the Deccan, but a very inferior general, d'Auteuil, defeated the East India Company's forces, and they broke, in shameful flight, deserting their allies, and leaving their artillery and camp equipage behind them. Had d'Auteuil led his men after them, that day's disgrace would have ended the war.

But d'Auteuil was old, and moreover was writhing in the throes of an attack of gout, and though he saw the English forces hurrying along the road to Trichinopoly, huddled together in disorder, everything forgotten save the blind impulse to flee, he would not pursue them until the next day.

The English were so demoralised that they could make no stand. They fled into an ambush, and were punished for it, as they deserved. Then they retreated across the Coleroon, and took refuge in Srirangam, an island formed by its junction with another river. Even there, they durst not wait the coming of the French, and they crept within the walls of Trichinopoly itself, while d'Auteuil took possession of Srirangam.

The only thing that can be said in excuse for the conduct of the English troops is that at this period they were commanded by a Swiss, who was as incapable as the worst officer on the French side.

Dupleix was urgent for an immediate attack upon Trichinopoly, before the garrison had rallied their spirits. Unluckily he had made a bad choice to relieve d'Auteuil, whose gout had obliged him to resign his post. The new commander, generally known in French and Indian records as "M. Lass"—in reality a Law of Lauriston, nephew of the financier—had been an excellent soldier under authority, but was one of "those who never see till next day what they ought to do on the evening of the day before." He hesitated to "throw away the lives of men" against the double walls and deep ditches that surrounded the town, and decided instead to blockade it, and starve the garrison into submission.

The Governor of Fort St David was then a Mr Saunders, who had been appointed in the previous year. To him, as to every one else, the plight of the English must have seemed hopeless. Only a remnant of their army was left outside the walls of Trichinopoly, incapable of helping the garrison, who could do nothing to help themselves. One little fort on the road to Fort St David still declared for Mohammad Ali, all the rest of the Carnatic was in the hands of Chanda Sahib and the French. It was merely a question of how long the dispirited men in Trichinopoly would sit behind their walls before hunger obliged them to surrender.

With all this in his mind, Mr Saunders was told that the Commissary of the force routed by d'Auteuil had arrived, and demanded to see him. In the panic after d'Auteuil's victory, Robert Clive had been conspicuous as one of the few who had vainly tried to rally the men. Instead of taking refuge with them in Trichinopoly, he had come to Fort St David with a plan of action which might yet save the town. If only Mr Saunders would give him the command of a few men, he would lead them to take Arcot, the Nawab's capital, which in the general preoccupation with Trichinopoly had been left almost undefended.

It may be a sound military maxim that the belligerent who cannot hold his own should carry the war into the enemy's country, but it was somewhat hazardous to leave Trichinopoly to its fate, and reduce the garrison of Fort St David to the lowest possible number, in order to send a handful of men into the heart of a hostile province, under the leadership of "an untrained civilian" of six-and-twenty. Saunders saw the danger as clearly as did those men at the outposts who, later on, were to strip themselves of their last soldier and their last gun, in order to send help to the camp on the Ridge of Delhi, and, like them, he was ready to take risks. Nothing could well make the position any worse than it was, and Clive's plan at least gave the chance of doing something, instead of sitting still till the English settlements in Madras were wiped out of existence.

It was early in September when Clive arrived at the gates of Arcot, "with 200 Englishmen, 300 sepoys, and three small guns," amid storm and thunder and rain, and finding no one to oppose him, marched in, repaired the fortifications, and waited for what might happen.

Dupleix had begun to feel the ebb of the tide; he learned that public opinion in France, influenced by the 'Mémoires' of the dead La Bourdonnais, was turning against him; his brother and only defender in Paris had died. He was struggling with a severe illness, but his head was clear, and he refused to be drawn into Clive's trap. Law received orders that no consideration was to be allowed to interfere with the conquest of Trichinopoly. Chanda Sahib, however, would not be withheld from sending 4000 of his best troops, under his son, to regain Arcot.

The story of the fifty days' siege that followed has been told by many pens. We all know how the reliefs sent from Madras were beaten back; how Clive refused to surrender on honourable terms, though a breach yawned in the wall; how, when provisions ran short his sepoys asked that the rice might be given to their English brothers, who needed more solid food, since they themselves would be content with the water in which it had been boiled; how, in an ecstasy of defiance, the garrison dragged a large gun, cast long ago by Aurangzib, to the topmost tower of the fort, and fired it once a day upon the enemy, until, to their great mortification, it blew in pieces at the fourth discharge; and how Chanda Sahib's son burst open the gates with elephants, only to be beaten back, after eighteen hours' hard fighting, leaving four hundred of his men lying dead about the walls.

"It was at Arcot that English officers taught their sepoys to follow them with the implicit confidence which superior skill and energy alone can inspire; it was at Arcot that they learned the lesson that in Asiatic warfare the question of numbers is merely a secondary consideration; that discipline, and the self-confidence born of it, are of infinitely greater importance; that there is nothing which a capable general, one who can impress his spirit on his soldiers, may not prudently attempt against an undisciplined enemy."[1]

Clive again put the lesson into practice when, the besiegers having broken up their camp and disappeared from Arcot on the day after the great assault, he followed in their rear. Twenty miles away, on the banks of the river Arni, he came up with them, and though they were now strengthened by French reinforcements from Pondicherry, they were beaten and driven back upon Gingi, leaving their guns to the conqueror.

## II.

Again Dupleix entreated Law to fall upon Trichinopoly; food was running short, the garrison were completely demoralised. But Law hesitated and wavered until another despatch came promising that he need not fear Clive, since Dupleix was taking measures to occupy him elsewhere. One hundred Europeans had been sent to strengthen Chanda Sahib's contingent, who were laying waste the country up to within a few miles of the town of Madras, and intended to surprise Arcot.

[1] Malleson.

Having failed in this latter design, with great astuteness the enemy doubled back and took up a position at Kaveripak, on the road by which Clive must march to Arcot. They concluded—as was the case — that he would pass when the sudden darkness of an Indian night was falling, and the trap very nearly succeeded as well as it deserved. The French artillery cut the little force to pieces, and Clive had been all but driven from the field, when one of his officers who could speak French contrived to bring some of the men past the enemy's sentries, and fall upon the rear of the camp. Taken between two fires, the French fled, leaving their guns.

It was a decisive victory. It needed not that Clive on his way back to Fort St David should raze to the ground Dupleix-Fateh-a-bad, "the place of the Victory of Dupleix," founded on the battlefield where the French had set their candidate on the throne of the Deccan. All could see that the star of France was declining.

The English in India had just received a reinforcement worth several regiments in Major Stringer Lawrence, one of the many who have helped to build up our Empire in the East whose names are almost forgotten by men of to-day. He had foiled one of the French attempts upon Fort St David. He had been the first to notice Clive's military genius when the young man was serving as a volunteer in an expedition against the Raja of Tanjore. During the last two years he had been in England, and he returned for the crowning triumph over his old enemy.

To pit against him Dupleix had only the inert Law, who at this stage was demanding leave to return to Pondicherry "pour assister aux couches de sa femme."

Then Dupleix wrote to him, giving the number of the men who were about to march under Major Lawrence from Fort St David to the relief of Trichinopoly, with many other details obtained by his spies, and urging him to intercept them with the main body of his troops, leaving only a few to keep watch upon the city.

It was a long road, and a difficult, for it led across eight rivers, one of which had to be crossed three times. There would be many opportunities for cutting off the enemy, who were convoying provisions and stores for the half-starved garrison, and could not move fast. But Law was to throw away this chance, as he had thrown away all the rest. He sent out only one-third of his whole force, and though Major Lawrence's guides led the English astray till they were beneath the guns of the fortress where this detachment was posted, and the convoy was thrown into disorder, yet the

French officer in command made no sally to complete the rout, but sat placidly behind his walls until the English had re-formed and moved out of range.

Then, when it was too late, Law drew up his men to a general action and was beaten back, while Lawrence and Clive brought the convoy into Trichinopoly. When he returned to camp he was as one distraught. Nothing would serve him but to retreat into the island of Srirangam—that island between the two rivers from which the French had chased the beaten English less than a year before.

In spite of the frantic remonstrances of Chanda Sahib, who cried out, with tears in his eyes, that no one would have dared such infamy had Dupleix been on the spot, the retreat was made—in such haste that a large part of the stores and baggage had to be abandoned and burned to prevent it from falling into the hands of the English.

Once more, as if in pity to Dupleix, fate gave Law a chance of retrieving their fortune. He learned through Chanda Sahib's spies that Clive had left his post at Simiaveram, on the highroad between Srirangam and Pondicherry, and was on the way to intercept d'Auteuil. By a forced march of ten miles he might take Simiaveram, and then fall upon Clive's force while they were busy with d'Auteuil. Again Law deliberately chose to send out only a small part of his army—seven hundred sepoys, and eighty Europeans, half of whom, it is grievous to confess, were English deserters.

Again they missed success by a hair's-breadth. Clive had returned from a bootless excursion after d'Auteuil, who had been warned of his movements, and was lying asleep in his palki in an open shed beside one of the two pagodas that sheltered his English force; his sepoys were encamped round them. The English deserters explained to the sentries that they were part of a reinforcement sent by Major Lawrence to Clive, and without more ado led the enemy into the midst of the sleeping camp.

A sudden volley crashing into the pagodas aroused Clive, and he ran out thinking that his sepoys had taken a false alarm, and were letting off their muskets regardless of their surroundings—a favourite weakness of the sepoy. Calling up some of the Europeans, he went towards the lesser pagoda, from which the shots came, shouting to the men drawn up before it. One of them attacked him, wounding him in two places, and then ran away. Clive, still believing them to be some of his own sepoys afflicted with that form of hysteria which sometimes runs through a whole camp at night, gave chase, and at last understood what had befallen when six French soldiers bade him surrender.

It was for the French to yield, said Clive, not for him; they were in his power, and of his mercy he had come to offer them terms; let them come and see for themselves how all his army waited for them outside.

Whereupon three of the soldiers laid their arms at his feet, while three undertook to bear his message to their comrades in the pagoda. The English deserters, fearing what might be their punishment, declared against surrender, and one of them nearly murdered Clive as he stood waiting for the answer. There was a sharp struggle, and then the pagoda was surrendered. Well had Clive earned the title of "Sabat Jung"—"the daring in war,"—by which he was remembered in India nearly a hundred years after the battle of Simiaveram.

The last chance for the French had failed. D'Auteuil was surprised, and obliged to yield with all his force. Law's native allies were deserting him, and food was running short upon the island. Chanda Sahib urged him to make a sally, and cut his way to Tanjore, sword in hand; Dupleix ordered it as the only course left to them. But Law would think of nothing but surrender. He made a pitiful attempt to save the life of Chanda

Sahib. Death assuredly would bė his portion were he to fall into the hands of his rival, Mohammad Ali, but a bribe paid down, and the promise of more, brought the general of the Raja of Tanjore to swear that he would protect him. If ever he had intended to keep his promise, the general soon found it beyond his power; Mohammad Ali, and the Maratha and Mysore troops who had been his auxiliaries, all laid claim to Chanda Sahib, and, "terrified at the commotions which would inevitably follow if he gave the preference to any of the competitors," the Tanjore general "saw no method of finishing the contest but by putting an end to the life of his prisoner."[1]

On June 13, 1752, Law's army surrendered. It was a triumph for the English, and it had been won not only by Clive's genius, but by his loyalty in working under Major Lawrence's command as whole-heartedly as when he was acting on his own responsibility. Had La Bourdonnais conceived duty as Clive did—had Clive fought for his own hand like La Bourdonnais—there might have been another story to tell.

[1] Orme.

# III.

# THE END OF A DREAM—1751-1754

"Sorti de l'obscurité, Dupleix devint en peu d'années presque un roi, et sans contredit le représentant politique le plus grand du génie français au dix-huitième siècle."—TIBULLE HAMONT, *Dupleix d'après sa Correspondance Inédite.*

## III.

## THE END OF A DREAM—1751-1754.

STILL, Dupleix would not acknowledge himself beaten. His obstinate jaw and straight mouth set more firmly as he reckoned up the points for and against himself. He had lost Arcot, and most of his conquests in the Carnatic; he had no longer a candidate to oppose to Mohammad Ali. The besiegers of Trichinopoly were prisoners, and save for a few invalids, he had no garrison for Pondicherry. On the other hand, he still kept Gingi, the fortress which none but Bussy could storm; Bussy himself was in the Deccan, and could be summoned at need. The Viceroy was his friend, and would help him. He had been beaten in the field, because he must give his plans to be worked out by officers, not one of whom could be trusted to obey orders; in diplomacy he had Mme. Dupleix at his side, and the two together were more than a match for thick-headed English or cunning Hindus.

Accordingly he set to work to sow dissension among the powers allied against him. Mme. Dupleix created a French party in the zenana of the Regent of Mysore, and in a little while the forces of Mysore were ready to fly at the throat of Mohammad Ali, the Marathas would have been equally well pleased to attack either, and the men of Tanjore had no wish but to return to their own land. While they quarrelled, Dupleix was receiving and drilling the first instalments of his annual draft from France. Then both Major Lawrence and Clive fell so ill that they must return to Madras, leaving the troops under the same Swiss whose incompetence had already cost them dearly.

French prestige revived. The Viceroy of the Deccan appointed Dupleix Nawab of the Carnatic —a dignity offered to him before, and refused by him in favour of Chanda Sahib. At the instance of the Directors of the Compagnie des Indes Orientales, Louis XV. created him a Marquis. The forces of Mysore and the Marathas, having quarrelled effectually with their late ally, Mohammad Ali, were blockading Trichinopoly on their own account, and undertook to help Dupleix when required, if he would not interfere with them. A ship was about to arrive from France with seven hundred men, and an experienced commander, M. de la Touche. Dupleix saw no risk in sending his nephew Kerjean to begin the siege of Fort St David, while he waited for them.

The news of the peril of the Fort was brought to Major Lawrence, and, ill as he was, he sailed at once to its help. The French numbers were considerable, and their position strong; Kerjean had only to sit still until his reinforcements came. But Kerjean was young and ambitious, and meant to have the glory of beating the English before he should be obliged to yield the command to La Touche. When Lawrence retreated to a post two miles from Fort St David, Kerjean could not refrain from going after him, and, in the security of an easy victory, encamped in a bad position without any of the usual precautions. At night Lawrence attacked the camp, and while Kerjean "amused himself by firing on the advanced guard," as Dupleix described it to Bussy, some of the enemy entered at the rear unperceived. "Nevertheless each stood his ground; but there was confusion. The bayonet played its part, and the enemy was about to fly, when the report of Kerjean's death spread abroad. There was no way to hold the soldiers or the sepoys. All broke, and it was not possible to rally the troops."[1] Kerjean and fifteen officers were taken prisoners.

[1] Dupleix to Bussy.

Still Dupleix cheered his Council, who were losing heart. Lawrence had gained a victory, but from illness or from some error in judgment he had not followed it up; Clive, after capturing the strongest fort in Southern India next to Gingi, with a force composed of the scourings of English jails, had been obliged to return to England for his health. When La Touche came, France would recover all her lost ground. But La Touche never came; the ship which was bearing him and his seven hundred men to India was destroyed by fire on the high seas.

At the time of the capture of Srirangam, Dupleix had already spent £140,000 of his private fortune in the service of his Compagnie, who grudged every halfpenny and every man sent to India. He still continued to spend what was left to him. Beset on all sides as he was, seeing from the walls of Pondicherry the smoke from the villages burned by Mohammad Ali and the English, he would not yet recall Bussy from the Deccan, where he was serving French interests. He chose rather to engage a body of Maratha cavalry, to divert Lawrence's attention, while the forces of Mysore invested Trichinopoly.

Happily for the garrison, it was no longer the Swiss officer who commanded in Trichinopoly, but Captain Dalton, a man not unworthy of the time.

The previous siege had lasted eleven months; this went on for a whole year. The Marathas outside exercised their usual tactics, swooping down on foraging parties, cutting off supplies, and intercepting communications. At Lawrence's approach they melted away, and no wiles of his could draw them into the open field. The Mysore army gradually encircled the town more closely, until it was cut off from the surrounding country.

Lawrence heard from Captain Dalton that provisions for three weeks only remained to him, and made a hurried march for Trichinopoly. The Mysore force retreated into Srirangam, whence he was unable to drive them, though he succeeded in revictualling the town. Meanwhile Dupleix sent reinforcements under M. Astruc to Trichinopoly, and sent an expedition under a kinsman of Chanda Sahib to recover some of the strong places in the Carnatic, which the English of necessity had left insufficiently garrisoned.

A severe illness obliged Major Lawrence to retire into the Fort, instead of remaining in camp outside Trichinopoly with his men, and Astruc took his advantage. To the south of the English camp were the heights of the "Five Rocks"—"the key of the surrounding country." The sepoys left to guard them suddenly found themselves surprised by Astruc, who set his men then and there to cover the base and flanks of the heights with fortifications, and made such speed that the work was finished by the time that poor Lawrence dragged himself out in a fruitless attempt to recover the position next day.

From the "Five Rocks" the French could prevent all supplies being brought in to Trichinopoly. If another height, the Golden Rock, were taken, there was no shelter between it and the city for Lawrence's army, already driven from its old camp. On a July morning, while most of his sepoys were receiving their rations, Lawrence heard the sound of firing, and saw French grenadiers swarming up the sides of the Golden Rock. Before he could collect his men, the French lilies were waving from the summit, and the French army was gathered at the base.

Before him were the rugged heights, where a triumphant band stood ready to hurl him back; behind him pressed the Maratha horsemen, eager to pull down their prey. From either flank of the rock came the rattle of the French artillery. On every side was death, whether he stood, or fell back, or advanced. "The Golden Rock is taken!" he cried; "it must be taken back!"

Astruc saw Lawrence draw up his men—only four hundred and twenty Europeans and five hundred sepoys in all—and lead them towards the left of the base of the Golden Rock, where the whole French army waited for them. If the Englishman preferred to end it quickly, so much the better; the French were ready, their right against the left spur of the rock, and the Marathas were moving at Astruc's command to take the English in flank and rear. Only fifty yards separated them, when a sudden blaze from the rock overhead threw the French line into disorder.

Unnoted by Astruc, Lawrence had picked out certain of his grenadiers and sepoys, and bidden them scale the rock on its front, while he advanced. Silently, without pulling trigger, the men scrambled up, till they stood on the summit; then they fell upon their enemy. It was death or victory, and they knew it, and they changed death into victory, and sent the Frenchmen over the opposite side of the rock.

As their shots crashed into the French below, Lawrence's men fired, and then charged with fixed bayonets—and the French army wavered, broke, and fled. In vain Astruc threw himself among the fugitives, trying to rally them; flushed with victory as they had been some few moments ago, the surprise for the time had broken their nerve, and they ran, while the Marathas covered their retreat.

A military expert gives the verdict that "No

finer feat of arms has been performed in any part of the world than the assault by a handful of grenadiers of the Golden Rock, held by an enemy that had just conquered it, and whose army was formed up at its base."[1]

In bitter mortification, Astruc went back to Pondicherry: his successor tried blockade and strategy with no effect, and was beaten in an attempt to intercept a convoy of provisions. Then Astruc returned with reinforcements, took back the Five Rocks and the Golden Rock, and recommenced a blockade. Lawrence waited till his own reinforcements arrived, and then on October 1st, 1753, marched out and offered battle. When Astruc declined it, Lawrence encamped for the night on the ground where his men were drawn up, and next morning won a decisive victory, driving the French across the Cauveri. Astruc was taken prisoner, with over a hundred of his army, and the rest retreated into the island of Srirangam.

"Je n'ai pas un homme de tête pour conduire la moindre opération," wrote Dupleix, after hearing of this reverse. For the time, he could do nothing to repair it, and his Directors were urging him to conclude the war. He began negotiations with the English, who were not averse to peace. They had

[1] Malleson.

not engaged in war, like Dupleix, led by a dream of empire, but to extend their trade, and military operations interfered with commerce. So they were ready to meet him half-way, save that they could not recognise him as Nawab of the Carnatic.

While they disputed this point, a new commandant at Srirangam had surprised the sleepy sepoys at one of the outworks of Trichinopoly before daybreak, and might have been inside the walls if the French troops could have refrained from firing off two captured guns with shouts of "*Vive le Roi!*" The garrison woke up and let off their pieces indiscriminately, by good luck killing an English deserter who had undertaken to guide the French. In the darkness the attacking party could not find the gate without his help. Some were killed, some leaped from the outwork at the risk of broken bones, the greater number were taken prisoners.

So sure had they made of success that a messenger had been sent to Dupleix as soon as the outwork was taken to announce the capture of Trichinopoly. "Had not French petulance made them too soon discover themselves," wrote Lawrence, "they perhaps might have had time to execute their designs." As it was, another messenger arrived some hours later to tell of the disaster.

Again Dupleix turned to diplomacy, and French and English commissaries met to arrange the terms of peace. Neither side was unreasonable in their demands, but the East India Company would not give up the cause of their ally, Mohammad Ali—since he had been their pretext for war, they scarce could do less—while Dupleix obstinately persisted in claiming the title of Nawab of the Carnatic. A letter from Dupleix to Bussy describes how the French commissaries duly exhibited firmans and documents in support of their claim, all of which had been forged for the occasion. This seems to have troubled him not at all, but he speaks with righteous severity of the unjustifiable behaviour of the English, who declined to exhibit any documents whatever, "either false or genuine," and expected their word to be taken without other formality.

Dupleix's obstinacy about a title is inexplicable in a man of his genius. Let who will call himself Nawab of the Carnatic, the Governor of Pondicherry, with Mme. Dupleix at his side, could make him dance to French piping. But he must have been overwrought by the long strain, and incapable of seeing clearly. Moreover, just at this time, Bussy had signed an agreement with the Prime Minister of the Deccan, whereby the French gained the provinces known as the Northern Sirkars, with four hundred and seventy miles of sea-coast and a revenue of £400,000. The practical effect of this was to give them the mastery of the Deccan; should Dupleix bow before Mohammad Ali when he could rule Mohammad Ali's lord?

"Seventy years later, the man whom he most resembled in ambition, in genius, in the power of compelling others, came, under similar circumstances, at Dresden in 1813 and at Châtillon in 1814, to a similar resolution."[1]

As with Napoleon, so with Dupleix, the resolution was fatal. The Directors of the East India Company had long bewailed to the English Government the restless ambition of M. Dupleix; the English Government made representations to France, regretting that one man should have it in his power to disturb the good understanding between the two nations, and let it be known that they were sending four ships and a regiment to India. It was nothing to the Directors of the Compagnie that Dupleix had nearly given France an Eastern empire; they saw their dividends falling, and they were weary of his urgency for men and money.

Thus it happened that France sent out a Commissary to treat for peace—a M. Godeheu, supposed to be the devoted friend of Dupleix, who had shown

[1] Malleson.

him great kindness, even to the saving of his life in youth. On his way to India Godeheu wrote protesting that he viewed his appointment merely as an opportunity of profiting by Dupleix's wisdom. When his ship arrived in Pondicherry Roads, Dupleix hurried down to embrace the man for whom he had waited with impatience as "the dearest of his friends." Once more he was hopeful, for two thousand troops were coming after Godeheu. The Raja of Tanjore, defeated by the Marathas, was half disposed to break with the English, thanks to his skilful manipulation, and he was dreaming of making perpetual alliance with Portugal and adding Macao to the possessions of the Compagnie.

Godeheu, surrounded by his guards, bowed coldly to the man who held out his arms to him, and produced a paper to be read at once. Dupleix unfolded it, found it to be an order for his immediate return to France with all his family, and turned to Godeheu for an explanation. Without allowing him time to speak, Godeheu put two other papers into his hand, one a demand for a detailed report upon the state of affairs, and the other an order from King Louis revoking his appointment as Governor.

At the first shock Dupleix grew pale, and made "a gesture of astonishment"; then he fixed his piercing black eyes upon the Commissary as he asked whether he had any further orders. The Commissary had an order for the arrest of Dupleix should he offer any resistance, but he did not think it necessary to produce this. There was one glance of contempt for the false friend, and one sigh, ere Dupleix turned away to summon the Council at Godeheu's request.

The Council was gathered in the vast hall with marble colonnades where Dupleix had received the homage of princes. The Commissary bade his guards clear away the crowd who had pressed after them, ere his commission was read aloud. The members of the Council gazed round them in consternation, drawing in their breaths and staring at Dupleix, who sat with bent head on Godeheu's right, silent and impassive, only betraying his emotion by some feverish movements of his hands. When Godeheu's voice ceased, a chilling silence fell upon the assembly, broken by a single cry of "*Vive le Roi!*" Dupleix was standing before them, his arm uplifted, and all echoed his cry. Then he left the hall and the Council followed him.

Ten weeks later he started on his homeward voyage amid general lamentation. "Your departure is a thunderbolt," wrote Bussy, who only consented to remain at his post at Dupleix's entreaty. The Viceroy of the Deccan bewailed "my uncle, Zafir Jung."[1] Throughout the country ran the word that the new Governor of Pondicherry understood nothing, and that it would be wise to make terms with Mohammad Ali and the English, who after all had gained the upper hand.

For Dupleix there were to be nine weary years of waiting, memorialising and petitioning to no purpose. The Compagnie refused to repay one penny of the £240,000 owing to him—aided and abetted by Godeheu, who threw Dupleix's chief witness into prison, and then reported to the Directors that the claim could not be established satisfactorily. Mme. Dupleix, for the first time in her life, failed her husband; she who had ruled as a princess in India could not endure poverty and neglect in France, and she died. His friends deserted him; Bussy broke off his marriage with Mdlle. Dupleix. "J'ai sacrifié ma jeunesse, ma fortune, ma vie, pour enrichir ma nation en Asie. Mes services sont traités de fables; ma demande est denoncé comme ridicule; je suis traité comme l'être le plus vil du genre humain. Je suis dans la plus deplorable indigence; la petite proprieté qui me restait vient d'etre saisie; je suis contraint de

[1] "Zafir Jung Bahadur"—"Victorious in Battle,"—the name given by the Viceroy to Dupleix.

demander une sentence de délai pour éviter d'être trainé en prison."

So Dupleix wrote in a last appeal, and the document lay unheeded with others at the Ministère des Finances until they were scattered in the street by the mob of 1830.

In the beginning of November 1763, a Commissary was sent from the Châtelet to take an inventory of the contents of a certain house in the Rue Neuve des Capucines, only a few doors away from the Paris headquarters of the Compagnie des Indes Orientales. In one of the rooms on the ground-floor he noted "a dead body, male, extended on a bed with low posts." It was the body of the Marquis Dupleix, Zafir-Jung-Bahadur, Commander of Seven Thousand Horse, Governor of Pondicherry, Nawab from the Kistna to Cape Comorin.

# IV.

## A JACOBITE EXILE—1754-1766.

"L'humiliation pour la France, Pondichéry ruinée, incendiée, detruite de fond en comble, un grabat pour Dupleix mourant, le tête de Lally roulant sous la hache de bourreau; voila le denoûment tragique de cette lutte de dix ans pour la possession de l'Inde. Aux peuples qui s'abandonnent, aux gouvernements qui n'ont ni la volonté des sacrifices, ni l'intelligence politique, ni la tenacité, ni le courage, le désastre à la fin."

—T. HAMONT, *La Fin d'un Empire Français aux Indes sous Louis XV.*

## IV.

# A JACOBITE EXILE—1754-1766.

At the outbreak of the Seven Years' War in 1756, the Directors of the Compagnie des Indes Orientales must have regretted the faithfulness with which M. Godeheu had carried out their instructions.

When Dupleix was treating for peace, a few months before his recall, Saunders had been willing to agree practically to everything that he required, save only in the matter of the title of Nawab of the Carnatic. The peace made three months after Dupleix had left India gave the English all that they had asked. The French had many native allies, the English at that time had only the half-hearted support of the Raja of Tanjore, yet both Companies agreed for the future to renounce all Moghul titles and dignities, and never to interfere in the differences of the princes of the country. Bussy had obtained a grant of the Northern Sirkars to the French, yet it was now agreed that they had no exclusive rights there; and certain other territories, already their property by right of gift or possession, were to be divided between the Companies. One thing only did Godeheu leave undone of the things that he ought not to have done. He did not recall Bussy from the Deccan.

These measures greatly weakened Bussy's credit with the Viceroy, who was indignant that the succession to the Carnatic should have been decided without reference to him. If the French were not strong enough, said the Viceroy, there must needs be an alliance with the English, since no one could hope to remain on the throne of the Deccan without the support of one Power or the other.

Bussy appeased him by driving a Maratha invasion out of Mysore, on condition that the Raja owned himself a vassal of the Deccan and paid arrears of tribute. Chased from the Viceroy's service by Court intrigues, he was back again in three months, reinstated in all titles and honours. But by good luck for the English, the three months chanced to be from the end of May to the middle of August 1756, when their settlements in Bengal were on the verge of being swept out of existence. Another opportunity for France had been lost—this time by no fault of her children.

Had Bussy then commanded the troops of the Deccan, it is possible that the flag of St George might not have been run up on Fort William at the New Year.

The next opportunity of retrieving the Compagnie's fortunes was ruined as soon as it arrived by the French Ministry, who were inspired by the outbreak of war in Europe to send out three thousand men to India, under a commander who was given superior rank to Bussy.

Thomas Arthur Lally, son of one of the "Wild Geese" who took flight from Ireland after James II.'s disastrous campaign and entered the French service, at first sight appears one of those gallant Irishmen who figure as the heroes of countless romances. A captain in Dillon's regiment at eight years old, he was taken by his father to a siege "that he might at least smell powder to gain his first step." Four years later, as "a holiday amusement," he was sent to mount his first guard. Grown to manhood, he went as unaccredited ambassador from Cardinal Fleury to Russia. For his services on the field of Fontenoy, when the Irish Brigade charged to the cry of "Remember Limerick," he was thanked by Louis XV. and the Dauphin in person, and nominated Brigadier. Had the War Office in Paris listened to his representations, France would have given better support to

Prince Charles Edward in the winter of 1745-46. Disguised as a smuggler, he made his way across to England in the wild hope of stirring an insurrection in the home counties. It was useless; the English Government had wind of the plot, and posted bills with his description at every cross-road between the coast and London. Back to the coast he went, and was impressed by a gang of smugglers. As they dragged him to their boat he heard them arguing whether it would not be a profitable speculation to hunt for this Lally, on whose head Government had set a great price. Thanks to his arguments in favour of the small profits and quick returns of smuggling, they decided upon a run across to France, and Lally's skilful pilotage ran them under the nose of a French cruiser. The smugglers were lodged in Boulogne prison, and Lally hastened to Versailles.

All that his Prince could offer him, an Irish peerage, Lally refused until the King should come to his own again. But he would never cease to serve Stuart interests wherever he might, and he would never lay down the sword against the English. "We dream of beating the English on this side of the water, since we cannot on the other," he wrote, and he went off to the campaign in the Low Countries, where he distinguished himself on every occasion. "His escapes were the talk of the army." The highest compliment paid to him was that of Marshal Saxe—"On peut dormir tranquillement, Lally est à l'ennemi."

In spite of all his gallantry, a more unwise choice seldom was made, even by a Ministry, than the selection of Lally to command in India. He was past fifty, without any experience of the East either in peace or war. The "great gentleness of manner" that Voltaire noted in him in earlier days, had vanished, and there remained only the "stubborn fierceness of soul" and uncontrolled bitterness of tongue that raised for him hosts of enemies wherever he went. Though an Irishman, he could neither flatter nor cajole to gain his object, and was entirely destitute of imagination—two fatal defects for a man in his position.

Evil omens were plentiful. There was a story—probably one of those that are remembered or invented after the catastrophe—that three young men, going through Paris at night, passed a house where a *bourgeois* was celebrating his daughter's wedding, and insisted on joining the party; that one of them grossly insulted the bride, and was obliged to save himself from the consequences by confessing that he was Captain Lally and the others were nobles of the Court. The girl's father threw open the door. "You say you are nobles of the Court. I am the public executioner. Go, and take heed lest it be not the last time you pass through my hands." There is no doubt about another story that when Admiral d'Ache at length brought his ship into Pondicherry Roads, having taken all but a year over the voyage, some of the guns which fired a salute from the city were loaded, and five balls went through the hull and rigging of the vessel which carried Lally. The sailors muttered gloomily, and many of the landsmen were dismayed.

Accordingly, all went wrong from the moment of Lally's setting foot on shore. As his French biographer says, it was no longer a question of picking up the crown of the Moghul Emperor to set on the head of the King of France, but of guarding a shop. Lally, who had dreamed in his young days of king-making, could not guard the shop. He had not the art of conciliating the rajas, and he never tried to conciliate the Council of Pondicherry, whom he made no secret of regarding as dishonest and imbecile. In many cases this was true, and he had some excuse for his stinging sarcasms when he found that not a man of the Council could tell him the strength of the English garrisons in the neighbourhood, or the number of rivers to be crossed between Pondicherry and a fort sixteen miles distant. But there were some points on which the Council could have advised him, if he had not determined against listening to them.

No sooner had the French fleet dropped Lally on shore than it was defeated by the English fleet, and driven back to Pondicherry. Lally atoned for this by forcing Cuddalore to surrender. Though he was short of food, ammunition, guns, and mortars, and of money, he took Fort St David within five weeks of his landing in India, and would have attacked Madras if Admiral d'Ache would have agreed to transport his army thither. Now was the time to strike, he said, while the English were discouraged by their losses. But the Admiral said that he had no provisions and his men were all sick, and he sailed away to Ceylon to watch for English merchant ships.

Then Lally committed the only blunder unachieved by Godeheu, and ordered Bussy to leave the Deccan and join him. Bussy was thunderstruck, knowing that to obey would mean the abandonment of all his plans against Bengal, and the loss of the Deccan. "Je frémis, monsieur," he wrote to Lally, "mais j'obéis."

Thus the only man who could have saved the remnants of French dominion in the East was dragged away from the outpost which he alone could hold, at the bidding of a newcomer who understood the situation so imperfectly as to write to the Governor of Pondicherry, "En quoy consiste le profit que notre Compagnie et notre commerce peuvent retirer des guerres et des paix de M. de Bussy?"

It was not likely that two such opposite natures as Bussy and Lally would work together, even if Bussy's heart had not been set upon a speedy return to the Deccan with the reinforcements for which he unavailingly importuned Lally. He had all the gifts which Lally had not. His geniality, blended with a high-bred dignity, and his charm of manner, his tact, coolness, and judgment, his skill in dealing with the men of all the varied races among whom he worked, wrought upon the officers under Lally's command, and they made no secret of their admiration. Lally jealously considered their homage as intended to spite himself, rather than as a just tribute to Bussy, whom he styled "le plus cupide, le plus avare, le plus menteur, le plus pillard de tous les hommes." Bussy, forced to stand by while the army with which he might have founded an empire was thrown away in enterprises foredoomed to fail, grew bitter and resentful. Dupleix, still penning memorials which the Directors never troubled to read, was avenged, had he ever known it, for Bussy's desertion.

The campaign opened well for France. The

native Governor of Arcot was bribed to surrender the town, and the army arrived at Madras at the beginning of December 1758.

As some writers have noticed, it is from Madras that the popular conception of India among the unlearned of this country has been derived. The impossibly blue sky, the dark-green rollers breaking upon a bright sandy beach, the tufted palm-trees and clustered banyans, the dark-skinned natives, all may be seen in the coloured pictures upon missionary boxes, or in missionary publications. The city is the oldest British possession in India: it was as long ago as 1639 that Mr Francis Day, on behalf of the Company, rented a strip of coast-land, a mile broad and six miles in length, and on the island between the heavy surf of the Bay of Bengal and the malodorous black ooze of the river Koum laid the foundations of Fort St George, or White Town. It was holy ground, for near it was the spot where St Thomas, the Apostle of the Indies, had suffered martyrdom: an early traveller, noticing the number of victims to elephantiasis in Madras, has no doubt that they were the descendants of the men who slew the blessed martyr.

Lally's first attack was upon the native quarter, Black Town, which was little defended either by men or by fortifications, and fell an easy prey.

The camp-followers enriched themselves with plunder, for Lally could not maintain the discipline enforced by Bussy, who had once mulcted a grenadier of a hundred rupees for picking an orange in a garden near his camp.

Within the walls of White Town was Stringer Lawrence; and the Governor, George Pigot, had the wisdom to leave the defence to him. An unpublished journal in the Record Office at Madras[1] thus begins the story of the siege: "In order to dispose the garrison with spirits and as a Reward for the Bravery, it is resolved to publish to them in case the enemy shall be either defeated or compelled to raise the siege, the sum of Rs. 50,000 shall be divided amongst them five days after their defeat or retreat." With truly British stolidity, after this they elected the Mayor and Sheriffs of Madras on the proper day, and fired the usual salute of nine guns, which were pointed at the enemy's quarters, "in honour of the new Mayor, and it is hoped with good effect upon the enemy."

One of Lally's best officers was taken prisoner, another mortally wounded, at the beginning of operations, and his army was entirely out of hand. The men who should have been at work in the trenches were hunting for treasure in the Black

[1] Quoted in Forrest's 'Cities of India.'

Town, and even some of the officers spent more time in guarding their plunder than in doing their duty. An English post had been left untaken on the way from Arcot, and its garrison now made constant attacks upon the French rear, aided by a detachment of cavalry from Tanjore. From the ramparts of Madras, French deserters, of which there were some two hundred within the city, held out a bottle of wine and a purse, or shot letters on arrows into the camp, tempting the besiegers to join them. The besiegers had neither powder, shot, or provisions; money and men sent from home were intercepted at the Isle of France by Admiral d'Ache, and supplies trickled irregularly and uncertainly from Pondicherry. Well might Lally write, "Le désordre ne se comprend pas, et il est sans remède. L'enfer m'a vomi dans ce pays d'iniquité."

When by incessant labour in the trenches he had succeeded in constructing two batteries, and had thrown shells by night and fired cannon by day for six weeks, almost at the same time as a breach was made in the walls, he heard that an English fleet was on its way from Bombay. He ordered an assault, in spite of his engineer officers, who declared it would be fruitless. All was ready for the night of February 16th, when in the afternoon the English ships were seen in the bay. It was hopeless; he had no bombs, and scarcely any powder, his native troops had disappeared, lacking their pay, and the Europeans were threatening desertion. Next day he broke up camp and retreated, and at Pondicherry the men whose inertness and ill-will had contributed to his failure, made open demonstration of rejoicing.

While Lally was staking everything upon the capture of Madras, the Deccan was lost to France. Three months after Bussy's departure, a petty Raja in the Northern Sirkars seized Vizagatapam, looted the French factory, and then ran up the English colours and appealed for English help. In the teeth of all his Council, Clive sent Colonel Forde to Vizagatapam, although it left Bengal almost undefended. Forde, confronted with a superior force, and with the army of the Viceroy on his right and a French corps on his left, captured Masulipatam, and obliged the army occupying it to surrender. Then came what the Viceroy had foretold: he was obliged to sign a treaty whereby he gave up Masulipatam and the Northern Sirkars, undertaking to dismiss all Frenchmen in his service, and to give no help or protection to the enemies of the English, who, on their side, agreed to protect him against his foes.

Misfortunes crowded thick and fast upon the French during 1759—that wonderful year in which, as Horace Walpole said, an Englishman was obliged to ask every day, "What new victory?" for fear of missing one in the Gazette. There was defeat and mutiny. Lally fell ill. D'Ache, beaten in a naval action off Fort St David, sailed away with his fleet, never to return. The English had captured the town and fort of Wandiwash; Lally regained the town by a *coup de main*, and while he was besieging the fort, with the assistance of Bussy, his Maratha scouts hurried in to tell him that Colonel Eyre Coote was at hand, coming to its relief.

As Coote advanced, the French guns played upon his line, and seemed to cause some disorder. Lally, sword in hand, called upon his European cavalry to charge. Not a man obeyed. It was not until he had displaced their two chief officers that the rank and file would follow him, and the delay gave time for the English to bring up two cannon. Only a few men were injured by the discharge, but panic seized the remainder, and they fled, leaving Lally alone with his A.D.C. a few paces from the English grenadiers.

Unhurt, but with his clothing riddled with balls, he galloped to his infantry, and they responded to his cry. Their charge broke the English line, which re-formed, and the columns were mixed in hopeless confusion. Bussy on the left, leading his men to recover an intrenchment carried by the English, had his horse shot under him and was taken prisoner. The French army fell back, the cavalry, who had regained their courage too late, covering the retreat of the infantry, and enabling Lally to save his park of artillery. All in turn had failed him, and as he returned for the last time to Pondicherry he heaped bitter curses upon the heads of those whose "infernal plot" had succeeded.

Bussy returned to France as soon as he was released. His life's work had been undone in a few months, and he was left with such consolation as could be derived from the considerable fortune that he had carried away with him.

Lally's work, too, was done. One after another, all the French towns and forts were taken by the English or surrendered by incapable defenders. The case of Pondicherry was hopeless. No help came from France, and the inhabitants would do nothing to save themselves now that the supreme hour had come. Some openly rebelled, some secretly conspired; all thwarted every one of his proposals. The town was covered with bills, accusing him of having sold the French to the enemy. A letter threatening him with death was found on his table. Suffering from the climate, and from an internal complaint, Lally struggled, for four months, to make head against his enemies within and his enemies without. But in vain he flung himself against the English lines: when a disastrous storm damaged the fleet and destroyed the siege-works and ammunition, he lay in bed, too ill to move, and the cowards who gloried in bringing all his plans to nought would not fall upon the enemy at the moment when they might have swept them from their position around the city. Neither the "eternal sarcastic smile" with which Lally had irritated their susceptibilities at his first coming, or the torrents of invective and entreaty which he poured forth in his extremity, had any effect.

In the afternoon of January 16th, 1761, the garrison of Pondicherry "drew up under arms on the parade before the citadel, the English troops facing them. Colonel Coote then reviewed the line, which, exclusive of commissioned officers, invalids, and others who had hid themselves, amounted to 1100, all wearing the face of famine, fatigue, or disease."[1] Pondicherry had surrendered unconditionally, and the garrison and inhabitants were prisoners of war.

The closing scenes were in keeping with the rest of the story. When Lally, half dead, was carried out of the fort in a palki, he was attacked

[1] Orme.

by a crowd, among whom were two members of his Council, and saved from being torn to pieces only by some English cavalrymen, who rushed up, sabre in hand. A quarter of an hour later, his intendant, an old man and nearly blind, was cut down as he tried to follow Lally, and his corpse stripped and dragged about the town. It was well known that he carried with him valuable evidence of the misdoings of the civil and military authorities in Pondicherry, and when these had been put where they could do no harm, no man troubled to look for his murderers.

Having done nothing to avert the disaster, Court, Ministry, and populace in France were furious that it should have occurred. Of course it was any one's fault but that of the men who had disgraced Dupleix for trying to give France an empire, and had subordinated Bussy to a chief who was unfit for an Eastern command. "Nous sommes trahis!"—then, as many times afterwards, it was the cry, and a scapegoat was soon found.

Lally had been set free on parole in September —on the day after that on which George III. had been crowned King of Great Britain and France, while Lally's Prince watched from a corner of Westminster Hall, vowing that he did not envy the young man. On arriving in France, Lally found none but enemies. In spite of past services to France, an Irishman was an alien, and every one was convinced that Lally had sold the French possessions to the English, and, moreover, could tell how much he had received for them. Even the coachmen in the streets would cry to an offending horse, "Hue, Lally!"

Warned by a pitiful few that a *lettre de cachet* was on its way, Lally would not escape. "I bring hither my head and my innocence" were his words ere he surrendered himself at the gate of the Bastille.

There was more than a year of imprisonment to be endured ere came the mockery of a trial before the Parlement of Paris. Without counsel, without a single friend to encourage him, the weary old man—he was past sixty—fought for his life before judges who were determined to condemn him. For over three years the torture continued, until Lally was adjudged guilty of having betrayed the interests of the king, of his state, and of the Compagnie des Indes Orientales.

One of his judges voted for breaking him on the wheel, and though this was changed to beheading, with confiscation of all his goods, he was made to suffer all that the vindictive hate of small-minded men could devise. Kicked by a jailer, dragged in a cart to the Place de Greve, his hands bound, a gag between his lips, he was hacked to pieces by a clumsy or brutal executioner.

"There is not another man in all India," wrote Eyre Coote on taking Pondicherry, "who could have kept on foot for the same length of time an army without pay, and receiving no assistance from any quarter."

"Lally était un grand fripon," wrote Mme. du Deffand on his execution, "et, de plus, il était fort désagréable."

The traveller to Pondicherry in these days will see nothing of the old fortifications which Lally defended; Eyre Coote's army blew them up before they marched away. But the language spoken is still French, and at the head of the pier still stand the eight grey pillars which Bussy brought to Dupleix, an earnest of his capture of Gingi. Bussy's tomb is in the old cemetery, near the Cathedral. To the west of the pier are piled some carven fragments from the Gingi temples, and upon them, towering over gods and dancing women and distorted monsters, is a figure in the court dress of the reign of Louis XV., one hand on his sword, the other grasping a half-rolled paper, the wide and lofty head thrown back, the eyes gazing far away. It is the statue of Dupleix, erected by France in remorse that came just a hundred years too late. The Pondicherry paper which described its unveiling in 1870 also told the public that the first Prussians had crossed the French frontier.

# V.

## SOME RULERS IN BENGAL—1756-1765

"Where the East India Company have Suffer'd here abroad by the Knavery in their Servants £1000, they Suffer'd at least £10,000 by employing of ffools."
—Governor PITT to the E. I. C.

## SOME RULERS IN BENGAL—1756-1765.

THE scene must now change from the south to Bengal.

Learned historians deny any foundation to the story that the English trade in Bengal owed its foundation to Gabriel Boughton, an English surgeon. The legend runs that the Princess Jahanara, daughter of Shah Jahan and the queen for whom he built the Taj Mahal, was grievously disfigured with burns, and the Englishman who restored her to health and beauty, when bidden to name his own reward, asked that his countrymen might trade in Bengal, duty free. At least the historians allow some credence to another story, that Boughton's cure of a lady in the harem of Shah Jahan's favourite son gained leave for the Company to build a factory at Hughli.

At first they were forbidden to fortify it in any way, but an opportune rebellion of certain rajas in the west, at the end of the seventeenth century, brought them instructions from Aurangzib to defend themselves, and they raised walls and bastions round a factory about twenty miles from Hughli, lately erected by a certain Job Charnock. One of the phantom emperors who succeeded Aurangzib was taken ill just as he was about to celebrate his wedding, and again a doctor in the Company's service was able to work a cure where the hakims had failed. William Hamilton's fee was a grant from the emperor to this factory of land extending for ten miles along either bank of the river, and the City of Palaces began to arise.

"Calcutta is a wonderful city," sings an Indian historian and poet, at the beginning of the nineteenth century—

> "Its buildings are heart-attracting and delightful.
> The hat-wearing Englishmen who dwell in them
> All speak the truth and have good dispositions."

Unhappily, some fifty years before he wrote his verses the hat-wearing Englishmen were not regarded with favour in Bengal, whatever their virtues might have been. For many years the ruler of Bengal and Bihar—nominally viceroy for the Emperor of Delhi, but in reality his own master—had been the great Nawab Aliverdi Khan, who lived from youth to the age of eighty years, hearing no music, abstaining from all intoxicating drink, and looking upon no woman who was not his wife. Cruel and unscrupulous, he was also wise, and in some degree just. So long as he lived the three European nations — English, French, and Dutch—who traded in Bengal, were unmolested, in spite of some of his counsellors, who looked jealously at their rapid increase of wealth. "They are like bees," he said, "who produce honey when left in peace, but attack those who foolishly disturb them," and his last injunction to his successor was to leave the English alone.

That successor, Siraj-ud-daula, the son of his daughter, was one of the few characters in history who seem to have had no redeeming qualities. About twenty years old at the time of his grandfather's death in 1756, he was already notorious for his lust and cruelty. His agents, in disguise, spied upon the Hindu women as they bathed in the Ganges, and carried them off. He was often seen at the ferry when the river was high, ordering the ferry-boats to be upset or sunk, so as to have the pleasure of seeing men, women, and little children struggling and drowning in the deep waters. His delight in torture and death was useful when reasons of state required the removal of some great noble or minister; Aliverdi Khan then would leave the business to his grandson, retiring to one of his houses or gardens outside Murshidabad,[1] that he might not be disturbed by the cries of the victims.

Siraj-ud-daula had a grudge of long standing against the English. "On certain occasions they refused him admission into their factory at Cossimbazar and their country houses, because, in fact, this excessively blustering and impertinent young man used to break the furniture, or, if it pleased his fancy, take it away." With the French, on the other hand, he was on good terms, and from time to time they cultivated his friendship with gifts, while the English did not even send the usual presents on his accession.

During the last illness of Aliverdi Khan, the Europeans in Bengal, fearing a contested succession, had repaired their old fortifications or added to them. The young Nawab's first act was to send an order that all new fortifications were to be pulled down. The French, who had taken care to send away the Nawab's spies with a bribe, submitted petitions, and were told that they were at liberty to repair, provided that they built no new fortifications. Mr Drake, the Governor of Calcutta, absolutely refused obedience. In the days of Aliverdi Khan, when the Marathas were raiding Bengal, leave had been given to the

[1] Then the capital of Bengal.

English to surround Calcutta with an entrenchment always known as "the Maratha ditch." Rumour said that Mr Drake had professed himself content to fill up the ditch, if it were the Nawab's wish, "provided that he might use the heads of Moors" (*i.e.*, Muslims).

It is unlikely that Mr Drake said anything of the kind, but whether the taunt were uttered by some thoughtless youth in his presence, or invented for the occasion, Mr Drake's refusal gave Siraj-ud-daula the opportunity he needed. Springing up in anger and pulling out his sword, he swore that he would exterminate all the Feringhis, and the only person who dared remonstrate was his mother. In vain she wondered that a soldier should stoop to war upon mere traders: her son was not to be moved. It was well known that many nobles, in fear of him, had fled to the English, or sent their treasures to Calcutta, thinking that he could not seize them there. Had not the son of one of his uncle's ministers escaped to Calcutta with all his private fortune, and the fortune of that same uncle—who was supposed to have been poisoned in order to clear the way for Siraj-ud-daula? There was wealth untold behind the walls that the stiff-necked English refused to raze to the ground at his bidding, and he meant to have it.

The English factory at Cossimbazar surrendered without firing a shot, and the Nawab demanded that M. Jean Law,[1] head of the French factory, should come with him to help in the attack upon Calcutta. "Calcutta is yours," he said. "I give you that place and its dependencies as the price of the services you will render me, but if you refuse the offer I make you, you will soon see me fall on you."

French and Scotch chivalry alike revolted, and Law replied that it was impossible to fight against the English, with whom France had no quarrel. The Nawab "swore he would have what he wanted, whether we wished it or not," says Law, who wasted much time in trying to appease him. At the risk of his own life, and of ruin to his Company, Law still refused to march to Calcutta, and the only part which the French took in the ensuing tragedy was to succour some of the English prisoners with clothes, food, and money, and to save two or three beautiful Englishwomen from the lust of Siraj-ud-daula. The Dutch, it may be as well to note, had refused to make common cause with the English against the enemy, and it is hardly necessary to say that no acts of mercy are recorded of them.

What took place at Calcutta in June 1756 is too

[1] Brother to the besieger of Trichinopoly.

well known to need a description here; those who have heard of no other event in Indian history know of the "Black Hole." After this the Nawab returned to Murshidabad, and levied contributions upon the French and Dutch factories, to indemnify himself for the trouble and expense of putting down the English. Great was now his contempt for all Europeans; "a pair of slippers," he said, "is all that is needed to govern them."

So great was the desire of all parties to see the tyrant humbled, that the French would not interfere with the vengeance of the English when it became known in Bengal, at about the same time that France and England were again at war, that Clive was coming from Madras with Admiral Watson's fleet.

The Hindu governor left in charge of Calcutta was at a nautch when he heard that the English had come back to claim their own. His garrison scarcely waited to exchange shots before they bolted, and he fled to Murshidabad to tell his master that the newcomers were very unlike those who had sailed down the river with Mr Drake, six months ago. His words were confirmed by a small force which went up the river past Chandernagore, without hindrance from the French, captured the fort at Hughli, then "the second city in the kingdom," and destroyed the magazines.

This news, to use the expression of a native historian, "took the cotton out of the ears" of Siraj-ud-daula, who marched from Murshidabad to Calcutta with his army and artillery. On a February morning he was roused from sleep by volleys of musketry; and if the thick fog had not hidden his tent, he would have been a prisoner in the hands of Clive. As it was, he suffered heavy losses, and was thankful to make peace upon the terms dictated by the English—restoration of all privileges that they had ever enjoyed, and full compensation for all they had lost by his seizure of Calcutta.

Again the Nawab tried for a French alliance; the French hated him, and would have preferred to remain neutral, but France and England were again at war, and they could not afford to reject an ally. Siraj-ud-daula might have taken action on their behalf but for a catastrophe at Delhi.

While all these things were happening in Bengal, Ahmad Shah Daurani, an Afghan who had been invading Hindustan with great industry and perseverance for some years past, had taken the capital and despoiled the inhabitants of everything that had escaped the notice of his old master, Nadir Shah. Siraj-ud-daula, "the most cowardly of men," fancied that he might be the next victim, and thinking the English the stronger party in Bengal, wrote in terror to Clive, promising him Rs. 100,000 a month in return for his protection.

Clive realised that there could be no peace in Bengal until Siraj-ud-daula was crushed, and he knew that a French alliance would make the Nawab inconveniently strong. He could not be generous to the French at the expense of his own nation and his own employers; he must act at once, and technically he was within his rights, since he knew that war had been declared between France and England. But if he remembered the generosity of the French at the time of the "Black Hole," he cannot have marched with a light heart upon Chandernagore, where they had their head-quarters in Bengal.

With Admiral Watson's help, it was no great matter to knock the crumbling fortifications to pieces. Driven from post to post, the French "stood to their guns so long as they had any to fire," as an English eyewitness recorded, and at last withdrew into the Fort. The batteries were covered with dead and wounded, the bastions undermined; there was no disgrace in hoisting the white flag. Civilians were allowed to go where they pleased, with their effects; the garrison were made prisoners of war.

Law was forced to leave Cossimbazar with his

garrison. The Nawab sent for him, and told him, "in a shamefaced way," that he must surrender to the English or leave Bengal. "Your nation is the cause of all the importunities I now suffer from the English. I do not wish to put the whole country in trouble for your sake. You ought to remember that when I had need of your assistance you always refused it. Take what road you please, and God protect you." Ever shifty, he tried to deprecate Law's anger with a promise to send for him again "if anything new should happen." "Send for me again?" was Law's scornful answer. "Rest assured, my Lord Nawab, that this is the last time we shall see each other."

It was a true prophecy. The Nawab's cruelty and greed had left him no friends. "He spared no one, not even his relatives, from whom he took all the pensions and all the offices which they had held in the time of Aliverdi Khan. Was it possible for such a man to keep his throne?" His nobles intrigued against him, and he was betrayed on all sides. "Scarcely had he formed any project when it was known to the lowest of his slaves."[1] Mir Jafar Ali Khan, his Moghul Commander-in-Chief, wrote to Clive offering to come over to the English in any general engagement if he might rule in Bengal and Bihar instead of Siraj-ud-daula.

[1] Law.

On June 23, 1757, the armies met at Plassey, and after hard fighting on both sides, an English bayonet charge put to flight the host of the Nawab. At the end of the day, Mir Jafar went over to the English camp, and the Nawab, who had mounted a swift camel, was on the road to Murshidabad.

"Misfortune has no friend," says the native chronicler in telling this story, and Siraj-ud-daula found it true. Even when he opened his treasury to his soldiers, it availed him nothing. Robbed and deserted, he fled away from Murshidabad with such jewels as he had been able to save, and took boat for Patna, where he hoped to find Law.

When he had gone some way, he ordered his servant to land and get a light for his *hukka*. The man saw a hut in the jungle and asked the occupant for fire. Now the owner of the hut was a man who had lately turned faquir, after having his ears and nose cut off by order of Siraj-ud-daula. He recognised the servant, who had the Nawab's bejewelled *chillam* in his hand, and asked him what he was doing in the jungle. The servant, either a fool or a traitor, told what had happened, and the faquir, leaving him in the hut, hurried with the story to the governor of the nearest town. Law arrived in the neighbourhood a few hours too late to save the wretched Nawab, who was seized and sent back to Murshidabad, where Mir Jafar's son took effectual measures to prevent his giving further trouble.

Mir Jafar was made Nawab in his stead on condition that he paid the expenses of the war. To dethrone one king and set up another over a country as large as Great Britain was no small feat for a body of merchants, who had been driven with shame from their settlement twelve months before they entered Murshidabad as conquerors.

## II.

After the first, the change of rulers seemed to have effected little improvement in Bengal. The new Nawab, forgetting that he owed his throne to the English, grew weary of being under Clive's tutelage, and bethought himself of another European alliance.

Accordingly, he made overtures to the Dutch to introduce a large European force into their factory at Chinsurah. The fact that England and Holland were officially at peace with one another in Europe did not prevent the Dutch Government from sending a fleet from Batavia, nor did it prevent the Dutch commander from seizing upon British vessels, hauling down their colours, and carrying off their guns and stores.

Clive had taken precautions beforehand by blocking the river, so as to prevent the Batavian fleet from entering it. He now seized the ships, and sent an expedition to cut off the Dutch troops before they could reach Chinsurah.

The expedition was commanded by Colonel Forde, just returned from his triumph in the Deccan. He was not concerned about the strength of the enemy, but he demurred to attacking a nominally "friendly" Power, and wrote to ask for an order in Council. The letter was brought to Clive as he sat at the card-table, and he took out a pencil and wrote on one of the cards in his hand: "Dear Forde, fight them immediately, I will send you the order in Council to-morrow." Then he called for another pack, and went on with his game, while Forde went in pursuit of the Dutch, whom he overtook within sight of Chinsurah, and beat in half an hour.

Shortly after this, Clive's health obliged him to return to England, leaving very incompetent successors, who fell out with Mir Jafar. The Nawab was an old man, becoming imbecile, and his habit of lavishing upon dancing-girls the money with which he should have paid his troops led to inconvenience and disorders. Nevertheless, it was unseemly that when he was deposed—"persuaded to resign" was the phrase used by the Council of Calcutta—in favour of his son-in-law, Mir Kasim, that part of the agreement with Mir Kasim should stipulate for a gratuity of twenty lakhs of rupees[1] for the Council.

Their punishment came swiftly. In a little while they were quarrelling with Mir Kasim over the customs duties of Bengal. The trouble had been caused in great measure by the insolence and dishonesty of certain Bengali agents whom the Company employed to carry on their inland trade. These men, "of no character or position," "lorded it over the country, imprisoned ryots and merchants," and gave legitimate grounds for Mir Kasim's bitter complaints. The dispute was aggravated by the unwisdom of Mr Ellis, head of the English factory at Patna, who openly proclaimed war, and seized upon the fort and the city. He held them for about six hours, at the end of which time the Nawab's troops recovered every position, and Ellis and his garrison were obliged to surrender.

In the war with the English that ensued, Mir Kasim's army was thrice defeated. "Furious and half-disordered in his mind," he commanded that all his English prisoners at Patna should be executed forthwith. His native officers refused to obey him. "Arm the English, and we will fight them like soldiers."

[1] £200,000.

Then the Nawab turned to a scowling fellow, who had once been in the service of the East India Company, and was now in command of two battalions in the Bengal army. In the province of Trèves, where he was born, he had been known as Walter Reinhard. When he came to India he called himself Somers; his morose look and sullen bearing made his comrades in the French army of Southern India turn this into Sombre, and the natives corrupted it into "Somru." He undertook to do what was required "with ardour and alacrity," and sent to the prison to borrow all the knives and forks from the English captives, declaring that he meant to invite them to sup with him next evening. When the hour for the meal was near, he surrounded the prison with two companies of sepoys, and sent for Ellis and eight others to come into a little outer court. "They were all terribly mangled, and cut to pieces, and their bodies thrown into a well in the square." Then the sepoys ascended to the roof of the house, and fired down upon the captives assembled below. Some took refuge in the inner rooms, and defended themselves with bottles, plates, bricks, and fragments of furniture, until they were overpowered. The sepoys themselves were horror-stricken; some refused to fire unless arms were given to the captives, vowing that they were soldiers, not butchers, but they were struck down by Somru, who set them an example by murdering the infant child of Mr Ellis. At length, by curses and blows, the sepoys were forced to complete their work. Neither age nor sex was spared, and certain natives of Patna, who had been taken prisoners with the English, shared their fate. The bodies were thrown into a well near that in which Ellis and his companions were lying.

The English were not slow in taking revenge; driven out of Patna, Mir Kasim fled to the Nawab of Oudh, accompanied by Somru, who saw clearly that his old master's day was over, and therefore plundered him of all that he could, and transferred his allegiance to Oudh.

"It was a rule," it was said, "with Somru, to enter the field of battle in column at the safest point; form line, facing the enemy, fire a few rounds in the direction where they stood, without regard to the distance or effect; form square, and await the course of events. If victory declared for the enemy, he sold his unbroken force to him to great advantage; if for his friends, he assisted them in collecting the plunder."[1] On the field of Buxar, seeing that the English were prevailing, he withdrew his brigades and guns from

[1] Sleeman.

action at a critical moment, and the united forces of Oudh and Bengal suffered a crushing defeat.

When the Nawab sued for peace, one of the conditions laid down by the Company was the surrender of Mir Kasim and Somru. The Nawab replied that he regretted he could not surrender Mir Kasim, as he knew not where he might be, having had him set upon a lame elephant and turned out of the camp the day before the battle. As for Somru, though his cautious tactics made him of little use as an ally, he was too dangerous an enemy to be attacked openly; but the Nawab would undertake to invite him to a banquet, and have him assassinated in the presence of any emissary whom the Company might send as a witness.

It surprised and annoyed the Nawab to find this offer rejected. Nevertheless, to his relief, the English did not farther press him for the surrender of the murderers, who, like the Nana Sahib and Tantia Topee after the massacre of Cawnpore, went each his way. Mir Kasim escaped into the Rohilla country, and after many years and many intrigues, ended his miserable life "unlamented even by his own family," says a native historian, in such dire poverty that his last shawl had to be sold to buy him a winding-sheet.

Somru wandered up and down the country, always carrying poison hidden in his clothes, for fear of falling into the hands of the English.

Mir Jafar was replaced in office, and when he died, which he did in a few months, he was succeeded by his son, an indolent profligate, who was glad to allow the Company to collect the revenues and provide for the defence of Bengal, Bihar, and Orissa, so long as they gave him a yearly pension. "Thank God!" he exclaimed, when the arrangement had been concluded, "I shall now have as many dancing-girls as I like!"

# VI.

# KINGS OF THE SOUTH—1761-1782

**"The defeat of many Braithwaites and many Baillies will not ruin the English. I may ruin their resources by land, but I cannot dry up the sea."**
**—HAIDAR ALI, 1780.**

## VI.

## KINGS OF THE SOUTH—1761-1782.

WHILE French and English were fighting it out in Bengal and the south, the young Raja of Mysore — who, be it remembered, had sent a force to help the English and Mohammad Ali at the siege of Trichinopoly — was extremely malcontent.

His kingdom extended over about half the territory of the modern State of Mysore, a fertile and wealthy State which had enjoyed long peace, thanks to its distance from Delhi, and the tribute that it paid to the Marathas. In his capital at Seringatapam he had wealth and jewels and elephants, and all that the heart of a prince could desire—save freedom. The real ruler of Mysore and of the Raja was the Prime Minister.

For some time the Raja had chafed under his tyranny, before the old Rani, widow of a former Raja, suggested that something might be done, with the help of a young man of Afghan descent, who had commanded the Mysore contingent in the campaign against the French. His name was Haidar[1] Ali, and he was wont to claim descent from the last of the Adil Shahi Kings of Bijapur, overthrown by Aurangzib; his father had been an officer in the Moghul service. He was wholly illiterate, "and addicted to low pursuits," but clever enough. He had profited by the confusion, after the head of the usurping Viceroy of the Deccan had been struck off upon the battlefield, to secure a good share of the dead man's treasure, before bringing his army home to Mysore, and he had succeeded in getting rid of the Marathas when a misunderstanding over the payment of chaut[2] had brought them into the Raja's territory. He was a keen soldier and sportsman, and all the thieves, scoundrels, and ruffians in the countryside were eager to take service with him, attracted by his "humble and agreeable manners," and his praiseworthy custom of making no deduction from a soldier's pay.

When the matter was set before him, Haidar saw no objections. With the help of a clever Brahman who kept Haidar's accounts—a necessary

[1] "The Lion."

[2] *Chaut*—the tribute levied by the Marathas as a condition of not attacking towns and districts—similar to *Danegeld*.

ally for the soldier who to the end of his days never achieved more penmanship than to scrawl an inverted H on official documents—a palace revolution was effected. The Minister was sent about his business, and the unlucky Raja found that he was no more his own master than before, Haidar having taken up the reins of government.

The first revolution having been successful, Raja and Rani now had the inspiration to try another. Haidar's Brahman was bribed to help them, and called in the Marathas, his fellow-countrymen, who attacked Seringapatam, and obliged Haidar to ride nearly a hundred miles in twenty-four hours to escape them, leaving his treasure, his artillery, and his family behind him. But the Raja enjoyed his freedom only for a little while. The Marathas were recalled to Poona; Haidar returned with a following, surprised the Mysore camp, and was acknowledged by the army. In return for life and a yearly income, the Raja was compelled to give him all authority, and henceforth had as little to say in the administration of Mysore as had the Emperor of Delhi in the Deccan or Oudh.

He was obliged, moreover, to surrender the Brahman who had been his confederate. The Rani and the ladies of the Palace begged earnestly for his life, and Haidar vowed to cherish the Brahman as if he were his parrot. A parrot is a favourite pet in Muslim households, and the queens thought this a figurative promise of kind treatment. The vow was kept; Haidar shut the wretched man in an iron cage, "like an inauspicious crow," says his Muslim biographer, and fed him upon rice and milk and bird-seed till he died.

For some years Haidar governed Mysore in the name of the helpless Raja, annexing weaker States, and harrying his neighbours, until the English agreed to unite with the Nizam and the Peshwa to suppress him as a public nuisance. They had undertaken more than they could effect, handicapped as they were by the treachery of the Nizam, who veered from side to side with the fortunes of war.

There were the usual blunders of the civil power, sometimes redeemed by the valour, pertinacity, and resourcefulness of the military chiefs, Colonel Wood and Colonel Smith. The latter having occupied Mulgabal, a fortress on the Mysore plateau, had left some of his own men to garrison it before going on to join Colonel Wood. In his absence the Madras Council substituted for his garrison a company of soldiers supplied by Mohammad Ali, Nawab of the Carnatic. Their commandant was bribed to yield the fortress to Haidar, and Colonel Wood, who hurried to the spot, could recover no more than the lower fort. He never dreamed that Haidar and his army were close at hand, till they came down upon him, horse and foot.

Haidar's guns were well served, the English were heavily punished, and had been taken by surprise. They were falling back, when Captain Brooke, who had been left in command of the baggage guard, effected a diversion. Somehow or other, he hauled and pushed two guns to the top of one of the great rocks that lay scattered as if a giant had been amusing himself with throwing stones, and discharged them upon the enemy, while his men shouted "Smith! Smith!" at the top of their lungs. Haidar at once supposed that Colonel Smith had arrived, and drew back for a little while. Ere he found out his mistake, Wood had taken up a better position, and was able to drive back his cavalry when they returned.

The Madras President and Council had interfered in Smith's operations, had failed to supply him with anything that he needed, and had recalled him in punishment for the failures caused by their stupidity and neglect. It was therefore no more than they deserved, when, having reconquered most of what had been taken from him, Haidar slipped past their army, and arrived at St Thomas's Mount, five miles from Madras. Of course they lost what little sense they had ever possessed, and made a treaty at his dictation, by which, amongst other stipulations, it was agreed that either party was bound to help the other in case of attack by a third power. Then Haidar marched back to Mysore, past the camp of the furious Colonel Smith, who was forbidden to attack him, having put the crowning touch to his audacity by affixing a most opprobrious caricature to the city gates.

It was not long before he claimed the fulfilment of the treaty. The Peshwa's army invaded Mysore, to claim arrears of tribute, and having surprised Haidar while he was holding a drinking-bout in his camp, cut his army to pieces. Seringatapam was besieged, and the Marathas had to be bought off with a very heavy indemnity. When Haidar appealed to Madras for help, Sir John Lindsay, the special ambassador appointed by Parliament to the Court of the Nawab of the Carnatic, refused to allow it, and made a treaty with the Marathas.

To his dying day, Haidar never forgot this breach of faith, and henceforth the object of his life was to be revenged. He increased his army, he engaged French officers to drill it, and maintained strict discipline with the aid of whip and cudgel. He was now strong enough to brave the discontent of his soldiers, and by ingenious calculations, based on the difference between lunar and solar months, he robbed them of more than half their pay. "Towards the end of his reign he abandoned all consideration for any persons, however respectable, . . . he gave them the vilest abuse, and for the least fault put them to death." If the officer in charge of an expedition was dilatory or unsuccessful, he was abused for his failure; if successful, he was abused for his rashness in throwing away the lives of his men. "In fact, in all his life, Haidar was never known to praise any one." His spies were everywhere, and he himself would go out at night, muffled in a blanket, through street or camp, to learn what citizens and soldiers were doing. "His old servants, and the people of the towns in his territory, dared not speak a word to each other in the street. . . . Cutting off the nose and ears of any person in his territories was the commonest thing imaginable; and the killing a man there was thought no more of than the treading on an ant. No person of respectability ever left his house with an expectation to return safe to it."[1]

The only person who went in no fear of him

[1] Mirza Ikbal.

was his senior wife, the mother of his son Tipu, and he frankly admitted to his intimates that he had not the courage to answer her, for she had "a long tongue and a high-sounding voice."

## II.

"Viewing the number of Haidar's troops, the splendour of his equipment, and the pomp of his Court," says an admiring contemporary biographer, "the thorn of grief and jealousy penetrated the hearts of the Nizam and the Chief of the Marathas, and to break down the power of that nourisher of the poor and dispenser of benefits, they exerted their utmost endeavours." So they sent embassies to represent that "the blood-shedding English" were daily increasing in power, having taken possession of Bengal, "the mole on the cheek of Hind," and that it was necessary to expel these intruders, "and then they might reign in peace, and without the intermeddling of strangers." The reader of Indian history will be able to imagine how much peace would be found where the Marathas, the Nizam, and Haidar were left to their own devices unchecked.

Some years before, the Marathas had made overtures to Haidar, proposing a campaign for the advantage of both, and he had then laid the matter before the Council of Madras, openly avowing his unwillingness to join in a scheme which was bound to increase the Maratha power to a dangerous extent. Unhappily Sir John Lindsay rejected his advances, and Haidar turned to a French alliance.

The power of the French had dwindled wofully since the time of Dupleix. But European officers and European-drilled troops, however few in number, were worth much in a campaign.

In 1778, war between France and England broke out once more, with the usual consequences in India. Pondicherry, which had been given back to the French by the Treaty of Paris, made a gallant defence for forty days before yielding to overwhelming odds. The Admiral of the French fleet, a more ineffectual creature than d'Ache, sailed away, and made no attempt to save Mahé, a little settlement which La Bourdonnais had won in battle for France. Haidar, who was in possession of all Malabar, except for the European settlements, intimated that he should consider an attack upon Mahé as an attack upon himself. Despite their former experience, the English made light of his enmity, and after taking Mahé, sent an embassy to present him with a rifle which could not be loaded, and a saddle which, being made of pigskin, could not be touched by any Muslim without defilement.

Unpropitiated by these gifts, Haidar led out his army to war in the autumn of 1780; he had no help from the Nizam, who shut himself up in his capital, on pretence of sickness, or from the Marathas, who made their own bargain with the English. If France could have realised her opportunity, and sent a fleet and an army to co-operate with Haidar, England, then absorbed in the fight with her American colonies, must have lost Southern India. The Ministry of Louis XVI., true to the principles of economy which have lost great opportunities to other nations besides France, sent only a squadron and a regiment; even so, the combination with Mysore was nearly fatal to the English.

The Madras Council, lapped in an imbecile security, made no preparations, and had no idea that Haidar had passed through the Ghats, until they saw the smoke of the villages that he was burning round St Thomas's Mount. Then one party proposed that the commander-in-chief, Sir Hector Monro, should remain, to give them a majority in the Council, while Lord Macleod should lead the army—amounting to six thousand—without an hour's preparation, against the eighty thousand or more that followed Haidar.

Macleod flatly refused; he was ready to march out at the head of his regiment, but he would not command the army until it was properly formed and equipped for service. "I have been a great many years in the service," he warned them, "and I have always observed that when you despise your enemy, he generally gives you a d—d rap over the knuckles."

The rap came, some six weeks afterwards, at Perambakam, where Haidar surprised a detachment, under Colonel Baillie, marching to join Monro. Baillie stood his ground bravely, though all the odds were against him, and Haidar would have retreated but for the representations of a French officer, who, having discovered the position of the English ammunition, fired a shot from a heavy gun at the tumbrils, which exploded. "Seeing this opportunity, the brave horsemen of the household cavalry, on one of the flanks, like a thunder-cloud in the spring season, rushing and shouting, charged the broken troops in a body. . . . On the other flank, the Sillahdars, like the blazing lightning, fell on and destroyed the harvest of the array of their enemies, and dyed their blue swords red as the ruby in their blood."

Baillie formed his men into a square, and, without ammunition, repulsed thirteen attacks of the enemy's squadrons, all the while under a devastating fire of cannon and rockets. At the end of an hour and a half, the English still held their ground, but the sepoys had broken, and could do no more. Baillie tied his handkerchief to his sword, and waved it to and fro, ordering Captain David Baird, his second in command, to cease firing. Some of the sepoys, bewildered and not understanding what was going on, still discharged their muskets, and Haidar's officers would not agree at first to give quarter. Then Baillie gave Baird the order to ground arms.

So soon as this was done, the Mysore cavalry, led by Tipu Sahib, Haidar's son, swooped down upon them, and slaughtered every man within their reach. Had it not been for the French officers, no Englishman would have survived the defeat. Doubtless in the long agony of captivity most of the two thousand English taken prisoners envied the seven hundred of their brothers-in-arms, and five thousand sepoys, who lay dead upon the field, where Haidar sat enthroned, distributing rewards of five rupees for every European head that was laid before him.

Under a burning sun, without a drop of water, the wounded prisoners were borne in doolies, or in rough carts, to the various places where they were to be confined. Their wounds were crawling with maggots, and "infected the air around"; they were half-starved, and almost naked. In one place where they halted, their guards took money from the country people who flocked to see the prisoners as if they had been wild beasts; and "indeed we were most miserable-looking creatures," records John Lindsay, one of the captives, a boy of nineteen.

David Baird, with two sabre wounds in his head, a ball in his thigh, and a pike-thrust in his arm, was sent with others to Seringatapam, where the official in charge of the prison served out irons weighing about nine pounds each pair. Captain Lucas, who spoke the language perfectly, represented that to fetter Baird's leg, crippled by an open wound, would be to kill him. The gaoler was inexorable; "the Sirkar" (Government) had sent as many pairs of irons as there were prisoners, and they must be worn. "Then put two sets on me," said Lucas.

The gaoler relented so far as to send to the governor of the prison "to open the book of fate." The messenger came back to say that the book had been opened, and "the Captain's fate was good," so Baird escaped the irons for a short time

Every one knows how, when it was told at Newbyth that Haidar's prisoners were fettered together, two and two, Baird's mother, thinking of her restless, active son, exclaimed: "Heaven help the chiel that's tied to our Davie!" What is not so well known, perhaps, is that "it is one of the most remarkable and beautiful features of this dreadful captivity that every man during its continuation seemed more anxious for his fellow-sufferers than for himself; and that every opportunity was seized by the whole party to ameliorate the condition of those who were at times even worse off than themselves."

In a large house at some distance were confined over a hundred privates of the 73rd Highlanders, who, hearing through native servants of the miserable plight of Baird and the rest, picked out the soundest and most wholesome part of the food supplied to them, and contrived to smuggle it in to the officers' mess. The sepoys who had been taken with them, cruelly treated and kept at hard labour, in their turn saved a part of their own miserable rations to give to their white brothers-in-arms.

Crowded together, suffering from horrible diseases, getting news from outside only when their captors could taunt them with an English defeat, tortured by such hunger that the sternest self-control was needed to prevent them from snatching the scraps of food out of each other's hands, the prisoners still kept up their hearts. The six books found among them—a volume of Smollett's 'History of England,' a volume of Pope, half of Johnson's Dictionary, a prayer-book, and Mrs Glass's Cookery—were taken from them every evening, "from the supposition that, with the assistance of books, in the night Europeans could do a great deal of mischief when left to themselves," but they manufactured cards, chess-boards, and other games to pass the long hours. Fettered as they were, when cheered by a dinner of stewed mutton, Lindsay and Baird had a wrestling match; Baird caught his foot in the chain of Lindsay's irons, and fell, scratching his face, while Lindsay narrowly escaped a thrashing from their surly Muslim gaoler, who insisted that the prisoners, being the property of Haidar, must not presume to injure themselves or each other.

Haidar continually tempted them with splendid offers: let them enter his service, and they should be taken from the prison to a palace, where they should receive three times the amount of their pay in the English army, and have as many horses, palkis, and wives as they desired. But the captives stayed in their prison, and as the fourth of June came round each year, they made what cheer they could with sherbet and plantains, and drank to the health of their king.

Many, including Lucas, were relieved by death. One Englishman who fell into Haidar's clutch, and survived to tell a grim story, was left chained to the dead body of his friend and fellow-captive while it rotted in the heat; but this extremity of cruelty seems to have been spared to the officers at Seringatapam.

They had a narrow escape when an unhappy man, who spoke the language of their gaolers, went out of his mind, and declared he had important secrets to reveal. He could have betrayed the few alleviations they had contrived or procured, and particularly the letters written with pens of fowl quills and ink made from the smoke of a lamp, and smuggled to other prisoners, one of which would have been the death-warrant of every man. Reasoning was useless, and his friends grimly debated whether it were not expedient to smother him in the night. Baird prevailed upon them to wait till the next morning, pointing out that the sudden death of a man who had promised to disclose secrets would certainly cause suspicion. Next day an official came to hold an inquiry. After much wild talk, the lunatic declared that his fellow-prisoners were in a conspiracy to murder him, and in proof of it, took from his pocket a piece of bread which he declared to be poisoned.

There was a general sensation, and the official

was obviously impressed. "The man is mad," quoth Baird, and seizing the bread swallowed it. As he was none the worse, the gaolers troubled no more about the revelations of the lunatic, and the captives were delivered from deadly peril.

Three years and eight months had dragged by, and all save Baird had renounced any hope of freedom, when one day the Brahman who doled out to the captives the sixpence a day out of which each man had to purchase food, clothing, and everything else that he required, came round with the gaoler, and ordered that Baird, Lindsay, and another should be freed from their irons and taken from the prison. Baird, who had been threatened with all manner of ill-usage, declined to stir until he knew for what purpose he was wanted, and Lindsay was equally resolute, until the gaoler replied that peace was proclaimed, and letters from home were waiting for them.

## III.

While Haidar's captives were enduring their sorrows, many things happened in Southern India.

Warren Hastings, the first to bear the title of Governor-General, was then at Calcutta, and on hearing of the disaster of Perambakam, he sent Eyre Coote to Madras. Clive's lieutenant was nearly sixty, and his health had broken under his labours, but his head was clear and his spirit high as in the days when he took Pondicherry. Ere he could arrive at Madras, Haidar had taken Arcot by assault, and was laying siege to the fortified places near—among them Wandiwash, where Lieutenant Flint held out with a courage and resourcefulness recognised in the warmest terms by Coote, but by no one else. The Court of Directors refused even to give the lieutenant a step in promotion.

As usual, Mohammad Ali was of little assistance to his friends the English. On arriving in Madras, Coote went to visit him and asked: "What have you done with your troops?" "Certain English gentlemen," replied the Nawab, "strongly insisted that one European or man of their country was equal to twenty men of this country, as had been often seen, and why should money be thrown away in employing such useless men? Relying on deceiving words like these, I have disbanded my troops."

The Muslim historian who tells this story asserts that "the General smiled"—which may or may not be true. He made short work with the repentant Nawab, who "hid the face of shame in the hood of patience," and took the horses out of his stables and the stables of his sons and relations, and the carriage-oxen of the merchants and citizens, for the force that he contrived to raise.

Having collected an army, Coote marched southward, revictualling the fortified places as he went, and raising the siege of Wandiwash just as Flint's ammunition ran out. There was nearly such a disaster as was to make the name of Saratoga hateful to Englishmen two years later. A French fleet with a French regiment on board was off the Coromandel coast, cutting his communications by sea; and Haidar, who had followed him closely, was between his army and the country inland. Madras, guarded by invalids, could do nothing to help him. Haidar, who perfectly understood the position, withstood all temptation to risk a battle. Let the French admiral merely remain where he was for a few days, and the last English army must be starved into surrender. "Never had France such an opportunity. It was an absolute certainty. Sir Eyre Coote saw it; Haidar Ali saw it; every man in the army saw it; every man in the fleet saw it, excepting one,"[1]—and that one was the Admiral, who sailed back to the islands, having done nothing for France or France's allies.

In June 1782, Coote and Haidar encountered each other near Arni. Coote was very ill, his men

[1] Malleson.

were tired with a long march, he had Tipu before him and Haidar at his rear, and yet he contrived to avert disaster, and even to capture a gun. Four days afterwards Haidar led the English into an ambuscade, and they suffered severely. It was the last time that the two old enemies were to meet.

The decisive action was to take place not on land, but at sea. France, too late, had sent out a fleet under the Commandant de Suffren, the most distinguished captain in her navy, and he planned to surprise Trincomali, and succeeded, in spite of being hampered with incapable subordinates. To lose Trincomali would be fatal to the English in Southern India; they had no "half-way house" such as the French possessed in the Isles of France and Bourbon, and it was at Trincomali harbour that their ships went to refit. Sir Edward Hughes, the English admiral, sailed from Madras as quickly as he could on hearing that the French fleet was dangerously near Ceylon, and, the wind being against him, arrived just in time to see the French fleet lying in the bay, and the fleurs-de-lis waving from the forts.

Much against the wishes of his captains, Suffren decided to go out and fight Hughes. He knew that Bussy was on his way from France, and was expected daily to arrive in the land where his triumphs were still remembered. If Hughes could be cleared out of the way, there would be nothing to prevent the French overrunning all India south of the Krishna. Moreover, he had ascertained that Hughes had only twelve ships to his fourteen.

So he weighed anchor and sailed away towards the English fleet, and his sulky captains formed line so badly that he signalled to them to reserve fire until they should be at close quarters. His signal was misunderstood as a command to open fire at once, and in a few minutes both fleets were hard at work. Still possessed with ill-temper, some of the French captains had manœuvred their ships so clumsily that only two were ready to support Suffren when his *Héros* bore down upon the English centre, where Hughes waited for him with five other vessels.

For an hour they fought hand to hand, and then Suffren could do no more against such odds, and signalled to two more of his fleet to come to his help. Neither obeyed.

At either end of the line, French and English were firing at long distances, without much display of skill on either side, rather to the advantage of the French. But after another half-hour, though in the meanwhile two other ships had come up to his rescue, the *Héros* was cruelly mangled. The hail of shot from the English ships brought down mainmast, fore-topmast, and mizzen-topmast, and the English cheered wildly, thinking that Suffren had struck his flag.

From his station on the poop, Suffren's voice was heard above all the hideous din of battle: "Bring flags! bring up all the flags that are below and cover my ship with them!"

The men leaped to do his bidding, and it was the turn of the English to feel distressed. Then Suffren was told that his ammunition had run out. But he still had powder, and continued to fire with that, in the hope of putting off the moment when, having spiked the guns, he would blow up his ship and those around her.

Then came a shift of wind, and the French vanguard came up to relieve the ships in the centre. Night fell, and the battle ceased before either side had prevailed, although the English were decidedly in evil plight. Both fleets anchored near the battlefield, too crippled and exhausted to fight more or to sail away. Next morning the French entered Trincomali, and the English steered for Madras.

The news of Suffren's capture of Trincomali came in time to cheer Haidar, who was dying of cancer. He also heard of the death of Eyre Coote, worn out by battles and marches, and, we are told, "sighed deeply, and said: 'He was a wise and an able man.'" In December 1782 "the lion-hearted Prince, whose disposition was mild as that of an antelope," according to his biographer, left a world in which "from morning till night he never remained a moment idle."

# VII.

# THE TIGER OF MYSORE—1782-1799

"The Nazarenes, on contemplating from the sea-shore the sagacity of our king, forget their own schemes and counsels.

"Owing to the justice of this king, the deer of the forest make their pillow of the lion and the tiger, and their mattress of the leopard and the panther."

—*Encomiastic Ode recited before Tipu Sultan.*

## VII.

## THE TIGER OF MYSORE—1782-1799.

It might truly be said of Haidar's son and successor that, where his father chastised men with whips, he chastised them with scorpions. Haidar was cruel as a matter of policy; Tipu from a beast-like love of cruelty. Haidar, as his story has shown, tried to keep faith with his enemies; Tipu betrayed even his friends, and took the first opportunity of murdering two nobles who had served his father most faithfully, their crime being that they were rich and powerful.

It is impossible to give the details of his cruelties. If some stories have been exaggerated by malice, his own memoirs and correspondence bear evidence against him. He was a vindictive persecutor of the Christians in his dominions, sixty thousand of whom he imprisoned at once. In a letter written to one of his officers, who was besieging a town, he orders that in case of an assault "every living creature in it, whether man or woman, old or young, child, dog, cat, or anything else, must be put to the sword," with the exception of one man, probably reserved for a worse fate. In another letter he instructs an official to promise release to a culprit provided that he sends for his family, and having thus secured them all, to throw every member into prison. Elsewhere, he directs the crucifixion of an offender, and of his nephew, "if he should be more than twenty-five years of age," and the confinement of his family in irons. A third official is warned that if people should persist in coming to his house to transact business instead of going to the proper place, the Kacchari, "their ears and noses should be dispensed with." An order to one of his generals to cross a river, during a campaign against the Marathas, is thus worded: "You must leave the women and other rubbish, together with the superfluous baggage of your army, behind." When some of the Nizam's cavalry had been captured, he orders concisely, "Let the prisoners be strangled, and the horses be taken into government service."

His father had been "the lion"; he would be "the tiger." The tiger's stripe was stamped on the binding of his books, engraved on his plate and firearms, woven into his soldiers' uniforms, and formed the watermark of the paper that he used. His throne stood upon a tiger, and tigers' heads of gold and jewels adorned the railing round it, and the tiger stripe gleamed in its pearl-fringed canopy, over which hovered a bird of diamonds, rubies, and emeralds. His favourite toy was an organ in the shape of a tiger mauling a prostrate British soldier. "I would rather live two days as a tiger than two hundred years as a sheep," was his favourite saying.

Unhappily for Southern India, he was to have more than two days.

The French alliance did not profit him as much as he had intended. Bussy arrived, in the March after Haidar's death, but not the General who had held the Deccan in awe: this was an ill-tempered old man, who shut himself up in his tent all day, and would do nothing that interfered with his comfort. The English were trying to regain Fort St David; Suffren by a daring manœuvre succeeded in running his ships abreast of the fort, in the place just vacated by Hughes, without firing a shot. Hughes was driven back to Madras, and Suffren landed to urge Bussy to attack the English at once. All the advantages of position, numbers, and equipment were with him. Bussy would not exert himself. "Do you expect me to take my ships to beat the enemy on shore?" cried Suffren, as he went back to his fleet.

When at length Bussy ordered a sortie, it was a failure. Tipu's biographer says that "Time, at seeing the killed, shed showers of tears, and Mars, from fear at the blood shed by these valorous men, fled to the fifth heaven." The English troops were driven to retreat, but the Madras sepoys formed up from the right and left, covering their backs with their own bodies, and drove back the French. The Colonel of one of the English regiments vowed that he could not understand why his men did not hold their ground, since all were tried men, having stood their trial at the Old Bailey.

Thanks to the Madras regiments, the French were repulsed with heavy loss, one of the prisoners being a sergeant in the regiment of Aquitaine, hereafter to be known as Charles John XIV. of Sweden, who always retained a grateful memory of the kindness of the English. A few days later came the news that preliminaries of peace had been signed between France and England. Suffren perforce went home, and was killed in a duel about four years later, thereby, in the opinion of experts, affecting the course of French and English naval history.

Tipu's memoirs records his fury with "Bussy, the worthless commander of the French, who, being in his dotage, had lost his wits—at least two-thirds of them," when "the two accursed ones concluded an accommodation." He worked off his rage in an expedition to the Malabar coast, where a force sent from Bombay under General Matthews had lately captured Bednore and other places. Matthews was forced to surrender to him, on condition of being allowed to retire with all his army, and nevertheless was made prisoner, with most of his officers and men. Two were cut to pieces by Tipu's orders; Matthews and sixteen others died in captivity, and it was said in the bazaar at Seringatapam that their food had been poisoned.

At last the war was ended by a treaty which bound either side to restore the places captured by the other, and to surrender all prisoners. Thus it was that Baird and his companions were released. Tipu acted with his usual treachery, retaining a great part of those who had survived their captivity, and the Madras Council had not the courage to insist.

Both sides realised that the peace could not last, and sought to make alliances against the day of battle. In spite of his disappointment with Bussy, Tipu still craved French support, and he sent an embassy all the way to Paris to ask it. But too much was happening in France for Louis XVI. to have time to think of India, even if his dull brain had been capable of grasping the issues at stake. Tipu gained nothing but empty promises in return for his embassy; Marie Antoinette gained some exquisitely fine muslin, such as only certain looms in India were capable of making, and when she drove on the last day of her life from the Conciergerie to the Place de la Révolution, she wore over her shoulders a fichu made from the gift of Tipu Sultan.

Tipu did not mean to wait for France's help, but to take what he could, whenever he saw an opportunity, and for the next year he was continually invading his neighbours' territories, or putting down rebellions in his own dominions. He now called himself Padishah, or King, and coined money without the name of Shah Alam upon it, some of which he sent to Delhi. This last proceeding was viewed as a piece of unexampled insolence, when even the Nizam stamped his coins with the titles of the Emperor. For some time the Madras Council, having burned their fingers severely, forbore to meddle with him, but when he attemped to seize the country of their faithful ally, the Raja of Travancore, desecrating temples and burning down towns and villages, Lord Cornwallis, the Governor-General, after vainly trying remonstrance, determined upon war. He captured Bangalore, the second town in Mysore, while Tipu fell back upon Seringatapam, and murdered the survivors of the English captives whom he had detained in defiance of the late treaty, lest they should tell tales. His capital was invested, and he was obliged to make another treaty, whereby he ceded half his dominions — including the province of Coorg, which he had subdued with fearful cruelty —delivered up all his prisoners, paid an indemnity, and gave over two of his sons as hostages for the fulfilment of all the conditions.

Again there was an interval of peace while Tipu plotted revenge. He ground down the wretched cultivators of Mysore, in order to raise the money for the indemnity, while he lost no opportunity of stirring up strife between the English, the Marathas, and the Nizam. Again he sought French help, sending an embassy to the Isle of France, to ask a fleet and an army to expel "the shameless, thieving, robbing English." There was a Jacobin Club among the Frenchmen employed in Mysore, and they planted a tree of liberty in the principal square of Seringatapam, vowing hatred to all kings, save "Citoyen Tipu, the ally of the French Republic," and singing "Amour sacré de la patrie." There was also a large French contingent in the Nizam's army, whose commandant, an ardent Jacobin, was

Tipu's friend. Revenge might be easy, if only a French expedition were sent from Egypt to India. The English knew it, and so did "Citizen Tipu," who had slept upon canvas ever since Cornwallis defeated him, vowing to lie upon his bed again when he should have set his foot on the necks of the English.

A new Governor-General, Lord Mornington (better known as Marquis Wellesley, and brother to the Duke of Wellington), was quick to act. The Nizam was obliged to disband his French contingent, and Tipu was required to renounce any French alliance. At first Tipu endorsed the Governor-General's letters—"No answer"; then he replied with protestations of friendship, and at the same time sent overtures to the French Directory. Offered the choice between peace and war, he chose war, and was utterly defeated.

He made his last stand within the walls of his capital. "Who can take Seringapatam?" he would say, and he thought to hold out there until the English were weary, or had work elsewhere found for them by the Marathas and others. But there was treachery within. Tipu was to reap the fruit of his cruelty and caprice, his habit of promoting men of low class, and putting down old servants of the state, his love of innovation, his self-confidence and arrogance. His own nobles were turning against him, and it is said that some of them betrayed him to the English. Without was the man—now a General—who for more than three years had endured captivity in the prison near the palace, and had seen his friends suffer and die beside him.

It was the night of May 3rd, and the English engineers had reported to General Harris that the breach was nearly practicable. "We have but two days' rice in camp for the fighting men," said the Adjutant-General, "and if we do not succeed to-morrow, we must go."—"Either we succeed to-morrow," answered Baird, who had volunteered to lead the storming party, "or you never see me more."

Before daybreak the troops were in the trenches, and Baird, passing along them, had recognised some of his fellow-captives and bidden them be of good cheer, for they would soon have a chance to pay off old scores. Long hours dragged away before the preparations were complete; it was not till past one o'clock in the afternoon that Baird stepped out of the trenches, and waving his sword, called aloud, "Now, my brave fellows, follow me, and prove yourselves worthy of the name of British soldiers."

He led them over the Kaveri, by the ford marked out during the night by a lieutenant, while the shot rained about him thick and fast, yet never touched him, and up to the breach, whence the British flag was waving in six minutes.

Meanwhile Tipu's astrologers were prophesying evil things, and the Sultan, forgetting his zeal for the religion of the Prophet, was making last desperate efforts to avert his doom, presenting an elephant to a Brahman, and dividing rupees and cloth among an assembly of poor men and women. Then he ordered his dinner to be brought, and had swallowed only a mouthful when the sounds of weeping and wailing arose without. He asked the cause, was told that one of his most trusted officers had been slain, and immediately left off eating and washed his hands, saying, "We also shall soon depart." Then he mounted his horse, and rode from his palace for the last time.

Baird had halted his column, to give them a little time to breathe, when a Muslim officer was brought to him, with news of twelve grenadiers of the 33rd who had lost their way and been taken prisoners in a night attack. They had been murdered, he said, in parties of three at a time, their heads twisted while their bodies were held fast, by order of Tipu.

As he marched to the palace, Baird vowed that, if the tale were true, Tipu should be handed over to the 33rd Regiment to be tried for murder.

But on second thoughts, he decided that the officer was lying for some private end—wherein he did him an injustice—and sent forward to offer protection to every one in the palace, including the Sultan, if an unconditional surrender were made at once.

The terror-stricken princes in the palace swore that they knew not where their father might be, and a search in every room except those of the zenana failed to produce him. He had been seen last upon the north rampart, firing upon the advancing columns with his own hands, while his attendants loaded for him, but no one could tell what had become of him.

At last an official of the palace admitted having heard a story that the Sultan had been wounded at a gateway in the north face of the fort.

It had chanced during the assault that part of the 12th Regiment, instead of going along the ramparts, as had been ordered, separated from the rest, and entered the body of the town. They advanced till they reached a postern gate, where they saw some of the enemy collected, and began firing on them from inside, while the rest of the regiment, having marched by the proper way and reached the other side of the gate, were firing from without. Caught on either side, the enemy had vainly striven to escape, and the gateway was choked with dead and dying.

Dusk had fallen, and it was by the light of lanterns that Baird stood while the heap of slain was slowly turned over, until a corpse was dragged forth and laid before him. The countenance was in no way distorted, but had an expression of stern composure, the large dark eyes were open, under the arched eyebrows, and the body was still warm, so that at first the bystanders thought that the life was yet in him. The ornamented turban, the rich sword-belt, and the light-coloured jacket that Tipu had put on in the morning had been stripped from him, but he still wore the wide trousers of flowered chintz, and dark red sash, and the talisman bound on his right arm. With three wounds in his body, and one through his right temple, "the Tiger" had fallen, "in the lost battle, borne down by the flying."

Next day he was borne through the streets of Seringatapam, to be laid beside his father's mausoleum, with all due ceremony, while fearful claps of thunder pealed overhead.

Wellesley wrote to Pitt that he expected either to be hanged or rewarded for the capture of Seringatapam, and that he would be satisfied in either case, since to him "an English gallows seemed better than an Indian throne." As luck would have it, Parliament chose to thank him, and he was made a Marquis in the peerage of Ireland. But General Harris, who had advanced the money from his own purse for equipping the Madras troops, was left for fourteen years with no reward but the consciousness of having saved the Presidency. It is one of the few pleasant things to be recorded of the Prince Regent that he made Harris a peer.

The rightful heir to the throne of Mysore—a baby of five years old—was restored, under British protection, to rule over a kingdom which exceeded in area that which Haidar Ali had seized, although both the English and the Nizam gained some accession of territory.

As for Tipu's sons, some were to give trouble in after years, but one survived till towards the close of the last century, "greatly respected as a Justice of Peace, and for his hospitality and charity."

# VIII.

# THE MARATHA CONFEDERACY—1761-1782

"Though most of the men in the Maratha army are unendowed with the excellence of noble and illustrious birth, yet, as they undergo all sorts of toil and fatigue in prosecuting a guerilla warfare, they prove superior to the easy and effeminate troops of Hind. Their food consists chiefly of cakes, with a little butter and red pepper ; and hence it is that, owing to the irascibility of their tempers, gentleness is never met with in their dispositions."

—TARIKH-I-IBRAHIM KHAN BAHADUR, 1786.

## VIII.

# THE MARATHA CONFEDERACY—
## 1761-1782.

A January day of 1761 was drawing towards evening, and on the plain of Panipat, where two hosts had been contending since noon, the sun's last rays were obscured by clouds of dust and smoke. Before the sudden darkness of night could cover them, "the gale of victory had blown over the flags" of one army, and the other broke and fled. Out of the press and the reek galloped little dark horsemen, shrilling "Har! har! Mahadeo!" their hands and faces stained yellow, one end of their turbans flying loose, and after them pressed large-boned hawk-faced men, whose shout was "Din! din!" Once more the Crescent had triumphed, on the plain where, sixteen hundred years before, Mahmud of Ghori had defeated the last Hindu King of Delhi.

For greater part of the first half of the eighteenth century, it had been of little moment to any, save the faction who played with him, whether one puppet or another sat in the hall where the Peacock Throne once had stood, and called himself Padishah, King of Kings, and Shadow of God. But while Lally and Bussy were making their last campaign against the English in the south, the heir to these empty titles, hereafter to be known as Shah Alam, had suddenly evinced unusual strength of character by going into rebellion against his father. Incited by the Nawab of Oudh, who longed to see the English driven from the Bengal provinces, he led an invading army thither.

Beaten back by Clive, he returned in the following year, by which time his father, according to the frequent precedent for the nominal ruler of Delhi, had been assassinated by a Prime Minister. Clive had returned to England, but, happier than Dupleix, he left representatives who were not altogether unfit to carry on his work. One of these, Captain Knox, sent to the relief of Patna, crossed the river with seven hundred men, charged an army of thirty thousand, and after six hours' fighting, with the help of a Rajput ally, led the three hundred survivors of his force in triumph into the city, "covered with dust and blood," while what was left of the Moghul host fled away.

While Shah Alam wasted his time, and such resources as he possessed, in fruitless attempts upon Bengal, the Afghan Ahmad Shah Abdali, whose occupation for some years past had been to invade the Emperor's territory, was preparing to drive the Maratha Confederacy from Delhi. As Ahmad Shah had sacked the city twice, and the Marathas had sacked it after him, tearing down the silver ceiling of the Hall of Audience and flinging it into the melting-pot, either side knew that nothing worthy of their attention could be left within the red walls; but for many years the ruler of Delhi had been overlord of Hindustan, and the tradition was not forgotten. The Marathas, swollen with pride, thought that none could stand against them, and that they were to drive the northern invader before them, as they had driven the Moghul troops from the time of Aurangzib. Their leader, commonly known as "the Bhao," was cousin and representative of the Peshwa of Poona, who was Prime Minister to the *fainéant* Raja of Satara, and head of the Confederacy; with him were various others whose fathers had risen from guerilla chiefs to be the lords of towns and villages,—the sons of Sindhia, who had been the Peshwa's slipper-bearer—the Gaikwar, whose forefather was a cowherd, and Holkar, son of a goatherd, a calling esteemed by his people lower than that of a shepherd. With Ahmad Shah were the Nawab of Oudh, always ready for evil, and the Rohillas, an Afghan tribe whose good qualities, if they had any, are not prominent in their history.

In their fortified camp at Panipat the Maratha host were safe from attack, but the Afghans blocked the approaches, and the last mouthful of food had been eaten in the dawn of that January morning before they came out to what, as they foreboded, would be the last battle that most of them were to see. At one time it seemed as if Ahmad Shah were to be the loser; then, at the crisis of the fight, Holkar and the Gaikwar rode from the field. The battle turned into a rout; thousands lay dead upon the plain, others were cut down as they fled, and their corpses lay strewn shoulder to shoulder from Panipat to Delhi.

Among those who hurried southward was a dark-skinned man of about thirty years old, upon a mare who "outstripped the cold winter's blast in speed." One by one, the friends and followers who fled with him were left behind, and he struggled on alone, while after him lumbered an Afghan trooper riding a heavy Turki charger. In vain did the Maratha urge his worn-out steed; she could do no more, and whenever he looked over his shoulder, he saw the charger "shaking his ears and coming straight on." In a last desperate effort, he set the mare at a ditch; she fell, and as the rider struggled on the ground the Afghan stood over them. "This shall give you a mark to remember for years to come," he swore, dealing his enemy a blow in the leg; then he stripped the young man of his rich dress and accoutrements, and spitting contemptuously upon him, rode away with the mare, for which the owner had given twelve thousand rupees.

Helpless, half-naked, and in agony, the fugitive lay by the wayside. That morning he had ridden forth with his brothers to lead their clan to battle; now they were dead, and he, the last of Sindhia's race, was at the point to die.

The history of India must have been written differently but for a waterman who came along the road to Delhi, driving his bullock. Muslim though he was, he pitied the wounded man, lifted him upon the animal's broad back, and carried him off to a place of safety. Night had fallen on the plain, and "the glad sounds of the kettle-drums were reverberating from the army of Ahmad Shah."

## II.

For some years after the battle of Panipat there was no longer even a semblance of empire at Delhi. Shah Alam, the rightful heir, was living in Bengal, under protection of the English; Ahmad Shah was so much exhausted by his victory that he withdrew from India with the remnants of his army. The great Maratha Confederacy had melted away like snow in harvest; the Bhao and many lesser chiefs were lying among the thirty-two mounds of corpses heaped on the stricken field. The Peshwa was dead of a broken heart, and his successor was a minor. All Sindhia's lawful heirs were dead, although there remained a son born out of wedlock, Madhaji, the wounded man whom the water-carrier had picked up by the wayside.

Among a race where purity of lineage is of the first importance, an illegitimate son is at even greater disadvantage than in the West, and Madhaji obtained the succession to his father's fiefs and commands merely because no other of his blood was left. He was handicapped, moreover, by his wound, which had lamed him for life, so that he could not rise from his seat without the help of two men. Yet, with all this against him, in a few years the slipper-bearer's unlawful son was to be the most formidable power of Hindustan.

His fief lay in the north of Malwa, the most fertile province of Hindustan.

> "In Malwa land you are always fed,
> One step water, the next bread,"

says a Hindu proverb. From his capital at Ujjain he could enter the country between Agra and Alwar, where the Jats, a Hindu tribe of "stout yeomen with strong administrative tendencies of a somewhat republican stamp,"[1] had established themselves, or the no-man's-land that by a polite fiction was supposed to belong to the Emperor of Delhi, or the deserts and mountain passes which alone were left to the Rajput princes. It was a good position, and Sindhia, having raised a strong body of cavalry, waited for the hour to use it to the best advantage.

His first opportunity for self-assertion came in a dispute with his overlord. Holkar died, four years after the battle of Panipat, to the regret of all his soldiers, whose shields he would fill with rupees when they had pleased him with some feat of arms; his only son had died before him, leaving a son by his wife Ahalya Bai, one of the family of Sindhia. Always weak and foolish, the lad

[1] H. G. Keene.

became actually insane during the eight months when he sat on his grandfather's throne, and in one of his paroxysms of rage, slew a man for an offence of which he was not guilty. "Beware how you kill me, for I will take vengeance upon you," the victim had warned him, but the prince took no heed. Too late the dead man's innocence was proved, and from that hour his vengeful ghost haunted the murderer.

Day after day and night after night did Ahalya Bai sit beside the bed where her son tossed and raved, praying to the gods whom she served devoutly from her youth up, or imploring mercy of the dead man's spirit that had taken possession of his slayer. "Release my son," she pleaded, "and I will build a temple to you, and settle lands upon your heirs for ever." But through dry lips the pitiless answer came, "He slew me innocent, and I will have his life."

It is possible that the end was hastened by some of the Brahmans whom the graceless youth had tormented by putting scorpions among the gifts that he was required to bestow on them. With him died Holkar's last male descendant; his sister, having married into another family, was considered to have foregone all claims upon the succession.

Holkar's Brahman prime minister now approached the Peshwa's uncle and regent, Raghonath Rao, whom the English—who were to have more than enough of him—called Raghoba. Let some male child be adopted as Holkar's successor, under the minister's guardianship; Ahalya Bai should be made to retire from public affairs—which were unbefitting a woman—with an ample provision for her needs, and Raghonath should receive a suitable reward for his consent to the arrangement.

But when the scheme was laid before Ahalya Bai, she turned in wrath upon the Brahman. If there were any adoption, she said, it was her right and her duty to make it, as wife and mother of the last of Holkar's blood: it was not for Raghonath to meddle, and no gift should be made to him with her leave.

Raghonath threatened to force her obedience, whereupon the princess advised him not to make war upon a woman, since it could not result in honour, and must bring disgrace upon him—and ordered bows and arrows to be hung in the howdah of her favourite elephant. Holkar's troops were ready to follow her to battle, while those of Raghonath were not eager to meet them. Raghonath called upon Madhaji Sindhia to join him, and Sindhia flatly refused. Ahalya was of his kin, and he had fought side by side with old Holkar in former days.

So the army mustered by Raghonath was employed in a raid upon Delhi territory, and for thirty years Ahalya Bai administered the Holkar dominions from Indore, which she changed from a village into the capital of her state. She appointed Takuji Holkar, of the same tribe but not the same family as her husband, to command her troops, and devoted herself to the government and to works of charity. Never once, we are told, was there so much as a dispute between them; he called her "mother," though she was the younger of the two, and to the last day of her life he behaved as a dutiful and affectionate son.

Rising at dawn to pray and read sacred books, holding her court every day, accessible to all classes of her subjects, inflexibly just, but refusing to use stern measures with evil-doers until conciliation had been tried in vain, Ahalya Bai was reverenced throughout India.

Long after her death men loved to tell how in the hot season the traveller on the road, and the weary oxen toiling in the field, would be refreshed with water sent by Ahalya Bai; how even the birds driven from the cultivator's land would find crops sown for them; how at every shrine of India, from the snows of Kedarnath to the babul-trees of Ramesvaram, pilgrims were sheltered in the rest-houses built by the saintly princess.

It was said that her fasts and prayers shortened her life; it is probable that she never recovered from the agony of beholding her only daughter become *sati*. Ahalya commanded as a sovereign, she pleaded as a mother, but the childless widow was determined to burn on her husband's pyre, and the mother stood to watch the sacrifice, "gnawing her hands in anguish."

There is a story that Raghonath's wife, as beautiful as she was wicked, once sent an attendant to the Court of Indore to report upon Ahalya Bai's appearance. "She has not beautiful features," said the woman on her return, "but a heavenly light is on her countenance."

To Sindhia and all of her own faith, the solitary woman, worn with fasts and toil, arrayed in the plain white robe that is the dress of the poorest Hindu widow, became something sacred, to be defended from all enemies. But enemies she had none; Muslims, to whom she showed kindness and tolerance, joined with Hindus in praying for her, and the common people believed her to be a divine incarnation, and worshipped at her tomb near Indore, long after she had "found freedom."

## III.

One of the first enterprises in which Sindhia and the forces of Ahalya Bai acted in concert was the restoration of Shah Alam to the throne of Delhi.

The memory of the defeat at Panipat still rankled in Maratha breasts, and having collected his feudatory troops to the number of three hundred thousand, the Peshwa sent them northward. They began as usual by laying waste part of Rajputana, then occupied Delhi. The ruler there was son of the Afghan whom Ahmad Shah had appointed governor, and he fled at their approach. From Shah Jahan's palace in the Fort, Takuji Holkar invited Shah Alam to return to the throne of his fathers, under Maratha protection.

The Emperor rose to the bait. For a long time he had wearied of his mock Court at Allahabad, where the English officer in command of the brigade appointed to watch over his safety objected to the din of his kettle-drums. The English had refused all his requests to be taken back to Delhi; here were the Marathas offering to do it of their own accord, and he would pay all they asked and grant all they wanted. So, regardless of good advice and warnings from the Government of

Calcutta, Shah Alam was escorted by Sindhia to the Maratha camp, and on Christmas Day, 1771, he was enthroned at Delhi.

In the disorder of the next twelve months, Marathas, Moghuls, Rohillas, and Jats alternately fought and plotted with each other, to the distraction of the country and the despair of all who try to read the history of the period. Then the situation was complicated tenfold by the death of the young Peshwa, one of whose last acts had been to free his uncle Raghonath from the durance which had kept him from meddling in affairs of state. Raghonath was supposed to have an affection for the rightful heir, the Peshwa's younger brother, and for a few months after his accession they seemed to work in concert. Ere long, however, the uncle went too far, and was confined in the palace under his nephew's own eye.

Then an order written by Raghonath found its way to the commandant of infantry at Poona. Raghonath himself vowed that when it left his hands, it authorised the commandant to seize his nephew. But when it reached its destination, the word "seize" (dhurawe) had been altered into "kill" (marawe); it was always said, by her own people, that the writer was Anandi Bai, Raghonath's wife.

The Peshwa was sleeping in the heat of an

August afternoon, when he was roused by shouts and trampling; his infantry had mutinied for their arrears of pay, and had entered the palace. He fled to the rooms where Raghonath was confined, pursued by one of the officers who had received the order, and flinging himself into his uncle's arms, begged piteously for protection From an inner chamber darted Anandi Bai, who tore the clinging hands asunder, and flung the youth to his murderers.

Raghonath, proclaimed Peshwa, soon found that all obstacles were not yet removed from his path. Among the least estimable of the late Peshwa's ministers was a certain deputy auditor and accountant, generally known as "Nana Farnavis," and he, discovering the widowed Rani's condition, removed her to a fortress under a strong guard, and proclaimed a Council of Regency. Lest any mistake should occur, however, he sent with her five other expectant mothers, which caused some natural doubt as to the parentage of the boy produced some three months later.

At any rate, he could be used against Raghonath, who, defeated by the child's partisans, made appeal to Sindhia and Holkar. Obtaining nothing from them—for Ahalya Bai, herself a widow, was not likely to take part against another widow—he proposed an English alliance, and promised in exchange for British troops to cede to the Bombay Government the harbour of Bassein and the Island of Salsette, which commanded the port of Bombay.

The Portuguese had a title to both places, but this mattered little to Raghonath or to Governor Hornby, who, without consulting his superiors at Bengal, signed a treaty at Surat, took possession of island and harbour, and sent troops under Colonel Keating to conduct his ally back to Poona.

Then the storm burst. Warren Hastings, then at the head of affairs in Calcutta, though he disapproved of Hornby's action, would have been content to order that the Bombay Government should "get clear of the war as soon as they could with honour and safety." But he was overborne by other members of Council, who despatched a furious letter to Hornby, pronouncing the war "impolitic, dangerous, unauthorised, and unjust," and wrote to the Maratha chiefs disowning the action of the Bombay Government.

This step, though it lowered the prestige of Bombay, did not affect the policy of its Governor, who continued to carry on the war, on his own account, with great success. Keating defeated the troops of the Regency in several engagements, and drove them across the Nerbudda, into which they threw their guns as they fled.

Philip Francis had then the majority in the

Calcutta Council, and being bent upon opposing Hastings in all things, sent an envoy to treat with the Regency, who arranged the Treaty of Purandhar, whereby the British forces were pledged to leave the field, and the Council acknowledged the child Peshwa, on condition of retaining Salsette.

Like the majority of treaties, this pleased no one concerned. The Regency objected to giving up Salsette ; Raghonath protested that as he had not been consulted, he was not bound to disband his troops, and the Bombay Government ostentatiously harboured him at Surat. An appeal to the Court of Directors in England resulted in a despatch that practically set aside the Treaty of Purandhar.

Another campaign proved disastrous to the Bombay forces. The military member of Council at their head was an imbecile, the commander understood war only as observed in the course of a short experience in Germany. They dawdled, quarrelled, and when they found Sindhia's forces enveloping them, twenty miles from Poona, they lost their heads, burned their stores, threw their guns into a pond, and after two days' desultory fighting, sent envoys to treat for peace.

Sindhia's terms were hard—the surrender of Salsette and all that had been gained during the last five years, and the abandonment of Raghonath, who with great tact "saved the face" of his allies by giving himself up without waiting to be surrendered. To gain time, the English agent pleaded that the Bombay Government had no power to make treaties unauthorised. "Then show me by what authority you broke the Treaty of Purandhar," retorted Sindhia.

Poorly as the English officers had figured, Sindhia had conceived from that time a deep respect for the English soldier. "What soldiers yours are!" he exclaimed, during the negotiations for peace. "Their line is like a red brick wall, and when one falls another steps into the gap. I hope one day to fight on the same side." Already it was crossing his mind that it would be an error in judgment to let Nana Farnavis become too powerful.

Accordingly, the next development was that Raghonath found himself again at large, and went back to British protection, carrying friendly messages from Sindhia. The Regency insisted that he should be given up, the English refused, and war began again.

The prospect was ugly for the English in India during the summer of 1780; Haidar Ali had proclaimed himself the ally of their enemies, the French, and had invaded the Carnatic; the

Council of Madras made no effort to oppose him. In Central India were rumours that once more the Marathas were forming a great confederacy, and would break the power of the English as they had broken that of Delhi. One man at least kept his head while the whole English dominion seemed toppling to its fall, and that man was Hastings.

One of the strongest fortresses in India was that of Gwalior, "a huge rock of sandstone, capped with basalt, one and a half miles long, rising from the plain like the hulk of a gigantic battleship."[1] In ages long ago, hermits and saints had dwelt in the caves with which the rock is honeycombed, but with the dawn of history kings and warriors had fortified it with scarp and wall, tower and bastion, until it was almost impregnable. Used as a state prison for royal captives by Akbar and the later Moghul emperors, it had been seized by the Rana of Gohad during the struggles of the moribund empire. Sindhia had taken it from the Rana; his men now garrisoned it, assured that no one could disturb them, and careless that three battalions under a certain Captain Popham were encamped within ten miles of them. For two months the little force had sat there, apparently waiting to be relieved as soon as the rains were over, and no one save Bruce, the engineer, knew

[1] A. H. Murray.

that Popham had any motive for gazing up where the exquisite blue and yellow tiles of Maun Singh's palace still gleam from the height.

It was a dark night in August when, acting upon information received through the Rana's spies, Popham took his men across the Chambal. Bruce was in command of an advance party, guided by the spies. Arrived at the rock, they lay in its shadow while the rounds passed overhead, then planted their scaling-ladders and ascended, their cotton-shod feet making no noise. A steep climb of forty yards brought them to the second wall, which was thirty feet high. The spies, who knew the place, secured rope-ladders, and in a few minutes the advance party were squatting down within the fort. Even when three of the sepoys "so far forgot themselves as to shoot some of the garrison who lay asleep near them," and thus gave the alarm, the Marathas had no stomach for fighting. Taken completely by surprise, they threw down their arms, and at sunrise the fortress was in Popham's hands. He had done what Sir Eyre Coote had pronounced it would be madness to attempt, when the project was discussed in the Bengal Council.

The effect upon British prestige was what Hastings had hoped when he resolved to divert Sindhia's attention by an attack upon his northern possessions. Friends and allies veered round; and when in the following year Bruce surprised Sindhia's camp in a night attack, and the Maratha fled, losing tents, elephants, horses, and baggage, it was evident that war with the English was no longer profitable.

In October, Gwalior, Ujjain, and all his previous possessions south and west of the Jumna were restored to Sindhia, on the sole condition that he should persuade the Poona Regency to make peace.

By his means a treaty was now arranged. The English were to restore all territory gained subsequent to the Treaty of Purandhar, and Raghonath was to be pensioned and live where he chose. Haidar Ali, who had joined the Maratha Confederacy, was to release all English prisoners and relinquish all his conquests.

At first sight this seems a poor return for so much trouble. But it was through this Treaty of Salbai that, "without annexing a square mile of British territory, the British power became virtually paramount in the greater part of the Indian peninsula, every province of which, with the one exception of Mysore, acknowledged that power as the great universal peacemaker. Indirectly, it was the corner-stone of the British Indian Empire."[1]

[1] H. G. Keene.

# IX.

# WHERE THE CARCASE IS—1782-1802

> "Or puoi, figliuol, veder la corta buffa
> De' ben che son commessi alla Fortuna,
> Per che l'umana gente si rabbuffa."

## IX.

## WHERE THE CARCASE IS—1782-1802.

HAVING come to an understanding, the two wisest men in India went each his own way — Warren Hastings to found an empire for his country, and Madhaji Sindhia to make a kingdom for himself.

There is no need to tell here the familiar story of Warren Hastings. "Truth, the daughter of Time," has vindicated him; and for all who are desirous or capable of forming a fair judgment, his reputation has been cleared of the mud flung by Irish political adversaries and Whig pamphleteers. "We know now, as they might have known then, that the account given by the Whigs of the Rohilla War was false from end to end; that Nuncomar was justly tried, and as justly punished; that Cheyte Sing was not unfairly treated; that the Begums of Oudh had appropriated money that was not theirs."[1]

[1] 'Blackwood's Magazine,' April 1913.

Sindhia had learned his lesson. So long as he lived there was peace between him and the English, and his kingdom was to be built with their help, not in their despite.

In Delhi all was misery and confusion. The spirit of Shah Alam's young days, when he led his army into Bengal, had withered away under the weight of the crown. Bullied by his ministers, plundered by his councillors, his dominions raided by Jats, Sikhs, and Rohillas, he was borne helplessly along the tide of events without attempting to struggle against it. When Sindhia presented himself before him at Delhi, the Emperor made no difficulty in granting two patents—one declaring the Peshwa Vicegerent of the Empire, the other giving command of the army to Sindhia as the Peshwa's deputy.

Having, as he hoped, thus secured peace for himself, the Emperor retired once more behind the marble screens of his palace to study the Koran.

But peace was the last thing desired by the princes of Rajputana, who were infuriated at this arrangement. Were they, the children of the sun and the moon and the flame, who had defied the great Akbar, to submit themselves and pay tribute to the Peshwa and to his slipper-bearer's bastard? The Muslim nobles, learning of Sindhia's purpose to investigate the titles by which they held their lands, joined cause with the Rajputs. After three days' fighting near Jaipur, Sindhia was defeated, fourteen thousand of his infantry deserting him.

Driven back upon Gwalior, he was saved from ruin by a loan from Ahalya Bai, who had not forgotten the time when Sindhia had stood between her and the Regent of Poona. Neither dreamed how in after years the loan was to bring trouble upon the whole Maratha Confederacy.

Meanwhile Shah Alam, forgetting his obligations to Sindhia, had chosen new friends, and showed his usual unwisdom in the choice. The Rajputs might again be the allies of Delhi as in the time of Jahangir and Shah Jahan, but there could be no alliance between the Emperor and Ghulam Kadir the Rohilla. Ghulam's father was son of that Afghan governor whom Ahmad Shah had left in Delhi, and it was said that after Shah Alam's restoration, Ghulam, then only a boy, made prisoner and taken into the royal household, had there received such treatment as no man could forgive.

Sindhia was beginning once more to hold his own, but he made no move when Ghulam, having allied himself with Ismail Beg, a Persian leader of cavalry, entered the imperial city, nominally as the friend of Shah Alam, in July 1788. Perhaps he thought well that the faithless Emperor should taste the fruit of his own devices.

Bitter fruit did it prove. While Ismail Beg encamped on the outskirts of Delhi, and took toll from the citizens, Ghulam insisted upon replacing the palace guards by his own men; it was useless to resist, but the Emperor thought to secure himself by making the bandit swear fidelity upon the Koran. Then Ghulam began his search for hidden treasure; he tore up the floors and stripped the royal apartments, regardless of the protestations of the Emperor, who wailed, "If there is any more money, you are welcome to it. I came out with a shirt and an old pair of trousers which I still have, but you know all about it." The princes were stripped and exposed to the sun, the princesses were scourged, the harem slaves were tortured, but former spoilers, Persian, Rohilla, Afghan, and Maratha, had done their work too well, and only a little gold and silver could be produced. In a fury of disappointment Ghulam flung himself upon the Emperor and blinded him with his dagger, kicking away the royal ladies who came from behind their curtains to beg for mercy. "Do you see anything?" he asked derisively; and the Emperor answered, "Nothing but the holy Koran between me and you."

Then followed weeks of horror. The ladies of the harem were stripped naked in the search for jewels, and exposed without their veils to the gaze of the Rohilla and his drunken fellow-ruffians; the princes were made to sing and dance before their enemy, as if they had been hired players. The Emperor and his household were left without food, so that several of the children died of hunger and thirst. His own associates sickened with horror, and warned Ghulam that a day of retribution was coming, but he mocked, and answered with threats too foul to be written here.

By the beginning of September the reckoning was at hand; Ismail Beg had decamped, and the Maratha forces were approaching. As a last effort, Ghulam set the Palace on fire and then hurried across the river.

Rana Khan, the water-carrier who had saved Sindhia after the battle of Panipat, now promoted by Sindhia's gratitude to be a general in his army, arrived in time to put out the flames before they had done much damage, and then joined with Ahalya Bai's army in pursuit of Ghulam. For nine weeks Ghulam defended himself in the fort at Meerut, then escaped with a few trusted followers under cover of night. In the darkness he was separated from his companions; his horse put its foot into a hole and fell with him; "the way bristled with thorny acacias, so that he knew not which way to turn." He went to the house of a Brahman, whom he would have bribed with a diamond ring to shelter him. But the Brahman's village had been ravaged by Ghulam in former days, and he handed the fugitive over to Rana Khan, who sent him on to Sindhia.

For several days, by Sindhia's orders, the Maratha forces were entertained with the sight of Ghulam Kadir being gradually cut to pieces. What was left of him after death was hung from a tree, some choice portions being sent as a present to the Emperor. "A trustworthy person relates that a black dog, white round the eyes, came and sat under the tree, and licked up the blood as it dripped," says a chronicler. "The spectators threw stones and clods at it, but still it kept there. On the third day the corpse disappeared, and the dog also vanished."

The crown jewels of Delhi were hidden in the lining of the saddle upon which Ghulam rode in his flight. They were never seen again; but a French officer in Sindhia's army having suddenly returned to his native land about this time, evidently with a large fortune, it was always believed that he had had the luck to capture Ghulam's horse.

The poor blind Emperor was replaced upon the

throne with due ceremony, and a revenue of about £90,000 a year allotted for his support. Court gossip declared that Sindhia's representative took such good toll of this that the imperial family seldom received more than £5000, irregularly paid, and that had it not been for a compassionate allowance made monthly by the English Government, his Majesty and his thirty children would have fared very ill. Nevertheless, one of the Persian poems with which Shah Alam beguiled his long hours speaks of "Madhaji Sindhia who is as a son to me," and by comparison with what had gone before, the years of Sindhia's administration were peaceful and prosperous for the dwellers in the Emperor's territory. Even if they were heavily taxed, it is a gain to have one spoiler in the place of many, and Sindhia allowed no one else to reap in his furrows.

The Rajputs also had met their master. Among the adventurers who came to seek fortune in India was a certain Savoyard, Benoît Boigne. He had served in the French and the Russian army, he had even served for a brief space in the Company's army in Madras, and narrowly escaped being made the prisoner of Tipu Sahib. Through the good offices of Warren Hastings he was introduced to Sindhia, and beginning as commander of two battalions of infantry, he became head of an army which he drilled and disciplined upon European lines.

In the spring of 1790 this army was to be tested. Ahmad Shah's son, Timur, was known to be meditating a descent upon the Punjab, and this was an irresistible temptation to Ismail Beg, Ghulam's former confederate, who raised a standard of rebellion, and was joined by the Raja of Jodhpur and the Maharaja of Jaipur. Ismail was at Patan, between Gwalior and Ujjain, where Boigne had blockaded him for several weeks, when the Kachwaha Rajputs of Jaipur arrived upon the scene. If they had fallen upon Boigne in the rear, they might have disposed of him once for all; but the Kachwahas are lightly esteemed as fighting men by other Rajput clans, and that day they deserved their reputation. Some say that the Rathors of Jodhpur had mocked them with a taunting song of a time when "the Rathors guarded the petticoats of Jaipur," and Sindhia's emissaries had no difficulty in bribing them to stand aloof from the fight. Ismail Beg made a sortie, and was heavily defeated. Boigne advanced to Ajmir, the key of Rajputana, captured the town, and invested the fortress of Taragarh, which crowns the sharp-pointed hill above it.

The Maharaja of Jodhpur tried diplomacy; let the General forsake Sindhia and join the Rajputs, and he should be invested with the fief of Ajmir. "My master has already given me Jodhpur and Jaipur," answered Boigne. "Why should I content myself with nothing but Ajmir?" Then the Maharaja led his Rathors to the relief of Taragarh, and Boïgne met them under the walls of Mairta, eighty miles away. The Maratha general would have fallen upon them at once, but Boigne shook his head. "The hour is late, the men are tired; let them have a good meal, and then sleep; there will be time enough in the morning."

The Rathors passed the first half of the night in festivity, and were asleep when a French colonel led three battalions to the attack in the mists of dawn. But the alarm was given, the Rathors armed, and sprang to horse. "Where can we fly, brothers?" cried the chief of Ahwa. "If there be one of us who prefers wife and children to honour, let him retire." None spoke in answer; each warrior raised his hand to his brow, and the chief gave the word "Forward." With the cry of "Remember Patan!" they cut their way past Boigne's brigade, up to the mouth of his eighty pieces of cannon. The grape showered around them, but they stayed not for it, galloping faster and faster, driving the Maratha squadrons before them in the headlong Rajput charge in which their forefathers had ridden since the beginning of history.

The Marathas scattered, the Rathors drew rein in triumph—and rode back through "a valley of death." Boigne had formed his infantry in the hollow square that is said to have been his own invention, and had wheeled his guns round. The Rathors had no reserve to support them, but the Savoyard General was gradually bringing up his battalions, under cover of the storm of grape. Out of four thousand Rathors who charged with the Ahwa chief, scarcely one was left in the saddle.

The modern and scientific method of fighting had demonstrated its superiority over the hand-to-hand struggle in which the best man had the best chance of winning. The Rajputs were left to mourn the last day of chivalry in India, as Bayard had mourned it, two hundred and fifty years previously, in Europe. Udaipur, Jodhpur, and Jaipur perforce humbled themselves before the Peshwa's slipper-bearer. Timur Shah postponed the invasion of India for a more convenient opportunity.

For the next few years Sindhia was the greatest man in India, although he affected to call himself no more than the Peshwa's servant, and when he paid a state visit to Poona, insisted upon carrying his slippers in full durbar, with the words: "This was my father's occupation, and it must also be mine."

Long after his death, it was a common saying in India that "Madhaji Sindhia made himself the sovereign of an empire by calling himself the headman of a village."

The young Peshwa showed him marked favour, thereby exciting the jealousy of his minister Nana Farnavis, "the Machiavel of India," who was known to be the lover of the Peshwa's mother, and suspected of being actually the Peshwa's father. He had been heard to remonstrate with the Peshwa, and to threaten to resign his office, if so much were made of this base-born adventurer who despised Brahmans, and preferred Rajput, Muslim, or even European to his own countrymen. When the news passed from mouth to mouth, in the February of 1794, that Madhaji Sindhia had suddenly died of fever near Poona, not many could be found to believe it. There were whispers of assassins sent by Nana Farnavis, who dogged the old chief's steps as he went home at night, and though beaten off by his attendants, contrived to deal him several mortal wounds. The one man who could keep order in Hindustan was dead, and the Maratha wolf-pack was left without a leader, just at the time when in France another wolf-pack, having pulled down all their foes, were beginning to fly each at the other's throat.

## II.

"They were continually levying a tax from the towns, and when the wretched townsfolk had no more to give, then burned they all the towns, so that well mightest thou walk a whole day's journey or ever thou shouldst see a man settled in a town, or its lands tilled. . . . Wretched men starved with hunger. . . . Every man plundered his neighbour as much as he could. . . . The earth bare no corn; you might as well have tilled the sea; for all the land was ruined by such deeds."

The lament of the Anglo-Saxon Chronicle of 1137 might have been written of Central India during what its historians call "The Time of Troubles"—from 1798 to 1818.

Had Sindhia lived out his threescore years and ten, or had he left a worthy successor, the time of troubles might have been less grievous. Despised by Brahmans and men of his own race, on account of the stain on his birth, he had given his favour to aliens and foreigners, and opposed the growing ascendancy of the Brahmans with all his might, regarding himself rather as the lord of Hindustan than as the leading member of the Maratha Confederacy. Now that he was dead, the influence of the Brahman ministers in the

Confederacy was supreme, and they, in the words of a Muslim historian, "converted the peaceful cord of their order into a bowstring."

There was none to check them ; Madhaji Sindia left no son, and Daulat Rao, the fifteen-year-old great-nephew who succeeded him, was cruel and treacherous as any of his race, but lacked the ability to make his treasons profitable. Ahalya Bai died in the following year, and her successor, Takuji Holkar, was rapidly becoming imbecile.

In the year of Ahalya's death, weary of the tutelage of Nana Farnavis, the young Peshwa threw himself from a balcony in his palace, and was dashed to pieces. He left no heir. Raghonath, whose claims to the succession had caused the first Maratha War, was dead, but unhappily he had a son, Baji Rao—a worthy child of the murderess whose name was accursed even among her own people.

No sooner was he established on the throne than he stirred up the young Sindhia to imprison the Nana, who had come to return a formal visit of ceremony. To prevent trouble with Sindhia, he then arranged for his assassination during a conference at the palace, but his heart failed him at the critical moment, and he did not give the signal.

Then the Raja of Satara, for many years a

negligible quantity, having been allowed to join in the conspiracy against the Nana, lost his head at finding himself of importance, and rebelled against the Peshwa, as did the Raja of Kolhapur, who, incited by Nana Farnavis, "was spreading fire and sword over the whole of the southern Maratha country." There was grave scandal about Sindhia's treatment of two of his great-uncle's widows, commonly known as "the Bais," who fled to the camp of the Peshwa's brother, and stirred up revolt. To crown the confusion, Takuji Holkar died, leaving two legitimate sons. It was arranged that the weakly elder son should administer the home government, while the younger led the army to battle. This suited neither party. The younger appealed to the Nana, the elder to Sindhia. A reconciliation was arranged under Sindhia's auspices, and both brothers swore upon the leaves of the sacred *bel*-tree,[1] the tree of Mahadeo, to lay aside their quarrel. That night, the younger brother's camp was surrounded by Sindhia's troops, and as he mounted his horse at dawn, he fell dead, with a ball through his forehead. Every man has his price, and Sindhia's price had been the restoration of the bonds given by his great-uncle to Ahalya Bai.

From the welter of confusion there emerged

[1] Ægle Marmelos.

Jeswant Rao, the unlawful son of Takuji. Left at his half-brother's death with a few horse and some of the family jewels, he fought and plundered his way upwards, until he was able to pose as Regent of Indore for its lawful heir, the dead man's posthumous son. Up and down Malwa he went, spoiling, burning, levying contributions from the wretched inhabitants, and the horrors of that war cannot be told. Either side outdid the other in atrocities. Jeswant's horde was the scum of the earth; though Boigne's stern discipline had done much to check the wanton greed and cruelty of Sindhia's army, the Savoyard general had left India soon after Madhaji's death, and Perron, his successor, was not concerned about the behaviour of his men except when they were in action. It is said that the wells round Indore were choked with the bodies of women, who had flung themselves down to escape torture and shame.

At that time the Governor-General was Lord Wellesley—"a nobleman resembling Joseph in beauty and Zohrab in the field of battle, lord of the country of generosity, and master of liberality and benevolence," as a Muslim historian describes him. Since his coming to India in 1798, he had effected many changes. He had delivered Mysore from its tyrant, and set the rightful heir upon the throne; he had assumed control of the Carnatic, after discovering that its worthless ruler had been in secret correspondence with Tipu. The south was at peace, recovering from the wastings of fire and sword; there remained to pacify Hindustan, now rapidly becoming a desert, between Marathas and Pindaris.

It casts a light upon Maratha usage to find Ahalya Bai eulogised by her subjects for allowing merchants and bankers to grow rich in her territories, without mulcting them of their gains. Her successors were Marathas of the old type, and if any man had scraped together a few coins during the "time of troubles," he hid them in the ground, and was careful to seem as near starvation as his neighbours. Commerce was at a standstill, whole tracts of country were falling into wildernesses. The wild beasts of the jungle walked boldly upon the highway, and a single tiger would often cut off all communication between the few villages still inhabited.

Wellesley's first efforts at mediation were not successful; Jeswant Rao Holkar had a blood feud with the Peshwa, who had not only ordered his brother to be trampled to death by an elephant, but had superintended the execution in person. The fact that the brother was a ruffianly freebooter and deserved his fate, naturally did not weigh with Holkar, though, thinking something might be gained by a momentary reconciliation, he appealed to the Peshwa to constitute him Regent of Indore. But the Peshwa went in fear of Sindhia's army, whose general Perron was the terror of every raja and chief from the Nerbudda to the Sutlej, and would not commit himself.

So the armies of Sindhia and Holkar, both officered by Europeans, fought out the quarrel, about ten miles from Poona; Holkar gained a victory, and the Peshwa threw himself upon English protection. On the last day of the year 1802, he signed the Treaty of Basain, whereby he agreed to maintain the British troops sent for his support, and to acknowledge the English as the supreme power. This, the third great treaty in the history of British India, gave to the English the Presidency of Bombay, as the fall of Tipu Sultan had given them the Madras Presidency, and the Treaty of Buxar, the Presidency of Bengal.

# X.

# A FREE LANCE FROM TIPPERARY—1778-1802

"The spider hath woven his web in the regal palace of the Cæsars,
The owl standeth sentinel on the watch-towers of Afrasiab."

—SAADI.

# X.

## A FREE LANCE FROM TIPPERARY—1778-1802.

ONCE upon a time there was a very beautiful woman, who was master of men.

To this day no one knows whence she came. Some said that she was the daughter of a Sayyad, or of an impoverished Moghul noble; others believed that her great dark eyes and fair skin were derived from Kashmiri parentage; others again, that Arab blood was shown in the small feet and perfectly moulded hands and arms. Whatever her birth, she was trained as a dancing-girl at Delhi, in the middle of the eighteenth century, when adventurers by the score came from overseas to seek their fortunes in Hindustan, and the destinies of some of these men were entwined with hers.

The first of these to cross her path was the gloomy "Somru Sahib," who had kept his gang of ruffians together l . .eans of what he had taken from his old master, Mir Kasim. With them he had gone from one place to another, now sent away because his temporary employer feared the English, and now because his villainies were too horrible for ordinary human beings to stomach.

At last he came to Delhi, and entered the service of the Emperor, receiving in fief the jaghir of Sardhana, about forty miles to the north. At Delhi he saw the dancing-girl, and he bought her, and took her to Sardhana. With her he passed the last miserable years of his life.

On every side he saw nothing but deadly peril. He knew that the English made continual applications for his surrender, and though they were refused once or twice, at any time the Emperor's ministers might find it expedient to grant them. His brigades were continually in revolt, beating and ill-using their officers, whom they stripped and grilled upon guns, if their pay were longer in arrears than usual. He could trust no human being save the dancing-girl, and at his death she succeeded to his jaghir, and to the command of his troops.

It seemed preposterous that a woman should be set over mercenaries, who had the reputation of being "the most mutinous troops in India." In a little while they learned that the "Begam

Somru," as they called her, a woman still young and beautiful, so small in stature as to be almost a dwarf, was more to be feared than Somru himself, with the blood of the murdered English upon his hand.

It happened one day that she was with the greater part of her troops in camp at some distance from Agra, having left a detachment to guard certain houses in the city where she kept her valuables, and lodged the widows, wives, and families of the chief officers in her service. News was brought to her that two of the slave girls left in charge during her absence had set fire to the houses, as a prelude to running away with two soldiers of the guard. The roofs, being thatched, blazed merrily, and the lodgers beneath them had a narrow escape of losing their lives, many of them being purdah women, who would have burned to death rather than expose themselves to the stare of the crowds gathered to see the fire. Before the flames could be extinguished much damage was done to property, although no lives were lost.

After this escapade the two slave girls were so incredibly foolish as to remain in the bazaar at Agra, where they were soon discovered and haled forth to the Begam's camp. "Had she faltered on that occasion," said an eye-witness who told his story, many years afterwards, to an English officer, "she must have lost the command. She would have lost that respect without which it would have been impossible for her to retain it a month." She did not falter; there and then she held an inquiry, and the slaves' guilt being proved, she had them flogged till they were senseless, and then buried alive in a hole dug in front of her tent. "For some years after," we are told, "her orders were implicitly obeyed."

The story was handed down from one to another, gathering horror on its way, until some forty years after the event, good Bishop Heber shuddered to hear that the "very little queer-looking old woman, with brilliant but wicked eyes, and the remains of beauty in her features," had watched an erring nautch-girl bricked up in a vault beneath the hall where she was about to give a splendid entertainment. The exact date of the execution is nowhere given, but it is to be hoped that it took place before the Jesuit fathers at Agra had received the Begam into the Church, some three years after Somru's death.

The next European who was to cross the dancing-girl's path was a man of a different type from Somru.

The Begam's troops being notoriously some of

the worst ruffians in the country, the command of a battalion was the last resort of the European adventurers who abounded in India at the close of the eighteenth century. Destiny for a time gave to the Begam the services of one of these men, whose story, sad and strange as any in Indian history, might be called "The Man who would be King."

It is a far cry from a Tipperary bog to an Eastern palace, but an Irishman once travelled all the way there, and some little part of the way back again. His name was George Thomas, and he was a sailor on board a British man-of-war, from which he deserted when it lay at Madras. After spending a few years among the lawless Polygars of the Carnatic, he was for a little while in the army of the Nizam of the Deccan. Tiring of this, he set out to walk from Haiderabad to Delhi.

A madder venture was never tried, not even by an Irishman. All Hindustan was the prey of contending factions; the roads were infested by armed bands who robbed and murdered at will, whether in time of war or of nominal peace. There was no attempt, scarcely a thought, of establishing order. In the universal chaos, it seemed to those who had any power to think that the end of all things was at hand. "All the world is waiting in anxious expectation of the appearance of Imam Mahdi, who is to come in the latter days," writes a contemporary Muslim historian. "Shah Alam sits in the palace of Delhi, and has no thought beyond the gratification of his own pleasure, while his people are deeply sorrowful and grievously oppressed, even unto death." To walk from the Deccan to Delhi would be a hazardous experiment in these days, when the traveller would not be likely to meet a worse enemy than sun and chill; George Thomas must have been in mortal peril every hour in the twenty-four. Unhappily, when he told his story at the close of his life, he never told how he succeeded in reaching Delhi unhurt; perhaps it was because he was taken to be a madman, and therefore under the special protection of Heaven.

On reaching Delhi, he volunteered for service with the Begam Somru's force. Above six feet in height, so strong that he could cut off a bullock's head with a single stroke of his sword, he was a recruit worth having. His manners are said to have been pleasing, and the "coarseness" which some English contemporaries noted in him is not likely to have shocked the woman who for several years had been at the head of a force recruited from the scum of the earth. Ere long Thomas was married to a girl named Marie, who had been adopted by the Begam, and set in command of a battalion.

Soon after this the Begam's troops were called to the help of the Emperor Shah Alam, who was trying to reduce a rebellious subject to order. The rebel's forces, however, were far better disciplined than the imperial army, and Shah Alam was in peril of his life during a night attack, until rescued by a hundred men under the command of Thomas, directed by the Begam herself, who was on the field of battle in her palki. In a durbar held in the afternoon of that day, the Begam was publicly thanked by the Emperor, who called her his "most beloved daughter," and gave her the name of Zeb-i-Nisa—"Glory of Womankind"—and Thomas received a valuable present.

For some years the Irishman continued to rise in the Begam's service, but he could not keep on terms with the other officers, most of whom were Frenchmen. They persuaded her that Thomas was plotting against her authority; Thomas was goaded into rebellion and defeated. His life was spared, and he was allowed to depart unmolested, to begin the world again—this time with fifty pounds in his pocket.

The money was spent in enlisting a number of "masterless men," like himself, ready for any desperate venture. With their help he plundered a large village near Delhi, and lived upon the proceeds for some little time, under the protection of the British Frontier Force at Anupshahr. "He took measures to acquaint the neighbouring nobility and gentry that he was prepared to execute orders for rapine and slaughter,"[1] and was engaged, accordingly, by a Maratha chieftain, Appa Khandi Rao, to collect his revenues. Of course there was no money to pay Thomas and his men, but certain districts were assigned for their support — a piece of great generosity on the part of Appa Khandi, who had never been able to collect a single anna from the population, who fled to the hills whenever his bands appeared in their territory. On his way to take possession Thomas had to pass through a jaghir belonging to the Begam Somru, and plundered it heavily, in order to keep in his hand, and to avenge his dismissal from her service.

For some years Thomas collected his new master's revenue with great success, sometimes rewarded by fresh grants of land belonging to other people, sometimes in difficulties, as when Appa fell into disgrace with Sindhia, and was deprived of some of his territory including districts bestowed upon Thomas, or when the mer-

[1] H. G. Keene.

cenaries refused to fight until they were paid, and had to be appeased by the sale of some of their leader's property. Appa himself alternately appealed to Thomas to get him out of danger, and planned to destroy him lest he should grow too powerful. Once, Thomas having refused to deliver up a Brahman prisoner who had surrendered upon conditions, Appa, who knew the man to be wealthy and intended to extort a heavy ransom, summoned the Irishman to his presence, and on a pretext of being confined to bed, induced him to come upstairs, leaving his escort below. Again Thomas was urged to give up his prisoner, and again he refused. Appa then left the room, which suddenly was filled with armed men.

Thomas sat and gazed upon them, silent and impassive, until one of them presented him with a paper demanding surrender of the Brahman at once. Then the Irish temper broke loose. Springing to his feet, he refused to give up his prisoner, and demanded to be taken at once before Appa Khandi. Hand on sword, he strode from the room, and none dared to stop him. He stalked into Appa's presence, made his salaam, and uttered the conventional phrases with which an inferior in the East takes farewell, and the terrified Maratha gave him leave to depart.

Once back in his own camp, Thomas sent an intimation that he and his men would no longer serve under Appa. The Maratha, who had need of his services, contrived to soothe him down for the moment; but a little later, when master and man quarrelled over the right of ownership in certain captured guns, Appa engaged a band of Hindu pilgrims to murder Thomas, who killed most of them in fair fight.

In the meanwhile the Begam Somru was in evil case. Among those who had driven Thomas from her service was a Frenchman, Le Vassoult, who gained great ascendancy over her, and is said to have married her. The other European officers were malcontent, especially when he refused to receive them at his table, saying that nothing should induce him to eat with men of such habits. Whereupon they stirred the rank and file to unbearable insolence, and the Begam, who had in vain urged Le Vassoult to civility, determined to seek the protection of the English, with her husband, leaving her troops to whatever fate their lawlessness might bring upon them. The battalions stationed at Delhi learned that Le Vassoult had been in correspondence with Sindhia, and with the Governor-General. They broke into mutiny, elected as their leader Aloysius Balthazar Reinhard, the half-imbecile son of Somru by an insane Muslim wife, and marched upon Sardhana. Word of their approach was brought to Le Vassoult, who roused his wife at midnight and implored her to fly with him. He would rather die, he said, than fall into the hands of the mutineers. The Begam vowed, if need were, to die with him. They fled at the dawn, Le Vassoult riding beside her palki. But with them, in heavy-laden carts, they dragged their money, jewels, and portable property, and the force at Sardhana, discovering their flight, rode after them to take the spoil. The fugitives had gone scarcely three miles along the road to Meerut, when they saw clouds of dust rising behind them. Le Vassoult, who might have saved himself by riding hard, asked the Begam whether she still preferred death to what awaited them at the hands of the soldiery, and she answered "Yes," showing him the dagger in her right hand. He drew a pistol from his holsters. The foremost of the pursuers came up with them, there were screams from the palki, a slave girl rushed along the road shrieking that her mistress was dead, and Le Vassoult, looking between the curtains, saw blood overspread the white handkerchief upon his wife's breast. He set the pistol to his temple, fired, and dropped from his horse.

All the indignities that the mutineers could devise were heaped upon his corpse, while the Begam, who was suffering from nothing more than a slight flesh wound, was taken back to Sardhana. Some say that she was weary of Le Vassoult, and deliberately feigned to kill herself, in order to get rid of him and regain her authority over her troops. If so, she suffered some retribution in the next few days; Aloysius and his crew of ruffians held indescribable orgy in her palace for a week, while she lay chained to a gun in the courtyard. Had it not been for a faithful ayah who sometimes stole out with food, the Begam of Sardhana would have starved to death.

In her dire extremity she remembered George Thomas, and contrived to send a letter imploring his help, and promising to pay any sum he might require if she were once more mistress of Sardhana. One of the French officers, who had no hand in the recent mutiny, made appeal to Thomas, who immediately sent 20,000 rupees to a Maratha commander, to induce him to move certain of his troops towards Sardhana. He then rode to the town with his mounted bodyguard, having sent a message in advance that, acting by authority of Sindhia, he would show no mercy to the rebels unless the Begam were reinstated at once.

By this time the effects of the debauch were

beginning to tell, and the mutineers had discovered the worthlessness of their lately elected chief. They submitted, and before sunset the Begam was set at liberty, and Aloysius Balthazar Reinhard on his way to Delhi as a prisoner. Thomas went back to camp without the 20,000 rupees, which were never repaid to him.

Never again was the thread of the Begam's story to become entangled with that of the Irishman. For the remainder of her life all prospered with "the Witch of Sardhana," as the country people called her. It is true that she sent five battalions to fight upon the losing side at the battle of Assaye, but as the greater part were set to guard the camp, four of them escaped, none the worse, and she atoned for her error in judgment by repairing at once to Lord Lake's camp to make submission.

Lord Lake, who, we are told, had just finished dinner when the Begam arrived, hurried to the reception tent, where, to the amazement of all the spectators, he took her in his arms and embraced her, as if she had been one of the male chieftains who visited his camp now that the star of the Company was in the ascendant. The English spectators were agape with consternation, the Begam's retinue were horrified, but the lady's presence of mind was unfailing as in the day when she had ordered the execution of her slave girls. "Receiving courteously the proffered attention, she turned calmly round to her astonished attendants. 'It is,' said she, 'the salute of a *padre* to his daughter,'"[1] and the excuse passed muster with the majority, who knew little of Christian usage, and were aware that the Begam had made profession of Christianity.

In her old age the Begam led a blameless life, respected by natives and English. She entertained governors-general and commanders-in-chief. Bishop Heber visited her, and Mrs Sherwood presented her with a Bible. Lord William Bentinck, on the eve of embarkation for England, wrote to assure her that her benevolence of disposition and extensive charity had excited in his mind sentiments of the warmest admiration, and that his prayers and best wishes would attend her. In the Roman Catholic Cathedral which she built at Sardhana, her white marble effigy sits upon a platform surrounded by allegorical figures, sculptured by a Roman artist. A folk-tale, still current in the Simla district, tells of the Begam Somru as a rich lady who laid up treasure in heaven by giving alms to the poor. A tradition of the Deccan speaks of the Witch of Sardhana who could destroy her enemies by throwing her veil at them.

[1] Colonel Skinner.

## II.

Shortly after his rescue of the Begam Somru George Thomas was again thrown upon the world. Appa Khandi Rao, stricken with a horrible disease, had committed suicide by drowning himself in the Jumna, and the Irishman was free to seek another master. Had he chosen, he might have obtained permanent employment under Sindhia; he preferred to roam the country as a free lance. When his men clamoured for their pay, he extorted it from the luckless towns and villages around him. In after years he confessed, without any apparent shame, how he had demanded a lakh of rupees from the governor of a town belonging to the Raja of Jaipur, and how, when it was refused, he stormed the town. The commandant of the fort, which still held out, offered him 52,000 rupees to go away, and he accepted the bribe, but in the meantime, "unfortunately," the town had been set on fire, "and burnt so fiercely that goods to the amount of several lakhs of rupees were totally consumed."

After several months of foray and pillage in this manner, Thomas was emboldened to play for higher stakes. "In every corner of the kingdom people aspired to exercise independence," says a native historian, and he who had seen one petty Maratha chieftain after another rise by murder and robbery to be the ruler of a state, aspired to carve out a principality for himself from the ruins of the Moghul Empire.

In the border country, between the Delhi territory and the sand wastes of Bikanir, where the wells are "four hundred feet deep and lined throughout with camel bone," lay a tract of over three thousand square miles, Hariana (Green Land), the history of which is not unlike that of the Debateable Ground along the Scotch and English border. Lying on the road from the gates of the north to the fertile central plains of India, its chief town, Hansi, had been sacked by many a conqueror's army since the days of Mahmud of Ghazni, and its soil had been watered by the blood of many battles. Now that the Moghul Empire had fallen into decay, no one had thought it worth while to lay claim to Hariana. A terrible famine had desolated the country, some twelve years before Thomas's arrival, the water-supply had failed, and—so it is said—only a faquir and two lions were left within the ruined walls of Hansi.

Hearing that a ruler capable of defending his own was flying his standard upon the old citadel on the summit of the great mound at Hansi, inhabitants gathered once more in the deserted streets, and rebuilt the mud dwellings that had cracked to pieces under the fierce desert sun. "By degrees," Thomas told his biographer, "I selected between five and six thousand persons, to whom I allowed every lawful indulgence." He set up a mint, and coined his own rupees, one of which sometimes falls into the hands of the collector—small thick coins, with the title of Shah Alam in Persian characters, and an English capital T. He cast his own artillery, and made muskets, matchlocks, and powder. "I wished," he says, "to put myself in a capacity of attempting the conquest of the Punjab, and aspired to the honour of planting the British standard on the banks of the Attock."

But, meantime, his men must be paid, and Thomas's only resource was in "excursions," as he calls them, into the territories of his neighbours—especially into that of the Raja of Jaipur, "which place had hitherto afforded a never-failing supply to his necessities." In one year he harried Jaipur and Bikanir, took part in a Maratha expedition against Udaipur, and chastised the Sikh Raja of Patiala, who had taken advantage of his absence to raid into Hariana.

"I explored the country," he said, "formed alliances, and, in short, was Dictator in all the countries belonging to the Sikhs south of Sutlej."

The "Sahib Bahadur" was beloved by his men, to whom he was generous at his neighbours' expense when he paid them at all, and feared by the whole countryside, who told tales of *Jowruj*[1] *Jung* long after he had ceased to lead his wild chase through their villages. A little discretion, a little common honesty, and he might have ruled in Hariana for many years to come. But it never occurred to him to fill his treasury in any other fashion than by taking it from his neighbours—any more than it would have occurred to a moss-trooping Scott or Elliot to fill his larder from any source than the byres across the Border.

The Sikhs to the south of the Sutlej, who, next to the Raja of Jaipur, were his chief victims, made appeal to General Perron, the commander of Sindhia's army,—originally Pierre Cuillier, a deserter from a French frigate. Though the Marathas were ready to murder, pillage, torture, and outrage, whenever it suited them, they would not brook that any other should dare to reap their harvest. In this they were not remarkable; Thomas himself animadverts severely upon the "thievish depredations" of the men of a certain district in Hariana.

Perron began diplomatically by inviting Thomas to a conference. Thomas went, but with a

[1] "George."

previous determination against any proposals that might be made to him. It was impossible, he said, that he and a Frenchman could ever act in concert or with cordiality. Invited to surrender his land in return for a monthly payment, and to take service with Sindhia, he replied that principles of honour forbade him from acting under the command of a Frenchman. If his head had ever been capable of connected and logical reasoning, it was now too confused with strong drink for him to realise that he could not retain Hariana in the face of all his enemies. Sindhia, the enemy of the English, could not allow an independent state, professing loyalty to King George, to exist anywhere within his sphere of action. Not one of the neighbouring states whom Thomas had raided but would rejoice at the downfall of the adventurer, and the English Government would not raise a finger to help him. As Sindhia's vassal, he had a chance of ruling Hariana; as an independent and irresponsible chieftain, he was certain to be crushed.

So when Thomas indignantly flung away from the conference, war was declared, and Perron called up his allies. Even then, Thomas's case was not hopeless, though the Sikhs were preparing to invade the north of Hariana, and the Begam Somru had sent a detachment to join Sindhia's force. Holkar, who had quarrelled with Sindhia, might come to the help of Sindhia's enemy, and Bourquin, whom Perron sent in command of the expedition against Hariana, was not only a coward but a fool.

Bourquin marched to the fort of Georgegarh, one of Thomas's chief strongholds, and learned that Thomas himself had gone towards the Sikh country. Leaving three battalions to besiege Georgegarh, the expedition went on in pursuit, while Thomas doubled back to his fort, marching seventy miles in two days, and cut up one battalion, leading his men to the attack, sword in hand, as in his prime.

Three days later, Bourquin, having discovered his mistake, arrived at Georgegarh, and found Thomas encamped in a strong position between the fort and the village. Bourquin's men were fasting, and weary with a long march, nevertheless their commander insisted upon attacking at once. Musketry and cannon showered upon them like hail when they came within reach of the line of sandbanks that covered Thomas's front, and their left wing was driven back. A few moments more and the victory would have been with the Irishman; but at the turning-point of the fight, Captain Hopkins, his second in command, fell mortally wounded, and Hopkins's battalion ran back, taking their leader with them. Bourquin's left wing then rallied, but the fire was so murderous that the whole line was ordered to sit down—and they sat till nightfall, unable to attack Thomas's men, who were protected by their sandbanks, and did not venture out.

Had Thomas possessed another officer like Captain Hopkins, he would have gained the day; had he sallied from his entrenchments on the morrow, and fallen upon the exhausted troops of Bourquin before they had recovered from their long march and their desperate fight, he might have destroyed them utterly, and marched upon Delhi before another force could have been mustered against him. There he could have made his own terms with Sindhia, and might have succeeded to Perron's command, for the Maratha was jealous of the Frenchman, and would have seized upon an excuse for getting rid of him.

Over and over again had men seen Thomas "rally panic-stricken battalions by the magic of his presence, and lead them to victory where they had but just fallen back in defeat."[1] They had seen him throw himself upon an enemy twenty times his strength, where a repulse meant ruin, and there was no retreat. They now looked for him to lead his men out from the camp, and drive Bourquin's worn-out force before him.

[1] H. Compton.

They looked in vain. To the amazement of all, there was no sign of activity in Thomas's camp, save that here and there more fortifications were thrown up. Hopkins was dead, the remaining officers were incompetent—and George Thomas sat drinking within his tent.

Yet before he had drunk away his kingdom and his army and his honour, Thomas wrote to Miss Hopkins, left destitute by her brother's death, sending her Rs. 2000, and promising more should it be needed.

Reinforcements came to Bourquin, and Thomas's camp was completely surrounded. "Skirmishes now took place every day, but he was always thrashed back into his lines. Supplies and forage began to get scarce; his soldiers became dissatisfied and began to desert." Thomas left off drinking and resumed command, but it was too late.

The enemy had captured the tank whence he drew most of his water. Treachery was at work amongst his men; his stacks of hay and stores of grain were set on fire. Then, on a November night, when the Marathas were making preparations for a general assault, Thomas with three hundred horsemen cut his way out of the camp, lighted by the blaze of the last haystack which the traitors within had lit as a signal to the enemy without. Away into the night he rode, with all the enemy's cavalry at his heels, and his escort dropped from him, until only four remained —two captains and two sergeants, all Europeans. The Persian horse on which he rode had borne him through many a charge, and it now covered a hundred and twenty miles "without halt or stay" till they reached Hansi.

All his baggage and guns at Georgegarh fell into the hands of the enemy. "His soldiers, having laid down their arms, were offered service, but they refused it with contempt. Several native officers who had been a long time in his service rent their clothes and turned beggars, swearing that they would never serve as soldiers again."[1]

The end of the story was very nearly reached. Bourquin with infantry, horse, and Sikh cavalry surrounded Hansi, and stormed the town with great loss, although Thomas, clad in a complete suit of chain-armour, led a hand-to-hand fight in the streets against the advancing columns. The citadel still held out, and finding that his guns produced little effect upon the solid mound of earth, Bourquin tried other measures, and shot letters upon arrows to the defenders, promising six months' pay and permanent service if they would surrender Thomas and the fort. Some of the garrison responded to these overtures, and

[1] Skinner.

Bourquin bragged openly how he would use "that blackguard Englishman" when once he had caught him. Happily for Thomas, Bourquin's European officers were all English, or country-born, and although they had no compunction in putting an end to his depredations, they revolted at the thought of his being imprisoned for life in a Maratha dungeon.

One of these officers was James Skinner, son of a Scotch ensign in the Company's service, and a Rajputni lady taken captive in war. His name will be remembered by all who have stood beneath the cream-coloured dome of St James's Church, built by him at Delhi in observance of a vow made to the God of his father when he lay sorely wounded upon a stricken field. He had run away from the printer to whom he was apprenticed as a boy, because he must needs be a soldier or a sailor, and through an old friend of his father's had obtained a commission in the Maratha army under General Boigne.

There he had soon risen to distinction, and had been joined by his younger brother Robert. The two had been sent to take part in the siege of Hansi, and in conjunction with the other European officers, "knowing Bourquin to be more of a talker than a doer," "managed to persuade him into offering terms, assuring him that he would himself gain a higher name by inducing Thomas to capitulate than by catching him by treachery."

"It was one day after tiffin, when the wine he had drunk had put him in high spirits and good humour, that we plied him thus, and at last he called out in his broken English, 'Well, gentlemens, you do as you like—I give power; he be one damn Englishman, your countryman, that treat their children very ill.' (He meant that the country-borns were very ill-used in not being admitted into the Company's service.)"

The officers at once sent one of their number to the fort, where he was received with great joy by Thomas, who knew what treachery was at work in his garrison, and was ready to accede to any terms that the English officers might make for him. With some trouble Bourquin was induced to grant that Thomas should be escorted to the Company's territory, with all his ready money, clothes, shawls, jewels, and household stuff, and that his soldiers should be allowed to march out with their private arms.

It was arranged that the fort should be given up in two days. Thomas and Bourquin spent two hours together, "and became great friends," the Frenchman inviting the Irishman to dine in his camp on the following day.

The story of the last pitiable scenes was told by James Skinner:—

"It was about seven in the evening when Thomas arrived with about fifty of his sowars, much affected, as it appeared, by his misfortunes. About eight we sat down; and after dinner did all we could to cheer Thomas, taking great care to avoid all conversation about our attacks or anything that might give him offence. By eleven o'clock all of us had got pretty merry with drinking bumpers to such toasts as 'General Perron,' 'George Thomas,' &c., and Thomas was quite happy; when, all of a sudden, Bourquin called out, 'Let us drink to the success of Perron's arms!'

"At this we all turned up our glasses, and Thomas, on hearing and seeing this, burst into tears, and, putting his hand to his sword, called out to Bourquin that it was not to him but to his own ill fate that his fall was due, and (drawing his sword), 'One Irish sword,' said he, 'is still sufficient for a hundred Frenchmen.'

"Bourquin, in terror at this, jumped from his chair and ran out of the tent, calling for his guard. Then Thomas's sowars, hearing the hubbub, also rushed in; and we, apprehensive of a row, called out to them to keep off, as it was only the sahib that was drunk; while Thomas, in the midst of us, kept waving his sword, and calling out in Hindostanee to look how he had made the d—d Frenchman run like a jackal!"

At the imminent peril of "some accident," as Skinner delicately words it, the English officers induced Thomas to sheathe his sword and to sit down at table once more. Then they made apology for Bourquin, urging that if the wine had made him forget himself, it was Thomas's duty to be magnanimous and forgive the slip. Bourquin was brought back, to shake hands and apologise, and in a few minutes Thomas and he were drinking together once more, the best of friends.

"Perceiving that they were getting still more 'jolly,'" with great presence of mind James Skinner rode to the town and instructed the sentries not to challenge Thomas's party on his return, since he would be in no condition to reply. Of course it was in the nature of things that Thomas went to the one gate which Skinner forgot to visit.

To the sentinel's challenge, one of the sowars replied, "Sahib Bahadur," which was Thomas's title among his men.

The sentry returned that he knew of no Sahib Bahadur, and that the party must halt until he had his officer's leave to pass them. Thomas, "much in liquor," turned round to his sowars, and asked, "Could any one have stopped the Sahib Bahadur at this gate but one month ago?"

"No, no!" they replied; whereupon the Irish

sword flashed once more from its sheath and smote off the sentry's right hand.

"Fortunately," says Skinner, "I was only a few yards distant from the gate, and on hearing the noise, ran up. There I found Thomas, walking up and down with his naked sword in his hand, and Hearsey, and several of his sowars, who had dismounted, endeavouring to lay hold of him. At length a rissaldar caught hold of him from behind, when the rest ran in, and taking his sword from him, sent for his palanquin and had him carried into the fort."

Next day, when sufficiently sober to be told of his exploits, Thomas had the grace to send for the man whom he had maimed for life, and give him Rs. 500, and to write an apology to Bourquin.

Little more than a week after, he parted from his benefactor, James Skinner. They were never to meet again. For rather more than a year, Skinner was to remain in Sindhia's army; when the outbreak of the Maratha War of 1803 caused the dismissal of all English and country-born officers from the Maratha service, he and his brother went to Lord Lake's camp at Aligarh, and "met with so much attention as seemed to them perfectly marvellous."

In spite of the prejudice generally felt by both races against half-castes, Skinner was trusted and respected by the English and the natives of India throughout his life. When a body of Perron's horse transferred their allegiance to the British, and the troops were asked whom they would choose for their commander, one and all declared that if "Secunder Sahib"[1] were there, he was the man. He accepted the command, on condition of never being employed against his old master, Sindhia; and his "Yellow Boys," in their dark-red shawl turbans and yellow tunics, proved one of the most picturesque and efficient corps of irregular horse in the Company's service. He closed his life as a Lieutenant-Colonel in His Majesty's service, and a Companion of the Bath "for the long, faithful, and meritorious services rendered to the Honourable the East India Company." When his body was escorted by his "Yellow Boys," and a great concourse of people, to its last resting-place near the altar of St James's Church, the crowds said that "none of the emperors were ever brought into Delhi in such state as Secunder Sahib."

Long before that day, George Thomas's sand had run out. He had saved from the wreck of his fortunes about a lakh and a half of rupees, and jewels and other property to nearly the same

[1] The natives of India cannot pronounce a double consonant; Skinner's prowess in arms made this version of his name the popular one. (Secunder = Alexander.)

value, and he meant to go back to the country that he had left as a boy. His eccentricities were somewhat pronounced, even for the Tipperary of the beginning of the last century, and perhaps it was well for all concerned that he was taken ill on the voyage down the Ganges to Calcutta, and died near the military cantonments of Bahrampur in August 1803.

He had sent back his wife and their four children to the Begam Somru, at whose hands he received her, with a lakh of rupees for their expenses. To do the Begam justice, she fulfilled the trust. One of the three sons commanded a regiment in the army of Ranjit Singh, the man who was to fulfil Thomas's dream of a Punjab kingdom.

Among the crowded tombs in the cemeteries at Bahrampur are many from which the name has been lost, and it is possible that one of these may cover the body of George Thomas. No other trace is left in India of "the man who would be king."

# XI.

# THE GREAT MARATHA WAR—1802-1803

"The lamp of Delhi has been long since extinguished, and the Marathas have taken possession of most of the cities of Hindustan; and the Rajas of Jodhpur, Udaipur, and other chiefs have become weak and pass their days as if they were nights."—SA'ADAT-I JAWED OF HARNAM SINGH.

## XI.

## THE GREAT MARATHA WAR—1802-1803.

THE immediate result of the Treaty of Basain was the Second Maratha War. Sindhia, Jaswant Rao Holkar, the Peshwa's brother whom Holkar had set on the throne, and the Bhonsla Raja of Nagpur were all united, for the moment, in their hate of the English. Sindhia undertook the Nizam of Haiderabad, with whom the Marathas were in a chronic state of warfare, while Holkar devoted himself to Benares and Bihar. The Bhonsla would attend to the fertile delta of Bengal, and the Rohillas, who had joined the confederacy, would pay off old scores against the Nawab of Oudh.

Against them were an Irishman, the Governor-General's brother, General Arthur Wellesley, who had taken part in the storming of Seringapatam, and an Essex man, General Gerard Lake, who had seen service in the Low Countries before coming to India.

Lake's first move was to Aligarh, a strong fort near the town of Koil, between Delhi and Agra. Perron was in Koil, with a force stronger than Lake's, but he had no heart for resistance. He knew that he was hated by all Marathas, that Sindhia was jealous of him, and intended to get rid of him at the first opportunity, and that his officers, French and English, were not to be trusted. So, bidding his son-in-law, Colonel Pedron, the commandant at Aligarh, remember that the eyes of millions were upon him, he rode away from Koil, after a brush with Lake's force, and made terms for himself.

Pedron was not unwilling to follow his example, but his garrison contained a large proportion of Rajputs, who, like all their race, knew how to die, and they put him into confinement and elected one of their number as commander. The fort was surrounded by marshes, and the only way into it was a narrow causeway over a deep moat, defended by an outer gateway, behind which were three other gates. Lake believed that Pedron had mined all the approaches, but he knew that every day's delay gave time for the enemy's forces to gather from Central India.

Before dawn on a September morning, a picquet of fifty men on guard with a gun before the fort were surprised by four companies of the 76th

Regiment, and six battalions of sepoys, guided by an Irishman once in Sindhia's service. The picquet ran to the wicket, and were admitted, while the assaulting party, having vainly tried to enter with them, remained outside, under a terrific fire of musketry and guns. It was useless to plant scaling-ladders, for the walls above bristled with pikemen. For a full hour they stood their ground, then, as the sun rose, they fell back a few yards, and Lake, watching from one of the batteries, cried out, "They run!"

It was only for a moment; rallied by their officers, they formed once more and came back, bringing the Maratha gun with them. "The God of Heaven certainly looked down upon these noble fellows," says James Skinner, who was at Lake's side, "for with two shots they blew open half the gate, and giving three shouts, they rushed in."

"The fort is ours!" cried Lake joyously, but no more than the first step had been gained; the Rajputs stood their ground, and every inch of the way to the second gate was won by hand-to-hand fighting. The second gate yielded with little trouble, and the storming party passed through the third gate with the fugitives; the fourth gate defied men and guns, and it seemed as if they had come thus far to no purpose. Then

Colonel Macleod of the 76th espied a little wicket gate, tried it, and found himself in the heart of the fortress, with his men—what was left of them —behind him. Aligarh was won, and Lake rode in triumph to the gate. "But when he saw his heroes lying thick there, the tears came to his eyes. 'It is the fate of good soldiers,' he said, and turning round, he galloped back to the camp."

There was commotion in Delhi. The officer commanding there was that same Bourquin who had overcome George Thomas, and on hearing of the fall of Aligarh, he spread abroad that Perron had gone over to the English, and forced Shah Alam to invest him as commander-in-chief of Perron's infantry. Lake, advancing from Aligarh, had come within six miles of Delhi; his weary men were scattered, some undressed, some cooking their dinner, after an eight hours' march, when at 11 A.M. he learned that Bourquin was upon him with twelve battalions of infantry, five thousand cavalry, and seventy guns, established in a strong position with a line of entrenchments in front and a swamp on either flank.

"That which in others would have been rash was in Lake prudent daring," says a military expert. Disregarding the smallness of his numbers and the weariness of his men, he sent out his cavalry to attack the enemy, and fall back as if beaten. Bourquin's men pursued, the cavalry retreated farther still, and then opened for the passage of the British infantry, led by Lake himself, who had stolen up under cover of the long grass. "It was one steady but desperate charge of the bayonet against the cannon—for the men, though falling in scores, never took their muskets from their shoulders till within 100 paces of the enemy, when orders were given for the charge."[1]

By seven o'clock in the evening the victory was complete. Lake wrote to the Governor-General, "I do not think there could have been a more glorious day, but as I may be thought partial, I will say no more."

Three days later, Shah Alam, released from a miserable confinement, sat under a tattered canopy in the Diwan-i-Khas, where, sixteen years previously, Ghulam the Rohilla had torn out his eyes, and greeted Lake his deliverer as "Sword of the State, Hero of the Realm, Chief of the Age." Though the Emperor was to the conquerors "an object of pity, stripped of authority and reduced to poverty," yet they knew that "almost every state and every class of people in India continued to acknowledge his nominal

[1] James Skinner.

sovereignty," that "the current coin of every established power was struck" in his name, and that he was everywhere regarded as the "only legitimate fountain of honours." The blind and feeble old man had the glamour of the past hanging about him, and when he acknowledged the English General as his protector and the commander of his army, it was not a barren compliment.

## II.

Meanwhile Wellesley had gone in pursuit of the united forces of Sindhia and the Bhonsla.

Some time previously, when Sindhia's Europeanised army was the envy of every Raja in India, an old Maratha chieftain had objected to Sindhia's intention of building cantonments at Ujjain. "Our fathers, the first founders of the Maratha power, made their houses on the backs of their horses; gradually the house came to be made of cloth; and now you are making it of mud: take care that in a very short time it does not all turn to mud, and is never rebuilt." "Who is there dares oppose me as long as I have my infantry and guns?" asked Sindhia, while his court derided the warning. "Beware!" answered the chieftain, "it is that very infantry and those guns that will be your ruin."

The warning came true. The Bhonsla would have kept to the old Maratha traditions, never risking a battle, hanging upon the enemy's flanks to cut off stragglers and supplies, melting away when he turned upon them—the tactics of the wolf-pack, which had broken the armies of Aurangzib. Jeswant Rao Holkar had sent a message—"If you fight like a sovereign" (*i.e.*, with a regular army), "you will be defeated; fight like a Maratha, and you will be successful." But Sindhia was vain of his battalions and his guns, and would prove them, although the last advice of Boigne, the man who made his army, had been to disband it rather than risk it in a conflict with the British.

On the 23rd of September, Wellesley beheld the enemy's line stretched along the northern bank of the river Khelna, their cavalry on their right, their infantry and artillery on their left, close to the village of Assaye. They were more than 50,000, and his men were only 4500. As he gazed on the long array, he was told that the enemy had neglected to guard the only ford across the Khelna. "They cannot escape us now!" he exclaimed, and he crossed the ford.

Even as he drew up his army for the attack,

information reached him that his native allies, the cavalry of the Peshwa and the Nizam, intended to go over to the enemy. He was unmoved. A little later, the officer commanding his right wing, when ordered to advance, sent word that the Maratha cannonade had killed his gun-bullocks and disabled his guns. Still impassive, Wellesley replied, "Well, tell him to get on without them."

They did "get on"; each man fought as if the victory depended on himself alone. The Maratha horse dashed down upon the thinned ranks of the 74th Regiment, and they parted to let the 19th Light Dragoons pass through them at full gallop. Cheered by the very wounded and dying over whom they rode, the dragoons "cut in and routed the horse, and dashed on at the artillery and guns." The infantry, covered by their charge, pressed forward, the enemy's first line was driven back, and Assaye was carried at the point of the bayonet.

"I cannot write in too strong terms of the conduct of the troops," Arthur Wellesley informed the Governor-General; he had certainly taken every opportunity of judging, having led two charges, and had two horses shot under him.

Sindhia, who had left the field after beholding

the defeat of his cavalry, had little heart to continue the war; the Bhonsla, who had not waited so long, made ineffectual efforts. The fortress of Asirgarh, on a spur of the Vindhya mountains, held to be the key of the Deccan, capitulated to General Stevenson in October, after an hour's cannonading, and the conqueror went on to Gawilgarh, a double fort commanding the main road across the mountain-range dividing Northern from Southern India. It was the gate of the Bhonsla's dominions, as the Bhonsla knew when he sent his army to fall upon the General. Unhappily for the Marathas, Wellesley was as well aware as they of the importance of Gawilgarh, and had effected a junction with Stevenson. At the village of Argaum he once more met the combined forces of Sindhia and the Bhonsla. The heavy fire of the enemy's guns at first disconcerted some of the sepoy battalions, although they had stood their ground at Assaye; but Wellesley rallied them, and they came back to their post, to hold it against a charge of the Maratha horsemen. Then Wellesley led three regiments of Madras native cavalry from the rear, and drove the Marathas before him, while on his right the 74th and 78th regiments received the *corps d'élite* of the Bhonsla's army, five hundred picked Arabs from the north, and "marching calmly forward, swept them, almost to a man, into eternity."

After this, there could be no hope of relieving Gawilgarh. A story told of Colonel Wallace, one of the officers engaged in besieging it, may help to show how it was that Wellesley and Lake were able to conquer what seemed overwhelming odds. A heavy gun had to be transported under cover of night over a steep mountain; the artillery officer in charge of it, after repeated failures, declared that it was impossible to carry out his instructions. "Impossible, sir?" exclaimed Wallace, "impossible? Let us see!" He then called for a light, pulled the instructions from his pocket, and, having read them, said, "Oh no, not impossible! the order is positive." The gun was dragged into place, and less than three weeks after the battle of Argaum, the fort was taken. The Bhonsla signed a treaty, in which, like the Peshwa, he acknowledged British supremacy, and undertook to levy *chaut* no more.

Lake on his side had been busy. "In the course of a month peace and tranquillity was restored from Aligarh to the gates of Delhi." The day after the battle of Assaye, Lake left Delhi for Agra, then held by a strong garrison, and protected by several battalions of Perron's army, which had not been admitted within the walls for fear they should claim a share from the treasure-chest. This greed proved the undoing of the garrison, for Lake first of all defeated the army outside, and then opened his batteries against the fortress, which surrendered.

He had still to deal with Sindhia's army. Its European officers had nearly all taken service with the English, tempted by the Company's offers, but the men were those who had kept Hindustan in fear, and at their head was a pundit, Abaji, who had the pertinacity and something of the genius of the early Maratha chieftains.

When Agra surrendered, Abaji made for the Jaipur territory, a favourite Maratha battle-ground, where he knew of a refuge among the Mewat hills, reached by a single pass which could be held against all comers. Lake hurried after him, and finding that he could not drag his heavy guns over the rain-sodden ground, left them behind, taking only the cavalry and infantry. On the night of October 31st he reached the camping-ground which Abaji had left in the morning; the pass was only thirty-three miles distant. At midnight once more Lake led on his cavalry, leaving the infantry to follow as they could; at sunrise he found the enemy posted about the village of Laswari. There was no time to be lost. Placing himself at the head of his advance-guard, he charged the enemy's left, while the 29th Dragoons and 4th Native Light Cavalry rode along the front of the enemy's line, raked by the fire of seventy-four guns, "formed up as steadily as on parade," and endeavoured to turn the right. "British and Marathas got into a mess together," as Skinner describes it, and the cavalry retired with heavy loss, unable to carry the entrenchments.

By this time it was noon; the infantry had marched five-and-twenty miles, and reached the spot, and were panting to be at the enemy. But Lake made them halt and eat their breakfast; then once more he led them to the attack.

It was a magnificent battle, such as can never be seen again. The first British line advanced through a deadly cannonade; for some reason, the second was late in following them. Regardless of this, Lake was leading his men "in face of a fire which, for intensity, has rarely if ever been surpassed," when Abaji hurled his cavalry against them. Still the line held firm, and Lake ordered a counter-charge. His horse was shot dead under him; his son dismounted to give him his horse, and fell at his side, severely wounded. Then the British cavalry made their charge; like a river in spate they rolled over the ground, and nothing could stand against them. The guns were carried, but still the Marathas held on grimly, like the dying wolves when the pack is broken up. When every position had been carried, and every gun taken, the survivors withdrew from the field.

As Lake rode back to camp, his men cheered him. "He took off his hat and thanked them, but told them to despise death as these brave fellows had done—pointing to the Marathas, who were lying thick around their guns."

Sindhia yielded to necessity, and made a treaty with his conquerors. That he broke it upon the first opportunity was probably no more than was expected by either side.

## III.

A Muslin writer has remarked upon the habit of the Marathas, after quarrelling among themselves, to unite against a common foe, "as we are told of the serpent when cut asunder, that the dismembered parts have a separate existence, and seek again incorporation."

The truth of this was shown after Jeswant Rao Holkar, who had been levying *chaut* in Malwa and Rajputana, declined to follow the example of Sindhia and the Bhonsla. Having paid his troops at the expense of one of Sindhia's towns, which he plundered of every article of value except the jewels that the women wore, he endeavoured to stir up the other princes of Hindustan to revolt. Failing for the moment, he moved towards Rajputana, and requested Lake to retire to Agra, "as your near approach to my victorious army appears likely to lead to unpleasant circumstances." Among his officers were three of English descent, and these he tortured and murdered, on a false suspicion that they were in correspondence with their fellow-countrymen.

Then Lake showed that he could beat Jaswant and his ally Amir Khan, the Pindari, in their own mode of warfare. "If they brought up guns, their guns were taken; if they attacked a district officer, he defended himself successfully with a handful of jail-guards and messengers. The armour-plated horsemen were overthrown or put to flight; the light cavalry could not always outmarch the British dragoons; the chiefs only saved themselves by the most headlong galloping."[1]

Unluckily, the lesson failed to strike home, on account of the disaster which befell Colonel the

[1] Keene.

Hon. W. Monson, who, having advanced far into Malwa, and taken a hill-fort by escalade, "a most gallant and brilliant exploit," not finding a detachment from Gujerat that he expected to co-operate with him, and running short of provisions, decided in an evil hour to retreat. It happened to him as it had often happened to the Moghul armies in a similar situation. Holkar fell upon his rear-guard, with whom were a band of Hara Rajputs under the chief of Koelah, Umr Singh. Dismounting from his horse, the chieftain stood with his men to defend the passage of the stream, which was soon choked with their bodies. He died upon the field, as became a Rajput; his next in command was taken prisoner by the Marathas, and forced to sign a bond for ten lakhs of rupees as a penalty for siding with the English.

Meanwhile Monson struggled on through mud and incessant rain. His guns sank into a quagmire, and had to be left to the care of another Hara, the Raja of Bondi. The wild Bhils, who, forgetting their own traditions, were the friends of Holkar, the Rajputs' enemy, murdered the wives and children of the sepoys while the force was trying to cross a flooded river, in which many were drowned. Holkar harassed them incessantly, and though driven back nearly every time, always returned. The baggage had to be abandoned. After three months of this misery, the survivors reached Agra "in flying and detached groups."

During the long retreat the older sepoys and native officers continually heartened the younger English officers, who were not so well seasoned as they, telling them, "Cheer up, for we will carry you safely into Agra." When some of these faithful comrades straggled back to Agra, long after the rest, their noses and ears cut off by Holkar's orders, because, when prisoners in his power, they had refused to take service with him, the fury of the English was almost uncontrollable. A little later, when Lake attacked Holkar's camp, his prisoners expected similar treatment, and were astonished beyond measure to be dismissed with the present of a rupee for every man, and the message, "Tell your chief that none but cowards are cruel to their prisoners."

Holkar, who had fled from his camp "at the first discharge of a galloper gun," now conceived an audacious plan—to surprise Delhi and secure the Emperor's person. Colonel David Ochterlony, the British Resident at the Emperor's Court, had for all defence between two and four thousand men, one-third of whom had to remain on guard in the palace. One corps of irregular cavalry went over to the enemy, and another had to be sent away, while a battalion of infantry mutinied. The remainder of the garrison had to defend a city seven miles in circumference, its only protection a ruinous wall, in many places too weak to support a gun, and surrounded on all sides by trees, scrub, and ruins.

For eight days and nights they held out against 15,000 infantry, backed by nearly 200 guns and 60,000 horse. Ochterlony, who knew the sepoy, served out a ration of sweetmeats to his men, who had no time to cook food, and promised them half a month's extra pay when the enemy should be repulsed.

On October 14th Holkar sat watching a nautch; in the centre of the room was a spear on which was transfixed the head of a private of the 76th Regiment, his prisoner, strangled by his order, and the nautch-girls danced round it. Next day Lake was at hand, and Holkar was in full retreat towards Bhurtpore, ravaging and burning the villages on his line of march.

Believing that he had left the English nearly forty miles behind him, he was again watching a nautch, when he received news that Monson had attacked the main body of his infantry at Dig, and defeated them, regaining fourteen of the guns lost in the retreat from Malwa. Before the next morning broke he was awakened by an explosion. It was the explosion of an artillery tumbril belonging to Lake's force, but he was told it was the morning gun from Fatehgarh, and believed it. His men, wrapt in their blankets, still slept in true Maratha fashion beside their horses, when showers of grape hailed upon them, and ere they could spring to their feet the 8th Light Dragoons were among them.

Holkar mounted his horse, and never drew bridle till he had left the camp eighteen miles behind him. Lake's cavalry, who had made a forced march of fifty-eight miles in the night, pursued the Marathas for ten miles more. They had lost scarcely twenty men; they had broken Holkar's army, and his prestige, so that never again did he muster half the number that he had commanded on the day before Lake surprised him.

All his forts in the Deccan were captured already, and Indore, his capital, had surrendered without resistance. Dig, belonging to his ally, the Raja of Bhurtpore, was stormed, and the only stronghold where Holkar might find refuge was Bhurtpore itself.

Popular tradition said that vast treasures were hidden within the fortified town, but hitherto its walls and bastions, and its deep moat, had kept out the attempts of all who would have possessed themselves of the wealth hoarded through centuries. "To take Bhurtpore" was the local equivalent for "Ding down Tantallon, build a brig to the Bass."

Nevertheless, Lake hoped that it might be taken by sheer audacity, like Aligarh, and did not lose hope till his men had been beaten back, in four separate assaults, with heavy loss. Then he sent for his battering train, and would have laid siege with all due form, if the Raja, who was becoming uneasy, had not sued for peace.

He obtained it, against the better judgment of many persons, because Sindhia was giving trouble again. It will be remembered that Sindhia's great uncle, Madhaji, had captured Gwalior from the Rana of Gohad. In the general redistribution of property Lord Wellesley had restored it to the Rana. Sindhia, who, by a great stretch of imagination, had persuaded himself that Gwalior was his ancestral property, took offence, and his ministers widened the breach. He plundered and imprisoned the British Resident in his camp, and received Holkar and Amir Khan with great demonstrations of friendliness.

Lord Wellesley had the impetuous Irish temper, and when crossed by his masters at home was in the habit of offering his resignation. More than a year previously he had consented, with great show of reluctance, to remain at his post for another twelvemonth. The British Ministry and the Directors of the East India Company were growing alarmed at the growth of dominion and expenditure, and resolved upon peace, retrenchment, and reform. They could hardly be blamed for taking Wellesley at his word, but at least they owed him the courtesy of telling him that his successor was appointed, instead of leaving him to hear it from private letters.

The successor was Lord Cornwallis, who, a few years before, had taken the field against Tipu Sahib at the head of the Company's army. Now old and feeble, as soon as he arrived he announced his intention of "giving up all lands west of the Jumna without reference to their political condition." Three months later he was dead, and was duly commemorated at Ghazipur by a monument so hideous that Bishop Heber suggested turning it into a campanile for a church.

His death brought no change for the better, since his post was temporarily filled by the senior member of Council, Sir George Barlow, who immediately proceeded to renounce all that had been won at great cost.

While Sindhia had been negotiating, Holkar had been perpetrating atrocities in the country near the Sutlej, until utterly defeated by Lake, and forced to sue for a treaty. He undertook to surrender Tonk, Bondi, and all places north of the Bondi hills—to none of which he had any claim except that of the strong hand. Under Wellesley, Barlow had been a zealous upholder of the "forward" policy, which may have occasioned some astonishment that his conscience now refused to allow him to ratify this treaty. Bondi was given over to the mercy of Holkar. Sindhia kept Gwalior and Gohad, and was left free to wreak his vengeance upon Jaipur, whose Raja had lent fitful assistance to the English during the war. The British Government undertook to enter into no treaties with the princes of Rajputana, or to interfere with "the arrangements" that Sindhia might make with them.

"This is the first time," said the envoy of Jaipur to Lake, "since the British government was established in India, that it has been known to make its faith subservient to its convenience."

Lake, whose clean soldier's mind was incapable of understanding political exigencies, resigned his civil power to Barlow, vowing that never again would he put his hand to treaties which were to be negatived at headquarters. His hands had been clean throughout his service, and when he went home, to die a poor man, English and natives alike united to give him such a farewell as no other public servant ever had received.

# XII.

# WHEN THIEVES FELL OUT—1805-1820

"In tempore vespere, et ecce turbatio ; in matutino, et non subsistet ; haec est pars eorum, qui vastaverunt nos, et sors diripentium nos."

## XII.

## WHEN THIEVES FELL OUT—1805-1820.

THE "Time of Troubles" was not ended; thanks to Barlow's masterly inactivity, Central India was in worse plight than ever.

The Marathas by themselves, in the degradation to which they had fallen since the deaths of Madhaji Sindhia and Ahalya Bai, were capable of ruining any state, and they had allies who could outdo them at their worst.

In the days before the last battle of Panipat the Maratha armies had been swelled by bands of freebooters of the worst type, commonly known as Pindaris,[1]—men of various races, with no common creed or interest, held together only by the lust of plunder. In later years both Sindhia and Holkar availed themselves of their services, which they paid by an occasional permission to

[1] The word was said to be derived from *Pinda*, an intoxicating drink.

the leaders to keep part of the lands they seized from other people, and a general leave to plunder "even beyond the usual licence given to a Maratha army."

Encumbered by neither tents nor baggage, carrying only grain for their horses and bread for themselves, the Pindaris would ride forty or fifty miles a day till they reached the district marked for their attention. Then, dividing into small bands, they swept the country systematically, never exposing themselves to danger if they could help it, but falling upon peaceful villages and defenceless cultivators. They ravished the women, they killed the children, they tortured the men in nameless ways in order to extract what little money they might have been able to hoard; they drove the cattle before them, and destroyed everything that they could not carry. If overtaken, they dispersed in all directions; but they could ride where regular troops might not follow, and they usually had finished their work before any force could be mustered to attack them—although, we are told, they would break off their labours five times a day in order to say their prayers.

"The very scavengers of Marathas," one who knew them well calls the Pindaris; and they richly deserved the name. The Maratha occasionally redeemed his treachery and cruelty by bravery, as on the field of Laswari; the Pindari had no redeeming qualities. "If any of our people ever had them," observed an intelligent Pindari to Sir John Malcolm, "the first effect would be to make them leave our company." If the Marathas were the wolves, the Pindaris were the hyænas.

The evil that they caused could not be measured only by the waste fields and burning villages and disfigured corpses left in their track; many of the lesser chieftains whom they harried, unable to protect their lands from the spoiler, became robbers in their turn and preyed upon others. "What else could we do?" asked the minister of a petty state in Malwa. "There was no other class but plunderers left in Malwa." The very Bhils, emboldened by the general anarchy, came down from their hills and forests to rob those weaker than themselves. In many districts the husbandman durst not plough his field without taking shield and lance with him, while a watchman stood on an earth-tower to give the alarm if any one were seen approaching. And all the while the Maratha armies were going up and down the land, levying contributions from towns and provinces, indifferent as to who might be the overlord, and Barlow sat still and made no sign.

Countries wasted by famine, or by evil beasts or tempest, have sought to propitiate their gods by a virgin sacrifice, as we know from such diverse sources as the legend of St George and the folk-tale of the Brown Bear of Noroway. There was to be a virgin sacrifice ere Malwa and Rajputana could be delivered from the scourge.

Had the Rajput princes held together they might have driven off the Marathas, or at least have made a good end. But it was the ill-luck of all the chief states of Rajputana to be governed at this time by rulers who were unworthy of all the traditions of their race. The Rana of Udaipur was weak, the Maharaja of Jaipur was a vulgar profligate, the Raja of Jodhpur was a ruffian. Each was at war with the other, and Sindhia and Holkar ravaged their dominions at will, and laid waste Kotah and Bondi to avenge the help given to the English, who would not lift a finger to save the kinsmen of those Haras who had covered Monson's retreat.

Now the Rana of Udaipur's daughter, the Princess Kishna, had grown to marriageable age in these troublous years, and was reputed to be the loveliest maiden in India. Sindhia himself had asked her in marriage; but though the fines levied by Sindhia and Holkar had reduced her father to such dire poverty that he had stripped the ladies of his family of their jewels, "the sun of the Hindus," the first among the Rajputs, could not stoop so low as to give his daughter to a Maratha. Rather than this, she should marry the Maharaja of Jaipur, who had asked for her, though his clan, the Kachwahas, were little esteemed in Udaipur, and the Maharaja was said to be the most dissolute prince of his age.

Then the Raja of Jodhpur claimed the princess: she had been betrothed to his brother, he said, who had died before the wedding-day, and therefore belonged to him by rights as his brother's heir.

It shows to what degradation the Rajput princes had fallen, that both the rival claimants appealed to the Marathas for aid. The Jaipur Maharaja backed his arguments with a bribe, and Holkar sent Amir Khan's Pindaris to his aid, while Sindhia lent some of his ruffians. Then followed war between the princess's suitors, while Amir Khan plundered the territories of both indiscriminately. There was battle and murder, and dead men's bones whitened the roads; and the English, to whom appeal was made, still sat inert, although by this time Barlow had been superseded by Lord Minto.

The Rana, helpless and broken, sued for peace,

and was told by Amir Khan that he should have it at a price. Let "the Flower of Rajast'han" die, and end the contention for her hand.

It was expedient that one should die for many; the father yielded. Royal blood might only be shed by royal blood, and therefore the Rana's half-brother was sent to the zenana. He looked on Kishna Bai, and at the sight his dagger fell from his hand and he confessed his purpose.

The women burst into cries and lamentations, while Kishna, serene as a virgin martyr, rebuked their clamour. "Why grieve, my mother? I fear not to die. Am I not your daughter? A Rajput maiden is destined for sacrifice, and often enters this world but to be sent from it. Let me thank my father who has allowed me to live till now."

Her father's sister undertook to compound a poisoned draught. As in the legends of the martyrs, twice the victim drank and received no hurt. When the cup was brought for the third time, she smiled, and wished that it might be the last. Then with the cry, "This was the marriage to which I was foredoomed!" she dropped down at the feet of her attendants.

## II.

The sacrifice of the virgin princess was the turning-point for Rajputana. "A shudder went through the length and breadth of the land," and in the following year reached as far as 'The Times' office, whence, in April 1811, came an obituary notice more remarkable for good intentions than for correctness, since it styled Kishna Bai "this second Helen." That such a deed should be done under the eyes of the English Mission in Sindhia's camp was felt as an intolerable disgrace.

The retribution for his sins soon fell upon Jaswant Rao Holkar. His temper, always violent, had become ungovernable through drinking cherry brandy, and working by day and night at the foundries where his cannon were being cast. At the time when Amir Khan was demanding the death of the princess, his master, after having been tied with ropes to prevent his murdering the women in the zenana, had sunk from a violent maniac to a speechless idiot, fed with milk like a baby. No cure could be found; some said that he was bewitched by an evil spirit in his palace; others recalled how, in one of his forays into Udaipur territory, he had plundered the shrine of Krishna at Nathdwarra —an insult to his own religion that had appalled every Hindu in his army.

Amir Khan seized upon the contents of the treasury, and a quarrel for the regency ensued between Tulsi Bai, the mistress of Jaswant, who had taken her from her husband, and various other disreputable persons. One of these, a certain Dherma, formerly Jaswant's servant, now promoted to command of the infantry, attempted a *coup-d'état*, and took possession of the lunatic, under the pretext of carrying him to the wonder-working shrine of Mahadeo, near Udaipur. Finding himself hard pressed by Amir Khan, he sent Jaswant, his son, and Tulsi herself, into the jungle, as a prelude to making away with them all. This was going too far; the army rebelled, and took Dherma prisoner. He had shown many of Holkar's qualities, and might have risen to an equal "bad eminence," but his opportunities were cut short by Tulsi, who ordered his immediate execution. The executioner, from stupidity or carelessness, slashed at his neck with one hand. Dherma looked sternly upon him: "Take two hands, you rascal; after all, it is the head of Dherma that is to be cut off."

Amir Khan was now indisputably the master, and he ravaged from Nagpur to Jodhpur, in the name of Holkar's unlawful son by a potter's daughter, whom Tulsi Bai and her confederates had proclaimed heir to the madman. The government was supposed to be in the hands of Tulsi, of whose unspeakable wickedness there is no need to tell; the Maratha ladies of her day had an evil reputation, and she was the most shameless of them all. With mutinies on one side and assassinations on the other, the regency continued to exist through a few squalid years, until the general upheaval.

Sindhia, in the meantime, was continuing his depredations wherever he thought himself secure from collision with the English. The Peshwa, under pretence of friendship, was contriving fresh mischief, inspired and abetted by his favourite, Trimbakji, once a spy, now his pander.

Everywhere the cry went up for the help of the English. "When will you take this country?" a faquir had asked Mountstuart Elphinstone in 1801. "The country wants you. The Hindus are villains." "All enjoy rest under the protection of the English, and all are comforted by their justice," sighed a Muslim chronicler, a few years later. Still the Directors at home clung to the policy of non-intervention. The Prince Regent had obliged them to send out his favourite Lord Moira as Governor-General. A man of nearly sixty, who had "no better record than that of a fair soldier and a zealous courtier," seemed a safe appointment, no doubt, and they knew nothing of the private journal in which Moira noted: "Our object ought to be to render the British Government paramount, in effect, if not declaredly."

He had not been long in office before the Pindaris went so far as to stir the blood of even a Court of Directors. In the cold weather of 1815-16, some 23,000 of them had been at work in the country between Nagpur and the Bay of Bengal, and in ten days succeeded in killing 182 of the inhabitants, wounding 500, and torturing over 3000, while doing damage to the amount of a million sterling. After this, Moira received permission to go so far as "repelling and chastising the invaders."

If the English broom was to sweep clean, there must be no holes and corners left where evildoers could harbour. Negotiations with the Maratha and Rajput states upon this question met with varying success. The Regent for the imbecile Bhonsla was easily brought to see where his best interests lay; Sindhia played fast and loose, now posing as the friend of the English, now trying to stir the other Maratha states and the Gurkhas to war. Amir Khan, on receiving a grant of territory, settled down into a responsible ruler and faithful ally. Nothing could be done with the Holkar regency, and the Peshwa was becoming little better than the Pindaris. His favourite, Trimbakji, had lately hired assassins to murder the envoy of the Gaikwar of Baroda—a most respectable Brahman, whose crime was that he had refused to allow his wife to visit the Peshwa's palace, in which no honourable woman could set foot.

The Resident at Poona was Mountstuart Elphinstone—one of the most honoured names in the history of British rule in India. His unflinching insistence at last brought the Peshwa to sign a treaty whereby he became the feudatory of the Company, and to yield up Trimbakji to the justice of the English.

The murderer was confined in the fort of Tannah, on that island of Salsette with which Raghoba had bribed the Bombay Council before the first Maratha war. To the fort, one day, came a Maratha horsekeeper asking for employment. When his service had come to a sudden end, it was remembered that he groomed his horses within earshot of the prisoner's window, and that he sang Maratha ballads as he worked.

One, evidently a favourite, as it was continually repeated, ran somewhat in this fashion :—

"Behind the bush the bowmen hide,
The horse beneath the tree;
Where shall I find a knight will ride
The jungle paths with me?
There are five-and-fifty coursers there,
And four-and-fifty men;
When the fifty-fifth shall mount his steed,
The Deccan thrives again." [1]

One evening the prisoner disappeared; he had escaped to the jungle paths, and in a few months was stirring up insurrection, with the connivance of the Peshwa.

## III.

In 1817, Moira (now become Lord Hastings) collected the largest army that had ever assembled under the English flag in India. The central force, under his own command, was to bar Hindustan against the Pindaris; the Madras army was to march up from the Deccan, under Sir Thomas Hislop, its commander-in-chief, while the Bombay army held Gujerat. The intent was not only to surround the Pindaris and sweep them

[1] Bishop Heber's translation.

up, but to overawe any of the native powers who might give trouble.

First of these was the Peshwa, who was sending his agents to corrupt the sepoys, and even the European officers in the British service, garrisoning his forts, and recruiting an army. As a good beginning, he proposed to get rid of Elphinstone, either by murdering him at a conference, as Sivaji had murdered the envoy of Aurangzib, or by setting Trimbakji to attack the Residency by night. All the English were to be murdered likewise, except a surgeon who had cured many sick among the Marathas.

A European regiment was on its way to Poona. To gain time was important, and Elphinstone seemed to credit all the Peshwa's civilities, while making what preparations he could against the storm. Long afterwards, old soldiers would tell of the strain of those days at the end of October and the beginning of November, how Elphinstone watched all one night on the terrace, knowing that the Peshwa's guns were yoked, and his horses saddled for an attack which happily was deferred, and how the sepoys, true to their salt, rejected the overtures of the Peshwa's agents, and brought his rupees to their officers.

They would tell "how the 'Old Toughs'" (103rd Regiment, now 2nd Battalion Dublin Fusiliers), "the only European corps within reach, marched seventy-two miles straight up over the ghauts to Poona, with only a single three hours' halt *en route;* how they closed up their ranks, and entered the British lines with band playing and colours flying; and how not a straggler dropped behind, for all knew 'that there must be a battle soon.'"

"Their arrival was the signal for the Peshwa to throw off the mask, and as the British Residency was untenable, our troops moved out to take up a safer position at Kirkee, about three miles from the city of Poona; and as they marched they saw all the houses of the Resident and his suite fired by the enemy, who swarmed out of the city. As they formed in line of battle, they anxiously watched the native regiments coming up on their flank, for that was the moment for successful treachery, if the native soldiers were untrue! Not a sepoy, however, in the British ranks wavered, though before the junction was complete a cloud of Maratha cavalry poured down upon them, dashed through the opening left between the two lines, enveloped either flank of the little army, and attacked the European regiment in the rear. Then, as a last resource, the European regiment faced about their second rank, and kept up such a steady rolling fire to front and rear at the same time, that but few of the eager horsemen ever came within spear's length of the British bayonets."[1]

A few days later, General Smith's arrival at Poona drove the Peshwa to Satara and re-established order in the city. It was just at this time that a new detachment arriving from Calcutta brought the cholera to Hastings's army, and in ten days twenty thousand officers, soldiers, and camp-followers were swept away. The track of the army through Bundelkhund was strewn with the dead and dying, and the Marathas thought that the pestilence had come to fight on their side.

It was too much for the newly-born virtue of the Regent of Nagpur, who had begun by doing all that was asked of him, in the hope that the English would allow him to succeed his imbecile brother, the Bhonsla. Mr Jenkins, the Resident, found his house surrounded by the Nagpur troops, called in the brigade of Madras Native Infantry from cantonments, and stationed it on the Sitabaldi hill, behind the Residency. Here they were assailed by the Nagpur army, led by a band of Arab mercenaries. The fighting went on from sunset till two o'clock in the morning, when the Arabs captured one of the twin peaks of the hill, and turned the gun stationed there upon the

[1] Sir B. Frere.

northern peak. Then the army closed round for a general assault, while from the sepoys' quarters, where the Arabs had broken in, came the cries of women and children.

With the brigade were three troops of Bengal native cavalry, under Captain Fitzgerald, who had been posted in the Residency grounds. Repeatedly, as he watched the danger thickening, he had asked leave to charge, and each time the commanding officer refused it. Now, when the day seemed lost, he sent yet another message, and received for answer, "Tell him to charge at his peril." "At my peril be it!" was Fitzgerald's exclamation, as he galloped out with his men. Down upon the main body of horse he charged, scattered them, cut the infantry with them to pieces, and rode back with the captured guns. The sight put heart into the sepoy infantry, who now charged in their turn. The Nagpur army was driven off—eighteen thousand men worsted by less than fourteen hundred.

In the beginning of December, Malcolm, then in hot pursuit of Chitu, the worst of all the Pindari leaders, entered Holkar's territory, and to his great surprise found himself withstood by Holkar's army. Tulsi Bai and her advisers had been professedly the friends of the English, but a political crisis had just occurred; the household troops were weary of her infamous rule and determined to end it. Having enticed Mulhar Rao from his tent, they seized upon the woman and her chief minister. On a December night they carried her down to the banks of the Sipra river; she begged for life, she cast the blame of her sins upon others, she offered her pearls as a bribe, and her shrieks roused the camp from slumber, but as an eye-witness testified, "not a foot stirred and not a voice was raised to save a woman who had never shown mercy to others." She was beheaded, and her body cast into the river.

A few hours later Malcolm crossed the Sipra at Mahidpur with scarcely 2000 bayonets, and engaged "20,000 of the best cavalry in India, with infantry and heavy guns." The result was a severe defeat for Holkar's troops, and his ministers were obliged to sue for peace, at the price of renouncing all claims upon Rajputana, and all territory south of the Satpura range.

The operations against the Peshwa cannot be told in detail; generally, it may be said with Skinner on another occasion, that "the British and the Marathas got messed up," for while the van of Hislop's Fourth Division was chasing the Marathas, the Maratha cavalry were sometimes pressing the rear-guard and baggage of the division.

On New Year's Day, 1818, Captain Staunton, in command of the 2nd Battalion 1st Bombay Native Infantry, was on his way from Sirore to reinforce the troops at Poona, then threatened with an attack from the Peshwa's army. By ten o'clock in the morning he reached the village of Koreigaom, built on a large mound overlooking the river Bhima, and saw the Peshwa's cavalry, twenty-five thousand strong, on the opposite bank.

In the centre of the village, where two ways intersect, was an open space where stood the village temple, and the rest-house for travellers. Here was the only shelter for the wounded through the long day when Staunton held the village with five hundred men and two guns against the host, while the Peshwa watched from an eminence overlooking the plain. There was no cover save a mud wall, breached in many places, and open on one side. There was no food, and no water; for though the sepoys could see the sacred Bhima running within a hundred yards of them, no man could cross that space under the fire of the Peshwa's army, and return.

The men had marched all night. The sun smote down upon them, half their officers were killed or disabled, and the enemy, having taken the temple, had slaughtered the wounded. The men were dropping with thirst and weariness, and still fresh assailants swarmed upon them, driven by the taunts of the Peshwa, who asked Trimbakji and his officers where were their boasts of defeating the English when they could not overcome one battalion?

Chisholm, the artillery officer, fell dead, and the Arab mercenaries rushed in upon the guns, and took one. The artillerymen began to murmur of surrender upon terms. Then from the place where he lay mortally wounded, with a shot through the body, rose the gigantic adjutant, Thomas Pattinson, son of a Cumberland clergyman. "Follow me once more!" he cried, and seizing a musket from a fallen sepoy, swung the butt of it against the Arabs, knocking them down right and left. His men, who adored him, followed, and the gun was brought back as he dropped, with another mortal wound.

By the evening no officer was left fit for duty except Staunton himself; "then the young assistant-surgeons, Wylie and Wingate, leaving their wounded, took their swords, and calling the almost exhausted men to follow them, twice led them to the charge." Wingate was killed. Then night came down, the attack weakened, and the men could draw water.

All next day Staunton stood waiting for another attack, and when night came again, retreated to

Sirore. In spite of having withstood the Peshwa's army, his men knew that they had failed to reach Poona, and we are told that "they came into cantonments with drooping heads." They were consoled by the welcome they received—all save Pattinson, who survived to reach Sirore with the rest, and could not be brought on his deathbed to realise anything but that the detachment had failed to obey orders.

In the following month, at Ashta, General Smith overtook and defeated the Peshwa, who escaped from the field. His chief adviser, Gokala, died, sword in hand, covering his retreat—a most undeserved sacrifice, since, in one of his attempts to negotiate with the English, the Peshwa had thought to conciliate them by offering to poison Gokala. The army was broken up, and the Peshwa was left to wander from place to place, without friends or resources.

Thus, one after another, all the refuges whither the Pindaris had been used to retreat were taken from them, and the cordon was drawn tighter until all the robber bands were dead or dispersed. "There was not one hour of their hunted existence when they tried to fight like men."[1] There was something of dramatic retribution in the fate of Chitu, who, from his lair in the forests between

[1] Keene.

the Nerbudda river and the Vindhya mountains, had terrorised all within his reach. The few followers left to him urged surrender to the English mercy. But Chitu feared that the punishment for his sins would be banishment from India, and would not face it; in his broken and miserable slumbers he was heard continually to shriek "Black water!" meaning the sea over which the English would send him. At the last, he was separated from all his followers, starving and alone, and the English were tracking him through the jungles by the print of his horse's hoofs. In a tiger's den they found a mangled body, and a sword and a letter-case, which proved that the wild beast who had preyed upon Central India had become the prey of a wild beast in his turn.

"The Pindaris were virtually, and as an institution, abolished"; the Peshwa threw himself on the mercy of the English. There remained to put everything into place, now that the sweeping was accomplished.

The Raja of Bondi at last was rewarded for his fidelity. All the districts taken from him by the Marathas—some of which had been alienated for fifty years—were restored. The other Rajput states were also delivered from the spoiler, and came under British protection. An English officer has described the condition of the state of Udaipur, when at length the argent snake of Sindhia on its orange field had been displaced. "In a space of 140 miles, all was desolate; even the traces of the footsteps of man were effaced. The babul and gigantic reed, which harboured the boar and the tiger, grew upon the highways; and every rising ground displayed a mass of ruins. Bhilwara, the commercial *entrepôt* of Rajputana, which, ten years before, contained 6000 families, showed not a vestige of existence. All was silent in her streets—no living thing was seen except a solitary dog, that fled in dismay from his lurking-place in the temple, scared at the unaccustomed sight of man."

Now that the spoiler was cast forth, the people assembled from all directions whither they had fled, and came back to rebuild their homes with joy and singing. In a very short time the effects of the sweeping were evident. "A year or two ago, if you had come this way, you would have been killed for the food you carried," said the dwellers in a wild region of Bondi to an Englishman; "now, you might travel with gold."

Nagpur passed under British administration, till the child who was heir to it came of age. The young Holkar was left under the tutelage of a Resident, with dominions considerably shorn.

The Peshwa was deposed, and spent the rest of his life at Bithur, on the Ganges, near Cawnpore; he left an adopted son, remembered to this day as "the Nana Sahib," who was to avenge his quarrel with the English.

One of the least-deserving actors in the story profited the most. Sindhia, whose double-dealing had been detected and exposed repeatedly, who had been withheld from open war only by the neighbourhood of a British division, was confirmed in the possession of various territories which his army had torn from their long-established owners in Bundelkhund, just before the Pindari War.

Elphinstone declined a baronetcy, as an honour which he "would have to share with half the aldermen of London," and was not given the Bath—which he would have accepted gladly—or any other distinction.

Trimbakji was consigned to prison, under a guard of Europeans and sepoys. He showed no anxiety about his children, for whose safety Elphinstone cared, but was much concerned over his weekly accounts, and once set the whole garrison in an uproar over some *ghi*[1] which, he declared, had been stolen from him.

[1] Rancid butter.

# XIII.

# THE MEN OF THE HILLS—1814-1826

"In this reign a war broke out with the British in the Terai, but, depriving them of wisdom, the Raja saved his country. Then, calling the British gentlemen, he made peace with them, and allowed them to live near Thambahil."—VANSAVALI (GENEALOGICAL HISTORY) OF NEPAL.

## XIII.

## THE MEN OF THE HILLS—1814-1826.

To the north of India, where the snow-covered peaks of the Himalayas form the barrier to the forbidden plateau of Tibet, the lower hills—in many places higher than the Alps—are intersected by rivers flowing down to the sacred Mother Ganges. In the valleys, a sturdy race, with the narrow eyes and high cheek-bones of their Mongol ancestry, had dwelt for many generations, before they were invaded by a people fleeing from the Muslim invaders who overran Northern and Central India in the twelfth century. The new-comers called themselves Rajputs; their chief claimed to be of the royal house of Udaipur, and distorted fragments of its history are embedded in the records of Nepal. Intermarrying with the inhabitants of the valleys, in course of time they lost the outward characteristics of the Rajput, while retaining his love of fighting. Their first capital was at a place named Gurkha, from which they took the name by which they are best known. Later on, the seat of government was at Kathmandu, on the bank of the river Gandak, surrounded by lofty mountains, a town indescribably filthy and extraordinarily picturesque, with wide-eaved houses covered with elaborate wood-carvings, and temples like those on a Chinese tea-tray, hung with tinkling bells and adorned with glittering brass. The staircase of every house was like a ship's hatchway, so that at need each householder could turn his dwelling into a fortress—a useful precaution in a land where fighting was the only recreation for men.

During the latter half of the eighteenth century the Gurkhas had made efforts to widen their boundaries, sometimes triumphant, sometimes defeated by their neighbours. Their aggressions upon Tibet brought an invading army from China, and they were driven to appeal to the English, from whom they obtained much good advice, and a commercial treaty. Seeing no advantage in either, the Gurkhas then turned their attention to districts either owned or protected by the English, and at the end of the year 1813 seized a tract including two hundred villages beyond the forests that bordered Nepal on the south.

Lord Moira, who had arrived in Calcutta to take office in October, represented to the Nepal Government that these villages were part of the territory of the Raja of Oudh, lately ceded to the English, and demanded their surrender within twenty-five days. The Nepal Government replied by sending troops over the frontier to attack the British post of Bhotwal, where they killed eighteen of the police force, and murdered the head officer who had surrendered to them.

Moira had come from England with instructions to continue the policy of peace and retrenchment; he had found the Calcutta Treasury nearly empty, and he knew that, sooner or later, he must sweep Central India clear of the Pindaris and reduce the Marathas to order. But to allow the Gurkhas to go unpunished would be to degrade British prestige in India to a level even lower than had been reached under the guidance of Sir George Barlow and the Court of Directors. So, after vainly requiring an apology from the Nepal Government, he prepared for a campaign at the end of the rainy season, during which it was impossible to bring troops through the Terai, the long strip of malaria haunted forest beyond the British frontier. Meanwhile, the Nepal Government, "with a baseness and barbarity peculiar to themselves," as the Governor-General's proclamation indignantly declared, "endeavoured to destroy the troops and the subjects of the Company on the frontier by poisoning the water of the wells and tanks in a tract of considerable extent."

To meet the expenses of the war two millions were borrowed from the Nawab of Oudh—a loan that was destined to bring no good to borrower or to lender.

Four divisions were employed against the Gurkhas' little army of twelve thousand men; the largest, eight thousand strong, under Major-General Marley, was to march direct upon Kathmandu, while the next largest, under Ochterlony, attacked the Gurkha positions at the western extremity of their line. Another division, under Major-General Gillespie, was to occupy the Dehra Dun, a valley above the first range of hills, and then move westward to Ochterlony's support; the weakest division, under General Wood, was to move from the Gorakhpur frontier through Bhotwal. On paper, it seemed an effective scheme for crushing a few thousand hillmen, undisciplined and imperfectly equipped, and it might have worked out more or less according to expectation, had not one of the commanders been rash, while two were inert.

The first division to move was that under Rollo Gillespie, whose story is more suggestive of a melodrama than of history in the days of stocks, pigtails, and breech-loading rifles. Born of Scotch parents in Ireland, he insisted upon becoming a soldier, in spite of his father's opposition. Before he was one-and-twenty he had fallen in love at first sight with a beautiful stranger, married her privately, and killed his adversary in a duel across a handkerchief. On his way to join his regiment, the 20th Light Dragoons, in Jamaica, he was shipwrecked, and, on his arrival, nearly died of yellow fever. Having volunteered for an expedition against the French in San Domingo, he undertook to go with a flag of truce to demand the surrender of Port-au-Prince, and after swimming on this errand from the English squadron to the shore, with his sword in his teeth, was on the point of being shot for a spy by the enraged governor, when it occurred to him to make a masonic sign, which instantly changed the enemies into friends. Wrecked again on his return to England, his next adventure was in a theatre at Cork, where he unbonneted one of the audience who refused to show the usual signs of respect at the singing of "God Save the King," and having handled his man severely in the consequent scuffle, was obliged to escape in the dress of a soldier's wife from the warrant issued against him for assault and battery. On a return to the West

Indies, being attacked in his house one night by eight assassins, he killed six with his sword and put the other two to flight, and did not die of his wounds afterwards.

He was on his way through the Continent in 1805 to join the 19th Light Dragoons, to which he had exchanged, when he was warned in a theatre at Hamburg by a muffled man, who proved to be no other than the notorious Napper Tandy, that the French were about to make a descent on Hamburg to capture him. Hiding at Altona till the danger was over, he pursued his way overland, with no worse *contre-temps* than that of nearly being carried off and sold as a slave on his passage across the Euxine Sea, and narrowly escaping murder at the hands of an Arab chief who had taken a fancy to Colonel Gillespie's arms, but being attacked with a sudden ailment, was propitiated by a dose of medicine from the Colonel's store, which "wrought like a devil unchained."

He had scarcely taken up the command at Arcot, when, at the incitement of the sons of Tipu, who had been sent to live at Vellore after the capture of Seringapatam, certain native regiments broke out in mutiny—a foretaste of the horrors of fifty years later. The July moon was rising in the sky when the European barracks at

Vellore were surrounded by men who poured in a deadly fire at every door and window. The sick in the hospital were butchered, and the officers in their quarters. Two officers and a remnant of the men contrived tc fight their way through the mutineers to the house above the city gate, and held out there, while a messenger swam across a ditch haunted by crocodiles to take the news to Arcot eight miles away.

Had it not been for an accident Gillespie himself would have spent that night at Vellore, and probably would have been murdered with the rest. As it was, he was taking his early morning ride, when a man on a staggering horse called to him that the devil was loose in Vellore. At once he rode to the barracks, and ordered the trumpeter to sound the call. With his dragoons and his galloper guns tearing after him, he was on the road to Vellore, where Tipu's tiger standard was floating in the morning breeze. It was Tipu's sons who had egged on the mutineers, and had feasted them at a banquet after the massacre of the English.

As Gillespie's small slight figure, far in advance of his men, came within eyeshot of the gateway where the survivors still held out, an old sergeant, who had served in San Domingo, exclaimed, "If Colonel Gillespie be alive, he is now at the head of the 19th Dragoons, and God Almighty has sent him from the West Indies to save our lives in the East!"

Standing beneath the house Gillespie called for a rope. There was none, but the garrison fastened their belts together and let them down.[1] As he rose in the air the enemy's bullets spattered round him like hail; not one hit its mark, and he leaped, unscathed, among the handful of men who were left of the garrison of Vellore.

Then came the crash and the roar of the galloper guns bursting the gates. The dragoons seized the fort, and the mutineers scattered. Some dropped from the walls and escaped, some were killed, many more were taken prisoners.

Tipu's sons were removed to Calcutta, but remained in receipt of the pensions paid to them by the Company.

After this exploit, a campaign against the Dutch in Java, in which he repeatedly carried positions by sheer audacity, had increased Gillespie's natural recklessness. He did not understand that in the Gurkhas he had an enemy as brave as himself, who would not of necessity retreat because he advanced.

[1] Modern critics deny this incident, tradition has always affirmed it. The story has been told by Mr Newbolt better than by any one else, and his version gives the belts.

Finding that the hill fort of Kalinga, the key to the Dun, garrisoned by a small force of Gurkhas, was in his way, he decided that it must be taken before he could advance westward to support Ochterlony. "The fort stands on the summit of an almost inaccessible mountain, and covered with an impenetrable jungle; the only approaches commanded, and stiffly stockaded. It will be a tough job to take it," he wrote to a friend, at the end of October, "but I think I shall have it, *sub auspice Deo!*"

The Governor-General, remembering what had happened when Lake attempted to storm Bhurtpore, had issued strict orders that every fortress should be bombarded. Gillespie was too much of an Irishman to obey orders that he thought unnecessary, and three days after the writing of that letter, his troops assaulted Kalinga at four separate points.

Impetuous to the last, finding that his batteries did not do as much execution as he intended, he gave the signal for the assault some hours before the time arranged, and the result was a pitiful fiasco. The King's Royal Irish, who took the lead gallantly, were obliged to fall back for want of proper support. Those who should have come to their aid did not appear, and afterwards pleaded in excuse that Gillespie's orders never reached them. Twice the assault had been repelled, when the General, seeing the men disheartened, put himself at the head of the storming party, vowing that he would take the fort, or lose his life in the attempt. As he stood within a few paces of the walls, waving his hat and sword, and calling on his men, a shot pierced his heart.

His division continued to besiege Kalinga, with the help of a battering train from Delhi, and was repulsed twice over with heavy losses, the garrison defending themselves with arrows, and with stones which the Gurkha women flung with a good aim. There were only seventy men capable of bearing arms left in Kalinga by the end of November, and they fought their way through the outposts one night, leaving the English to take possession of the ruins.

One day, while the siege was in progress, a Gurkha was seen standing on the breach, making signs with his hand. The firing ceased, and the man advanced, and explained as best he could that the English had broken his jaw with a round-shot; would they mend it for him? The regimental surgeons did their best, and were able, after some time in hospital, to discharge the patient as cured. Asked what he would do, the Gurkha replied that now the English had made him whole, he would go back to his own corps and fight them again. Apparently, he made the reputation of the English doctors, for, after this, it was a frequent event for a wounded Gurkha to demand their help, in order that he might be in better trim for fighting next day.

## II.

Meanwhile, Gillespie's death seemed to have struck a paralysis into his colleagues. General Wood, having succeeded in beating a force much below his own in numbers, took panic, and ordered a retreat, leaving the Gurkhas with all the advantages of a victory. After this, he did nothing with great skill for several months, and then retired upon Gorakhpur.

As for General Marley, he remained on the frontier, waiting for more artillery, through the month of December, without fortifying his outposts. The consequence was that on New Year's Day 1815, they were attacked by the Gurkhas, with a heavy loss in men, guns, and stores. This disaster seemed to produce something like imbecility in the General; though heavily reinforced, and receiving almost daily orders from the Governor-General to bestir himself, he sat where he was, and let the enemy burn villages over the border, and throw up stockades close to him. Finally, one morning in February, he mounted his horse before daylight, and took the road to his headquarters, without telling any one what he intended, or making any arrangements for his division during his absence. By this time, Moira had lost patience, and another commander was on his way to Nepal; unluckily, the new-comer proved of little more use than his predecessor.

Meanwhile, in India all these things were noted. The Marathas were restless, Amir Khan was collecting his bands, near Agra, and Ranjit Singh, the ruler of the Punjab, gathered an army at Lahore.

For relief, at this crisis, the Government of India was indebted to two men—a Scotchman and an Irishman.

The first of these was David Ochterlony, who had seen nearly forty years' service in India, beginning with the war with Haidar Ali, when he had been taken prisoner by the French. It was he who had held Delhi against Holkar's army, in the second Maratha War, and one of the first acts of Barlow's administration had been to remove him from the Residency "as a mere soldier who could not be expected to understand certain civil duties which were to be attached to the situation."

There was work for a "mere soldier" in Nepal.

The general confronting Ochterlony was Amar Singh, the best officer in the Gurkha army, who was encamped among broken hills, each ridge of which afforded a series of positions. An attack on his principal fortress was repulsed, and Ochterlony began to feel doubtful of succeeding. Nevertheless, he kept his doubts from his subordinates, "nor," we are told, "could his most familiar associates detect in his manner the slightest interruption of that cheerful flow of spirits for which Sir David was characterised through life."[1]

Now came the turn of the Irishman. Among the many European adventurers flocking into India at the end of the eighteenth century was the man said to have been the original of Thackeray's Major Gahagan, William Linnæus Gardner, who had left the British army to take service with Ahalya Bai. He remained with the Marathas when most of the other officers went over to the Company's army, and according to his own account, was ill requited; Jaswant Rao Holkar, having sent him on a mission to Lake, grossly insulted him in durbar on his return. "Drawing my sword, I attempted to cut Holkar down, but was prevented by those about him. Ere they had recovered from their amazement,

[1] Thos. Smith.

I rushed from the tent, sprang upon my horse, and was soon out of reach of my pursuers." The rest of the story is quite in keeping with its beginning. Captured by a Maratha force, Gardner was sentenced to execution, but on his way thither, flung himself over a cliff fifty feet high into a stream below, swam and dived till he had escaped pursuit, and having obtained a disguise, after various adventures, reached Lake's camp, and was given command of a cavalry force.

In the spring of 1814, he had ventured into the Dehra Dun to fish and to shoot, and had narrowly escaped being shot as a spy by the Gurkha officer in command there. From what he had seen of Nepal, he was able to grasp the weak points of the enemy; the army and the country were admirably fitted for guerilla warfare, but the line of defence was too long.

His cousin, the Hon. Edward Gardner, who had been prevented from sharing in his sporting expedition, was at Delhi with Metcalfe, the Resident, and to him Gardner wrote in November 1814, urging the immediate occupation of Kumaon, a province recently conquered by the Gurkhas. Its inhabitants were averse to the new yoke, and the Gurkhas, relying on their peaceable disposition, had left few troops there.

A few days later, the two cousins were on the way to Kumaon, at the head of a compact force of native infantry, "with some light guns," and supported by a column under Major Hearsey, one of the two officers who went with George Thomas on his last ride to Hansi. In the present campaign his support was of little worth, since he was captured by the Gurkhas, and taken prisoner to Almora, the chief fortress of Kumaon. There they kept him and treated him kindly, believing "that he was a Frenchman, and could procure them foreign help."

In April 1815, while in Europe the kings were gathering their armies for a last struggle against Napoleon, David Ochterlony was making his way further into Nepal, and by the middle of the month had established himself among the heights where Amar Singh's force was stationed. He had learned to fight the enemy in their own way, and it was the turn of the Gurkhas to be discouraged, while the invading army triumphed. Meanwhile, Almora was captured, and Amar Singh, as Gardner had foreseen, was cut off from his supplies. The chiefs began to desert him, Ochterlony closed the roads about him, and only two hundred men were still with him when he signed a capitulation in May, engaging to surrender all the Gurkha conquests west of the Jumna, and to evacuate the hill country between Almora and the fortress of Malaun, where he made his last stand.

Once upon a time, it is said, a Raja of Nepal unjustly put to death his prime minister; the dead man's wife became *sati*, and as the flames were lit about her, she spoke her curse—"May there never be sound judgment in this Durbar!"

How this has been fulfilled may be seen, over and over again, by any one who studies the history of Nepal. The curse was at work now, for the Durbar sent envoys in one direction to treat for peace with the British Government, and in another, to implore the help of the Chinese against the white barbarians, who had invaded the frontier of the Chinese Government.

With the Pindaris growing daily more troublesome, Lord Moira was so anxious to bring the war to an end that he yielded to nearly all the demands of the Gurkha commissions, consenting to give up most of the disputed territory, except what was in actual possession of the British. The family priest of the Raja of Nepal, who had full power to act, signed a treaty to this effect in November 1815. In the next month, believing that the Chinese army was at hand, the Nepal Durbar was again making ready for war.

Ochterlony—now a baronet, in consideration of his services—returned to the hills. A band of smugglers showed him a track unknown to any servant of the Nepal state. His force climbed by night through a narrow ravine, where a handful of men on the crags above could have destroyed them by rolling down loose stones, and emerged in safety at the hour when, according to the Nepalese saying, "the tiles on the roof of a house can be counted, and the hair on the back of a man's hand can be discerned against the sky." They had traversed the first range of hills, and in a few days they took the Gurkhas by surprise and defeated them.

Again the envoys came to sue for peace, and again they found a generous enemy. By the treaty to which they had agreed, the English were to retain all the territories actually in their possession at the time of its ratification. The Nepal Durbar had not ratified that treaty in November. In March the territory occupied by the British troops had extended widely, and to yield it would rob Nepal of nearly half its revenue. Whether quixotically, as some said, or wisely, the Governor-General did not hold to the letter of the agreement, and the territory actually ceded was small compared to what he might have claimed, and the Gurkhas were ready to surrender.

When that year's rainy season had ended, two

high officials from China appeared in tardy reply to the summons of the Nepal Durbar. They professed themselves satisfied with the Governor-General's statement of the case for the English, and administered a round scolding to the Nepal envoys sent to confer with them. "You Gurkhas are a mischievous race, and have caused the ruin of many rajas. You have been punished justly."

## III.

Edward Gardner was established at Kathmandu as Resident. Commercial relations were not encouraged by the Durbar, for the Nepalese have a proverb: "With the merchant comes the musket, and with the Bible, the bayonet." But the war was no sooner over than the Gurkhas began to enlist in the Company's army, and less than ten years after they had been in arms against each other, Gurkha sepoy and British soldier were fighting side by side at the siege of Bhurtpore.

Bhurtpore was besieged because the Governor-General, Lord Amherst, thought fit to disavow a course of action taken by Ochterlony, and was in consequence obliged to send a commander-in-chief and twenty thousand men to settle a difficulty that the "mere soldier" could have conquered with such troops as were at his disposal, if the supreme authority at Calcutta had not interfered.

The Raja of Bhurtpore, whose stronghold Lake had failed to capture, had put himself under British protection, and become our good friend and ally. His successor, having no son, adopted a boy relation, for whom he asked the recognition of the British Government. Ochterlony, then Resident at Delhi, obtained the authority from Calcutta, and invested the boy as the heir of Bhurtpore. A few weeks later the old Raja died, and his brother murdered the Regent, usurped the throne, and defied the British Government. Ochterlony issued a proclamation denouncing the usurper, and ordered out troops for the young Raja's protection. The wicked uncle thereupon renounced his claim to the succession, humbly pleading to be allowed to rule for his adopted nephew until the boy came of age. The storm might have subsided but for Lord Amherst, who had already determined "on making some arrangement by which Sir D. Ochterlony should retire from active employment." To effect this, he issued a severe official reprimand to Ochterlony, condemning his action as "precipitate and unjustifiable," and denying the young Raja's claim to protection, in the face of the treaty made with his predecessor.

The disgrace broke the old soldier's heart. The dishonesty which repudiated obligations that it was inconvenient to keep, the insult to his fifty years of service, weighed him down with shame. He would neither argue nor protest; he resigned all his public offices and retired. Three months later he was dead, and the Government of India were officially regretting the loss of a valued public servant, while Lord Amherst contributed "a handsome sum" towards a monument for the victim of his "arrangement." A better monument was the title by which Sir David was long remembered in Indian tradition—"Loni-Attah"—"Butter and meal,"—a corruption of his own name, which bore witness to the days of plenty when he ruled Central India.

Ochterlony had not been six months in his grave when Lord Amherst found his views of the Bhurtpore question "materially altered." The usurper was becoming a centre of disaffection, and the Maratha chiefs and others were showing a restlessness that was likely to produce dangerous results. So obligations were remembered, and an army was sent to take Bhurtpore.

For six weeks the siege lasted, to the great enjoyment of the Gurkha contingent, who were usually stationed with the 59th in the last angle of the trenches, "sniping" over the parapet at the enemy. With no language in common, the men were the best of friends, and the 59th shared their tobacco with the "little Gorkees," who grinned their thanks.

Then came the day of the assault, when the defences were hurled into the air by the explosion of our mines, and the crash was felt at Agra thirty-five miles away. The Gurkhas had received the order to follow the 59th, but when they saw their friends rushing at the breach, nothing would hold them back, and six-foot grenadiers and little hillmen entered Bhurtpore side by side.

"The English are brave as lions," said the Gurkhas next day; "they are splendid sepoys, and very nearly equal to us."

"You bully us, but go and take Bhurtpore," had been for twenty years the taunt of the native rulers with whom the British Government had any difference. Bhurtpore was taken, and restless spirits subsided for an interval of a few years.

# XIV.

## THE LION OF LAHORE—1805-1839

"The very type and embodiment of the species Sikh is a highwayman in possession of a castle. Take any man of that nation—I care not who—and give him a mud tower as his earthly portion, and next week he will be the Captain of Forty Thieves. Let him alone—that is, don't overmatch him with kings and other great policemen—and he will die a great man. It is the history of the Punjab in a nutshell."—Sir H. EDWARDES.

## XIV.

## THE LION OF LAHORE—1805-1839.

IT was at the close of 1805 that Mr Metcalfe, the Political Agent, sat in Lord Lake's camp beyond the frontier of the Punjab. While Sir George Barlow was arranging his ill-judged treaty with Sindhia, Holkar suddenly had separated himself from his ally, and hurried towards the country about the Sutlej, whither Lake's army had followed him. It was a critical moment, and the man who could influence it was the Sikh, Ranjit Singh, Maharaja of Lahore—"The Lion of the Punjab," as men called him—whose territory both armies had invaded.

As Metcalfe sat in his tent, he was told that "some Sikh troopers had come out of curiosity to see the Sahibs." It was all-important to conciliate Sikh goodwill, and Metcalfe received them with friendliness, and took them round the camp, showing them everything that they wished to see.

One of them was noticeable in contrast to all the rest, as being small and ugly, with none of the swagger of the Sikh trooper. His dark-brown face was deeply pitted with smallpox, which had destroyed the sight of an eye; nothing, however, seemed to escape the glance of the remaining one. When he spoke, his voice was unusually soft and pleasant for a common soldier.

Their sight-seeing concluded, the Sikhs took farewell of their host, who kept his suspicions to himself. When they were back at Amritsar, the little ugly man told his Durbar that he saw it would not be to his advantage to quarrel with the English, and that therefore he would not give Holkar the support which had been demanded. The Sikhs might chafe at this decision, but would not rebel against their temporal head, the greatest man in all the Punjab.

It was now more than a hundred years that the Sikhs had been a thorn in the side of the rulers of Hindustan. The Emperor Aurangzib had made great efforts to put down this heretical sect, who, while disregarding the barriers of caste, and teaching that God was One, read a book called the "Granth" instead of the Koran, and revered certain teachers or "Gurus." One of these Gurus, Teg Bahadur, imprisoned in Delhi by the Emperor's orders, refused to save his life by working a miracle for the amusement of the Court. He was brought forth to execution, accused of daring to gaze from the roof of his prison towards the royal harem. "O King!" he cried, "I gazed not at the apartments of thy queens, but at the white race from over-seas that shall tear down thy purdahs, and slay thy sons in the streets of Delhi."

Guru Govind, his son and successor, swore vengeance for his father's death. The mystical brotherhood of which former Gurus had preached was changed into an armed confederacy; men of all races, castes, and creeds might enter it, did they undergo the rite of baptism, by which each man became one of the Khalsa, or elect, not only a "Sikh" or disciple, but also a "Singh" or lion.

For the next hundred years their fortunes varied. At one time defeated, their leader and chief men put to death with horrible tortures, they were driven to skulk in the waste places, the holes and dens of the earth, until the chaos produced by Nadir Shah's invasion allowed them to steal from their lairs to plunder both sides indifferently. Then for a season they were masters of Lahore and the sacred city of Amritsar, where they built their Golden Temple with marble from the tomb of Shah Jahan; then, driven out from the cities, they took refuge in the forts with which they had dotted the Punjab, and bided their time for another stroke at the hated Muslim, were he Moghul governor or Afghan invader.

By the end of the eighteenth century they were divided into twelve great confederacies, six holding lands to the south of the river Sutlej and six to the north.

In such leisure time as they could spare from warring with their Muslim neighbours, these clans fought among themselves. One of the most powerful among them, the Kanheyas, had a long-standing feud with a lesser clan, in the course of which their chief's eldest son was killed. The chief died of grief and mortification, and, according to Sikh custom, the leadership of the clan devolved upon the slain man's widow, Sada Kour.

The widow had no son; she had a baby daughter, who, contrary to the usage of her people, had not been put out of the way at birth. Sikhs as well as Rajputs refused to burden themselves with girls, and in one noble house of the Punjab there is no instance of a daughter living to be married till the year 1871. It may be said, in extenuation of this practice, that the Sikh women of whom anything is known were generally of such a disposition that the men might well fear to be troubled with any more of them.

Sada Kour was ambitious, and aimed at more than the headship of the Kanheyas. Before her father-in-law's death, she had wrung his consent to an arrangement by which her daughter was married to Ranjit Singh, the little son of the chief of the rival clan. Ranjit was no more than twelve years old when his father died, killed by his own excesses, and Sada Kour became virtually the head of both clans. To keep the power in her own hands, she arranged that Ranjit should grow up in total ignorance, unable to read or write, and encouraged him in all manner of shameful excess, so that his will should be softened and his constitution broken.

The only person who interfered with her was Ranjit's mother—not from tenderness to the boy, but because she wished to rule herself. Then Sada Kour contrived that Ranjit should learn of the scandal caused by his mother's lovers. Some say that Ranjit avenged the honour of his house by slaying the wretched woman, as his father is believed to have slain his own mother in like case; anyhow, she troubled Sada Kour no more.

In spite of his mother-in-law's education, Ranjit soon proved that he had both wits and energy.

His first great opportunity had come six years before his visit to Lake's camp. Shah Zeman was hurrying back to Afghanistan to suppress one of the chronic rebellions which had broken out during his absence in India, where he had been leading invading armies for several years, after the example of his grandfather, Ahmad Shah. The river Jehlam was in flood, and he was obliged to leave twelve of his heavy guns behind him. Ranjit Singh, who had paid homage to Zeman through a deputy, being engaged in turning the invasion to his own account by raiding the territory south of the Sutlej, received a promise that if he could recover the guns and send them after the Afghan army, he might call himself Raja of the city and district of Lahore.

It was a grant that cost Shah Zeman nothing, since Lahore was not his to give, being still in the possession of the descendants of the Sikh chieftains who had taken it by surprise from the Muslim governor some thirty years before. But the permission was enough for Ranjit, who led his army to Lahore, and was welcomed by the townsmen, who were very weary of their rulers, and thought that any change might be for the better.

Three years later, he drove another Sikh clan from Amritsar, and seized the city and all its treasures, including the great gun Zamzama, cast for Ahmad Shah Daurani, which whosoever owns is master of the Punjab, and which may still be seen outside the Museum at Lahore. One by one, as time served, he reduced other clans and chiefs, now in open warfare, now by seizing upon the lands of defenceless widows or newly-made orphans, until he became the head of all the Sikhs.

Sada Kour might well be proud of her work, but one fatal defect was likely to undo everything: her daughter had borne no child to Ranjit, and to make matters worse, a younger wife had given him a son—the only one of the many children attributed to him of whom he was the father. Sada Kour was desperate, and when Ranjit returned from one of his forays, she told him that her daughter had given birth to a son in his absence. He accepted the child with such philosophy that when it died in babyhood, Sada Kour was emboldened "to try the effect of twins."[1]

Every one, including Ranjit himself, knew that the two boys had been purchased for the occasion, and that the one was the son of a washerman, and the other of a carpenter. Ranjit durst not openly repudiate them. for he could not afford

[1] L. Griffin.

at the moment to quarrel with his mother-in-law, but he refused to give them the place and dignity of sons, and waited an opportunity for vengeance upon the woman who had dared to trick him.

## II.

Three years after his stolen visit to the camp, in defiance of all his sirdars, who had told him that the very sight of an Englishman would be unlucky, Ranjit was to meet Mr Metcalfe again.

There were two excuses for sending an envoy to the Court of Lahore. The dread of a French invasion of India was making the British Government anxious for a good understanding with all independent native rulers; and the Sikh chieftains between the Sutlej and the Jumna, alarmed by Ranjit's gradual "eating up" of his neighbours, had sent a mission to the Resident at Delhi begging for protection.

If Ranjit were to be the ally of the English, he must be paid for it, and his price was that he should be acknowledged as suzerain of all the Sikh states. When Metcalfe owned himself unable to grant so much, the Maharaja broke up his camp, and defiantly began to raid in Malwa and Sirhind.

The Governor-General, Lord Minto, lost patience;

the Maharaja must understand that all Cis-Sutlej chiefs were under British protection, and must restore at once all the territories he had seized in the last few months. In former years Ranjit himself had fixed the Sutlej as the southern boundary of his kingdom; he must keep to it.

Ranjit was furiously angry; why should the English interfere with him when he was ready to be their friend? By what right were they to come between him and the wish of his life? He mustered troops and collected ammunition; he prepared the fort at Amritsar for a siege; he even made some recognition of the spurious children that Sada Kour had imposed upon him in order to insure her support. The fate of the Punjab was hanging in the balance when the Muslim festival of the Moharram came round, and the Mahommedans in Metcalfe's suite at Amritsar went forth to mourn for the slaughtered Hussain and Hosein.

There was a certain sect among the Sikhs, the "Akalis" or Immortals, whose fanatical devotion resembled that of the Mahommedan Ghazis. Clad in little beyond their blue turbans, they would hurl their steel quoits and dash themselves headlong against an enemy's ranks, careless of death, if they might kill ere they were killed. Even Ranjit was unable to control them, though he made use of their enthusiasm in the day of battle.

About three or four thousand of them gathered round the place where the Envoy's soldiers were erecting the tinsel shrines to the martyrs of Kerbela, and began to destroy the biers. Finding peaceful persuasion of no use, Metcalfe collected the five hundred men of his escort and attacked the mob; a few were killed or wounded, the rest fled in disorder back to the city, while the sepoys resumed their ceremonies, in no way discomposed by the interruption.

Ranjit Singh had arrived at the close of the skirmish, shaking his cummerbund as a signal for peace, and had seen his "Immortals" put to rout by a tenth of their number. The lesson was not thrown away upon the Maharaja; until his troops were disciplined to the English standard it was hopeless for him to think of resistance.

There is a story that one night he sat with Metcalfe upon his palace roof. The Envoy urged the wisdom of an alliance with the English; Ranjit, sullen and wrathful, still chafed at having to resign his conquests. At last he broke away, without a word, and Metcalfe, looking down, saw him riding like a madman on the level ground beneath the palace walls. Then, springing from his horse, he came back to the roof, to give assent to all that was asked of him. All his fury of thwarted purpose seemed to have spent itself in that wild gallop, and he was courteous and reasonable as heart could wish.

In April 1809 he signed the treaty: perpetual friendship was to exist between the British Government and the State of Lahore; the British Government was to refrain from any interference with the territories and subjects of the Maharaja to the north of the Sutlej, while the Maharaja was not "to commit or suffer any encroachment" to the south.

It had been a hard struggle to bring himself to accept the treaty, but when once it was accomplished, Ranjit kept it faithfully to the day of his death. For nearly thirty years he was the staunch ally of the English, even when his sirdars urged him to join the anti-English Confederation, and on his refusal, tried to sting him into action by laying woman's apparel before him in durbar.

There were momentary fits of petulance when the old lion himself chafed against the English. Once he asked the son of one of his chiefs, who had received some sort of an English education, to show him the Punjab on a map. The Maharaja's one glittering eye followed the direction of the lad's finger. "What are those red marks?" he asked, and was told that they indicated British territory. "Soon it will be all red!" cried Ranjit, and he kicked away the map.

Withheld from extending his borders towards the south, the Maharaja tried to paint the north of his own colour. Most of all, he had set his heart upon wresting the town and province of Multan from the Afghan governors who had held it since the days of Nadir Shah. The fortress was supposed to be impregnable, and contained shrines which make it a holy place to all good Muslims; the city maintained a flourishing trade with Kabul, and its silk manufactures were renowned through Central Asia. In spite of a heat which seemed to bear out the legend that the sun is a spear's length nearer to Multan than to any city in the world, its gardens produced finer fruit than those of Hindustan, and it was shaded by groves of date-palms, sprung, says a legend, from the date stones thrown away by the army of Nadir Shah.

Four times had Ranjit's arms invested the city, and four times had the governor Muzaffar Khan held the fortress against them. No help could come from Afghanistan, where brother was fighting against brother for the throne of Ahmad Shah, and the English, to whom Khan and Maharaja alike had appealed, would not interfere. In February 1819 eighteen thousand Sikhs camped round the citadel, where two thousand Afghans waited for them. The great gun Zamzama was dragged up from Lahore, and the gates were blown in, but the garrison entrenched themselves behind earthworks. The women and children took refuge in the great mosque, the dome of which was strong enough to keep out the Sikh balls. Food ran short, and the garrison dwindled hour by hour. Some lay dead, and some lay ill; some yielded to the bribes of which Ranjit was lavish, and went over to the besiegers. Up to the last, he offered lands and honours to Muzaffar Khan in return for the surrender of the crumbling walls and ruinous defences through which Zamzama had made wide breaches; and up to the last his offers were refused. Only three hundred men, nearly all of the Khan's own tribe, remained within the citadel, and they, like himself, would not sell their honour. Then came a June morning when an Akali, drugged with opium, led a handful of men into an outwork of the fort while the worn-out garrison slept; the Sikhs in the trenches followed; they pressed through the breaches, and carried the fortress by storm.

One of the chief officers of the garrison went to take farewell of his wife before going to meet the enemy for the last time, and found her digging a hole in the ground to bury her jewels. "Woman, would you be taken for the wife of a Jat zamindar?" was his stern rebuke. "Put on your ornaments, that you may be known for the wife of a Pathan. Of what use are jewels to her who has lost her husband?"

Muzaffar Khan, his long white beard and hair streaming in the breeze, waited for the enemy at the gate, his eight sons beside him. "Come out, man to man!" they shouted, as the Sikhs levelled their guns upon them. "Let us fall in fair fight." The Sikhs durst not come within hand's reach of desperate men, and the old hero, obstinately refusing quarter, was shot down by their matchlocks. Five of his sons and a daughter died with him.

The wealth stored in Multan was said to be enormous, and Ranjit was ill-pleased on receiving no more than two lakhs of rupees for his share when the army returned to Lahore. So he made proclamation that "the plunder of Multan was the property of the state," and that every man, officer or common soldier, in possession of money or valuables taken in the three days' pillage of the fort, was to bring the same in to his treasury. Some five lakhs was the result of this high-handed proceeding, and it was said that there was much more which remained with private owners. Little good did the spoil of Multan bring to any of its possessors, nearly all of whom are said by popular tradition to have come to a bad end.

Kashmir, which had also been the object of

how to wring the last coin from the wretched cultivator. Nevertheless, he was not actually driven off the land. "The Sikh farmer of revenue did not wish to kill the goose that laid the golden eggs, but he plucked its feathers as closely as he dared."[1] The accounts were audited severely by Ranjit himself. "A true statement he does not reckon among possibilities, so that when the accounts seem all fair and square, and the revenue rendered even exceeds the stipulated sum, he always disallows a certain percentage, the tenacity of his memory enabling him to follow out the most complicated statements."[2]

There are horrible stories of the cruelty of some of the Sikh governors, such as Gulab Singh, who would flay men alive, and Avitabile, the Italian, who introduced hanging as a punishment at Peshawar, and was guilty "of the ostentation of adding two or three to the string suspended from the gibbet on special days and festivals." Ranjit himself was not cruel, according to the standard of his race and his time. He never ordered an execution in cold blood, and he almost invariably provided for the families of his conquered enemies. He was thoroughly selfish, and could treat a faithful follower with shameless ingratitude, but

[1] Sir L. Griffin. [2] Sir H. Lawrence.

there was a certain amount of rough justice in his ordinary methods. He had many favourites, but even when half paralysed and broken, he was strong enough rather to govern them than be governed by them, and one of his amusements was to stir them up to quarrel in his presence, so that he might learn their true characters. There was sometimes a certain grim humour in his methods—as when he sent word to a family that had been boasting of the lavishness with which one of its daughters had been married and dowered, that "those who could spend so much on a marriage must be able to afford to give him fifty thousand rupees."

"In the respectable virtues he had no part," says Sir Lepel Griffin, and after reading how Ranjit kept his troops twelve months in arrears of pay from sheer avarice, how he despoiled the sons of men who had served him truly, and how he paraded through the streets of his capital during the Holi festival, on an elephant, in shameless drunkenness, with a woman of undeniable reputation at his side, it is difficult not to agree. Yet, for all his failings, he was king and soldier, and was feared and respected to his very last hour, even after speech had gone, and he could command by signs only.

## III.

Upon at least two occasions in his life Ranjit must have enjoyed a triumph thoroughly.

One was the discomfiture of Sada Kour. As the Maharaja's power waxed, hers had waned. When Prince Kharak, Ranjit's true heir, was married with great ceremony, she alone of the royal family was not present, and it was said that her mortification at her failure in imposing the spurious "twins" upon her son-in-law had kept her away. One of the boys was almost an idiot; but the other, Sher Singh, was handsome and spirited enough to please any father, and as he grew up, he clamoured to have a fief of his own and a separate establishment. Ranjit bade him apply to his "grandmother," who called him her heir, but was resolute that what he needed should come from his reputed father. At the age of twelve, Sher Singh, who was as brave as he was stupid, was sent with a force against the Hazaras, and behaved with great courage. When he returned, the Maharaja visited Sada Kour, who was then in camp a few miles from Lahore, and suggested that she was growing old, and should be released from the cares of this world; let her give up her property to her "grandsons," and be free to think upon her latter end. The princess durst not refuse; she signed the deed which settled half her lands upon the two boys, but when this was done, she hurried to one of her estates, whence she applied for leave to dwell under protection of the English beyond the Sutlej.

Ranjit soon heard of this project, and summoned her to Lahore to answer for intriguing with the English, who had interfered once with him, and might do it again. She escaped by night in a covered palki, but was overtaken by a troop of his horse, and sent to imprisonment for the rest of her life. She beat her breast continually in her despair, she cursed the son-in-law whom she had helped to a throne; but the prison walls held her close for the little remaining time that she had to live. Thirteen years had Ranjit waited to pay his debt, and he was not one to forgive.

The crowning triumph of Ranjit's policy was in the winter of 1838, when the Governor-General, Lord Auckland, visited Lahore in state. In June had been signed the Tripartite Treaty by which the East India Company and the Maharaja undertook to replace Shah Shuja upon the throne of Afghanistan, and it was necessary above all things to flatter and conciliate England's ally and partner in an extremely hazardous experiment.

Ranjit made great display of all his troops and his treasures, to impress his new allies. Miss Eden, Lord Auckland's sister, writes of "thousands all dressed in yellow or red satin, with quantities of their led horses trapped in silver and gold tissues, and all of them sparkling with jewels"; of driving for two miles and a half through a lane of Ranjit's bodyguard, half of them dressed in yellow satin with gold scarfs and shawls, half in cloth of gold, and all bearing gold arms, and shields and lances studded with gold; of a line of troops extending four miles and a half, which at first she took for a white wall with a red coping. In the midst of all this splendour, the Maharaja wore "a red stuff dress, with a little edging of the commonest grey squirrel fur, and a common red muslin turban," and looked "exactly like an old mouse with grey whiskers and one eye."

He was in the highest spirits at the Governor-General's visit, laughed and jested, and nearly poisoned some of the gentlemen of the suite by plying them with his favourite drink—a spirit distilled from dried grapes, saffron, and cardamoms, mixed with pearls ground to powder. He astonished his sirdars by taking the Governor-

General into the fort of Govindgarh where all his treasures were kept. Up to the last moment no one would believe that he would really admit Lord Auckland within his gates, which had been closed against all visitors, and when Governor-General and Maharaja went in together, "even the common soldiers said that they now saw that the Sikhs and English were to be one family, and to live in the same house." Jealous and suspicious as he had always shown himself, Ranjit at last had made up his mind that the English were to be trusted.

If his life could have been prolonged, the history of the Punjab for the next few years might have been less dismal to tell; but although his constitution was of the toughest, it was breaking under the strain of the life that he had led. He was half paralysed, and had to be lifted on to the back of the horse that he still rode with ease and grace. During Lord Auckland's visit, he had one or two alarming attacks of illness, which the English doctor was unable to do much to relieve, as the Maharaja always refused to take any medicine unless he first tried its effects upon some of his *entourage*, and then, if the results did not please him, declined it altogether.

He lingered into the summer, his mind clear, though his speech had failed. "By a slight turn of his hand to the south he would inquire the news from the British frontier; by a similar turn to the west he would demand tidings from the invading army." He struggled hard for life, but the "musk, ambergris, pounded pearls, sandal and almonds" of the native doctors availed him as little as the dispersion of his hoarded treasures among Sikh and Hindu shrines. "What will become of us if you give everything away?" wailed Kharak Singh and the sirdars, sitting round his bed; the Maharaja wept also, but dread was stronger than avarice, and his jewels, his elephants, and his horses were sent, one after another, to propitiate the gods, until on June 27th 1839, the end which he had greatly feared would be held off no longer.

# XV.

## CHIEFS IN THE NORTH—1773-1841

"Dost Mohammad is calm, prudent, and wise in cabinet, and an able commander in the field. In treachery, cruelty, murder, and falsehood he is equally notorious. . . . On the whole, whatever odium may be attached to the Amir of Kabul, it is an unquestionable fact that he is the only person fit to rule Kabul."—MOHUN LAL, *Life of Dost Mohammad.*

# XV.

## CHIEFS IN THE NORTH—1773-1841.

THERE are certain gems which are said to influence the fate of their possessors. Some, as they pass from hand to hand, bring good fortune—but the greater number bring a curse. Among the latter was the great diamond of the Moghul Emperors of Hindustan.

Some would trace its story back to the misty days when the Five Brothers dwelt on the plain where the cities of Delhi rose, one by one, in after time. But leaving myth and tradition aside, it is certain that a very great diamond came into the possession of Shah Jahan, who placed it upon the Peacock Throne. When Nadir Shah came down from Persia, and for nine hours the gutters of Delhi ran with the blood of its slaughtered inhabitants, the treasure which he coveted most of all was the diamond. Great was his wrath and disappointment when, having forced the wretched

Mohammad Shah to surrender the Peacock Throne, the most valuable of its jewels was found to be missing.

Every one, of course, professed ignorance of its hiding-place, and Nadir chafed in impotent fury, until a woman of the Emperor's harem, bribed to betray her master, revealed that the diamond was hidden in a fold of Mohammad's turban.

Nadir bided his time, until the hour when he was to take formal leave of the Moghul Emperor before returning to his own land. There, in the despoiled Hall of Audience, sat the miserable descendant of Akbar, surrounded by his nobles, longing for the moment when they should see the last of their terrible guest. The Persian embraced the Moghul, with the assurances of friendship. "Henceforth we are brothers; in pledge thereof, behold my turban."

An exchange of turbans has long been the pledge of friendship in Eastern lands. Mohammad durst not refuse. It was his destiny to lose the diamond, as he had lost all else, and no expression of his face betrayed what he felt while he took the turban from his head. The Persian's greedy fingers were already searching amongst the folds, and as he drew forth the jewel from its place of concealment, he involuntarily burst into the exclamation, "Koh-i-Nur!" (Mountain of Light), by which name it has been known ever since that day.

The greatest diamond in the world belonged by right to the strongest hand. It had brought no luck to the Emperor Mohammad, who died in such poverty that he was buried in an old clock-case; and it brought no luck to Nadir Shah, whose life henceforth was made wretched by his distrust of all around him, including his own son, whom he blinded on a false suspicion. He was planning the slaughter of every Persian in his army when some of his own nobles, wearied of his insane cruelty, assassinated him at midnight in his tent; his empire fell to pieces, and his treasures were parted among new owners.

In the confusion that followed, Ahmad Shah, an Afghan of the Daurani tribe, contrived to lay hands upon the diamond, which he had long marked for his own. At the age of three-and-twenty he was elected King of Afghanistan by the wild tribes of the north, the Abdalis, the Ghilzais, the Biluchis, the Hazaras, and Kizilbashis, who had determined to break loose from Persia after the death of Nadir Shah. It is not many who have been able to rule the Afghan tribes, who call no man master, and whose natural occupations are war, murder, and plunder. But Ahmad Shah understood the art of governing his fellow-countrymen. Fight they must, and to keep them quiet at home they must have war abroad. He seized Kabul, Ghazni, and Herat; four times did he invade India; he destroyed the great confederate army of the Marathas on the field of Panipat; his son's bride, a princess of the royal house of Delhi, brought the Punjab and Sind as her dowry. But before he was an old man he was attacked by cancer in the face. "Cure it," he bade his physician. "I can cure it," answered the wise man, "but the cure will kill you."

At his death, in 1773, he was succeeded by his second son, Timur, a strong man like his father, but preferring peace to war. His aim was to decrease in every way the power and influence of the tribal chiefs, and to keep all the real authority in his own hands. A well-regulated civil service and well-ordered finances might be desirable in other countries: the hill-men were not in a state to profit by them. Outlying provinces revolted; there were rebellions and conspiracies; the kingdom was seething with discontent, when Timur died after a reign of twenty years, leaving no instructions about the succession, but leaving three-and-twenty sons who might dispute it.

It was the opportunity of the tribal chiefs, and

they did not let it slip. They were weary of being governed by the strong hand. "We are content with discord," confessed one of them to Mountstuart Elphinstone; "we are content with alarms; we are content with blood, but we will never be content with a master." One son of Timur after another was set upon his throne, the puppet of one of the great chiefs, who paid off old scores against rival clans in the king's name. During the greater part of the next forty years the condition of Afghanistan may be described in the words originally applied to the kingdom of Poland, "a state of anarchy tempered by frequent revolutions."

Zaman Shah was first to be chosen king, thanks to the intrigues of his mother, who sent her veil to the chief of the Barakzai clan—the most humble entreaty that a woman could make,—begging him to support her son. Deposed, betrayed to his enemies by the Mulla with whom he took refuge, he found an opportunity of hiding his most precious jewels in the wall of the room where he was made prisoner. Blinded and a captive, he yet hugged the knowledge that the brother in whose name he had been cast down knew not where to find the Koh-i-Nur. It was not until that brother had been deposed in his turn, to make room for a third, Shah Shuja, that some official, happening to touch the wall of the room where Zaman had been confined, scratched his hand against something sharp-pointed. He picked at the crumbling plaster, in idle curiosity, and discovered the fatal diamond, which Shah Shuja, the new king of Afghanistan, wore henceforth in a bracelet on his arm.

Shah Shuja was an Arabic scholar, and might have won credit as a minor poet; as a ruler of Afghanistan he was not successful. After revolts and civil wars, extending over several years, he was obliged to flee from the country, and fell into the hands of the rebel governor of Kashmir, who tried every means of persuasion to induce him to part with the few jewels he was supposed to have secreted.

Meanwhile, his chief Begam and some of his family had sought refuge with Ranjit Singh at Lahore. The shrewd old Maharaja was always ready to take advantage of other men's troubles for his own ends. He meant to profit by the confusion in Afghanistan to extend his own frontier, and he would not protect Shuja's family without gaining something for himself. So he set to work upon the Begam, and, other arguments proving ineffectual, placed a guard about her house, so that her servants could bring no food to her.

At the end of two days she yielded so far as to surrender some of her treasures, amongst them the great balas ruby which Timur the Lame had carried away from Delhi at the end of the fourteenth century. But she would say nothing of the diamond.

Then Ranjit, fearing to what lengths an obstinate woman's determination might carry her, and not wishing for the scandal of her death, changed his treatment, offered bribes instead of threats, and the Begam condescended to name her terms. Her husband must be relieved from captivity, and there must be pensions for herself and certain others whom she named.

Forthwith word was sent to Kashmir, and the captive was released and brought to Lahore. But having gone so far, Ranjit was in no haste to keep his promise about the pension, and the Begam suddenly recollected that neither she nor her husband was in possession of the stone any longer: it had been pawned to a merchant at Kandahar.

Whereupon the Maharaja replaced his cordon of guards, and for a month the exiles endured semi-starvation. The Begam was dauntless as ever, but Shuja's spirit had been broken by his misfortunes, and he sent word to Ranjit through a confidant that he was ready to yield up the diamond for a consideration.

Ranjit himself came to visit his guests, and swore "by the Granth of Baba Nanak and his own sword" to grant certain fiefs to Shuja and his heirs for ever, and to help him with troops and treasure to regain his lost throne. For an hour the two sat opposite to each other, neither speaking a word; then Ranjit's patience gave way, and he bade the confidant remind Shuja of his promise. Shuja made a sign to a slave, who laid a packet on the carpet at an equal distance between them. Ranjit ordered it to be opened, and cried out in exultation when the diamond flashed out upon them.

"At what price do you value it?" he asked Shah Shuja, who answered, "At good luck, for it has ever been the associate of him who has vanquished his foes."

If the unhappy prince had hoped to break the spell of his ill-fortune by giving up the diamond, he was mistaken. He was stripped of everything else that was worth having, including the exquisite green enamel scent-sprinkler, with its pattern of white jasmine flowers, made long ago for Shah Jahan, and borne away with the spoils of Delhi by Nadir Shah.[1] Treated as prisoner, not as ally, he thought of Ludhiana, where his brother, Shah Zaman, had been living for some

[1] Now in the India Museum.

time under British protection. The ladies of his harem were disguised, and smuggled in covered carts out of Lahore. A stricter guard was set in consequence upon Shah Shuja, who was watched day and night. The few trusty attendants left to him bored through seven other chambers to the outside of the building; one remained in bed to impersonate him, and two more followed as, disguised in a beggar's dress, he climbed through the holes in the walls into the street and made his escape from the city by the main sewer.

Once beyond the gates of Lahore, he dreamed of recovering his kingdom; but such forces as he could muster were driven back from Kashmir by a heavy fall of snow, and he came disconsolate to his family at Ludhiana. Later attempts upon the throne of Kabul proved equally fruitless, until his evil destiny, or the spell of the diamond, brought him back for the last time—only to perish miserably.

## II.

There are certain pages in the history of the English in India which Englishmen would rather leave unread. It is small consolation to say that they are very few, and that there are many more in the history of other dominant nations. The pages are there, and nothing can blot them out. They shall be turned as quickly as possible, but let it be noted that even on the blackest page may be found certain passages which light up the blackness. If the heroism, the honesty, the unselfishness of certain men could not wipe out the ill-doing of a few in high places, they went far to atone for it.

Early in the nineteenth century Russian aggression was the bugbear of English politicians. Russian influence was paramount in Central Asia and Persia. England looked uneasily towards the "buffer states" to the north-west of her possessions in India. The most important of these were Afghanistan and the Punjab. Ranjit Singh long ago had made up his mind that his interests could best be served by alliance with the English, and he professed himself ready to stand with them. But Afghanistan was an uncertain quantity.

After many years of civil strife under the nominal rule of one or other of Timur's three-and-twenty sons, the greater part of the country was now enjoying peace—as the term was there understood—under Dost Mohammad Khan, of the clan from whom the prime ministers of Afghanistan were chosen. At first he and his elder brother, Azim Khan, had set up rival claimants to the throne in the persons of two otherwise negligible sons of Timur Shah; Dost Mohammad's nominee was murdered by Azim's nominee, after which the two brothers joined in an expedition against the Sikhs, apparently the best of friends, until word came to Azim that Dost Mohammad had secretly allied himself with Ranjit. Azim knew his brother too well to neglect the warning; he fled precipitately, dying before he could reach Kabul. Dost Mohammad, after some years of stress and toil, and after conscientious attempts on the part of all the chiefs concerned to establish the public peace by the assassination of rivals, succeeded in making himself master of Kabul Ghazni, Jalalabad, and Kandahar. In 1835 he had been proclaimed Amir at a great durbar in Kabul—modestly avowing that his poverty would not allow him to call himself Shah, after the example of the Daurani rulers.

A tall handsome man, with the marked Jewish features which have caused some persons to derive the Afghans from the Ten Lost Tribes, in his good points—of which he was not destitute—as well as in his vices, he was a type of his countrymen. He was entirely uneducated; before becoming Amir, his life had been a scandal to all with an elementary sense of decency or morality. He was recklessly brave, and first attracted the notice of his elder brothers by slaying an enemy of their house in broad day in the crowded streets of Peshawar when only fourteen years old. Even when power and responsibility had taught him better, he knew no higher law than his own will. A strong, reckless man, he respected strength in others, however it might be manifested, and first learned to esteem a wife forced upon him by necessities of state when he saw her eat fifty eggs at a sitting. By dint of industriously stirring up the innumerable blood feuds of the chiefs, he contrived to keep them too busy with each other to have leisure to combine against him. His cruelty was notorious. An English officer once asked him, "Is it really true that you have caused twelve thousand of your subjects to be flayed alive?" "Never!" exclaimed the Dost, in visible horror. "At the utmost, it was only three hundred."

It was to his court at Kabul that both Russia and England sent a mission in 1837. Our envoy was Captain Alexander Burnes of the Bombay Infantry, a keen soldier, a great Oriental scholar, who had previously visited Kabul in 1835, when making a tour through Central Asia. He was now sent with instructions to conclude "a commercial treaty" with Afghanistan.

At first Dost Mohammad received him with

great cordiality, and the fact that certain of the chiefs—amongst them his own brothers—inclined to the Russian alliance, made him all the more anxious for a connection with England. It seems incredible that we should have thrown away this opportunity deliberately, but so it was. The one point upon which the Amir insisted was that we should put pressure on our ally, Ranjit Singh, to restore Peshawar, upon which he had seized at an opportune moment when the ruler of Afghanistan was incapable of holding it. Lord Auckland refused to allow this, and censured Burnes for having shown too much favour to the Amir.

Then came the turn of Russia, whose agent, Captain Vikovich, at first received coldly, and scarcely admitted to the Amir's presence, was overwhelmed with attentions when he promised money and support. The Amir was bitterly mortified by our refusal to do anything for him except to prevent Ranjit from attacking Afghanistan—which, as he well knew, the Maharaja was far too astute to attempt under present conditions. "I had a turban of muslin," he complained, "and I had thought that the English would help me to change it into one of shawl." And he repeated, "It is not I who have abandoned the English—it is the English who have abandoned me."

All concerned in this ill-fated experiment were destined to be abandoned or betrayed. Burnes' despatches were garbled before they were given to the printer, so as to make it appear he had represented Dost Mohammad as hostile, and had urged for war. The fraud was exposed, twenty years later, when Burnes had been hacked to pieces in Kabul. Vikovich, on his return to Petersburg, was disowned by Count Nesselrode (with whom our Government had been expostulating) as "an adventurer lately engaged in some unauthorised intrigues." He went back to his hotel, wrote a few lines of reproach to those who had first made use of him and then cast him aside, burned all his other papers, and shot himself.

Having committed one act of folly by quarrelling with Dost Mohammad, the British Government now proceeded to crown it by arranging to depose him from his throne, and replace Shah Shuja in his stead. "They proposed to depose the ruler who out of chaos had evolved at least a semblance of order, a form of government, and, most certainly, a respect for authority, . . . and to replace him by a prince who had already enjoyed the opportunity of ruling and who had failed; who had twice attempted to force his return, and been driven back; and who, when at one time victory was in his grasp, had preferred flight to making the effort requisite to gain it."[1]

But the siege of Herat by the Persian army was filling English statesmen with alarm; the nominal pretext was the desire of the Shah to wrest the city from the Afghans, but there were Russian officers in its ranks, and the attempt was held to have been inspired by the Russian Ambassador at Teheran. The Russian Cabinet denied this, but without succeeding in convincing public opinion of their good faith. For ten months the siege dragged on; within the walls was a young lieutenant of Bombay Artillery, Eldred Pottinger, and it was he who inspired and led the resistance of the garrison, until the great army drew back, baffled and discomfited.

The "Russian terror" then subsided, but too late to save us from the consequences of our actions. Lord Auckland had already signed the Tripartite Treaty of Lahore, with Ranjit Singh and Shah Shuja. Our forces and those of the Sikhs were to co-operate in replacing Shah Shuja, who undertook to prevent all other foreigners from invading Sikh or British territory; Ranjit was to keep Peshawar and the states on the Indus in return for his support.

[1] Malleson.

## III.

It was a triumphant "Army of Occupation" that marched into Kabul in August 1839. In their midst, on a white charger, trapped with gold, his royal robes covered with jewels, rode Shah Shuja, and with him were the British Envoy, William Macnaghten, and Alexander Burnes, who had been appointed to the Mission.

Good reason had they to be proud. Kandahar had been entered without opposition; the strong fortress of Ghazni, deemed impregnable by the Afghans, had been carried by storm in a few hours. Dost Mohammad was a homeless fugitive; Koran in hand, he had ridden out among his troops, and besought them in the name of Allah and the Prophet to make a last stand against the Feringhi dogs. "You have eaten my salt these thirteen years; if ye will have a new master, grant me a last favour—let me die with honour." Only a small handful of men had come to his side; the rest had determined to worship the rising sun. The Dost saw that nothing was to be saved but life; his disorderly troops were surging to and fro, his guards had melted away, his servants were already cutting his carpets to pieces and rifling his tent. "Take all that you find within," he cried, and urged his horse to the mountains. Captain James Outram rode hard at his heels, with Lawrence, Broadfoot, and certain other picked men, but they were thwarted by one of the Afghan chiefs in their company, who had betrayed every leader whom he ever served, and now contrived to delay the pursuit until the Amir was over the Afghan border, beyond which they might not follow him. All his family, except two sons, were in our hands.

So fair was the prospect, that it was generally expected that the English forces were about to withdraw and leave Shah Shuja and his subjects to themselves. But there was a fear that Dost Mohammad might find allies among the chiefs of the Hindu-Kush, and descend again upon Kabul. It was therefore arranged that for the present the greater part of the army should remain in Afghanistan.

Dost Mohammad continued a source of alarm for the next few months; as he said of himself, "I am like a wooden spoon; you may throw me hither and thither but I shall not be hurt." At one time he was a prisoner in Bokhara; then he escaped, and led General Sale up and down Kohistan. There was universal terror when in an engagement early in November he rode with his blue standard into the front of the battle, and drove the 2nd Bengal Cavalry before him in headlong rout.

Next day, Sir William Macnaghten was returning from his evening ride, dolefully meditating upon a letter just received from Burnes, who considered that nothing was left for the force but retirement on Kabul. As he came near the Residency, a horseman rode up to him and asked whether he were the Envoy. When assured of this, the stranger announced, "The Amir is here." "What Amir?" asked Macnaghten. "Dost Mohammad Khan"—and the Dost rode up, sprang from his horse, and gave his sword into the Envoy's hands.

In spite of his success, he had realised that the game was ended for the present, and he knew that the English would be fantastically generous to a vanquished foe.

For ten days he remained in Kabul, as guest rather than prisoner, visited by all the officers of the garrison, who, we are told, "did all they could to soothe his feelings." When he was sent down under escort to India, there was general regret that such a "wonderful fellow" should have been deposed in favour of Shuja.

His last act in Kabul was characteristic of the man. Macnaghten, to assist in the process of soothing his feelings, sent a shawl-merchant to his tent, with instructions that the Dost was to choose any shawls that he pleased. The prisoner carefully selected the best, pricing them himself. When the English officers were all out of the way he sent again for the merchant. "I have made the Feringhis pay twice the value of the shawls; give me the half of your profits on them."

With our most dangerous enemy a prisoner in Ludhiana, all seemed fair weather. When it was evident that our occupation of Kabul was to be prolonged, officers had sent for their wives and families to enjoy the cool, bracing air of the north. Lady Macnaghten was there, and Lady Sale, the wife of the General. English and Afghans enjoyed each other's sports, the Afghans entering horses for the English races, or watching cricket and football, the English betting on fights of cocks or quails. Wrestling matches were popular, and when the lake near Kabul was frozen over, the Afghans, who could beat the Englishmen in sliding, were amazed at seeing them skate. Afghan chiefs received English officers at their houses, and were entertained in turn. Plays acted by the English were a great amusement to an Afghan audience, when translated as they went on, by Burnes, who was still at Kabul, as he said himself, "in the most nondescript of situations"

—his employment being "to draw a large salary every month, and give advice that was never taken."[1]

In August 1841, Macnaghten could write, "The country is perfectly quiet from Dan to Beersheba."

Yet signs of storm had been plain from the beginning to those who had eyes to see. Some had been foresighted or honest enough to protest against the whole proceeding, but their warnings were unheeded. Our Sikh auxiliaries were mutinous; the old Lion of the Punjab had died on the very day on which our forces had left Kandahar for Ghazni, and the weak hands of his successor could not hold the reins. It was all too evident that Shah Shuja was not popular with his subjects; he was haughty and miserly, too proud to give his daughters in marriage to the chiefs, but keeping them within his palace, unwed. Dost Mohammad, whatever his shortcomings, had at least been accessible to gentle and simple; any man might cling to his skirt, when he rode forth, and call for justice. But this King was never to be seen unless surrounded by white-faced infidels, who helped him to gather in his taxes.

So there were revolts and insurrections all over the country; the Khaibaris were discontented, the Ghilzais rose, right and left; Akbar Khan, son of

[1] Kaye.

the Dost, heedless of his father's injunctions to come in and make peace, was moving about on the Bamian frontier.

Worst of all, the Government of India was beginning to find that a puppet king is a costly toy. At least a million and a quarter a year were drained from their Treasury for the support of Shah Shuja, and they were beginning to feel that they did not get their money's value. The Court of Directors, therefore, urged Macnaghten to cut down expenses.

It has always been characteristic of English policy to be extravagant where there is no need, and to be miserly where the occasion calls for lavishness. Macnaghten had begun by scattering gold with both hands; now, to save a few thousands, he cut down the stipends of the chiefs of Kohistan, whose duty it was to keep the mountain passes open, and answer for any outrages committed within their jurisdiction. "At a time when the maintenance of our position in Afghanistan depended on our army, and our army alone,"[1] we broke our compact with the men who had it in their power to cut off communications with India.

The Ghilzais had ever refused to submit to a conqueror. In the days of Nadir Shah they had

[1] Malleson.

fled to the depths of their hills, where for months together they lived upon such roots as they could dig out of the snow, sending him a handful with the message, "So long as we can find these, we will not submit." While their pay was continued, it was to their interest to be the friends of the English; but if bribery was no longer to be used they had little fear of coercion. Accordingly, the word was passed round, and at the beginning of October, 1841, the Kurd Kabul pass was blocked.

This was doubly inconvenient, as Sir William Macnaghten was on the point of returning to India, having been appointed Governor of Bombay, in recognition of his services. With him was to travel General Elphinstone, who had applied to be relieved from the command at Kabul. Loved and respected by nearly all who knew him, he had two fatal defects—he had no Indian experience, and he was almost helpless with fever and rheumatic gout. For a time he had struggled to do his work, but after three months of "almost incessant severe illness," he had realised that to remain "would be useless to the public service and distressing to himself."

The journey had to be postponed—"for a fortnight," they said, little guessing that it was to be for ever. Hints of their danger were given on all sides, but no one in authority would heed them.

It was known that Shuja's own servants were conspiring with the enemy; a friendly chief warned an English officer, who sent on the intelligence to Burnes, that "all Afghanistan was determined to get rid of the Feringhis, and that the whole country was ready to break out."

But nothing was done—no attempt even was made to strengthen our position at Kabul. At first our troops had been quartered in the strong fortified palace called the "Bala Hissar," but in the previous year Shah Shuja had demanded this for his harem, and Macnaghten had yielded. The cantonments were in the worst possible position, on a piece of low swampy ground, commanded on all sides by hills and forts, and the commissariat stores had been placed outside, in a detached building, which would be practically indefensible in the event of an uprising.

It was small wonder if the Afghans believed that the infidels had been blinded by God, and given over to them for a prey.

# XVI.

## THE ILLUSTRIOUS GARRISON—
## November 1841–April 1842

"Trust in God, but tether your camel."—*Arab Proverb.*

## XVI.

## THE ILLUSTRIOUS GARRISON—

### NOVEMBER 1841–APRIL 1842.

SOME time before the Afghanistan campaign, the 13th was reckoned among the worst of all regiments in her Majesty's service.

The greater number of its men died from the effects of the Burmese climate, and the ranks were filled up with the offscourings of the London streets and jails—a sullen, ill-conditioned rabble, whom the first taste of discipline impelled to covert mutiny. Several officers were shot; there were attempts to stab others, and letters poured in upon the Colonel, Robert Sale, threatening to serve him in like manner.

After receiving one of these, the Colonel would put it into his pocket, ride down to parade, and give the order to the regiment to load with blank cartridge and fire, sitting unmoved before them, an easy target—then turn away, remarking, "Ah, if you don't shoot me, it's not my fault."

It took what modern disciplinarians would consider an inhuman amount of flogging to reduce the regiment to order; but it was done, with the result that the 13th became "as quiet as lambs" (excepting when they were called upon to fight), and adored their commander, whom they had nicknamed. "Fighting Bob."

His habit of riding two miles ahead of his men, and engaging hand to hand in every action, made for popularity with the rank and file, though it caused needless anxiety to his staff, who repeatedly urged that a general was not required to do the work of a private. To all remonstrances Sale returned promises of amendment, but was certain to be in the forefront of the next battle, his vivid blue eyes dancing with excitement.

He had marched to Kabul in 1839, having by this time become a brigadier-general. When his regiment stormed Ghazni, he fought his way through the breach, and was gripped by a gigantic Afghan, in whose embrace he rolled over and over, among fallen stones and shivered beams, until for a moment he came uppermost, and was enabled to cleave the chief's skull with a blow of his sabre.

In the shower of honours that descended upon the Mission after the occupation of Kabul, Sale was made a K.C.B. Experts have decided that he was nothing of a general, avoiding responsibility, and lacking dash and initiative. He had at least enough military knowledge to protest against giving up the Bala Hissar to Shah Shuja's harem, and quartering the Mission in cantonments.

Reliefs having come up to Kabul, it was arranged that Sale's brigade should go down to India, and accordingly they started at the beginning of October. The force included the 13th and the 35th Native Infantry, a squadron of the 5th Bengal Light Cavalry, and a hundred of the very irregular and highly efficient Corps of Sappers, whom Captain George Broadfoot had raised among the broken clans of the hills, some of whom had begun by fighting against the English with almost as much energy and goodwill as they were to display in fighting for them.

They found the passes blocked—for the reason already explained,—and had to fight their way through the Butkak gorge and the Tazin valley, down to the military post of Gandamak, having sustained a certain number of casualties, and lost great part of their baggage in the skirmishes with the Ghilzais.

It was while they rested at Gandamak that disquieting rumours began to be spread abroad. No news had reached them from Kabul for nearly three weeks; the tribesmen of the valley, who at first had been eager to make their submission and bring supplies, were now swaggering with more than their usual insolence, and swept off most of the cattle turned out to graze beyond the walls. On November 10th came ill news. There had been an insurrection at Kabul; Sir Alexander Burnes had been murdered in his own house, with his brother and William Broadfoot, and their bodies cast into the street; Shah Shuja was besieged in the Bala Hissar, and the English Mission in its cantonments. Macnaghten sent orders that Sale was to return to Kabul "at all risks."

Whether the majority of the council of war that decided to disobey this order were right or wrong, is a question for military experts. So far as Sale was concerned, the return to Kabul must have been what he most desired; his wife, to whom he was devoted, and his lately married daughter, had both been left in the Mission cantonment. But he was too honest to deny his conviction that the return was, "in a military sense, impracticable." There were three hundred sick and wounded, whom he durst not leave at Gandamak, and could not take back to Kabul; the whole of the camp equipage was destroyed, he had little transport, and only a limited amount of ammunition. He could not even remain where he was, since he was unable to command food or water for a day, and was hemmed in on all sides by hostile tribes, who might at any moment seize upon Jalalabad, and cut off his little force entirely.

So the decision was made, not to return to Kabul, but to march upon Jalalabad before the Afghans had taken possession of it.

The citizens of Jalalabad imagined that the English were on their way down to Hindustan, and when on the 12th of November they beheld Sale's brigade marching in at one city gate, they fled helter-skelter through another, too much surprised to think of resistance. The city and all it contained was in the hands of the English, without a shot having been fired.

Yet, when they came to examine their prize, there seemed little reason for exultation. The old winter capital of the Daurani kings had fallen into complete decay. There were three circles of ramparts around it, all broken or embedded in houses. The ditches were filled up, "to the consistency of thoroughfares," and roads led across and over the ramparts into the country. "There was a space of four hundred yards together, on which none of the garrison could show themselves excepting at one spot; the population within was disaffected, and the whole enceinte was surrounded by ruined forts, walls, mosques, tombs, and gardens, from which a fire could be opened upon the defenders at twenty and thirty yards."[1]

The stocks of provisions amounted to just one half-day's supply of flour, and some barley and Indian corn. All private baggage perforce had been left at Gandamak, and had been pillaged and burned by a regiment of Shah Shuja's cavalry quartered there, who made common cause with the rebels as soon as the brigade departed. Nothing had been brought on the march except such ammunition, hospital and commissariat stores as they had been able to collect.

As the wearied troops lay down to rest by companies, with their officers beside them, the tribesmen were flocking round the walls, fierce as wild bees disturbed from their nests. Their fires blazed in all directions; their wild dances and shouts of "Huk! huk!" resounded in the night. Some crept under cover of the ruins within earshot of the sentries, threatening the

[1] Sale.

infidels with death in hideous tortures if the town were not surrendered.

The first step in the defence was to put all ranks, soldiers and civilians alike, upon half-rations, and then to make each man do the work of four. George Broadfoot, appointed garrison engineer, set his men to collect wood from ruined houses and iron from the surrounding country. Foraging parties brought in firewood and provisions, so soon as a sally of eleven hundred of the garrison, three days after their arrival, had beaten off some five thousand of the enemy.

The defenders were greatly assisted by the Afghans themselves, who, in an access of excitement, set fire one night to every building within their reach—thereby destroying their own cover, and relieving Sale of one of his worst anxieties.

Towards the end of November the enemy began again to invest the walls and to harass the working parties; another sortie relieved this annoyance for the time, and the garrison had an interval in which to strengthen their defences and to add to their supplies. They had achieved so much against such odds that they might have been hopeful for the Kabul garrison; but the air was heavy with rumours of ill. No better authority could be found for any of the stories than "They say"; only this much was certain, that on December 17th Sale received a despatch which he read and put into his pocket without a word.

"All quiet," is the entry in a diary kept by one of the garrison on January 1, 1842. Next day came a letter from Eldred Pottinger, written from Kabul on Christmas Day:—

"We have had a sad Comedy of Errors, or rather tragedy, here. Macnaghten was called out to a conference and murdered. We have interchanged terms on the grounds he was treating on for leaving the country; but things are not finally settled. However, we are to fall back on Jellalabad to-morrow or next day. In the present disturbed state of the country we may expect opposition on the road, and we are likely to suffer much from the cold and hunger, as we expect to have no carriage for tents and superfluities."

On the heels of the messenger came another, to say that the brigade which had marched from Kandahar to the relief of Kabul, had found the roads beyond Ghazni impassable from snow, and had fallen back. And then an intercepted despatch was brought in, addressed to one of the neighbouring chiefs by Dost Mohammad's son, Akbar Khan, now commanding the insurgents at Kabul, which proclaimed a Holy War against the infidels, "whose chief I have slain with my own hand, as you, I trust, will in like manner slay the chief of the Feringhis in Jalalabad."

The next week was spent in anxious waiting for the arrival of the Kabul force. Some hoped that they might fight their way through the passes, like Sale's brigade, which had only mustered a quarter of their strength; but Sale had not been encumbered with helpless women and children, and thousands of servants and camp-followers. None could feel very hopeful; and most convinced of ill was Colonel Dennie of the 13th, who had shown conspicuous gallantry during the march down to Jalalabad, and in command of the sortie on December 1st. Ever since the first ill-tidings came from the Mission, he had prophesied that the force would be annihilated. "You'll see," he repeated, "not a soul will escape from Kabul except one man; and he will come to tell us that the rest are destroyed."

On the 9th a flag of truce appeared at the gate of Jalalabad, borne by a few horsemen who proclaimed that they had come from Kabul, and bore a letter from General Elphinstone addressed to Captain Macgregor, the Political Agent with Sale's brigade.

It was ill reading for the Council of War hastily

summoned by the Agent and the General. The agreement for the evacuation of Afghanistan had been concluded; it was therefore the wish of Major Pottinger and General Elphinstone "that the troops at Jalalabad should return to India, commencing their march immediately after the receipt of this letter, leaving all guns, as also such stores and baggage as there may not be the means of carrying away."

The heads of the Jalalabad garrison wasted little time in debate. Macgregor's spies had told them that the tribes upon the road had been warned by Akbar Khan to attack the English as they retreated from Kabul; they knew that, to use Sale's own words, "the convention was forced from our Envoy and military commander with the knives at their throats." They therefore decided to remain where they were until ordered to retire by the Governor-General in Council.

On hearing the decision of their superiors, the men cheered loudly, and set to work with renewed vigour. All through the 11th and 12th they were busy digging a ditch to protect the north-west angle of the town, their arms piled close at hand, and the cavalry, with horses saddled, ready to sally to their help if any marauding party of the enemy should attack them.

A little after noon, on the 13th, the sentry posted on the ramparts looking towards Gandamak, called out that he saw a mounted man coming down the Kabul road. Officers crowded to the ramparts, and strained their eyes across the arid plain. The pony was wounded, stumbling, scarcely able to put one foot before the other; the man clung to its neck, unable to sit upright. As they looked, they saw by white face and tattered uniform that the rider was an Englishman. "Did I not say so?" cried Colonel Dennie. "Here comes the messenger!"

## III.

The pony lay dead beneath the walls of Jalalabad; the man, Dr Brydon, sorely wounded but clear in mind, was telling his tale to the garrison. Some sixteen thousand men had left Kabul on January 6th; so far as he knew, he was the sole survivor.

Utterly demoralised, in spite of the bravery and coolness of individuals, the Envoy murdered, the General a helpless invalid, the next in command contumacious and insubordinate, the army out of heart and out of hand, instead of throwing themselves into the Bala Hissar, where they might have held out for a year, the Mission had come to terms with Akbar Khan. Dost Mohammad was to be released from captivity; English and Sikh troops were to evacuate the country immediately, being assisted in their retreat by the Afghans "with money, protection, and provisions." Shah Shuja had permission to live where he pleased.

After Macnaghten's murder by Akbar Khan on the 23rd, the demoralisation of the force was complete. There was neither food nor forage left. Lady Sale's last meal in Kabul was cooked with her own mahogany dining - table. On January 6th, after the troops had been standing about, without food, in the deep snow for half the day, the retreat began.

We all know what followed—how the camp-followers, the sick, and the wounded dropped by the way, and lay down to die in the snow, Akbar Khan bidding his hordes not to blunt their knives on the worthless Hindus, but to follow up the English to the last man; how the tribesmen waited in the Khurd Kabul Pass and reaped their harvest of death, and the little children amused themselves with cutting the throats of wounded grenadiers; how, on the 9th, the women and children—some wearing no more than their night-dresses, and fasting since they left Kabul—

were delivered to Akbar Khan as the only means of saving their lives. Certain officers were also taken by him as hostages. The rest of the force —what was left of it—had struggled along under the Afghan fire from Khurd Kabul to Gandamak. On the right of the road at Gandamak is the hill where the survivors of the 44th Regiment, with only two cartridges left, made their last stand. They clubbed their muskets, and when they lay down for their last sleep, a ring of the enemy was piled dead around them.

Some few pushed on towards Jagdallack, to find a six-foot-high barrier of prickly holly barring the road. Many more dropped here—among them a Captain Dodgin, who, disabled as he was —having lost one leg, — nevertheless killed five Afghans before he was pulled down.

Only half a dozen mounted officers were left to struggle on towards Jalalabad on the morning of January 13th. Dr Brydon, who had lost his horse, owed his life to an old subahdar who saw him stumbling along on foot. "I am wounded unto death, sahib, and can go no farther; take my pony, and save yourself." Soon after Brydon had mounted, the pony was shot through the loins, but still it bore him on. His sword was broken by a Ghilzai's stone, and when an Afghan attacked him he could not defend himself.

Wounded in several places, he fell forward on his empty holsters; the Afghan thought he was going to draw a pistol, wheeled his horse and rode off. For the rest of the way the pony never went beyond a shuffling trot. Three more men had ridden with him to within four miles of Jalalabad; then one had dropped wounded, the other two had turned back to help him, and neither of the three was seen alive again. A squadron of cavalry sent out from Jalalabad brought in their dead bodies.

As the officers in Jalalabad listened to the story, perhaps some of them may have had ironical recollections of a passage in a letter of instructions sent from Kabul to their division ere it marched through the valley of Tazin: "Our security must depend mainly upon our own prudence and vigilance."

For the next three weeks, the garrison exercised prudence and vigilance in comparative peace. The foraging parties collected cattle and sheep; every tree and bush that could give cover to an enemy was cut down. All able-bodied camp-followers were enrolled, and armed for the most part with pikes made out of scraps of old iron; spare muskets and rifles were few, and ammunition was running short, so that when a salute was fired on February 12th, on hearing of the birth of a Prince of Wales, "the guns were loaded with very small charges."

Sale was indefatigable, going out with his gun to the walls and firing at the enemy, as did the other officers, to save ammunition. He was no marksman, and the bullet usually went wide. "Ah, General, now," would come the dutiful exclamation of his Irish orderly, "wasn't that a beautiful shot? Sure, you nearly did for him!" To which Sale would make reply, "You lie! I didn't; it was a d—d bad shot."

When off duty the old man would sit for hours in silence, thinking of his wife and daughter captive among the Afghans. One of his officers told how he had seen the General sitting mute, with the tears running down his cheeks, until some alarm was given. "He was up in a moment, cheering and encouraging everybody."

Once his resolution failed, when on January 21st came the news that Colonel Wild, ordered to march from Peshawar to their relief, had been beaten back at Ali Masjid. Then he told his subordinates that he was convinced that they had no more hope of relief, and must make terms with Akbar Khan. Macgregor was of the same opinion. George Broadfoot was not, but in spite of his fierce opposition, it was agreed by the majority to treat for surrender. "I must congratulate you on the figure you will cut if a relieving force should arrive just as you are marching out," said Broadfoot grimly, as the Council dissolved.

Colonel Dennie declared that in such a case he should not go.

"We should make you," was Broadfoot's stern answer; "faith must be kept."

And though he knew that a letter had gone to Akbar, proposing terms of surrender, he set his men at once to dig a ditch round the works. Meanwhile he wrought upon the officers' minds to such good purpose that when Akbar's reply came, requiring them all to set their seals to the agreement in pledge of faith, several were ready to declare with Broadfoot that this suspicion of their honesty was adequate ground for a rupture.

General Sale, who had made up his mind to surrender, did not relish opposition, and expressed himself with such vigour that the Council had to be adjourned for an hour to give every one time to cool down. It says much for all concerned that, after weeks of nerve-destroying toil and strain, they still retained such self-command as to meet again in perfect friendliness. By this time, all but Sale and Macgregor were convinced that the only possible course was to hold on, and die sword in hand, and Sale allowed his opinion to be overridden by the majority. Macgrégor gloomily hoped that they might not be brought to regret the terms he had made for them.

On the very next day came messengers from General Pollock, who had been appointed by Lord Auckland to command at Peshawar, promising that in no circumstances should the garrison at Jalalabad be forced to make a disastrous retreat.

Sale and Macgregor sat down to write to Pollock. Communications were usually carried on in French, for fear of their being intercepted, and the General strove to express himself in that language with indifferent success. His letter concludes: "After writing the above, the dreadful earthquake of this day a fait tomber deux bastions et plusieurs autres sont culles."

It was too true; at about eleven o'clock on February 19th, "the fruits of two months' labour were destroyed in a minute."[1] The loss of life was small, but "the parapets were completely ruined, the ramparts in some places cracked, five bastions thrown down, three breaches made in the walls, and one of the gates almost thrown down."

The plight of the garrison might now seem hopeless. Their defences were ruined, and the enemy were closing down again upon them. Just

[1] MS. diary of Lieut. Frere.

across the river they could see the white English tents, part of the spoil from the Kabul Mission, where Akbar Khan had pitched his camp to invest the city. But the shock was scarcely passed, when they seized spade and pickaxe. "Before night, a parapet of dry clods was thrown up, all round the town, and the breaches made impracticable. In a week, the whole was almost in as good a state of repair as before," and the enemy, seeing no trace of the damage, vowed that English witchcraft was very potent, since Jalalabad was the only place that had not suffered from the great earthquake.

The siege dragged on for the next few weeks. There were almost daily mild shocks of earthquake, and incessant harassings from the besiegers. Sometimes there were false alarms, as when all the troops were under arms to repel an attack, and found the enemy to be "two old walls, which in the moonlight had the appearance of compact bodies of men." On March 15th they rejoiced at the news that "Akbar had been wounded," but it proved to be merely an accidental injury from the discharge of a gun by one of the chief's servants, who in consequence was burned alive with his brother. Then a Mullah in the camp having prophesied that an earthquake would knock down all the city walls on a certain date, the enemy turned out to wait for it, but were disappointed, as, though the earthquake came at the proper time, it was too slight to do any harm.

In order to divert the enemy's fire from the working parties, some of the officers dressed up a dummy in uniform, put a cocked hat on his head, and raised it above the parapet. This answered well enough until the Afghans discovered the trick. The bullets which the enemy wasted were thankfully picked up by the garrison, who had plenty of powder, but little else. One officer collected in a single day as many as a hundred and thirty bullets.

By the end of March, the garrison were nearly desperate; the stock of grain had run so low that the combatants only received quarter allowance; there was none for the camp-followers. The supply of salt meat was coming to an end, and not a single sheep or bullock was left. Up to this time the general health, in spite of incessant toil and short rations, had been excellent; now the camp-followers began to fall ill, and it was only a question of time for the sickness to spread among the fighting men.

A favourite manœuvre of the enemy at this time was to drive flocks of sheep, under an escort, as near as within six hundred yards from the crest of the glacis, in order to entice the garrison from their defences. On the first of April a sortie succeeded in carrying off five hundred head of sheep, with the loss of one man killed and two or three wounded, in the very teeth of the enemy. When the sheep were distributed, the 35th Native Infantry sent a deputation to Sale; they were not used to much animal food, and could do without it—might their share be given to their English brothers, the 13th Regiment?

A little animal food was sorely needed to put heart into the garrison in the next few days; contradictory rumours of Pollock's movements came from one quarter and another, until, on the evening of the 5th, Macgregor's spies declared that he had been defeated and driven back from the Khyber Pass. Next morning the hills around Jalalabad were booming and echoing with the thunders of a royal salute from Akbar's camp, evidently in honour of some good news.

It seemed that the last stage had come, and the defenders of Jalalabad were ready to face it, as they had faced all else. Food was nearly all gone, ammunition was running short; it was better to make an end quickly. At daybreak next morning, they would throw themselves upon the enemy; it might be that they should clear the road for Pollock, after all—for a wild rumour had come in that Akbar Khan was breaking up his camp in order to suppress a fresh revolution at Kabul; it might be that, even though Pollock were defeated, they would cut their way down to him. At any rate, they would die like men, not wait for the Afghans to crush them like flies.

Akbar was ready for them next morning, his army drawn up between a fort and the Kabul river. Only twelve men were left on guard at each gate of the city; the camp-followers manned the walls, and the garrison moved down to what might be their last fight. Colonel Dennie, leading his men to the attack, was shot, and died before he could be taken back to the city, and before he could know that the day was won. The troops manœuvred with as much coolness and precision as if they were on a field-day, and fought with a desperation that nothing could withstand. "The battle was over and the enemy in full retreat by about 7 A.M. We have made ourselves masters of two cavalry standards, recaptured four guns lost by the Kabul and Gandamack forces, the restoration of which to our Government is a matter of much honest exultation among our troops, seized and destroyed a great quantity of material and ordnance stores, and burnt the whole of the enemy's tents."

So wrote Sale, flushed with the pride of a "complete and signal" victory, gained at the cost of eleven killed and about fifty wounded. The only member of the garrison who had reason for dissatisfaction with the day's work was George Broadfoot, who, having been shot through the thigh in the month of March, was not sufficiently recovered to take any part in the action.

The tide had turned; the country-folk crowded to the gates of Jalalabad, bringing food and supplies. On the 14th came news that Pollock had succeeded in doing what the army of no ruler of India, from the great Akbar himself up to that time, had ever achieved, and had forced the Khyber Pass. On April 16th, the band of the 13th played him into Jalalabad, to the Jacobite air, "Oh, but ye've been lang o' coming."

# XVII.

# THE END OF AN EXPERIMENT—1842

"There is another world for the expiation of guilt; but the wages of folly are payable here below."—LORD ACTON.

## XVII.

## THE END OF AN EXPERIMENT—1842.

If Pollock had been "lang o' coming" to the relief of the beleaguered city it was not his fault. On his arrival at Peshawar, he found almost complete demoralisation. The disastrous repulse of Wild's brigade at the mouth of the Khyber Pass had put the finishing touches to what the fate of the Kabul Mission had begun. Our allies, the Sikhs, were openly disaffected, refusing obedience, and tampering with the sepoy regiments. The sepoys were horror-stricken at the sight of the miserable camp-followers, survivors from Kabul, some of whom had straggled back to Peshawar, mutilated and frost-bitten. Moreover, they feared to lose their caste in Afghanistan, where "red mutton" (beef) was often the only food to be had. In the brigade of four regiments, no less than one thousand men were returned as sick. The demoralisation had spread to some of the English officers, who publicly expressed the opinion that to force the Khyber would be to lose more than half their men, and that it would be better to leave Jalalabad to its fate rather than to risk another advance.

Happily there were still some Englishmen in Peshawar ready to take any odds. There was Mr Mackeson, for instance, whose capture of the fort of Ali Masjid, in the heart of the Khyber, was a feat worthy of the Black Douglas, or of Du Guesclin. Sent with a small party of friendly Eusafzais to make a survey in the neighbourhood, it had occurred to him that it might be possible to surprise the fort, and he proved it. When he and his men had settled themselves in the place of the Afghan garrison, they discovered that Ali Masjid's one strategic defect was the absence of any water-supply. So Mackeson proclaimed to the tribesmen swarming round the fort, upon whom his men practised their shooting, that he would restore to them the bodies of their dead, in return for two skins of water apiece. This process of barter went on for some time, to the satisfaction of both parties. Mackeson fell ill, and, unable to walk, was carried on his rounds, until the provisions ran out. Then, as Wild's repulse forbade all hope of securing more supplies, the garrison of Ali Masjid cut their way back to Peshawar. There, in spite of being only a civilian, Mackeson was appointed to command a levy of native pioneers, with whom at length he marched to Kabul.

But for one like Mackeson, there were many who openly declared that all was lost. Pollock, kindliest and most even-tempered of men, had need of all his tact and patience. He visited the sick in hospital on the day after his arrival; he ordered warm stockings and gloves to be supplied to the shivering sepoys. He forbade the Sikh troops to enter his camp. He personally expostulated or reasoned with those who were notoriously faint-hearted. A lesser man, eager for self-advertisement, or overcome by the urgency of the need at Jalalabad, might have ruined all by a precipitate advance; Pollock would not stir until he could trust his forces.

He never would have been able to write, after the first action in the Khyber, "The sepoys behaved nobly; they are in the highest spirits, and have a thorough contempt for the enemy," if he had not taught them to trust him within Peshawar.

Once at Jalalabad, he was again doomed to months of inactivity—this time, not through the fault of his men, but through the policy of the Governor-General. Lord Auckland had sailed for England, his last recommendation urging the rescue of the English prisoners; Lord Ellenborough, his successor, arrived committed to a policy of peace, and seemingly indifferent what price he paid for it. He had written a warm letter of appreciation to Sale, calling the defenders of Jalalabad "that illustrious garrison"—a name which has clung to them ever since; otherwise he was weary of the whole Afghan imbroglio, and only wished to get it off his hands as quickly as possible.

There was a certain amount of excuse for withdrawal in the fact that our puppet had been broken to pieces. Left at Kabul after January 6th, still nominally King of Afghanistan, he had been torn hither and thither by contending interests, now vowing to the chiefs to lead a holy war against the infidel, now writing long and plaintive letters to the Governor-General, swearing unalterable faith, and begging for money. His own people distrusted him, and hated his parsimony; the Government of India, having no more money to throw away, could only be liberal with advice.

"I always said to Sir William Macnaghten that this affair would end badly," he complains in one of his letters; and it was to end badly for him as well as for those who had tried to use him for their own ends. Forced by the chiefs to leave Kabul, in order to place himself at the head of the army to be sent against Jalalabad, he was carried in a chair of state from the Bala Hissar to the camp. As he went towards his tent an ambush fired upon him. He sprang from the chair, and ran across a field, trying to shelter in a ditch. "For God's sake, save me! What offence have I done?" he vainly cried. The murderers finished their work; the body was taken back to Kabul, where it remained unburied for months, until it was thrown into a ruinous mosque. The cannons that had wakened the echoes of Jalalabad on April 6th, were fired by Akbar on receiving the intelligence of the murder.

From first to last, jewels play a part in Shuja's story. He had been in the habit of carrying those which he most valued in a small bag at his girdle; as he ran from his assassins, he cast it from him. An Afghan, coming to look at the dead king, picked up the bag, and showed its contents to a townsman of Kabul, who persuaded him that they were only coloured glass, and made a favour of giving him ten pounds for them. The Afghan, a "savage hillman," was pleased with his bargain; so was the trader, who had acquired what was worth many thousands at a trifling expenditure—until he was summoned before the chief who had slain Shah Shuja, and bidden to disgorge, if he would not be blown from a gun. Once more the king's jewels changed hands, and the unhappy trader was dismissed without repayment of the ten pounds.

Shah Shuja for the time was replaced by his second son, but the Government of India were not prepared to do anything for his assistance. They had enough to do to pay for imposing one poor king upon a people who did not want him. On April 29th, Pollock received instructions; Nott was to evacuate Kandahar and retire upon Quetta, while he was "to withdraw every British soldier from Jalalabad to Peshawar."

As for the prisoners in the hands of the Afghans, the women and children, and the hostages, they were to be left to their fate.

"A soldier only knows his orders"; but happily some soldiers have known how to obtain the orders they desired. Knowing that to disobey might be his ruin, Pollock, nevertheless, on receipt of this letter, wrote at once to Nott, requiring him on no account to retire, whatever commands he might receive from other quarters, until he should hear from him again. "Stopping Nott for a few days after his receipt of orders to retire, was perhaps a very bold step," Pollock wrote in after years, "but I looked upon it as the only safe course to pursue, and it succeeded. If it had not succeeded, I knew that I might lose my commission, but I felt pretty certain that if we worked together in earnest, the game would be ours."

Nott was of a different type to Pollock. A man of no birth, soured by having been passed over for promotion in favour of others with better connections or manners, his crabbed temper and habit of telling unpleasant truths without consideration for his superiors' feelings had prevented his being sent to command at Kabul in the previous year. He hated the thought of retiring from Afghanistan as much as any man could, but had seen no alternative; he now gladly undertook not to move without Pollock's sanction.

In the meanwhile Pollock had written to the Governor-General, boldly asserting that in his opinion it was essential to remain or even to advance "to uphold the character of the British nation," and such a storm of resentment was rising in India, and at home, that Lord Ellenborough, although he affected indifference to public opinion, was obliged to bow to it. Pollock's astute representations as to the difficulty of moving in the height of summer, gained him leave to remain where he was until October. On July 4th, Ellenborough wrote to him and to Nott, suggesting that "perhaps General Nott might feel disposed to retire from Kandahar to the provinces of India by the route of Ghazni, Kabul, and Jellalabad;

and that perhaps General Pollock might feel disposed to assist the retreat of the Kandahar force by moving forward upon Kabul." But if done at all, it must be on their own responsibility.

A glance at the map will show that there was justification for the comment of certain persons that this was to recommend a retreat to London from York by the route of Edinburgh.

Sale wrote at once to Nott, asking what course he meant to adopt. Historians say that there is no truth in the tradition that his message was in two words only—"Advance, Nott." By the middle of August, a reply came to say that Nott was about to adopt the Governor-General's suggestion as to the line of his retreat.

The force at Jalalabad had been suffering cruelly from the inevitable reaction. The water was bad; bare food was procurable, but no luxuries of any sort. A plague of flies poisoned everything. Men dropped in scores with dysentery and fever, and those who were still able to drag themselves about, looked like ghosts. But at the news of the advance, all was changed. Sir Robert Sale, "so excited that he could scarcely write," assured the General that he would take no carriage from the commissariat, and that his officers were ready to "double up four" in one of the little sepoy tents, generally considered inadequate protection from the sun for English soldiers. He and Pollock were so luxurious as to take one of these tents apiece. Broadfoot offered to take his Sappers up to Kabul with no tents at all. As for carriage, at Pollock's suggestion, the mounted troopers could carry grain in their spare pairs of trousers.

Thus they made their way up through the mountain passes, where the dead bodies of Elphinstone's army lay so thick where they had fallen that the guns had to be driven over them. In many cases the features were "hideously perfect," and could be recognised. In the valley of Tazin, Pollock's forces had a decisive encounter with the Afghans, who, occupying the high ground, fired down upon them as they charged up-hill. The heights were won by the bayonet, and Broadfoot's Sappers distinguished themselves by "clambering up the steepest ascents under the hottest fire." Meanwhile Nott had advanced from Kandahar, retaken Ghazni, and reached Kabul, the day after Pollock had planted the flag on the Bala Hissar.

Akbar had fled towards the Hindu-Kush, and the chief to whom he had entrusted the greater part of his captives was susceptible to the arguments of George Lawrence and Eldred Pottinger, especially when backed with substantial bribes.

A few days after arriving at Kabul, Sir Robert Sale was noticed to be unusually excitable and restless, spending the day in excursions from his own tent to Pollock's, and back again. He had heard that Lady Sale and his daughter were actually on their way to Kabul, with several other ladies and their children, and some officers and privates who had shared their captivity. It was on the 20th of September that Sale met the captives in the hills to the south-east of Kabul. No one could speak, least of all Sale himself, who twisted his face into horrible grimaces, and galloped away when one of the officers tried to congratulate him.

After this, there was no more to detain the army in Kabul, and after blowing up the bazaar in which Macnaghten's mutilated body had been exposed, and the mosque built by the Afghans to commemorate their triumph, the homeward march was begun.

All the fruit of the Mission to Afghanistan was a pair of sandal-wood gates, which Lord Ellenborough had commanded Nott to bring away from Ghazni, being persuaded that these were the gates which Mahmud the Idol-breaker had carried off from the temple of Somnauth. Unluckily, it was discovered that they were of a later date than the eleventh century, and so, instead of being restored with great ceremony to the Brahmans, they were left in the Fort at Agra, where they may be seen to this day.

Our prestige was gone, our honour stained. Sikhs and sepoys had learned that we could be worsted outright, and were to apply the lesson within a few years. As for Afghanistan, in a little while all was as before our intervention, save that certain chiefs, who had been more or less friendly, were left, as they complained, "in the mouth of lions," to reckon with Dost Mohammad.

Finally, the affair had cost the Government of India more than eight millions of money.

The principal actors in the story met with varying fates. In October 1842, Dost Mohammad, released from a nominal captivity, returned to Kabul, where he ruled with great success, and by one of the strangest of Time's revenges, was destined to stand our friend at a time when the English dominion in India was trembling in the balance.

Sale came home, to be feasted and honoured, then returned to India to die a soldier's death in the battle of Mudki; his daughter married again, and she and her second husband were among the first victims of the Indian Mutiny.

Dr Brydon, being in Lucknow in 1857, was

severely wounded, but survived the siege, and ended his days in England.

Pollock was over eighty years of age before he was gazetted Field-Marshal, as a tardy recognition of his services; Nott was invalided home to die, about a year after the Afghan campaign.

George Broadfoot was made a Companion of the Bath, and first appointed Commissioner of Moulmein, then made Agent to the Governor-General on the Sikh frontier. At the battle of Ferozeshah he was mortally wounded—"an irreparable loss," as Sir Henry Hardinge testified.

Lord Ellenborough was created an Earl, as Lord John Russell pointed out to the House of Commons, for supplying provisions to the troops already collected by Lord Auckland, and for "not preventing" the forward operations against Ghazni and Kabul.

# XVIII.

# THE HEIRS OF RANJIT SINGH—1839-1845

"There are perhaps no characters in history more repulsive than Rajas Gulab Singh and Dhian Singh. Their splendid talents and their undoubted bravery count as nothing in the presence of their atrocious cruelty, their avarice, their treachery, and their unscrupulous ambition."

—Sir L. GRIFFIN.

# XVIII.

## THE HEIRS OF RANJIT SINGH—1839-1845.

THE lion was dead, and his prey was left to the jackals.

Miss Eden's lively pen has described the principal personages at Lahore in 1838. There was Kharak Singh, the half-imbecile heir-apparent, and Nao Nahal Singh, his son, "very interesting-looking, with enormous black eyes"; Sher Singh, "a very jolly dog," always ready to sit at table and drink with the English Mission, though he declined eating with them, and his seven-year-old boy, Pertab Singh, "a dear, good child, with eyes as big as saucers, and emeralds bigger than his eyes." There was Ajit Singh of the great Sindhanwalia clan, whose extraordinary cleverness made a great impression upon the Governor-General; there were Hira Singh, "a handsome boy, loaded with emeralds and pearls," Dhian

Singh, Hira Singh's father, the Prime Minister, "uncommonly good-looking," and his brother Suchet Singh, "the great dandy of the Punjab."

Had any one with second-sight looked upon these chiefs during the festivities given in honour of Lord Auckland's visit, he would have seen the winding-sheets rising high about them all.

Dhian Singh, Suchet Singh, and their brother Gulab Singh, were the evil geniuses of the Khalsa. Their rise dated from the time when Gulab Singh, a common *sowar* or trooper of the Dogra tribe, having killed his enemy in a feud, took refuge in Ranjit's tent during a review of the troops. His audacity pleased the Maharaja, who took him into favour, and with him rose his two brothers. Of Gulab Singh no one appears to have had any good to say. Dhian Singh's pleasing manners gained him a certain amount of liking, which wore off upon a better acquaintance. Next to Ranjit, he was the most able of all the Sikhs, and, like him, he was wholly illiterate.

In the last years of Ranjit's life Dhian Singh's influence was paramount; no one was allowed to enter the Maharaja's presence without his leave, and even Kharak Singh and Sher Singh were obliged sometimes to wait for hours and to bribe attendants before they were admitted. Ranjit made a great favourite of Hira Singh, whose chair was set in durbar when every one else must stand, and would scarcely let him out of his sight. Both father and son were allowed to enter Ranjit's zenana at their pleasure, and the women feared and served Dhian Singh more than their own lawful master. Dhian lost no opportunity of impressing on Ranjit that Prince Kharak Singh was an idiot, and expected that the old Maharaja's fondness for Hira Singh would cause the boy to be appointed as his successor.

All his schemes were upset when Ranjit on his deathbed proclaimed Kharak Singh to be his heir, telling Dhian Singh that the only return he expected for his past favours was that the Prime Minister would be loyal to the new Maharaja.

The day after Ranjit's death, his corpse was burned on a sandal-wood pyre before the palace gates. Four of his queens, and seven Kashmiri slave-girls of great beauty, dressed in their richest *saris* and jewels, burned with him. The chief Rani, ere she died, took the hand of Dhian Singh, and placing it on the breast of the dead Maharaja, bade him swear to be true man to Kharak Singh and his son, and faithful to the Khalsa; then Kharak Singh, in his turn, swore to be true master to Dhian Singh. The women, sitting round their dead, neither wept nor shrieked as the flames rose; but Dhian shed tears, and four times strove to spring upon the burning pyre, and four times was held back by those who stood near him.

It would have been better for the new Maharaja, and for the country, if the Prime Minister had been allowed to fulfil his intention. There were varying opinions about the measure of Kharak Singh's imbecility; "some people say he only affects it, to keep Ranjit from being jealous of him, but it looks like very unaffected and complete folly," says Miss Eden. He was certainly not equal to his Prime Minister, with whom he fell out in a few weeks. Their differences began with his forbidding Dhian Singh and Hira Singh to enter the royal zenana for the future; when Dhian Singh protested that he could no longer govern the Punjab if he were not conversant with all the intrigues of the women, Kharak listened to a favourite who declared that if the Prime Minister would not do his duty, others might be found to take his place.

At the beginning of October, rumours, fathered by the Dogra brothers, were flying around the bazaars, that the Maharaja was going to put himself under British protection, to pay six annas out of every rupee in the revenue to the Company, and to disband the army of the Khalsa. The soldiers were furious, and when Nao Nahal Singh made a rapid journey from Peshawar to Lahore, summoned by a messenger from Dhian Singh, he and the three brothers had no difficulty in getting into the palace by night, killing the favourite, and sending the Maharaja prisoner to the fort.

From that time, though Kharak Singh sometimes appeared at durbars in his royal robes, he was to all intents a prisoner, and all authority was in the hands of the young prince. It is said that Dhian Singh widened the breach between father and son by carrying false reports of one to the other, and by contriving that they should not meet, even when, in his dying agonies, the Maharaja called upon his son to come and receive his forgiveness. Some say that Kharak Singh died of a broken heart; the process may have been hastened by the acetate of lead and corrosive sublimate mixed with his food.

One solace was left to him in his captivity, the Koh-i-Nur, which he wore upon his arm. It is said that Ranjit had come to dread its curse, and though he could not bring himself to part with it during his lifetime, he ordered upon his deathbed that it should be sent to a Hindu temple, in spite of the remonstrances of his sirdars, who pleaded that such a diamond would purchase Hindustan itself. But the Court jeweller refused to part with it, unless the order were signed by the Maharaja, who by that time was unable even to make the impression of his five fingers on paper, and the diamond passed to Kharak, who wore it until his agonies were cut short by death, thirteen months after his deposition.

Nao Nahal Singh was not yet twenty years of age, capable, energetic, with much of his grandfather's ability but with little of his shrewdness. He disliked the English, and is said to have drawn his sword in open durbar and vowed to use it against them. It is certain that during his regency, the arsenals at Lahore were filled, anti-English emissaries were stirring up strife in various quarters, and it was debated whether the English troops should be allowed to pass through the Punjab on their way to and from Afghanistan. Nothing but the watchfulness, tact, and diplomacy of George Russell Clerk, then Political Agent for Sikh affairs, could have prevented a rupture. As it was, wiser counsels prevailed; Dhian Singh, though he fervently hated the English, saw that it might be fatal to pick a quarrel with them, and the new Maharaja had not declared war when he attended the funeral ceremonies the day after his father's death.

The corpse was burned near the mausoleum of Ranjit Singh, and with it burned three slave-girls, and one of Kharak's ranis, Ishar Kour, a most beautiful woman whom Ranjit had sent to his son from his own zenana. Kharak's principal rani, Chand Kaur, always jealous of her "sister-wife," now forced her to become *sati*, in spite of her entreaties. The sun was hot, and Nao Nahal grew very weary, and insisted, in defiance of etiquette, in going down to the bank of the Ravi to make the ceremonial ablutions, before the pyre was consumed. As custom forbade him to ride past the burning place, his elephants waited for him at a little distance. The washing was done, and the Maharaja walked back, hand-in-hand with his favourite companion, the eldest son of Gulab Singh. "He had to pass first through a gateway, then across a courtyard, and lastly through a deep archway leading from this courtyard to the spot on which the corpse had been burned, and near which the elephants were now in waiting."[1] On the threshold of the archway, he called for water, but there was none. All the sacred Ganges water brought for the funeral rites had been sprinkled upon the pyre. "An evil omen!" murmured the sirdars; the Maharaja laughed. At that moment came a crashing sound; the parapet wall collapsed, and beams, stones, tiles, and bricks fell upon the heads of the two who stood beneath the archway.

Gulab Singh's son was killed instantaneously by the largest of the stones; the Maharaja was still

[1] Carmichael Smyth.

breathing when Dhian Singh lifted him and placed him in a palki. He was carried to the garden-house of the fort, the doors were locked, and not even his wives allowed to enter.

Letters were sent to Multan, to Peshawar, and even to Mr Clerk, to say that the Maharaja was injured but expected to recover. According to one story, his mother, Chand Kaur, came and beat at the gates of the fort with her own hands, and was not admitted. Dhian Singh pacified her with an assurance that she should reign in her son's stead, if she would hold her tongue for the next few hours. Meanwhile he was sending messengers post-haste to Sher Singh, who was then some eighty miles away, and placing relays of horses all along the road for his use. When the prince arrived, it was acknowledged that Nao Nahal Singh had died within an hour of the accident, and his body was burned with two of his ranis.

There were ugly rumours that the fall of the masonry was caused not by accident but by the arrangement of Dhian Singh, who had found the young Maharaja unfriendly and intractable, and that when the parapet wall failed to kill, he had completed the business in the garden-house. So many crimes can justly be laid to Dhian Singh's account, that it is not worth while to argue the ase for and against him over this one.

## II.

Whether the Maharaja's death were a murder or a casualty, it was necessary to conceal it until Sher Singh's arrival, if the throne were not to be seized by the rival claimant, Chand Kaur.

There is a custom among the Sikhs that, in default of male issue, a widow succeeds in preference to a brother. Chand Kaur was a spirited woman, who had already seized upon the Koh-i-Nur, and she was ready to do battle for the throne. She had her supporters, among them Ajit Singh, her lover—for she was still comely though no longer young, and growing very stout. On the other hand, though every one knew the true story of Sher Singh's birth, even a spurious son of the great Maharaja made appeal to the army, with whom he was popular. Finding herself likely to be worsted, she declared that her daughter-in-law, one of Nao Nahal Singh's surviving widows, was expecting the birth of a child, which would necessitate a regency for at least six months.

Then followed wranglings as to who was to be regent. Sher Singh's party declared that fighting men could not be governed by a woman. "England is ruled by a queen," retorted Chand Kaur "why should it be a disgrace to the Punjab to be governed by a rani?" and either her reasonings or other arguments prevailed so far that she was appointed regent until her grandchild should be born.

Then came disaster. Dhian Singh, who had been working all the while for his own ends, went to Jammu on a hunting expedition; the army, to whom the Rani had omitted to distribute largesse, began to mutiny. Sher Singh appeared at the gates of Lahore; most of the troops went over to his side, and the city surrendered to him. But Gulab Singh held the citadel for the Rani, and his nephew Hira Singh joined him, in spite of the fact that Dhian Singh was fighting upon Sher Singh's side. "The intent of this manœuvre was, that by ostensibly becoming enemies to each other they were enabled to become the leaders and controllers of the contending parties, whereby their object was secured, whichever side was successful."[1]

After seven days' siege, the citadel was surrendered with the honours of war. Chand Kaur renounced all claim to the regency, and was given a grant of lands in compensation.

The events of the next few days cannot be

[1] Carmichael Smyth.

described. Disappointed of the plunder of the fort, the troops fell upon the city and plundered and murdered indiscriminately. "Every man gratified his private revenge; officers were killed by their men; shopkeepers by their debtors. It was many days before the troops were pacified, and the licence which they then enjoyed, they never forgot."

In the meantime, Gulab Singh had loaded his ammunition-waggons with the treasure in the fort, and marched back to Jammu. The Koh-i-Nur was recovered from Chand Kaur and presented to Sher Singh, who was enthroned as Maharaja. To secure himself better, he renewed the offer he had made directly after Nao Nahal Singh's death, of marrying Chand Kaur by the Sikh rite called "throwing the sheet," which was used for widows and wives of inferior station. He was told by Dhian Singh that the Rani considered he must be mad or a fool to dream that one of the Kanheya clan would think of marrying the son of a washerman. Whether Chand Kaur really said it or not, the taunt was fatal. Sher Singh and Dhian Singh alike were anxious to get rid of her. When for a year she had been living at Lahore, secretly intriguing with the sirdars and the army to replace her upon the throne, and making overtures, through Ajit Singh, to the English, four of her slave-girls were promised a large reward if they would kill her. At first they tried poisoning her drink, but she suspected the taste, and threw it away; then, while they were supposed to be dressing her hair, they battered her head to pieces with a heavy stone. Thus was avenged the dying agony of Ishar Kaur. The Rani died, unconscious, within two days, and the slave-girls disappeared; whether they also were put out of the way, or merely lost their hands, ears, and noses, is a disputed point.

The army by this time was thoroughly disorganised. The regimental officers had no authority, and took their orders from the "Panches"—"a deputation of the five cleverest blackguards in a Sikh regiment, who took their seats in the midnight parliaments of the Khalsa army, where measures were concerted for keeping the Lahore Government in the hands of the soldiers, putting up or deposing and murdering a Vizier, voting themselves extra pay, gold necklaces, &c."[1] There were continual mutinies and assassinations; General Ventura, and most of the European officers who had trained the army in Ranjit's day, left the Punjab. Dhian Singh, now paramount at Lahore, tried to mend matters by discharging some of the worst regiments and

[1] Edwardes.

enlisting men from the hills in their stead, with the result that the disbanded troops swelled the gangs of robbers that infested the country and sometimes raided into British territory.

Sher Singh was no match either for the army or for Dhian Singh, whom he had begun to suspect of a design to depose him. To propitiate the army, he recalled from exile the Sindhanwalia chiefs, Ranjit's kinsmen, Ajit Singh and Lahna Singh. Ajit Singh had been the lover of the Rani Chand Kaur, and had a score to pay off against her murderers. Adopting Dhian Singh's favourite tactics, the Sindhanwalias persuaded the Maharaja that his Minister was about to murder him, and brought him to sign a paper authorising them upon a certain day to murder Dhian Singh. Then they showed the paper to Dhian Singh, and arranged with him to substitute the Maharaja for the Minister. On the day appointed, they entered the summer-house beyond Lahore, where Sher Singh was listening to state papers, saying they had come to show him a new gun; as he put out his hand to take it, Ajit fired both barrels into his breast. Only four words did he gasp before he died—"What treachery is this?"

They killed or wounded his attendants before going on to the garden close by, where Pertab Singh, the Maharaja's son, the most promising of all the royal family, was at prayer. Lahna Singh rushed upon him with a drawn sword, and the poor boy—who was only twelve years old—cried out, "Babaji, I will remain your servant." "Your father is slain," answered the sirdar, and ran him through the body.

Meanwhile Ajit Singh had ridden to meet Dhian Singh and tell him that all was well. The two rode back to Lahore side by side, and went up to the fort, talking of the succession. "Who is to reign?" asked Ajit; and Dhian answered, "Dhulip Singh shall be Maharaja and I Wazir, and the Sindhanwalias shall enjoy power." Again Ajit asked the same question, and again Dhian obstinately made the same reply. Then Ajit's fury broke forth. "You are the murderer of the Rani Sahib," he cried, and fired his pistol at the Minister. Dhian Singh fell dead from his horse, and the attendants hacked his body with their swords, and flung it into the rubbish-pit of the gun foundry in the fort.

An attempt to complete the day's work by inveigling Suchet Singh and Hira Singh to a conference in the fort, was a complete failure. The news of what had been done was flying through the district, and Hira Singh was haranguing the troops, promising gratuities and increase of pay to all who would follow him to punish the murderers of his father, who had sworn to deliver the country to the English and disband the Khalsa army. Leaving the supper which the cooks were preparing at the moment, the indignant soldiers gathered round the fort, and before the close of another day it was carried by storm. Ajit Singh and Lahna Singh were killed, and Ajit Singh's head was taken to Dhian Singh's widow, who had sworn not to burn with her husband's corpse until his murderers lay dead at her feet.

Next day the Panches of the army proclaimed Hira Singh, "the lapdog of Ranjit," as Prime Minister, and the boy Dhulip Singh as Maharaja.

Of all the spurious children fathered upon Ranjit, Dhulip Singh was the most barefaced attempt at imposition. There was a certain woman in Ranjit's zenana named Jindan, the daughter of a trooper, or, as some said, a dog-keeper in the Maharaja's service. Shameless and abandoned, she enlivened the drinking-bouts at the palace with her coarse buffoonery, and was in great favour with Ranjit in his latter years, until her impudence went so far as to imitate her betters by presenting him with a "son." If Dhulip Singh were indeed her child, his father was a water-carrier at the Palace; but he may have been procured from outside, like Sher Singh. He was certainly not the child of Ranjit, and Jindan was never married to the Maharaja.

Just before Dhian Singh's murder, he seemed to be meditating a *coup d'état*, to depose Sher Singh and set up the six-year-old boy in his stead, and now Hira Singh carried out his father's designs.

The new minister did not enjoy a long or a prosperous reign. The country was almost in a state of anarchy, the army entirely out of hand, and the woman whom he had raised to the rank of queen-mother was intriguing against him, aided by her worthless drunken brother, Jawahir Singh. It is impossible to tell all the story, which is unspeakably loathsome. The end of it was that, after little more than a year, there was another revolution at Lahore; Hira Singh was murdered, and the government was carried on by Jawahir Singh, the Rani Jindan, her lover, and her favourite slave-girl. Murders, revolts, and a terrible visitation of the cholera added to the misery and disorder of the country, while such scenes were passing at the Court as must be left undescribed. On several occasions no business could be done, because Jawahir Singh, the Rani, and even the little Maharaja, were all drunk. Then Jawahir Singh was murdered by the soldiery, though he strove to protect himself by taking the young Maharaja on his elephant.

When Jawahir's widows came in the evening to burn upon his pyre, they were treated with brutality by the soldiers—although a *sati* is sacred, and her curse can drag down to all the hells. The money which they would have thrown among the crowd, according to rite and custom, was snatched out of their hands; their jewels, their ear-rings, and their nose-rings were torn from them when they mounted the pyre. As a crowning outrage, one of the soldiers tore the embroidery and gold fringes from the trousers of one of the women. Then, among the smoke and flames, a tall figure rose and cursed those who had insulted her last hour; ere the year was out, the Sikhs should be conquered, their land desolate, and the wives of the Khalsa army should be widows.

# XIX.

# THE TAIL OF THE AFGHAN STORM—1838-1843

"Cui licet finis, illi et media permissa sunt."

## XIX.

## THE TAIL OF THE AFGHAN STORM—1838-1843.

AT a crisis in one of Great Britain's recent wars, timely help was given by certain reinforcements which had been embarked at Karachi.

It is due to the foresight and wisdom of Bartle Frere, Commissioner of Sind sixty years ago, that Karachi has a harbour ranking "among the most convenient as well as the most important in the world." That Sind itself, on the shortest route between England and India, and commanding the road through the Bolan Pass and onward to Central Asia, should be British territory, is due in the first instance to Lord Auckland's Afghan policy.

Except for strategic advantages, the triangle formed by the delta of the Indus was not a desirable territory. At the base was the sea, and on the other sides were rainless deserts.

Inland stretched mile after mile of sandy waste, where occasional patches of tamarisk jungle marked the beds of rivers filled only in the rains, or ridge after ridge of low undulating stony hills covered with prickly-pear bushes. Here and there were the ruins of ancient cities and forts crumbling to dust and forgotten. The annual rising of the Indus turned great part of the plain into a level flood, which, as it subsided, left wide tracts of swamp to breed malaria and fever.

Towards the end of the eighteenth century a Biluchi chief had established himself in Sind. He succeeded in having his title established by a firman from Kabul, and took his younger brothers into partnership with him. All but one of the "Four Friends" (Char Yar), as local history calls them, left male descendants, and these, known collectively as "the Amirs," were ruling Sind at the time of the Tripartite Treaty.

According to some authorities, the Amirs were good-natured, if hasty and not always to be trusted, and their government, though despotic, was patriarchal. According to others, the Amirs were monsters, as cowardly and treacherous as they were debauched and cruel. Without leaning to one side or the other, certain facts may be admitted. The Amirs did not profess to govern Sind for its own good; their exactions were ruining the cultivators of the soil, who had to pay nearly two-thirds of the produce to the tax-collector. They laid waste fertile land to make preserves for their game, which it was death for any man but themselves to kill or injure. Neither they nor their Biluchi vassals, who were the upper class in Sind, saw any harm in cutting a wife to pieces, or in stifling a child whose further existence was inconvenient.

Uglier crimes than these were laid to the charge of the Amirs; if the worst that was said of them had been proved in every detail, it scarcely could justify the way in which they were treated by the British Government at the time of the Afghan war.

Already several commercial treaties had been made between the Amirs and the Company, by which free passage through Sind was granted for merchants and travellers, while it was laid down that ships of war and military stores were not to be carried on the Indus.

Unhappily for the Amirs, Ranjit Singh refused to allow the British army to pass through his territories on the way to Afghanistan. Lord Auckland durst not offend "our old and faithful ally," as he styled the Maharaja, so he directed Colonel Pottinger, the British Resident at Haidarabad, to inform the Amirs that the army must pass through Sind, and therefore "the article of the treaty with them prohibitory of using the Indus for the conveyance of military stores, must necessarily be suspended."

But more was to be taken from the Amirs than the control of the river of which they were keenly jealous; funds were wanted for the expedition. It was as impossible to get money from Ranjit, who had hoards of treasure, as from Shah Shuja, who was without resources. Accordingly, Pottinger was instructed that the Amirs must pay several lakhs of rupees to Shah Shuja as the price of his acknowledgment of their independence; the exact sum, he was told, had not been settled, but "the Amirs may be supposed wealthy."

This letter was written by William Macnaghten, then Secretary to the Governor-General. For any part that he may have played in this business he was to pay in full, some years later, upon the blood-stained snow on the plain of Kabul.

The Amirs protested indignantly that Shah Shuja was the puppet of the British, incapable of taking one rupee without their help. They produced releases from his supremacy, signed by himself upon the Koran in former days.

"How this is to be got over, I do not myself see," wrote Pottinger. He saw the method when a British force, having obtained possession of the island fort of Bakkar, the key of Sind, began its march southwards to Haidarabad, where another British force was making demonstrations.

The threat was enough; the Amirs submitted, hoping, said one who knew them, that when once the English army was in Afghanistan, they might prevent its return to India. It has been told how that army returned.

## II.

Relations between the Amirs and the British Government became more and more strained after it had been decided to evacuate Afghanistan. For a time the Amirs of Upper and Lower Sind forgot their disagreements with each other, and combined against the hated English. "They interrupted the river navigation; they levied duties contrary to the treaties; they even passed an insolent decree that all the traders who had established themselves on the skirts of our cantonments should have their houses razed and their goods confiscated."[1] To some extent they had been checked by James Outram,

[1] A. Innes Shand.

the Political Agent in Upper Sind and Khelat, whose achievements in maintaining peace, in keeping open the road to Kandahar, and in sending supplies to the generals in Afghanistan, had been rewarded by removal from his post. In his stead, with full civil and military powers, had come a small peremptory man of sixty years old, with flowing grey hair and beard, hooked nose, and eyes as bright and fierce as those of a hawk, flashing behind a large pair of spectacles, which the Amirs amused themselves with trying on, at their first interview.

The Amirs did not like Sir Charles Napier, or his business with them. He had none of Outram's dignified courtesy and conciliatory manner. He was irascible, vehement, making no allowances for the tortuous methods of Eastern diplomacy. He upbraided them with treachery, denouncing their secret correspondence with the ruling powers at Lahore and Multan; he required them to sign another treaty, by which, though they were relieved from the payment of the tribute and subsidies, they were obliged to cede territory to the British, and to the Nawab of Bhawalpur to whom part of it had once belonged. There was much talk of "improvement in the administration," and the Amirs, like many better men, had no zeal for improvements that were to be carried out at their expense. So they made their dispositions, hoping for the support of some of the neighbours whose wrath against the English they had been fanning since the beginning of the Afghan war.

In all time of trouble the Amirs of Upper Sind could take refuge in their fortress of Imamgarh, in the very heart of the desert. No European had ever beheld it, none knew exactly where it stood. Few Sindians would dare to attempt the way thither by the desert tracks that changed from time to time as the scanty watersprings disappeared from the wells, to trickle up again in some other patch of sand, far away. In the desert prowled the Biluchi horsemen, ready to attack all comers. Within the fortress was a garrison of two thousand, with food, water, and ammunition. Once in Imamgarh, the Amirs could defy any foe, since those who escaped from the horsemen would be smitten down by the sun, or perish more slowly of hunger and thirst among the whirling columns of dust that overwhelm camels and dry up waterskins.

Imamgarh, "the base and place of arms for the main army" of Upper Sind, was held by a son of the old Amir Rustam, lately the wearer of "the Turban" that gave pre-eminence in Sind. Rustam had been tricked into resigning the Turban to an ambitious brother, Ali Murad, and believed that Napier, who had advised him to "trust to the care" of that brother, was responsible for his downfall. Napier considered the Amirs "the greatest ruffians he ever met with, without any exception," and was convinced that the annexation of Sind was inevitable and desirable—"a very advantageous, useful, humane piece of rascality." But he was incapable of double-dealing, and the villain of the piece was Ali Murad, who studied how to embroil the other Amirs with Napier, and to represent their actions in the worst light, so that he might become sole ruler in the land.

Another son of Rustam was holding another fort in the eastern desert near the border of Jeysulmer. Rustam, when called upon to make his sons keep the peace, blandly replied that he had invested them with authority to hold the forts, and that his cession of the Turban to Ali Murad was null and void. Ali Murad announced an intention of reducing his kinsmen to order, but seemed in no haste.

The Biluchis were gathering in Upper Sind; Rustam himself hovered on the borders of the desert where food and water could be had, and other Amirs were said to be upon the road to Imamgarh with thousands of followers. It was

January 1843, and in a little while the fearful "hot weather" of Sind would begin.

Napier was as well aware of this as the Amirs could be. His own summary of the situation is not unfair to them, if unjust to Outram. "I found that all the politicals had gone on from the beginning, trifling. Sometimes letting the Amirs infringe the treaty without notice; at others pulling them up, and then dropping the matter: in short, I saw it was a long chain of infringement — denial — apology — pardon, over and over. I therefore resolved not to let this which old Indians call '*knowing the people*' go on. . . . As letters from the Ameers were intercepted, proposing to other powers to league and drive us out of Scinde; Lord Ellenborough thought, and I think justly, that a new treaty should be entered into, which he sent me. . . . I cannot enter upon our right to be *here at all* —that is Lord Auckland's affair. Well! I presented the draft of the new treaty. The Ameers bowed with their usual apparent compliance, but raised troops in all directions. These I was ordered by the Governor-General to disperse. To disperse irregular troops, they having a desert at their back, and four hundred miles of river to cross and run up the mountains, and all this with their chiefs swearing they submitted to everything, to get me into the *hot* weather when I could not move, and thus cut off all our communications at their ease, was no trifle. In short, it was to attack a 'Will-o'-the-wisp.'"

The words were written as he returned from a chase after the "Will-o'-the-wisp."

Even the wild beasts—the hyæna, the boar, the deer—dared not penetrate far into the wastes surrounding Imamgarh. "The sandhills stretched north and south for hundreds of miles, in parallel ridges rounded at top, and most symmetrically plaited like the ripple on the sea-shore after a placid tide. The sand was mingled with shells, and run in great streams resembling numerous rivers."[1] Across the ridges toiled a small force of men, mounted upon camels—350 of the 22nd (Queen's) Regiment, 200 irregular cavalry, dragging two howitzers, and led by Napier himself, who was enjoying the desperate venture with all his heart. It cost him nothing to march light, since he had often demonstrated his maxim that no soldier needs much baggage beyond two towels and a cake of soap; but when the forage failed, and water was scarcely to be had, on the second day of his desert march he was obliged to cut off more than superfluities, and sent back 150 of his cavalry.

[1] W. Napier.

Rustam, with seven guns and a force ten times as large as Napier's, was on his flank, but still the march continued. Outram, sent back from Bombay by a sudden caprice of the Governor-General that he might help the negotiations for the treaty, had reached Napier's camp in time to take part in the expedition; he was sent to reason with Rustam, and Napier rode further and further "through an ocean of sandhills."

Water was not always to be found, the camels grew weak, and the men must help to drag the howitzers. They went by a way that they knew not, uncertain whether they went right; but on the eighth day they saw the walls and the round towers that encompassed the square keep of Imamgarh.

It was empty; the young Amir and his garrison had fled with their treasure, two days before, southwards to the Indus.

To save trouble in the future, having wrung an unwilling consent from Ali Murad, Napier used the powder left in the magazine to blow the fortress to pieces. Then he set off on the return march to the Indus, thinking not of war and battle, but of his dead mother. He notes in his diary, on the day when Imamgarh was destroyed, that in a dream he saw her "beauteous face"—that face which, eighty years before, had almost won a throne for Lady

Sarah Lennox when she played at making hay in the grounds of her uncle's house.

## III.

While Napier was bringing his force back to camp by another way through the desert, without a single case of sickness or the loss of one man, Outram was traversing ninety miles of hostile country with an escort of two Biluchi horsemen, endeavouring at the eleventh hour to make the Amirs decide for peace. He could do little. Rustam received him civilly, but when assured that the territory remaining to the Amirs was to be settled, "as much as possible, fairly towards all parties," retorted, "What remains to be settled? Our means of livelihood are taken."

Not one Amir from Upper Sind came in answer to Outram's summons to meet him by January 25th. The Amirs of Lower Sind ostentatiously sent deputies to the British camp, while secretly commanding their allies and feudatories to come with all their fighting men to Haidarabad.

Outram prevailed upon Napier to allow him to go down to Haidarabad to plead with them, and to extend the time of grace until February 6th. Though Napier was the first to give Outram the title of "the Bayard of India," he was finding that chivalry might be somewhat inconvenient. Having honestly made up his own mind that the Amirs intended treachery, and that they must be swept out of the way, he could not understand how any one could hold other views. "I confess not to like those who differ in opinion with me," he openly declared, at a time when he and Outram were in complete accord. Later on, it is: "Outram provokes me; he pities those rascals, who are such atrocious tyrants that it is virtuous to roll them over like ninepins." Nevertheless, he now wrote to Outram: "I am sure they" (the Amirs) "will not resist by force of arms, but I would omit no one step that you, or any one, thinks can prevent the chance of it." It was too late to persuade the Amirs that the General was not bent upon fighting them, whatever they might do. The nature of his methods of diplomacy was such as might be imagined from an order written soon after his arrival in India to the officer in command of a regiment reported to be in a state of mutiny: "I expect to hear by express that you have put down the mutiny within two hours after receipt of this letter."

At Haidarabad, Outram won the chiefs to a semblance of submission. A Durbar was summoned for February 12th, at which the Amirs would sign and seal the treaty. Incidentally, they designed at the same time to murder Outram.

"Blindly went Outram to the intended slaughter-house, and if he escaped, it was only because the Ameers, thinking the General was as reckless as his Commissioner, hoped for a greater victim." Outram probably was not so blind as William Napier chose to consider him; he knew his influence over the savage Biluchis, and he trusted to it to bring him unscathed from his last attempt to ensure peace.

The treaty was signed by all the Amirs save one, who was absent, and Outram went back to the Residency through a howling, cursing mob, that was restrained from violence only by the armed escort sent by the Amirs.

Next day, the Amirs were bewailing their inability to control their soldiers, to which Outram replied that they would be responsible for their subjects' conduct, and that he had no intention of retiring from the Residency, and would not post one additional sentry at his door.

Two days after this, eight thousand horse and foot attacked the Residency with six guns, but failed to force the "imperfect low-walled enclosure of 200 yards square," although Outram had only a hundred men to defend it, and each man had only forty rounds of ammunition. After four hours' fighting, "seeing nothing more could be done," the garrison crossed the few hundred yards dividing the Residency from the Indus, and embarked on the two little steamers belonging to the Company, which carried them up the river to the advanced guard of Napier's army.

They had given what Napier termed "a brilliant example of defending a military post," and the great battle for which he had been longing ever since his arrival in the country was now inevitable. There was probably not a happier man in India than the old General on the night of February 16th. "Not to be anxious about attacking such immensely superior numbers is impossible; but it is a delightful anxiety." "Let them be sixty or one hundred thousand," he exclaimed, when reports were brought in that the enemy were massing in increasing numbers, "I will fight!" He brought his journal up to date; he wrote last letters to kin and friends; he visited the outposts, and at midnight he lay down to sleep.

## IV.

Over a level plain of smooth hard sand ran the road to Miani. Here and there a few stunted bushes broke the whiteness of the surface, and to the right and left of the road, about three-quarters of a mile apart, were the Shikargahs, the woods which the Amirs had made for their hunting.

It was for other sport than hunting that they had brought out their army of thirty thousand men early on this February morning, and drawn it up within the dry bed of the Fuleli river. In front of the bank which sloped down to the plain were their guns; the right wing rested on an entrenched village, the left on a shikargah covered by a wall with one narrow opening.

Thus Captain Jacob of the Sind Horse found them, when Napier sent him on a scouting expedition at about seven o'clock on the morning of February 16th.

At three o'clock the bugles had sounded "Fall in," and Napier with his little army began the advance towards Miani. Outram was not with him, having been detached to set fire to the woods in which it was supposed that the enemy's left flank was posted. As the enemy had moved during the night, no one was the worse for the manœuvre save Outram himself, and the two hundred men with him, who missed the battle; but the smoke of the burning woods was the signal for Napier to form his line at nine o'clock.

The whole of Napier's force, including the officers, amounted to no more than two thousand four hundred men; and some of these must be told off to guard the camp-followers, who were formed into a circle surrounded by recumbent camels and bales of stores. Only one European regiment was there, the 22nd.

The line was formed, and the General gave the signal to advance across the thousand yards that separated the two armies. Already the Biluchi guns were playing on his line, and shots from the marksmen who lay hidden in the dry watercourses that seamed the ground, were driving through clouds of dust. Eighteen hundred men were to be led in frontal attack against more than thirty thousand, who had nearly every advantage of position.

As he rode forward with his staff, the General noted the opening in the wall enclosing the Shikargah on the enemy's left. He "rode near this wall, and found it was nine or ten feet high; he rode nearer, and marked it had no loopholes for the enemy to shoot through; he rode into the opening under a play of matchlocks,"[1] and saw there was no scaffolding, and therefore that the enemy could not fire over the top of the wall. Calling Captain Tew, he bade him take the grenadiers of the 22nd; they must bar the way for the enemy who would try to issue from the

[1] W. Napier.

opening and fall on the British line in flank and rear. Tew was killed at his post, but his men held on, keeping six thousand Biluchis blocked within the wall.

Meanwhile the army had advanced across the plain, the charge was sounded by the bugler who ran all day at the General's stirrup, and the infantry dashed forward, regardless of the fire from the guns within fifteen yards of them. A shout and a rush, and the 22nd were on the top of the bank, looking down upon the mass of the enemy. "Thick as standing corn, and gorgeous as a field of flowers," the Biluchis filled the river-bed; "they clustered on both banks, and covered the plain beyond. Guarding their heads with their large dark shields, they shook their sharp swords, beaming in the sun, their shouts rolled like a peal of thunder" [1] as they dashed over the bank.

The battle raged round the bed of the Fuleli, as musket and bayonet met sword and matchlock. The Biluchis leaped the banks like a swelling river; "they gave their breasts to the shot, they leaped upon the guns and were blown away by twenties at a time; their dead went down the steep slope by hundreds; but the gaps in their masses were continually filled up from the rear." The 22nd and the sepoys could not hold their ground against the

[1] W. Napier.

sheer weight of numbers; they were broken, they were driven back, but they rallied, and stubbornly regained their place. Wherever the fight was fiercest could be seen the little wiry figure of the General, cheering his men by voice and gesture, his waving grey hair singed by the guns. He was unable to defend himself because a day or two before the battle, seeing a camel-driver brutally ill-treating an animal, he had clouted him over the head, thereby dislocating his right wrist, without making any impression upon the offender. Once, in the press of the fight, he was separated from all his men, and surrounded by several of the enemy, "who stalked around him with raised shields and scowling eyes," but forbore to touch him, so that he came back unhurt amid the wild cheering of the 22nd.

After three hours of this work, Napier recognised that his men could not stand much more. Nearly all the European officers were killed or wounded, and the sepoys, as brave as the bravest when led by the men whom they knew and trusted, could not stand without them. The men's muskets were clogged with powder. Where ten of the enemy had fallen, it seemed that twenty swarmed in their stead. "There was no time to be lost," wrote Sir Charles in his despatch, "and I sent orders to the cavalry to force the right of the enemy's line."

Across the plain galloped the 9th Bengal Cavalry and the Sind Horse, and drove the Biluchis from the entrenched village. The ground was intersected with nullahs and ditches, and fifty men were thrown from their saddles in the charge, yet they rode through the guns, and over the high bank of the river, through the mud and water that filled its bed, up the bank on the opposite side, to divide on the plain beyond. The 9th fell upon the infantry to the left, the Sind Horse crashed into the camp of the Amirs, "spreading confusion along the rear of the line of battle." Then at last the Biluchi centre began to waver. "The 22nd first saw their masses shake, and leaping forward with the shout of victory, pushed them backwards into the deep ravine, and there closed in combat again." Sepoys and Madras Sappers crowded after them, and the forces within the Shikargah joined them in the river-bed for the last struggle. Through the clouds of dust and smoke now emerged the bright-coloured turban of a Biluchi, now the dirty white cotton cover that shaded the forage cap of a soldier of the 22nd.

Then from the choking haze began to thrust masses of Biluchi swordsmen at a swinging stride which they would not break into a run, though grape and shells were pouring upon them from the English guns. The flying cavalry were pursued by the triumphant Sind Horse for three miles, but the infantry yielded their ground so slowly that Napier thought it well to leave them alone, when once they were full in retreat.

He made his camp beyond the river, and rode over the battlefield at night while his soldiers slept. Nearly a sixth of his force had been killed or wounded, but more than five thousand of the enemy lay stretched on the plain, or heaped one upon another in the river-bed. After returning to his tent, he slept so soundly that when a false alarm roused the camp, Outram was obliged to pull him off his bed before he could be awakened.

Next morning the Amirs sent messengers to ask what terms he would grant. "Life, and nothing more," was the General's reply; "and I want your decision by twelve o'clock, as I shall by that time have buried my dead, and given my soldiers their breakfasts." Six Amirs thereupon rode into camp and laid their swords at his feet. The swords were for ornament rather than use; none of the wearers had exposed himself on the field of battle where their soldiers had fought to the death.

## V.

The campaign was not finished when Napier occupied Haidarabad a few days later. One of the Amirs, "the Lion," Sher Mohammad,[1] who had not been present at Miani, was at large, and gathering an army. His skirmishers raided up to the city gates, and drove away camels from under the noses of the pickets.

"Quit this land and your life shall be spared," was the message that his envoy brought to Napier in March, "provided you restore all that you have taken." As the words were spoken, the evening gun was fired. "You hear that sound?" answered Napier. "It is my answer to your chief. Begone!" And he turned his back upon them.

A friendly proposal to assassinate Sher Mohammad, made by "the Lion's" own brother, met with no gratitude from Napier, who sent warning at once to the chief. His own position was none of the pleasantest, with Sher Mohammad's forces surrounding his camp and dividing him from the reinforcements for which he was waiting, but he played the game of bluff, and played it well. With the help once more of Jacob and the Sind Horse, he succeeded in getting eight hundred sepoys, several squadrons of cavalry, and a battery of horse artillery, past the enemy into his lines. The day after their arrival, sitting at breakfast with his staff, he suddenly exclaimed, "Now my luck would be great if I could get my other

[1] Sher = Lion.

reinforcements; but that cannot be—they will not be here for a week, and I will not let 'the Lion' bully me any longer, I will fight him to-morrow." The words were hardly out of his mouth when an officer exclaimed, "There are boats coming up the river!" All ran out of the tent; the reinforcements from Bombay, coming up-stream, were entering the port, and in the distance, coming down-stream, were boats bringing other reinforcements.

Next day, March 24th, at another spot on the banks of the Fuleli, within a few miles of the field of Miani, the promised battle[1] was fought, and "the Lion" was put to flight

He fled into the desert, whence he was hunted by Jacob, who broke up his force, and drove him back to the Indus. The news of this victory reached Sir Charles at the time when he had dropped down with sunstroke, on going out of his tent. Thirty-three European soldiers who fell at the same moment, as from the discharge of a shell, were dead in three hours; the intrepid old General, having been bled in both arms, was making a hard struggle for life, when the horseman came with Jacob's despatch. "I felt life come back," said Napier.

[1] Generally known in history as the battle of Dubba, but inscribed as "Hyderabad" on the colours of the regiments engaged.

"The tail of the Afghan storm," as he called it, had now passed away, and he turned all his energy to civil administration. "I have to collect revenue, administer justice, arrange the troops, survey the country, project improvements, form civil officers, and appoint proper functionaries." He organised police, he forbade the carrying of weapons by any but the chiefs, and he put down wife-murder with a strong hand, to the bewilderment of the culprits and their friends, acting always on his own maxim that "the great recipe for quieting a country is a good thrashing first, and great kindness afterwards."

Meanwhile the Amirs were prisoners of state, and Outram vainly pleaded their cause in England. Nothing could be done. The Court of Directors passed resolutions condemning the policy which had resulted in the annexation of Sind, but Sind henceforth remained part of British India. Outram could only record his protest, and give all his share of prize-money—three thousand pounds—to charities in India.

For more than three years Napier governed Sind, a terror to evil-doers. Then, after a few months' holiday, came his appointment as Commander-in-Chief in India. Always at strife with some one or other, his chief antagonist was now Lord Dalhousie, who would pay no attention to his prophecies of a mutiny in the sepoy army, and their contention rose to such a pitch that he resigned his post. There were two years of peace at home, and then Charles Napier died quietly on his camp-bed, surrounded by those who loved him, while his son-in-law waved over his head the colours that the 22nd had carried to victory in Sind.

# XX.

# ON THE BANKS OF THE SUTLEJ—
## 1845-1846

**"I don't think that men ever could have been more attached to any commander than to old Gough, and there is little wonder he was looked upon as a father more than as a military superior."**

**—Sergeant P. KEAY, Bengal Artillery.**

## XX.

## ON THE BANKS OF THE SUTLEJ—1845-1846.

THE Sikh army had an overweening belief in their own strength, trained as they had been under Ranjit's eye by European officers, and the recent disaster in Afghanistan had shown that the English were not invincible. In every revolution at Lahore it had been proclaimed that the vanquished party were intriguing with the English to disband the army of the Khalsa. The army was athirst for vengeance upon the English, and the Rani Jindan, who for all her sins "had more wit and daring than any man of her nation," made no effort to restrain them, believing that, if thoroughly defeated, they would give her less trouble in the future. In December 1845, sixty thousand Sikhs crossed the Sutlej and invaded British territory.

It was an anxious moment for the Government

of India. The sepoys of the Company's army were for the most part Bengali Brahmans, whose caste rules were a continual hindrance to their efficiency, incapable of enduring the hardships and fatigues of which the Sikhs made light, and no longer confident that their Sahibs would lead them to victory. That experiment in Afghanistan had lost us our prestige, as well as a few millions of money and many valuable lives.

Through all the revolutions that had distracted the Punjab the last six years, the Government of India had exercised continual forbearance. "It is desirable," wrote Sir Henry Hardinge, the Governor-General, "that nothing should be done by us to indicate that the internal affairs of the state of Lahore are matter for our concern." Certain preparations had been made unostentatiously; Gulab Singh, now Raja of Jammu, and suddenly become our friend and ally, sent warning that war was inevitable. With the Sikhs encamped near Ferozepore, it was impossible to avert it by any feat of diplomacy. On December 12th, Sir Hugh Gough, the Commander-in-Chief in India, started on his march through sand and jungle to Mudki, about twenty miles from Ferozepore.

Sir Hugh was a tried soldier. He had begun his career in his father's militia corps at the age of thirteen, and, after obtaining his commission, had seen service at the Cape, in the Peninsula, in China, and lately in the Gwalior campaign. Impetuous, fearless, with a quick temper that sometimes exploded when he was furious, "as only Sir Hugh Gough could be furious," and a generous spirit that neither danger, calumny, nor injustice could quench, he was respected by all who knew him, and adored by his soldiers. He may not have been a complete military strategist, but his men followed wherever he led; and even when his leading seemed to have cost them dearly, their faith in him never wavered, and wounded and dying cheered him "when they had scarcely heads left upon their shoulders to cheer with."

It was on the 18th of December that his forces arrived at Mudki, soon after noon. The cooks were busy preparing dinner for the weary men, the camp was being made upon the sandy plain, when clouds of dust began to rise in the distance, and gradually came nearer. The Sikhs had detached 10,000 cavalry and 2000 infantry to cut off Sir Hugh's army before it could be reinforced by Sir John Littler, who was at Ferozepore.

It was plain from the first that the Bengalis could not stand against the men of the Khalsa. It was the English cavalry and infantry that drove back the enemy with cold steel. The Sikhs fought desperately, neither giving nor taking quarter. When night brought an end to the slaughter, after the fighting had been carried on for an hour and a half in the dim starlight, amid clouds of dust, the Khalsa had been driven from every position, and had left seventeen pieces of artillery behind them.

Our troops, too exhausted to follow up their victory, rested upon the plain and buried their dead. Reinforcements came in, and on the 21st Sir Hugh led out his army to attack the entrenched camp of Lal Singh at Ferozepore. Another portion of the Sikh army, under Tej Singh, was mounting guard over Littler at Ferozepore, and Sir Hugh's instructions were that Littler should effect a junction with him, unperceived by this force.

It is a question for the military experts—who have decided it variously—who was to blame for the errors of that day. Unfortunately for Sir Hugh's plans, Sir Henry Hardinge had accompanied our forces, and had been so much impressed by the bravery and discipline of the Khalsa at Mudki that he forbade the Commander-in-Chief to engage the enemy when they found themselves face to face with Lal Singh's entrenchments, on the morning of the 21st, until Littler's contingent should arrive. The men, who had only snatched a hasty breakfast after countermarching and being arrayed in new formation, were tired and hungry when the action at last began, about half-past three in the afternoon.

The enemy's guns were more numerous and heavier than our own. Littler's division made a premature attack, and was so fearfully punished that it had to retire. When part of our forces by repeated charges had won their way into the Sikh camp, a powder magazine exploded, and increased the damage already wrought by shot and shell. Sir Harry Smith succeeded in taking the village of Ferozeshah, in the middle of the Sikh position, but after holding it for several hours, was dislodged between two and three in the morning.

As darkness fell, the Sikh camp took fire in many places, from the explosion of packets of ammunition. The English army was recalled to a position between the burning camp and a low scrubby jungle, within reach of the Sikh artillery, which played upon them occasionally through the long winter night. Most of our men had been under arms for four-and-twenty hours; they suffered cruelly from hunger, and still more cruelly from thirst. Even some of the officers "of rank and in important situations" lost heart, and two came to Sir Hugh, as from the Governor-General, to urge retreat upon Ferozepore. "I shall go to the Governor-General," he replied, "but my determination is taken rather to leave my bones to bleach honourably at Ferozeshah, than that they should rot dishonourably at Ferozepore." Sir Henry Hardinge denied having sent any such message, and was resolute as Gough himself not to retreat, though he had little hope to do more than make a good end. He sent away the sword of Napoleon, given to him by the Duke of Wellington, and wrote instructions to his secretary to destroy all the State Papers left at Mudki, in the event of defeat at Ferozeshah.

In spite of his harassed night, Sir Hugh avowedly saw nothing to make him despond when the daylight showed him friend from foe. The infantry formed line, the Sikh entrenchments were once more attacked, and the enemy dislodged from the whole position. Then "the line halted as on a day of manœuvre, receiving its two leaders" (Gough and Hardinge) "as they rode along its front with a gratifying cheer, and displaying the captured standards of the Khalsa."

It was towards the evening of that day that intelligence was brought that Tej Singh was marching from Ferozepore with fresh battalions and a large field of artillery. Owing to the explosions in the past night, not a shot was left to our artillery, and the cavalry horses were "thoroughly done up." "For a moment then I felt a regret as each passing shot left me on horseback," says Sir Hugh. "But it was only for a moment."

The storm of shot and shell that now broke over our forces was too much for the sepoys, and even the English troops were staggered. Then Gough, in the white coat that he insisted upon wearing in the day of battle, rushed forward, his A.D.C. at his side, an easy mark "to draw a portion of the artillery fire on us from our hard-pressed infantry." "We, thank God, succeeded, and saved many unhurt," wrote the Commander-in-Chief to his son.

The day was saved by what seemed an irreparable disaster The British lines still doggedly held their ground; the Sikhs, always more ready to entrench than to attack, had lost their impetuosity. An officer on the staff, dressed in pyjamas, because, he said, "his overalls had been so riddled with bullets that they had dropped off," delivered an order to our artillery and cavalry to retire on Ferozepore. The poor man was suffering from sunstroke, and the order was the invention of his own crazed brain; but it was obeyed. Tej Singh took it into his head that the movement was part of an elaborate device to cut off his retreat, turned tail, and left the British forces upon the stricken field.

We buried our dead—nearly seven hundred—at Ferozepore, while the Sikhs fled back to Lahore. They left many men in the Sutlej, many more were robbed, abused, and beaten by the country people of the districts through which they had to pass, "even the women of the villages turning out to rail at them and strike them as they hurried along."

By January they had regained their spirits, and were massing again near Ludhiana. Sir Harry Smith routed them at Aliwal, and they fled back over the river. "Never was victory more complete," he wrote, "and never was one fought under more happy circumstances, literally with all the pomp of a field-day; and right well did all behave." The sound of the cannonading was heard near Sobraon, where Gough and Hardinge were watching the fortified camp of the Sikhs, on the right bank of the river. An officer asked the Commander-in-Chief what he thought of it. "Think of it! why, that 'tis the most glorious thing I ever heard. I know by the sound of the guns that Smith has carried the position and silenced their artillery." When the news of the victory reached him, "he was nearly frantic with joy"; two minutes afterwards an officer found him on his knees in his tent returning thanks to the God of Battles.

## II.

The Sikh camp at Sobraon was garrisoned with not less than thirty thousand men; its seventy pieces of cannon were supported by batteries on the other side of the river, and a good bridge ran from bank to bank. Nevertheless, others besides the Commander-in-Chief were of opinion that it could be taken by a direct attack. The weakest place was on the right of the Sikh entrenchments, and hither Sir Robert Dick led his division on the morning of February 10th, as soon as the heavy river-mists had cleared away.

The battle began with an artillery duel, in which the sixty British guns were no match for the Sikh artillery. After two hours' cannonading, an officer hurried to tell the Commander-in-Chief that only a few rounds of shot were left. "Thank God!" was Sir Hugh's ejaculation; "then I'll be at them with the bayonet!"

At this point, an officer on the Governor-General's staff rode up to urge, in Sir Henry

Hardinge's name, that if Gough were not sure of success, and anticipated much loss, he should withdraw his men and work up to the entrenchments by regular approaches.

"Loss there will be, of course," returned Sir Hugh. "Look at those works bristling with guns, and defended as they will be; but, by God's blessing, I feel confident of success."

The officer rode back, and presently returned to repeat the same message, to which Sir Hugh made the same reply. But when the messenger returned again, Sir Hugh rounded upon him, his silvery hair bristling, his small figure quivering with impatience. "What! withdraw the troops after the action has commenced, and when I feel confident of success? Indeed I will not! Tell Sir Robert Dick to move on in the name of God!"

It was nine o'clock in the morning when Dick's first line began the advance. Dick was killed, but his division was established within the entrenchments. Sir Harry Smith's division on the right was less fortunate; the way led over rough ground, intersected by water-courses; their first advance was repelled, and as they formed up again under heavy fire they could see the Sikhs butchering the wounded whom they had left behind them. Once more they charged, and this time they were not driven back.

Meanwhile the central attack had been repulsed twice, with heavy loss. The entrenchments could not be climbed without scaling-ladders; so they turned to the left, where the defences were not so high: one man climbed on the shoulders of another, and the guns were taken.

For nearly an hour the battle raged hand to hand at every point. The Sikhs stood their ground, even regaining some of their guns for an interval. Then the British cavalry swept through the openings that the sappers had made in the entrenchments, and the 3rd Light Dragoons, "whom no obstacle usually held formidable by horse appears to check,"[1] cut down the Sikh gunners, who, as in former actions, were resolved to die at their posts. The fire slackened, then ceased, and what remained of the Sikh host was in flight to the Sutlej, which had risen seven inches, while our horse artillery mowed them down. "Hundreds fell under this cannonade; hundreds upon hundreds were drowned in attempting the perilous passage." By eleven o'clock the battle of Sobraon was over.

More than once on that day was it proved that all the Khalsa was not composed of the dissolute ruffians who had torn the kingdom of Ranjit Singh to pieces, and made the name of Sikh

[1] Gough.

abhorrent from the banks of the Sutlej to the hills of Kashmir. There was a white-clad figure in the Sikh camp that for honour, loyalty, and dauntless courage might have stood beside the white-coated Commander-in-Chief. Sirdar Sham Singh was the son of a father who had given his life for Ranjit by taking a sickness of the Maharaja's upon himself, as Babar did long ago for Humayun. He had been one of the first in the breach at Multan, and had fought in many engagements. Though his daughter was married to Nao Nahal Singh, he took no part in politics, and from first to last had protested against the war with the English, pointing out that it would be the destruction of the Khalsa. In answer to his warnings, he only received the taunt that he was a coward, and afraid to die. So he rode to the camp at Sobraon, knowing that he rode to his death. On the night before the battle Tej Singh sent for him, and advised that they should fly together when the English made their first attack, and when he rejected the advice, said in anger, "If you are so brave, you had better take your oath about it, for I believe you will come with me after all." Then Sham Singh swore upon the Granth never to leave the trenches alive. Next morning, dressed in white and mounted on his white mare, he exhorted his followers to die as became sons of the Khalsa rather than to give back before the enemy. In the thick of the fight his voice called upon the Sikhs to quit themselves like men. "It was not till he saw that all was lost that he spurred forward against the 50th Regiment, waving his sword, and calling on his men to follow him. Some fifty of them obeyed the call, but were driven back into the river, and Sham Singh fell dead from his horse, pierced with seven balls."[1]

After the battle, when his servants swam back across the river to search for his body, it lay where the dead were thickest, marked out by the white dress and long white beard. His widow knew he was sworn not to outlive a defeat, and when the news of the battle came to her, she burned herself with the clothes that he had worn on their marriage day—the last *Sati* in the Punjab.

After Sobraon, the way was clear. The British army crossed the Sutlej, and the young Maharaja, accompanied by Gulab Singh and some dozen other chiefs, came to make submission to the Governor-General.

The terms of peace were not hard. The Government of India had no wish to annex the Punjab, and only desired that their territory and that of

[1] L. Griffin.

their allies should be secure from raids in future. Some of the worst disturbers of the peace were dead, and it was hoped that under proper guidance Dhulip Singh might grow up to rule with more credit to himself and less inconvenience to his subjects. Lahore, for the present, was to be garrisoned by English troops; the country between the Beas and the Sutlej was to be ceded to the Company; and an indemnity of a million and a half sterling was to be paid.

When this treaty was ratified, at a Durbar held in Hardinge's tent, "a small tin box enveloped in a shabby cloth" was passed from hand to hand. Within it was the Koh-i-Nur, which Dhulip Singh, as Maharaja of Lahore, had the right to wear.

In great state he was escorted back to his capital; the courtezans of the Sikh soldiers looked from every window as British troops marched through the narrow dirty streets; "and on every roof and in every gateway the soldiers themselves were throwing dice, and gambling away the memory of their defeats."[1]

[1] H. Edwardes.

# XXI.

# THE ADVENTURES OF A SUBALTERN—1847-1849

"The Heroical Vein of Mankind runs much in the Souldiery, and courageous part of the World; and in that form we oftenest find Men above Men."
—Sir THOMAS BROWNE, *Christian Morals.*

## XXI.

## THE ADVENTURES OF A SUBALTERN—1847-1849.

HAVING shattered the Khalsa, the English, with their usual stolidity, began to put the pieces together again.

The Rani Jindan was still to be nominal head of the Durbar, with Lal Singh as Wazir, and two British officers to support and advise them. One of these was Major George Macgregor, who as Political Agent at Jalalabad, had been one of the heads of the "Illustrious Garrison," and his superior was Colonel Henry Montgomery Lawrence, to be remembered for all time as the defender of Lucknow in a still more desperate siege. Sir John Littler was in command of the British forces at Lahore. With three such men at his back, if Lal Singh had set himself to reorganise the army, and reduce the power of the Sikh chieftains, he might have established a government worthy of the name. But "he reformed with one hand and peculated with the other." Having discharged some soldiers without paying them, their clamour terrified him so greatly that he dared discharge no more; and his confiscations of the chieftains' lands failed of their moral effect, because all the fiefs were transferred to himself.

As soon as the war indemnity began to be considered, it was evident that two millions and a half could not be paid from an empty Treasury, with the pay of the army in arrears, and the civil population already stripped bare with cess and dues and customs. It was therefore decided that instead of paying the indemnity in money, the Government of Lahore should cede the districts of Hazara and Kashmir to the British.

At this point Gulab Singh, still posing as the friend of law and the ally of the English, came forward with an offer: let them give Kashmir to him, and he would undertake to pay three-quarters of a million sterling for it. Seeing that the greater part of his resources had been derived from his plunder of the citadel at Lahore after the death of Nao Nahal Singh, the audacity of the proposal would have overpowered any one except the Government of India, who actually—upon a notion that Kashmir was too far off to be garrisoned—

delivered the country over to a man whose cruelties were as notorious as his treachery.

It was doubtless wrong of Lal Singh to bribe the Governer of Kashmir to hold the province for the Sikhs, instead of surrendering it to Gulab Singh, and to deny the proceeding in the face of his own letters with which he was confronted. At the same time, if all his shortcomings had had as much excuse, there would have been more regret when he was deposed after this, in favour of a "Council of Regency composed of leading chiefs and sirdars, acting under the control and guidance of the British Resident." To those who know the English manner of dealing with a fallen enemy, it will not seem remarkable that this Council included Tej Singh, who had commanded the army of the Khalsa at Sobraon, and several others who avowedly detested the English. The Rani had no longer any share in the government, but was given a pension.

One of the first subjects brought before the Durbar was "the outstanding revenue" of Bannu. "The Chancellor represented generally that Bannu was a place on the other side of the river Indus, in the midst of the hills, and peopled by Afghan tribes, whose peculiarly barbarous ideas of freedom had hitherto rendered it impossible to confer on them the blessing of a Sikh governor. Consequently, no tax-gatherer found it convenient to reside in that part of the kingdom, and the revenue (which was 65,000 rupees a-year) was always allowed to fall into arrear for two or three years, until the amount was worth collecting, when a force was sent from Lahore to *ask* for it; and if the answer was either short or evasive, they just took what they could, and came away again. 'Now,' said the Chancellor in conclusion, glancing at his notes, 'there are two and a half years' revenues due at this moment, so it is high time to send an army.'"

Colonel Lawrence agreed that as Bannu was part of the Maharaja's dominions (having been part of the territory ceded by Shah Shuja to Ranjit Singh), it was lawful to enforce the payment of revenue; but he advocated conciliation, if possible, and to that end the force sent to Bannu was to be accompanied by a British officer. The man whom Lawrence chose for the work was a young subaltern in the Company's service, Herbert Edwardes.

It was not an easy task. The expedition started in February; it was a month's march from Lahore to Bannu, and the hot season would be in full blast in April. "I had therefore at best a month allowed me to talk over people who had resisted

Sikh supremacy for a quarter of a century," says Edwardes, "and I think it is not very surprising that I signally failed in the attempt."

But the expedition was not a failure; it was true that he only succeeded in collecting less than one-third of the amount due, and that it was evidently hopeless to expect that the people of Bannu would ever pay anything of their own free-will. But he had gained the value of many lakhs of rupees in proving that Sikh soldiers could be taught not to touch what did not belong to them. For the first fortnight he did nothing but punish offenders; "the Sikh soldiers could not believe that they were no longer to be allowed to help themselves from every farmer's field, pull their firewood from every hedge, and drag a bed from under its slumbering owner, in order that they might take a nap on it themselves." Some of them had pulled the roof from one of the Raja Hira Singh's palaces in order to make the beams into bedsteads; why should any one trouble because a zamindari's young corn was taken for the horses and elephants, or the tree under which the village elders sat was chopped down for fuel? By dint of reproofs, fines, imprisonment, and floggings, they learned discipline. The country people, though deprecating any question of revenue, flocked into the camp, and talked with the expedition as friends; and the Sikhs, even when dropping down under arms for want of food, refrained from helping themselves. It was an object-lesson in English methods which the wild tribes of Bannu were to remember for our advantage in the hour of need.

After leaving Bannu, Edwardes moved from place to place upon the Punjab frontier, dealing out even-handed justice, everywhere making friends among the tribesmen, who conceived great respect for the law of the English, but considered it unnecessarily strict about trifles. A sixteen-year-old boy one day came to him, in much uneasiness because his tribe had heard that there was to be a law against murder. "What does it signify to a lad like you?" laughed Edwardes. "How many men have you killed?" He replied modestly, "Oh, I've only killed four, but father has killed eighty." "Yet," observes Edwardes, "*cæteris paribus*, in Bannu they are rather respectable men."

Edwardes did not waste time in formalities when bringing his ruffians in order. A certain Afghan merchant, Shahzad Khan, head of the Nassur tribe of Powindahs, refused to pay the tax for pasturage of camels levied by the Sikh Government upon all his fellows, and added contumely to his refusal; he had defied the Amir of Kabul and other potentates; "was it to be supposed he would knuckle down to the dogs of Sikhs?" He refused to come and talk the matter over, or to leave the Sikh territory. So Edwardes rode to the Nassur camp one night, with two hundred Dauranis and sixty Sikhs at his back, and on arriving within sight of the watch-fires, found that in the darkness the men, misliking their errand, had slunk away, and only seventy or eighty remained to him. Of these, only fifteen followed when he charged through the camp. It was impossible to capture Shahzad Khan, but Edwardes had not ridden so far to go home empty-handed, and catching sight of the Nassur herd of camels, he dashed upon them. The Nassurs were busy exchanging shots and abuse with the Sikhs and Dauranis; the camels, with true camels' instinct for embarrassing their owners, tore themselves free from their fastenings, and Edwardes drove the whole herd before him, aided by one of his few remaining followers, a highwayman whom he had pardoned a few days previously, "who entered heart and soul into the business, giving them a professional poke with his spear which set them stepping out gloriously." The Sikh troopers came to his aid, and kept off the Nassurs, and Edwardes rode away with his spoil.

When they had put about a mile between themselves and their pursuers he called a halt to examine the wounded, and found that a Khan who was one of his most staunch allies had been knocked off his horse and left in the camp. It was useless to return, even if any one would have followed him, as his appearance merely would have incited the Nassurs to murder the Khan, if he still lived. "A follower, well versed in this kind of work, suggested a reprisal"; another Nassur camp was surprised, and two Nassur chiefs secured, and exchanged for the Khan, who returned none the worse for his wounds or for the surgery of the Nassur women, who had sewed up the cuts with hairs pulled out of his own horse's tail. The sale of the camels realised a handsome sum in satisfaction of Shahzad Khan's arrears of taxes; Shahzad henceforth avoided the neighbourhood so long as Edwardes remained in India, and no other Kabul merchant dared refuse to obey Sikh laws so long as he was on Sikh territory. The pleasant recollection of that night sustained Edwardes's spirits under a very severe reprimand from an official superior, who did not approve of reprisals in kind, and was shocked to think of the inconvenience that would have been caused to his betters if the young man had been killed in his raid upon the Nassur camp.

In the meanwhile, another British officer, John Nicholson, a tall black-bearded man, who had been one of the garrison of Ghazni in 1842, had been sent by Henry Lawrence to put the fear of the law into the Pathans, Rajputs, Gujars, and other races dwelling in the tract between the Jhelum and the Indus, and was working very much upon Edwardes's lines. George Lawrence, Henry's brother, was keeping order at Peshawar. All over the Punjab a new era of peace and prosperity seemed beginning, though Henry Lawrence himself had been obliged to take leave to England. "India," said the London 'Morning Chronicle,' "is in the full enjoyment of a peace which, humanly speaking, there seems nothing to disturb." Neither the editor nor any one else troubled about the Rani Jindan, who had been removed to a fort some twenty-five miles from Lahore, where she could no longer corrupt her son, or intrigue with "a venal and selfish Durbar." Henry Lawrence had urged that she should be removed from the Punjab, but his advice was not taken, and though Edwardes discovered "that Jezebel" sending a slave-girl on a secret embassy to Multan in the summer of 1847, he accepted "her impudent excuse that she wanted a white âk-tree[1] for enchantments."

[1] *Calotropis gigantea*—sacred to Ravi or Surya.

## II.

Ranjit Singh had appointed a certain Sawan Mal as Viceroy of Multan. He must have been a man of extraordinary abilities, for while generally beloved for his justice and his kindness to the poor, he regularly transmitted the revenues to Lahore, and amassed the sum of £900,000 to be divided among his sons when a shot from a mutinous soldier ended his twenty-three years of office. He was succeeded by his son Mulraj, from whom the Lahore Durbar demanded the sum of one million sterling in death duties. The ensuing dispute was prolonged by the murder of Jawahir Singh and the consequent anarchy at Lahore, and in 1846 Henry Lawrence arranged a compromise. Mulraj was to cede part of his district, and pay eight lakhs of rupees at once, and ten more in instalments, besides an annual tribute.

This agreement did not long satisfy Mulraj; it seemed to him that he was paying too heavily for only a part of his father's district. Moreover, the people of Multan, seeing that the vexatious transit and town duties had been abolished in the Punjab, were dissatisfied with the fiscal system upon which

Sawan Mal had grown rich. Worst of all, it was impossible to keep them in order in these days when they had the right to appeal to Lahore, where the extravagant English notions about even-handed justice between man and man were being enforced. Therefore Mulraj determined to resign. John Lawrence, Henry's brother, then Acting-Resident at Lahore, attempted to dissuade him, but was emphatic that "no authority could be permitted to exist in the Punjab independent of appeal, and unaccountable to the law," and Mulraj was very wroth with the law which had lately obliged him to release certain prisoners, and to pay certain Muhammedan soldiers who claimed arrears. Finally his resignation was accepted; Sirdar Khan Singh, "an intelligent man," was appointed Governor in his place.

A Political Agent was appointed for Multan, Vans Agnew, "a man of much ability, energy, and judgment," [1] "remarkable for carrying his kindness to natives almost to excess," [2] and greatly beloved by them and by his own countrymen. His assistant was Lieutenant Anderson of the 1st Bombay European Fusiliers, an excellent Oriental scholar, endowed with "peculiarly conciliating manners," who had travelled through the whole of the Multan district. On the 18th of April 1848 they met

[1] Sir F. Currie. [2] Sir H. Edwardes.

Khan Singh at Multan, and encamped in the Idgah, a strong building within cannon-shot of the north face of the fort. Mulraj came from his own residence, a garden-house about a mile away, to receive them, and arranged to take them over the fort on the following day.

On the evening of April 22nd, Edwardes was sitting in his tent at Dera Fateh Khan, on the banks of the Indus, taking the evidence of sundry scoundrels who were "robbers, robbed, or witnesses to the robberies of their neighbours," when the feet of one running hard were heard outside, and a breathless and streaming messenger entered with the crimson letter-bag that means urgent correspondence. It was from the Sahib in Multan to the Sahib in Bannu (General Cortlandt, an American officer in the army of the Punjab); but since Edwardes was here, the runner considered he might as well read it.

Within was a large sheet of paper on which a native clerk had begun an official report to Sir F. Currie, at Agnew's dictation. On passing out of the fort, Agnew and Anderson had been attacked by two of Mulraj's soldiers; all the Multan troops had mutinied. Agnew had scrawled a few lines in pencil at the bottom of the sheet and on the back, addressed to Cortlandt:—

"My dear Sir,—You have been ordered to send one regiment here. Pray let it march instantly, or, if gone, hasten it to top-speed. If you can spare another, pray send it also. I am responsible for the measure. I am cut up a little, and on my back. Lieutenant Anderson is much worse. He has five sword wounds. I have two in my left arm from warding sabre cuts, and a poke in the ribs with a spear. I don't think Moolraj has anything to do with it. I was riding with him when we were attacked. He rode off, but is now said to be in the hands of the soldiery.

"Khan Singh and his people all right.—Yours in haste,
P. A. Vans Agnew.

"19th, 2 p.m."

For the next hour Edwardes sat in his tent, calm and impassive, turning over ways and means, while the Biluchis entangled themselves in perjury. Then he broke up the Court, and sent for Foujdar Khan, the officer in charge of the ferry of the Indus—"How many boats can you get for me by midnight?" The Khan told off upon his fingers every ferry-boat within twenty or thirty miles, and horsemen were sent out to fetch them. The whole camp was warned to be ready to cross the Indus. Edwardes was so crippled by a blow on the knee received during his camel-raiding that he could neither ride nor walk, and he lay in a palki on the river bank, in the burning sun, watching the boats toiling from side to side. Ninety miles ("chiefly sand") lay between him and Multan.

He entered the town of Leia unopposed, and there learned that it was too late to save the two Englishmen. Only broken fragments of the story reached him, and it was not for some time that he heard the whole truth. Whether Mulraj had determined his course beforehand, or whether, as seems more likely, he was hurried into it by the mutinous soldiery, he refused to seize the culprits and come himself to the Idgah, when invited to do so by Agnew, and Agnew's messenger found him sitting in Council with the Sikhs, who were binding the scarlet war bracelet upon his wrist. Next morning, the guns of the fort opened upon the Idgah; all the Sikh escort who had come with the Englishmen deserted them, excepting Khan Singh, some eight or ten horsemen, and their servants and clerks. At sunset they heard the roar of the mob from the city coming nearer and nearer. Khan Singh proposed waving a sheet and asking for mercy. "The time for mercy is gone," replied Agnew; "let none be asked for. They can kill us two if they like; but we are not the last of the English. Thousands of Englishmen will come down here when we are gone, and annihilate Mulraj and his soldiers and his fort."

In burst the mob, a motley crowd — soldiers, townsmen, and the scum of the bazaars—brandishing any weapons that they had found to their hand and yelling for blood. They seized Khan Singh, they knocked aside the servants with the butts of their muskets, and surrounded the bed where Anderson lay helpless, with Agnew sitting at his side and holding his hand. The two were hacked to pieces, and Agnew's head was flung at Khan Singh. "Take the head of the youth you brought down to govern at Multan." Then followed horrors of which it is impossible to write, until what was left of the bodies was buried in a hasty grave near the Idgah, from which they were twice disinterred by the people of Multan, in order to strip them of their clothes.

Once committed past all hope of retrieving himself, Mulraj openly proclaimed war with the English, and called all the disaffected to take part with him. The country was swarming with mercenary swordsmen, Biluchis and Pathans, and Edwardes's position was most critical. As he said himself, he was "very much like a Scotch terrier barking at a tiger," and he knew that, with a dash across the Chenab, Mulraj could sweep him and his men away and return to Multan, or ever help from

Lahore could reach him. But Leia was an important city, and so long as he could sit there with his little force, Mulraj's prestige would suffer throughout the countryside. "If a week only passes over, I shall have got together enough men to hold on," he wrote to Lahore. "If not, we are in God's hands, and could not be better placed."

Meanwhile he was enlisting recruits right and left among the tribesmen, many of whom had been in rebellion themselves only a few days before, and they answered to the call. Pathan hated Sikh, and the Sahib who was such a fearless enemy was likely to be a good ally. The Sikh regiment with him was not to be trusted; their co-religionists at Multan were sending letters urging "all who trust in the Guru" to join them, and relieve the Maharaja and his mother from the thraldom of the English. Edwardes intercepted the correspondence, but was warned by two native officers that his Sikh regiment were holding meetings, bearing themselves with "an unusual kind of swaggering air, such as the Sikh soldiers used to have at Lahore before the Sutlej War." It would have been madness to wait for the arrival of the force which Mulraj sent across the Chenab at the end of April, when Edwardes knew that the price of treason was actually fixed—12,000 rupees to the regiment for joining the rebels in the battle, and 12,000 more if they brought his head with them. So he retreated across the Indus to Dera Futteh Khan, to the indignation of the conspirators, who avowed themselves ready to hold Leia against twenty times their number. Let the Sahib trust them, and he would never repent it. "Which was probably true," is Edwardes's comment, "for they would not have given me time." Next day, General Cortlandt brought his detachment from Bannu, and Mulraj retreated.

The Commander-in-Chief in India was still Hugh Gough—now Lord Gough—and his decision not to take the field against the rebels until after the rainy season, was approved by the Government of India and by the Duke of Wellington. The heat of Multan had always been a bugbear, and that summer was unusually early and hot; many of the troops were absent on furlough, and it was not safe to lessen the numbers of our force at Lahore. It was therefore determined to send a Sikh army under Sher Singh, a member of the Lahore Durbar, to assist Edwardes in confining the rebellion to the province of Multan, until it was possible for English troops to brave the climate.

It was lucky for Edwardes that he had enlisted the support of the loyal Nawab of Bahawalpur in his operations against Mulraj, for the Sikh troops failed to appear. He had other allies won by his own personality, and English justice. At the outbreak of the war he had ordered the chiefs of Bannu to send him their sons and brothers, nominally as volunteers, but really as hostages for the good behaviour of the valley, and these men now brought guns upwards of two hundred miles to his assistance. There were sundry skirmishes, and many marches up and down, before he joined with Cortlandt and was engaged by Mulraj's army at Kaneri. It was an anxious moment. "A young lieutenant who had seen but one campaign—alone, and without any of the means and appliances of such war as I had been apprenticed to, I was about to take command, in the midst of a battle, not only of one force whose courage I had never tried, but of another which I had never seen; and to engage a third, of which the numbers were uncertain." His hesitation "came and went between the stirrup and the saddle." "I knew that I was fighting for the right. I asked God to help me to do my duty, and I rode on, certain that He would do it." Besides, it was Waterloo Day, and Edwardes felt "no Englishman could be beaten on the 18th of June."

After nine hours' hard fighting, Edwardes sat

down on the ground occupied by Mulraj in the morning, and "had the honour and satisfaction" to report to Lahore that the enemy had sustained a complete defeat, and were in full flight to Multan, leaving their camp and ammunition and most of their guns behind them. He was "unable to do justice to the gallantry" of his men, many of them enlisted but a month before.

As for the men, they had enjoyed themselves thoroughly, and even the wounded were in excellent spirits, though there was no doctor. Each was surrounded by the men of his own clan, who brushed the flies from him, and Edwardes's appearance to "see how they were all going on," "was followed by a general removal of bandages, which, for all our sakes, might better have been kept on." Even when writing his despatch on the field, Edwardes was interrupted by the arrival of the Khan whom he had ransomed from the Nassurs, who wished the Sahib to admire his wounds, and another wounded hero, with his brain laid open, would allow no one to dress the injury till the Sahib came.

Another victory on July 1st, and Mulraj was beaten back to Multan, Edwardes halting his troops almost under the walls of the city.

## III.

Now that fortune seemed to be with the British, Raja Sher Singh brought up his column, which should have been acting in concert with Edwardes's force all this time. The very day after their arrival, one of his colleagues frankly confessed that if their column had been ordered to advance against Mulraj before the battle of Kaneri, it would have refused, or gone over to the enemy. The neighbourhood of about five thousand disaffected men was a serious danger to Edwardes's little army, when Mulraj was writing to Sher Singh and his colleagues, welcoming them to his "poor city of Multan," and inviting the rank and file to come into his bazaars whenever the Englishmen were hard up for provisions. The arrival of General Whish, with an English force to open the siege of Multan, brought matters to a crisis. In an attack on September 12th the besiegers gained so much ground as to be "within battering distance" of the city walls. A few more hours might have seen them within the city walls, if Sher Singh had not suddenly gone over to the enemy with all his force. He had made some efforts to withstand the urgings of his soldiery, but his father, the Sikh governor of Hazara, was already in revolt, and filial duty was too strong for him.

It was the spark to the powder, and all the Punjab was aflame. The Rani Jindan was now removed to the religious quietude of Benares, but her white âk-tree was bearing fruit. Her emissaries had been preaching sedition everywhere, calling upon all true Sikhs to expel the English who allowed the Mahommedan dogs to flaunt their religion in the face of the Khalsa, and who would take their weapons from them and send them back to the plough,—the most awful threat that could be held over a Sikh warrior. There was a prophecy that the English dominion should last only for two years and a half; that time was now up, and as Guru Govind had prophesied, the Khalsa should conquer East and West. "Every petty Sikh horseman raised his head, and seized his own village in the name of the Khalsa, with the old cry of 'Wah! Guru-ji-ke fatha!'"[1] Dost Mohammad was to be bribed with Peshawar to send his armies against the men who had hunted him up and down his own land. At Lahore, the Durbar prepared for war. In Bannu, the Sikh soldiery revolted, murdered the commandant whom Edwardes had left in charge of the newly-built fort of Dhulipgarh, and marched to join Sher Singh. The

[1] Victory to the Guru.

Sikhs at Peshawar deserted in a body, and George Lawrence was a prisoner. Lastly, Gulab Singh of Kashmir was said to have fomented rebellion with great assiduity, and was certainly sheltering the families of the rebels, and allowing their troops to draw supplies from the territory which we ourselves had given to him.

For three tedious months the siege of Multan had to be raised until reinforcements could arrive. Edwardes and Cortlandt could do no more than stand their ground, in bitter disappointment. At the end of December, a division came up from Bombay, and a few days later Edwardes was displaying his levies to Sir Henry Lawrence, who had hurried back from England on hearing of the outbreak of war. On January 2, 1849, the final assault was given; the city was taken, and Mulraj with three thousand men withdrew to the citadel, which in less than three weeks was a wreck, from the constant storm of shells. The greater part of the garrison deserted, and Mulraj was driven to surrender. "The whole affair originated in accident," he pleaded. "Of my own free-will I would never have done what I have. I ask only for my own life and the honour of my women." To which General Whish replied that he had no authority to take or give life, and that the British Government warred with men, not with women.

On the morning of January 22nd, in a violent thunderstorm, Mulraj gave himself up to justice. He begged Edwardes to be his advocate at his trial, but Edwardes, who had already refused to act for the prosecution, would not consent. He was tried for the murder of the two officers, and found guilty, and, his sentence of death being commuted by Lord Dalhousie into one of imprisonment for life, was sent down to Calcutta, where he died in the following year.

Before our army left Multan, the bodies of Agnew and Anderson were taken from the hole where they had been flung, wrapped in Kashmir shawls, and borne by the soldiers of Anderson's own regiment to an honoured resting-place on the summit of the citadel. "By what way borne? Through the gate where they had been first assaulted? Oh no! Through the broad and sloping breach which had been made by the British guns in the walls of the rebellious fortress of Multan."[1]

Eight days before Mulraj's surrender Lord Gough had fought the battle of Chillianwalla—one of the deadliest in which the British army has ever been engaged. Not only was the loss in killed and wounded heavy out of all proportion, but though the enemy were driven back, they

[1] Edwardes.

took with them four British guns and the colours of three regiments. The Sikhs had suffered very severely, and conceived such a wholesome dread of our infantry charges that, when they next met in the field, they did not attempt to withstand another.

At the end of January came the news of the capture of Multan, and Sher Singh offered to treat. When his overtures were rejected, by a masterly piece of strategy he turned the flank of the English, unobserved, and hurried towards Lahore. Gough overtook him at the village of Gujerat near the Chenab, and won, as he said, "his last battle and his best." There was terrific fire from the British guns, and then a general advance. "We stood two hours in hell," explained a Sikh, "and, after that, we saw six miles of infantry."

It was a decisive victory, won at very little loss to ourselves. The campaign was at an end. In March, sixteen thousand of the flower of the Khalsa army surrendered at discretion at Rawal Pindi, the tears rolling down their cheeks as they flung their weapons at the feet of the conquerors. "To-day Ranjit Singh is dead!" they murmured as they turned homewards. They did not foresee the day when some of the English who now looked on at their humiliation, should lead them victorious through the streets of Delhi to fulfil Teg Bahadur's prophecy.

It was evident that the only chance for the Punjab was to pass under English rule, and Dhulip Singh resigned his throne, receiving instead a pension. The Koh-i-Nur was presented to Queen Victoria, after a sojourn in John Lawrence's waistcoat pocket—and, as some say, a visit to the *dhobi* while in that hiding-place.

Lord Gough was remembered long after he had retired to the Irish home, where he died, full of years and honours. An officer at the siege of Delhi in 1857 was always asked by the Gurkha troops, "When is the Lord Sahib coming?" To which he replied, "He is coming very soon now." But one day it occurred to him to ask, "What Lord Sahib do you mean?" when there was an instantaneous shout in reply, "Lord Gough Sahib, to be sure! If he comes he will win victory immediately, and no one but him can take that place. Why is he not sent for?"

"Since the days of Clive," wrote Henry Lawrence, "no one had done as Edwardes." There were other and more substantial honours for the subaltern, besides this appreciation from the chief whom he reverenced. He was created a Brevet-Major and a C.B., and a special gold medal was struck by the Company in his honour.

A few years later he negotiated a treaty with Dost Mohammad, the value of which was soon to be proved in the crisis of the Mutiny, when our old enemy loyally kept his agreement not to attack us.

When for a brief space in the summer of 1857, John Lawrence lost heart, and proposed to fall back beyond the Indus, it was Edwardes who, with Sydney Cotton and John Nicholson, withstood a retreat that would have meant ruin. Edwardes was ready to play the game as in the days when he had ridden at the head of his irregular levies to conquer an army, and, as before, his fearlessness saved the situation.

# XXII.

# THE LAST DAYS OF JOHN COMPANY—1848-1858

"The East India Company had not deserved its fate. Its rule had been better and purer, more adapted to the circumstances of the great dependency than would have been possible had its acts and orders been subject to the fluctuations of party feelings."

—G. B. MALLESON, *History of the Indian Mutiny.*

## XXII.

## THE LAST DAYS OF JOHN COMPANY—1848-1858.

"THE infamous son of a yet more infamous Persian pedlar" founded the kingdom of Oudh, in the evil days when the Moghul Empire was falling to pieces at the beginning of the eighteenth century. His successors, like himself, called themselves Nawabs of Oudh, affecting to rule in the name of the Emperor of Delhi.

During Lord Wellesley's administration, the reigning Nawab ceded certain provinces to the Company which he was incapable of protecting against Afghan invasion, or attack from Marathas or Sikhs. If he had ceded all his dominions, like the last Nawab of Bengal, in return for a settled income to spend upon dancing-girls, his subjects would have profited, for the administration of Oudh was a crying scandal throughout India.

It will be remembered that a Nawab of Oudh

lent two millions to the Company for the expenses of the Nepal War.[1] On the strength of this loan he styled himself "King of Oudh," as none of his predecessors had ventured to do, and had the help of the Company's troops to terrorise his wretched subjects, whom the tax-gatherers ground to the dust. Many sold their garments to buy swords, and turned dacoit, since no other way of getting a living was open to them—as did the people of Malwa in the "Time of Troubles." Every landed proprietor built a fort; the ryots twisted thorn hedges round their villages. The sovereign in whose name they were oppressed, starved the elephants in his menagerie to death, rather than buy food for them, and would have starved the widows of his predecessor, but that "they fairly broke loose from their prison,"[2] and plundered the bazaar, crying that they had pawned all their jewels and most of their garments for bread, and were dying of hunger, and that the King must pay for what they took.

The King is said to have been weak rather than wicked; his evil genius was the Prime Minister, formerly his *khansamah*, who knew no shame. A Rohilla chief owned lands in Oudh; his wife was famed for her beauty. The Prime

[1] See page 270. [2] Bishop Heber.

Minister seized by force upon the lands, and carried off the wife to his zenana while the husband was away. The chieftain rode to Lucknow, and scaled the walls of the garden where the Prime Minister's two boys were at play. He seized upon the children, and cried to the trembling servants that their father should come and speak with him. When the Prime Minister, aghast, came down into the garden, the chieftain, still gripping the boys, announced his terms. Let the British Resident be sent for, as a guarantee of good faith, and in his presence let the stolen wife be given back to her lawful owner, or the children should be slain before their father's eyes.

There was a long and terrible pause, while the chieftain waited and the boys shivered in his rough grasp; then the Resident appeared, followed by the chieftain's wife. Her husband took her hand and led her away from the garden.

Soon afterwards, to escape the Minister's vengeance, the chieftain surrendered to the English, preferring captivity in Allahabad to assassination in Oudh.

The death of the old King brought no relief to Oudh; his successor, "stained with every vice," made his chief favourite of his barber, who had learned how to curl hair in London, and it is impossible to tell what took place in the palace in his time. He died, poisoned by some of his own kin. His successor was too old to effect reforms, though he honestly attempted them, and the next King tried none. Then came the last and almost the worst of the line, who on his accession in 1847 was warned by Lord Hardinge that the Company would assume the administration of Oudh unless some improvement were visible within the next two years. The Company were better than their word; nine years passed, and it was not till February 1856 that the wretched King was deposed.

"Millions of God's creatures would draw freedom and happiness from the change." So said the Governor-General, Lord Dalhousie, whose last important act it was. But in East and West there are certain people so wrong-headed as to prefer a tyranny whose motives they understand, to a paternal government whose point of view is entirely different to theirs, and the natives of Oudh were not grateful for the improvement in their lot. Not even the appointment of the soldier-saint, Henry Lawrence, as Chief Commissioner of Oudh, could quell the storm, although his foresight and steadfastness enabled the garrison of Lucknow to weather it when it burst.

There was discontent and restlessness all over

India, and not in Oudh alone, at this time. There had been other annexations, and everywhere men were uneasy, doubting the good faith of the English, and watching the red circles spread over the map of India, as Ranjit Singh had foreseen. A more conscientious man than Dalhousie was never set in high place. Not from vulgar greed of dominion, but from an enthusiastic belief in the advantages of Western civilisation, he was convinced of the duty of the Company to annex any state where the ruler died without an heir. He carried out this principle in Nagpur, in Satara, in Jhansi, and elsewhere; and the price of some annexations was other than he thought. It was paid with interest on the day when the English at Jhansi—man, woman, and child—were butchered by the Rani's orders, and in the weeks when, having raised the countryside, she led her army against the English, until she ended her stormy life in a cavalry charge below the walls of Gwalior—"the bravest man on the side of the rebels."

There were other grievances beside the annexations. Former Governor-Generals had prevented the Indian widow from winning heaven for herself and her husband through the flames of his pyre, and had forbidden a father to put his new-born daughters to death. Lord Dalhousie went further, and would encourage the widow to marry again. His zeal for sanitation, education, and other Western fetiches roused terror in the hearts of the people, who were convinced that the English meant to break their caste, and do away with their religion.

Some of Dalhousie's passion for reform might have been spent with advantage upon the Bengal army, which notoriously wanted it. Our prestige with the sepoys had never recovered from the Afghanistan disaster. They were alarmed by the new rule that they should be required to serve out of India, believing that to cross "the black water" would be to break their caste. There were many grievances to be righted and abuses to be corrected; but beyond drawing up a series of Minutes on his departure, Dalhousie made no attempt at reforming the army, whose unsatisfactory condition was by that time made worse by the number of Oudh sepoys in its ranks.

If to these and other causes for disquiet be added the prophecy long current in India, that the dominion of the Company would be brought to an end one hundred years after the battle of Plassey, there is matter enough to excite a jealous and suspicious people without the pretext of the greased cartridges, which were generally assigned as the cause of the Mutiny.

## II.

The last territory left to the Moghul Emperor of Hindustan in the year 1857 was enclosed within the red walls of the Fort overlooking the Jumna at Delhi, where he and about twelve thousand subjects lived in squalor. Since Lord Lake had rescued Shah Alam from the Marathas, a pension had been paid by the Company, enough, with proper management, to support the Emperor becomingly. But no one of the Emperor's Court was able or honest enough to administer it, and twice the amount would not have sufficed for the hundreds who claimed a share of the blood-royal. "Here are crowded together twelve hundred kings and queens, literally eating each other up," wrote an English officer, who visited Delhi in the time of Shah Alam's son Akbar. "Kings and queens of the House of Tymour are to be found lying about in scores like broods of vermin, without food to eat or clothes to cover their nakedness."

Akbar died in the year of Queen Victoria's accession, and his successor, Mohammad Bahadur Shah, poet and devotee, was the feeblest of all shadow kings. A very old man, he and all Delhi knew that the existing conditions must end with his life. Lord Dalhousie had notified that on his Majesty's death the mock Court would cease to exist and the whole imperial family must vacate the Palace.

For every reason, moral and sanitary, it seemed advisable to clear the fort of its present inhabitants. No man then alive could remember the days when the Emperor of Delhi was anything but a name; no one could be really the worse if the name itself ceased to exist.

Dawn was breaking over the city on Monday, May 11, 1857, when certain mounted men rode over the bridge across the Palace moat, and called aloud upon the Emperor's name. They had galloped through the night from Meerut, thirty-six miles away, leaving smoking roofs and rifled houses and dead bodies behind them, and they summoned the Emperor to place himself at their head and strike with them for the faith. A hundred years or more counts for very little in India, and if the English had forgotten, the sepoys remembered the days when the lord of Delhi was lord also of Hindustan. One of the Hindu regiments in the city mutinied, a few hours later, to the cry of "Prithvi Raj-ki jai!"—going back seven hundred years to a time when a Hindu king was ruler in Delhi.

The poor old Emperor, not knowing what to do,

sent for Captain Douglas, the commandant of the Palace guards, who spoke to the men and bade them disperse. They obeyed indeed, but as they went their fierce insistent cry of "Din! din!" roused the Palace. Others in the city took up the cry. Two hours later, Captain Douglas and all the English in the fort were murdered, the prisoners in the gaol were set free, and the mob were killing the English in the city, and firing their houses. By the evening, triumphant mutineers were bivouacked in the great Audience Hall, and the Emperor Mohammad Bahadur Shah reigned in Delhi.

Four weeks later—on Monday, June 8th—an English army had occupied the Ridge overlooking the city, and the last struggle for Delhi had begun.

## III.

There is no space here for the story of the months from May 1857 to August 1858. It has been told over and over again, by those who were in the thick of the struggle, by those who watched it from afar, and in these later times by those who have studied it in every detail, and can offer a more or less complete picture of it. However often it may be told, nothing can lessen the wonder and amazement that when the revolt was ablaze at Agra, Lucknow, Cawnpore, Allahabad, and twenty other places at once, through the furnace-heat of summer, with help from England of necessity very long in coming, a handful of men could prevent the English rule in India from being wiped out of existence.

At first every post brought news of some fresh calamity. All Oudh had risen; the river at Cawnpore was running red with English blood; the garrison of Lucknow were in the last extremity. On September 14th the tide turned —again on a Monday—when the British columns fought their way into Delhi. On the following Sunday they were holding their thanksgiving service in the Diwan-i-Khas. "It's a far cry to Delhi," but at length they were within its gates as conquerors. On the last day of September Outram and Havelock made their entry into Lucknow, to relieve the garrison that had kept the flag flying from the Residency tower for eighty-seven days.

The crisis was past. Many reasons are given for its existence, as many more might be given for its defeat. There is a story that Exeter Hall held a meeting to give thanks for the suppression of the Mutiny, at which certain persons were invited to state what they considered to be the greatest mercy vouchsafed during the struggle. Among them was John Lawrence, who uprose and said, "The crowning mercy was that the telegraph-wire was cut between me and Calcutta,"—and sat down again.[1]

Only those who at an outpost of Empire in time of deadly peril have been thwarted, checked, goaded, by prohibitions and commands from official superiors with little or no understanding of the situation, can appreciate John Lawrence's crowning mercy to the full. Thanks to the deficiencies of postal and telegraphic communication in 1857, it was often necessary to leave the men on the spot to mind their own business—and they usually completed it successfully.

There were other factors—such as Edwardes's treaty with the Amir of Afghanistan, which prevented an attack on the North-West Frontier at the time when every available man and gun was on the Ridge at Delhi. Most of all, there was the personal touch, of even greater value with Eastern races than in the West. "There were giants in the earth in those days"—

[1] The story is told as it was handed down to me by oral tradition.

giants such as Henry Lawrence, and John Nicholson, and Neville Chamberlain—who could sustain the falling house upon their shoulders, while the earth heaved and quaked below their feet.

One consolation was left for those who had trusted to the prophecy of the hundred years after Plassey. Some one must pay for the Mutiny. "If India had at that time been under the rule of the Crown, the natural scapegoat would have been the Ministry of the day. As it was, the blow fell upon the grand old Company which had nursed the early conquests on the eastern coast of Hindustan till they had developed into the most magnificent empire subject to an alien race which the world has ever seen." [1]

"For divers weighty reasons, We have resolved"—so runs Queen Victoria's proclamation, publicly read at every civil and military station in India—"to take upon Ourselves the government of the territories in India, heretofore administered in trust for Us by the Honourable East India Company."

[1] Malleson.

# EPILOGUE

# THE MEN AND THE WORK

"Quasi cursores vitai lampada tradunt."

# EPILOGUE.

## THE MEN AND THE WORK.

On the 2nd of August 1858 the East India Company ceased to exist.

Its last hundred years of life had been spent to some purpose for great part of the dwellers in India. No longer did gangs of robbers infest the roads to murder the peaceful traveller. No longer did armed hordes sweep through a countryside, leaving their trace in wasted lands, burning villages, smoking fields, the bodies of men tortured until death was a relief, and women who had slain themselves to escape worse than death. Pindari and Thug had been hunted down, Sikh and Maratha were kept within their own border, and even the wild tribes on the North-West Frontier had learned to respect the Law of the English.

It is impossible to read the history of the last hundred and twenty years of the Company's existence without a feeling of amazement at the work done, and of deep reverence for the men who did it, both soldiers and civil servants. Those men for the most part are forgotten. Such names as Henry Lawrence, Mountstuart Elphinstone, Robert Clive, John Nicholson—to take a few at random—must live as long as the British Empire. But there are many known only to the student who has put together their story from fragments and chance allusions; and there are many more whose names survive perhaps in distorted tradition on the scene of their labours, and in no other place.

It cannot be said that all the East India Company's servants did honour to their service. Some were incompetent, some cared only for enriching themselves, by fair means or foul; some were a disgrace to the country whence they came and to the religion that they professed. But, seeing what were the conditions of service in the East up to the time of our grandfathers—the lifelong separation from family and religious influences, the slowness and the expense of communications with home—it must be acknowledged that, in proportion to the whole, the black sheep were very few in number.

Nor can it be said that all the work accomplished by the best men was entirely for the good of the natives of India, even when intended directly for their benefit. There is a certain simplicity about the British mind, which cannot but imagine that whatever is good for one race must of necessity be good for another. In the spirit of the little boy who crams sweets into his baby brother's mouth, he forces Western theories upon Eastern people, and meaning for the best, cannot understand why the results are not what he expected.

That some among them did wrong, that nearly all made mistakes—that is to say that the men who laid the foundations of our Indian Empire were human beings. But no other service in the world can show such a record of patience, of single-hearted loyalty, of devotion to a high ideal maintained through years of loneliness and neglect, of unflinching steadfastness in the face of misrepresentation, misunderstanding, and calumny.

Looking back, not upon the scattered units to be found in histories and National Biographies, but upon the countless host who toiled and suffered unknown to the great ones who are concerned with the destiny of the parish pump at home, figure after figure rises to the memory. Men who gave their best years to the service of an alien land, who bore perhaps lifelong separation from wife and children and kindred, who took the risk of death as indifferently as other men take the risk of catching cold when playing golf, who learned to see with other eyes, and to understand other ways of thought, and yet kept their own ideals intact,—it was such men as these who made "the justice of the English" respected and feared throughout the land. Many died at their posts; some came home, and after ruling over tracts of country as large as England or Scotland, perhaps found that their names were unknown to the great man whom Destiny had placed temporarily in charge of the India Office.

If a momentary thought is ever spent upon such men, their womankind should be remembered with them. Certain novelists have brought into prominence a type of the Anglo-Indian "Mem-Sahib"—idle, extravagant, dividing her time between brainless or spiteful gossip and shameless flirtation. The picture is received without question in many English country neighbourhoods, where gossip is as mischievous and silly as anywhere in India, and where flirtations are limited only by the scarcity of men. It is a misfortune that less has been written of another type of Mem-Sahib whom India has known for many generations, in the days of "John Company" as in the twentieth century.

She did not often wear the beautiful garments

of the novelist's heroine, because, with children at school in England, there was very little money to spend on herself, and her own beauty usually did not survive several "hot weathers" spent with her husband in the plains. But for all that, she was good to see, when revolt was in the air, and she must let her husband go to his work every morning, not knowing whether he would return to her—or when she was nursing some lonely stranger, with no claim upon her but that of white blood, through some deadly and probably infectious illness—or in less tragic moments, when she was battling against countless obstacles, to make a home in the most unhomely surroundings. It is difficult to reckon up the work done by British men in India; it would be impossible to say how much of the credit for it is due to the women who stood behind some of them.

We are now told that India is undergoing a change more fateful than any that have passed over her since the days of the Moghul Emperors, and that she can no longer be ruled by the same methods or the same type of man as in former times. It well may be, for everywhere the civilised world is moving to a different tune, and men must change step or fall out of the ranks. Whether the tune be better or worse than that to which their fathers marched, is a question to which our generation cannot know the answer. But for those who have to carry on the work under the new conditions, there can be no better wish than that they may prove themselves worthy of the men who went before them on the road.

# INDEX.

PRINTED BY WILLIAM BLACKWOOD AND SONS.